D0757990

BLIND SPEED

Also by Josh Barkan

Before Hiroshima

JOSH BARKAN

BLIND

a novel

SPEED

TRIQUARTERLY BOOKS
NORTHWESTERN UNIVERSITY PRESS
EVANSTON, ILLINOIS

TriQuarterly Books
Northwestern University Press
www.nupress.northwestern.edu

Printed in the United States of America

10   9   8   7   6   5   4   3   2   1

Library of Congress Cataloging-in-Publication Data

Barkan, Joshua, 1969–
    Blind speed / Josh Barkan.
        p. cm.
    A novel.
        ISBN-13: 978-0-8101-2493-6 (cloth : alk. paper)
        ISBN-10: 0-8101-2493-9 (cloth : alk. paper)
    I. Title.
    PS3552.A6164B58 2008
    813.6—dc22
                                                2007049775

BLIND SPEED

CHAPTER 1

(A little background first.)

When he was born, Paul Berger was already a little ugly. His mouth was big, and by the age of thirty-four his lips bulged up and outward. His cheeks were chubby, his blond hair short in an uncombed—don't wake me up or bother me now, I might be recovering from some drugs or from a night out—kind of way.

He had been in a fairly successful band, not just in high school and college but professionally. (They cut a few albums, one on a real label, opened for some Top 40 alternative bands, and Paul was the drummer.) But when he was twenty-seven it became clear they would never quite make it to the big time. They just weren't good enough. Paul didn't use the excuse the public wasn't ready for their kind of music—or that commercialism had ruined the whole industry. He might have believed the part about commercialization, but he also knew they just didn't have the talent. That simple. "It was just *that* clear," he would tell others.

Yet he was still a fan. He would still pony up two hundred dollars—even though he didn't have a lot of dough—to sit in the front row at the Orpheum in downtown Boston, for the right group. And if circumstances had been just a little different, his band might have hit the big time—by that I mean if they'd had just an ounce or two more talent.

(Now to the less serious, less manipulative, more sarcastic, funny part.)

What he did now—at the beginning of this book—is teach Am. Stud. at B_____ Community College. And because he liked history, especially the history of pop culture, he swerved off highway 2 into Concord when he saw a sign announcing a BATTLE REENACTMENT OF THE SHOT HEARD ROUND THE WORLD.

"You know, somehow I don't think it was heard round the world," Paul said to his fiancée, Zoe, and he guffawed as they decelerated from the blind speed of the highway, past blurred spring maple leaves, toward the town center. "Seven Americans die and we think everyone is interested. But two thousand people die in an earthquake in El Salvador and no one gives a fuck. 'Course, I'm not saying there wasn't something different here—something metaphorical. A few good *lads* dying to take on tyranny." He went into a Colonial accent. "Long live these our great *United free States. Death to King George.* But I mean, really. Talk about self-aggrandizement. And wasn't it all just really about taxes?"

In the center of Concord they did a half circle around a granite obelisk inscribed with the names of patriotic heroes, then continued out of town past Revolutionary-era wooden houses gussied up in red, white, and blue bunting and down a small road lined with old oak trees and white pines to a parking lot a hundred yards from the Old North Bridge, jammed with cars.

The Daughters of the American Revolution had planted a long rectangular garden of red, white, and blue pansies and tulips at the far end of the lot, complete with an arched wire grating six inches high along the edge of the flowers, and as Paul squeezed between a Cadillac and a VW SUV, he parked his worn-out Toyota Corolla with one tire over the victory garden.

"Careful of the flowers," Zoe said.

Paul peered over the hood of the car, winced at his mistake, and shrugged. "Nothing I can do now." He pulled his sunglasses out of the beat-up glove compartment and popped the frame over his regular lenses. It was sunny, the air crisp, the sky so blue. It was one of those New England days when you could put all of your troubles away for a couple of hours. They always crept back in.

"Did you get a load of the tall guy when we came in the lot?" Paul said. "Fuckin' A. Seven feet tall, a beanpole, and they made him the drummer boy."

The lot was crowded with Revolutionary War reenactors, tourists, Concord locals, and kids pulling their parents' hands to approach one reenactor or another. Some of the soldiers cleaned their muskets. Others tugged on Revolutionary-era leggings and belts with cartridge boxes. They sifted gunpowder into powder horns. They straightened their three-cornered black felt hats and pulled flags out of pick-up trucks. The redcoats stood at attention in two tidy rows on a grass field beside the parking lot and swung their muskets through firing drills in unison. Their commander, who had a red handlebar mustache, over-enunciated and bits of spit flew. "Fire, men! Fire 'til you take every last one of them."

The main event was supposed to start in thirty minutes, but the minutemen were engaged in some kind of disagreement as to who should play John Buttrick—the leader of the Colonials—when they came down from Punkatasset Hill to the Old North Bridge. And who would order the first shots at the king's men?

Paul looked across the parking lot, then further across the road they had driven in on, and he noticed the Ralph Waldo Emerson house. He had visited the Old Manse a couple of times before—a walnut clapboard with red, white, and blue cloth over the door. Inside the cozy home Nathaniel Hawthorne had churned out *Mosses from an Old Manse,* and in a moment of passion—or so it was said—he had inscribed his love to his wife using her diamond wedding ring on one of the upstairs bedroom windows, in fucking *cursive* no less. There was something else amusing about the house: the irony that the most important battle of the American Revolution—the shoot-out at the Old North Bridge—had taken place just outside the residence of the pacifist Ralph Waldo Emerson. True, Emerson was born after the battle, in 1803, but his grandfather had been living in the house at the time of the Revolution, and the juxtaposition of such pacifism against such violence struck Paul as a symbol of an eternal truth about American history: Nixon, that goofy Vietnam War mortician, was right: the silent majority ruled (not the rebellious, pacifist fringe); the majority killed for their property; and there was nothing really revolutionary about the minutemen, who won a war and took over the entire country to ultimately build fast-food restaurants and Disneyland while abolitionists, pacifists, hippies, and environmentalists were left to make well-intended flatulent noises—to write poems such as Ginsberg's "Howl"—in books for other defeated noisemakers.

A throng of reporters surrounded a man at the entrance to the Emerson house, obscuring him so that not even his forehead could be seen. The man was making some kind of speech. It was ten thirty in the morning—robins and cardinals were trying to maintain their identities, splicing their birdcalls between the fifes and drums. TV lights floated above the reporters, and cameras flashed around the journalists with bolts of white light, spearing the man at the center. The journalists pushed recorders toward the man, and when he was done with his statement, voices overlapped firing questions. The rays from the TV lights formed a corona around the reporters, and a ring of vacationing onlookers surrounded the reporters like secondary planets circling the sun.

Paul heard two reenactors next to him speculate about the identity of the man. "What's going on over there?" he asked them. They turned their attention hesitantly away from the reporters. The pupils of their eyes were still tight from the burning lights. One of the soldiers was the awkwardly tall drummer boy. Certainly Paul had never seen so tall a soldier in the good ol' days of the educational slide shows about the American Revolution he'd been forced to watch in elementary school. The tall soldier had a thin, pointy mustache, and he played with the wax at the tips. "You know, I've been on TV a coupla times befo-" he said with a thick south Boston accent, "for other reenactments and *import'nt* events like this one, and I know most of the pepul who participate in these battles, but I can't make out who it is over they'r-." He grunted and put his hand over his crotch. "But I gotta tell ya, whoever it is, is gonna get a good run in the sack tonight. I mean it! My wife saw me on TV last year at the battle over at Fort Warren and she nearly ate me like an a-phro-di-siac." His buddy next to him, a comparatively dwarfish redcoat with a Vietnam MIA pin attached to the leather pouch of his ammunition belt, nodded.

What would you do with soldiers like this? Paul thought. *What would you do if you were their lieutenant? Nice, horny, dumb.* But he hoped to get laid, just like them, when the day's wedding preparations were over.

"I'm going to go check out who it is," Paul told Zoe. She'd caught up to him, finally, after putting grape-colored lip gloss on in the car.

"It's probably just the mayor of Concord," Zoe said. "Isn't the reenactment going to be over there?" She waved in the direction of the river to indicate she'd rather go straight to the bridge.

By day she worked at Mass General Hospital as a nurse, and in the evening she acted in the few theaters of Boston. Reporters came in front of the hospital all the time to cover famous patients, and she'd grown tired of the press unless they had something to do with the theater. But her real aversion to TV cameras, Paul thought, was that she was afraid of being caught less than fully beautiful on tape. She told him all the time the camera made everyone put on ten pounds. At the beginning of her career she'd been on a national soap opera in L.A. for six months, until her character was poisoned. After that she couldn't find okay work, and she'd eventually ended up East.

Behind the Emerson house, to the right, down a pathway lined with ancient white pines, a replica of the Old North Bridge spanned the tiny Concord River, a half a wagon wheel rising in a pastoral arc over the river. Grandmothers and grandfathers, parents and children meandered down the path toward the bridge, where the reenactment would eventually begin.

"It can't be the mayor," Paul said. "The way they're asking him questions is too intense. I'm going to go see what's up."

Zoe looked at her watch. They were due at the caterer's in an hour to finalize the menu. (The wedding was scheduled in thirteen days and the first course had yet to be settled.) She was exhausted by all of the planning, but Paul thought she looked phenomenally good, even though she was clearly impatient with him (and had every right to be, he thought). She had on a pair of purple see-through imitation Gucci plastic sunglasses over her large, glassy, dark-brown eyes, a hand-embroidered peasant blouse that left her shoulders bare, dark tight jeans, and her thick hair, touched with henna highlights, was pulled back into a high ponytail that accented her cheekbones.

"Who knows?" Paul said. "It could be David Mamet. Or Arthur Schlesinger Jr. or some other famous director or historian. Maybe Henry Kissinger is telling us he's decided to become German again!"

But he knew almost no one cared about historians or Henry Kissinger anymore except the viewers of C-Span, PBS, and Book-of-the-Month Club hobby historians who took summer trips to Gettysburg in RVs, and to Concord, too, of course. The Old North Bridge at Concord was hobby history central. (Although he theorized the Civil War excited people more than the Revolution. Northerners preferred to hear how they'd kicked the shit out of the South, and Southerners loved to hear how they'd fought the North in order to preserve their plantation "culture and honor." They liked to think they would have won, too, if it hadn't been for a few twists of fate. And studying the Civil War gave Southerners the opportunity to argue that it hadn't been about slavery. No, they loved their niggers, they were so good to their Negroes, they understood their niggs; the war had plainly been all about states' rights.)

It was this loop of stalemated arguments that caused Paul to teach only post–World War II American studies: the present had yet to be mantra-fied. A young scholar of the recent past could do more than simply challenge historical "truths," writing obscure articles, adding only tiny pebbles to the stone soup of history. A young observer of recent times could come up with an original *grand explanation,* an account that might last, like Thucydides' *Peloponnesian War* (though nothing lasted forever, really . . . and besides, the trick now was not to document the main battles but rather the fringe characters and trends that bordered on the mundane yet which people could identify with). Yet, seven days ago in a meeting with the chairman of his department, his grand plans and ideas had spontaneously combusted. Chairman Kominski had informed him, choosing his words as carefully as a surgeon employing a scalpel, leaning his bony butt against his battleship-gray desktop (the same desk they had in every office): "Now Paul . . . I know B_____ Community College isn't always the be-all end-all. And for this reason, we're usually more than accommodating to a young professor who needs a little more time. But your seven years are up . . . True, you brought in fresh air when you came. I still remember your first term here. And big ideas almost nonexistent in a place like this . . . You were brutally good then, perhaps because you were an outsider from the 'normal' academy, and I had high expectations for you . . . But you've got to understand the pressure from the other members of the department who've already earned their permanent positions, and from the other candidates coming up who want tenure. The faculty has demanded we hold a final up or down vote . . . So unless you can finish a manuscript and get a publisher by the end of June, or at least write a significant article—just one—I don't have to tell you what the outcome of the meeting is likely to be."

The words sounded like a horn at the end of a long tunnel warning of a crash rapidly approaching. Paul had been told when he took the job that tenure wouldn't be a problem, and for the most part his students liked him. And wasn't this a community college? It was hardly a research university. He found his voice, at last. "And that's what I want to do, too, Chuck. Finish my book. I mean, *of course* I'll finish it. The manuscript is halfway through. Or at least a quarter. I'm just temporarily blocked." He threw his hands up in the air, as if to say, *What do you want me to do about it? It's out of my control.*

And it was out of his control, wasn't it? He found it impossible to write after the first forty-five pages. He'd been blocked for six years now—something even he had to admit was a feat for someone only thirty-four years old. But his incompetence didn't stem from having no research. He had piles of note cards and videotapes, reams of material detailing American conspiracy theories, the origin and development of popular how-to sex books, the history of American studies of sexual dysfunction, the development of the modern porn industry and private gun collecting as characteristics of American paranoia and feelings of inadequacy and the search for nirvana—but none of it was molded into any cohesive structure.

I must be a fucking idiot, he told himself as he left Chairman Kominski's office. *Just a fucking, plucking idiot. A failed nin-com-fucking-poop.* Of course, he didn't really fully believe this, yet. Did he? But it was becoming harder and harder not to. Hadn't he dropped out of a losing band? Hadn't he frittered away seven years without producing an article, let alone a book? He'd planned to tell Zoe last night about his meeting with Kominski, an encounter he was well aware had already taken place a week ago, but he found it impossible. Wouldn't she just think he was even *more unworthy* than she already probably thought he was, just before the wedding? Yet he did try to tell her last night when they were in bed. He twisted the words through his mind. But before he was able to find the courage to speak, she'd turned away, pushing her down pillow behind her head like a wall, blocking him with her elbow as he lay in bed. And so he stared up in the darkness of the room, at the ceiling, and said nothing except to himself, *What a lame mother-fucker, what an absolute loser I might become if I don't do something about my lameness.*

"OK," Zoe said unwillingly. "Go check it out." She waited to see if Paul would capitulate to her unsubtle plea that he stick with her. And he might have. He started to cave. But as if to rebuff him, Zoe beat him to the punch. "I'll see you later," she said. "I'll meet you over by the bridge." She headed away, and Paul stood in the middle of the crowd of reenactors and tourists with a pocket of air next to him where Zoe had stood.

And the man in front of the Emerson house—who was he? Paul approached him without Zoe, aware of the absence of her perfume, her fruity lip gloss, and her heat, but he felt some unspoken liberation, too, and he moved close enough to the crowd that he could finally see the star *attraction,* the man surrounded by reporters.

And it was his brother! How could he have failed to notice him before? What was he doing here? His brother was the kind of person you recognized instantly, not only because he was famous but because he radiated some kind of aura, some kind of crazy certainty. His brother always attacked and cajoled the press and his audiences, toying with them, berating them, telling them, Shame on you! You ought to know better, and that soon everyone would come to see the obviousness of the wisdom he was bestowing. The frequent truth of his words, and the unhesitant moral certainty with which they were spoken, had led to a massive grudging respect among the U.S. public. He was one of the most recognized lawyers in America, one of four or five whose names appeared as regularly in the tabloids as in the *Times.* He had defended major athletes accused of murder and theft (but who had been freed on account of tainted evidence gathered by incompetent police and outright racists); he had led Jewish survivors of Nazi death camps when they took on big German companies demanding compensation for slavery; he had, almost contradictorily, defended neo-Nazis in Chicago to guarantee their right to free speech. He had won multibillion-dollar lawsuits against the tobacco industry for its lies in advertising and then defended the right of citizens to smoke in bars. He lurked behind most of the high-profile free speech and individual liberty cases in America. Was he a libertarian? Not really; he believed the government had a role to play. After all, without a strong government, he claimed, only sheer might ruled. But when terrorists threatened the safety of the U.S., he demanded individual liberties be protected. So he often expounded upon individual freedoms that must be guaranteed and the need to curb the force of well-meaning but misguided or corrupt police and military officers. For the most part, right-wingers hated him, but then sometimes they found him on their side.

At the age of thirty-eight, he was a tenured professor at Harvard Law School, with eleven books published, and he had a large office with a Swedish leather executive chair surrounded by shelves of books (all of which he had actually read), including translations of his books and bound copies of legal articles he had written, along with current research clippings put together by three research assistants. His office view from the top floor extended over the oaks of the law school court-yard to the church steeples and blue cupolas of Harvard's broader campus. On the door to his office he had taped the hate mail that he found amusing and disgusting, the letters of men (rarely women) who wished to destroy the Constitution and other liberties. The letters revealed not only what he was battling but attested to his fame and to his love of fame. He had framed pictures from U.S. presidents—whom he had advised—and life-size caricatures of himself drawn by leading political cartoonists; a basketball signed by the best player in the NBA; various plaques with honorary degrees from major universities and one from the National Bar Association. He had three framed covers of major magazines: *People* magazine's cover fell into one of its rare forays into the "intellectual sphere," which was OK, because wasn't he more than some kind of intellectual, a cultural figure?

Paul's brother held forth in the middle of the crowd of reporters. "Isn't it time we put some of these slimeballs in jail? We're talking corruption on a scale almost never seen before. We're talking BILLIONS of dollars lost in pension funds for the small guy. And all of this because the president's unwilling to put some teeth into defending the right of every person in America, big or small, at the SEC, to free and accurate information. I mean, who are these CEOs kidding? Pro forma earnings? Let me tell you what *pro forma* means—that's Latin for 'I can get away with whatever I want.' It's fantasyland! Free speech *doesn't* mean public figures can engage in misleading statements. These are not *private* individuals. These are not people without any responsibilities. These are the CEOs of major U.S. corporations, and when they lie to the American public and to their boards, and to their stockholders, somebody needs to go to jail."

True, Paul thought, *but what about your own crimes?*

Cyrus gestured almost imperceptibly for Paul to wait until he was done with the press conference. Paul was attuned to the commands of his older brother.

"And so, that's why I've come here today," Cyrus said, pausing to let the full heat of the white lights buzz above the unusual moment of silence. A hush came over the reporters, who sensed an important announcement was about to be made, the kind that would lead to a real story, to something more than the violent robbery at a convenience store in Roxbury, or upcoming school cutbacks, or the persistent rain they had been having all spring until this first bright day, the nineteenth of April, when, in 1775, two hundred and twenty-nine years ago, a group of Colonial minutemen had taken on the British soldiers. Cyrus moistened his lips. He raised his hand with his index finger heavenward, not looking at the reporters but straight into the TV cameras. "For the sake of this community. For the sake of disinfecting the rotten stench in Washington and the moblike politics in Boston. For the sake of bringing back the rule of law to this—what can always be our great land, but a land that, to remain great, must be defended and protected and never taken for granted. For the sake of the kids in Roxbury, who don't have a chance compared to the people with their nice lawns and Volvos who live out here in Concord. Yet for the sake of the people here in Concord, too, who mean no harm but who just need to be reminded of their duties. For genuine promises, and real hope, and liberty, and in the hope of emulating the honor and tenacity of the minutemen who fought here at Concord, I, Cyrus Berger—" he pointed his finger into the cameras, "have decided to enter the race for the Ninth Congressional District. And I promise a tough and fair, all-out, knock-'em-down race that will leave the opposition speechless! So whether you're a Republican or Democrat against me, I say to you today, 'Bring it on.' And whether you're a Republican or Democrat for me, I say to you, 'I am ready to serve you! Let us go forward.'"

A number of tourists, and even some reporters, clapped. The language was clichéd, Paul thought, yet genuinely inspired; but what filled his more conscious mind was sheer shock, slight awe, and wonder. He'd had no idea Cyrus intended to run for Congress. Cyrus had never really shared such plans with the rest of the family. He simply showed up for the Passover and Christmas gatherings that had lasted until his parents separated after the death of their brother Andrew.

One more trophy in the case, Paul thought. When they were kids growing up in North Cambridge, in a small house with a chain-link front fence and a roof that often leaked—not because they were so poor (although they were low on money), but because their father always felt he had "better" things to do with his time, like stay in the basement of the house casting a series of small lead statues of Greek satyrs and other mythical figures—Cyrus had built a large glass case in his room to display his trophies. Cyrus started a computer consulting business when he was fourteen. He developed a system for encoding legal cases that he eventually sold to LexisNexis, and a plaque with appreciation from the company stood prominently in the glass case next to the shofar he blew at Rosh Hashanah services, surrounded by dozens of other trophies.

Cyrus ended the press conference abruptly. The reporters shouted: How have you suddenly come to this decision? Does this mean you'll be giving up your position at Harvard? Does this mean you won't finish with the Pete Delmacio case currently on trial? Does this mean you're disappointed with the new president of Harvard?

But he refused to answer any more questions. He stepped into a black limousine waiting by the side of the Emerson house, on the driveway next to the garden where Henry David Thoreau had often come to visit Emerson to inspect his beans and to steal many a meal. Cyrus motioned to Paul to get in the limo with him.

"I can't," Paul said. "Zoe's waiting by the bridge." He said the words softly, mouthing them more than anything, since he knew Cyrus wouldn't be able to hear him with the reporters crowded around the limo. Cyrus flicked his forefinger at Paul, up and around in the air then down to his feet, calling him to come sit in the limo. He put his palm out, flashed five fingers, then pointed at his watch. He sat in the back of the car, face forward as he spoke to the driver, waiting for Paul with the door open. A few cameramen took last-minute close-ups. The mirrored glass of the driver's side window next to Cyrus rolled upward smoothly and then shut.

"Five minutes only," Paul insisted, and he got into the back of the car. Even with the door open, the beige leather interior already muffled the voices of the reporters. "Zoe's back at the bridge," Paul said again.

"Just get in for a couple of minutes," Cyrus said, and the driver stepped out and shut the door. "I'll drop you off at the back of the museum on the other side of the bridge in a couple of minutes." It was silent in the limo except for the smooth rush of air pumped into the hermetically sealed interior. The lighting was a soft incandescent yellow. There was room for four in the back of the limo, facing each other, and a drinks bar. The last time Paul had been in the back of a limo like this was after a concert his band had given in Detroit eight years ago. The limo pulled out of the gravel driveway, nudging carefully but persistently through the crowd of reenactors and tourists—pushing those who got in the way to the side—as tourists gawked at the windows of the limo and moved away like the parting of the Red Sea, in a pleasant way Paul had almost forgotten; then the car turned down a country road bordering the Minute Man National Historical Park. The driver steered smoothly, sliding the limo along an old stone fence that lined the road.

"You want a drink?" Cyrus said.

"I don't know," Paul said. "Do I look like I need a drink?"

"You look a little tense. Relax. The wedding will be fine. Take off your vest." He pointed at Paul's orange down vest. Paul left the vest on and put his hands in his pockets.

"That's funny," Paul said. "I don't feel tense. What are *you*? Suddenly an expert on weddings?"

"Maybe. At least I have two of them under my belt. Two is better than none. But you'll figure that out soon. The advantage of two marriages is that you know when a marriage is over." He looked wistful and remorseful for a moment.

"So how are things with Rebecca?" Paul said. The last time he'd met up with Cyrus was at a XXX theater in Chinatown a month ago. Cyrus had called him to the theater drunk and asked him to take him home so that no one, including any taxi driver, would know.

"Fine. Rebecca's there. The kids are fine. They're there." He rubbed a finger in one of his ears to see if there was any wax. It was one of the peculiarities of Cyrus that he could be so savvy and diplomatic in front of figures of power—that he could even be obsessed with manicuring and cutting his nails perfectly—yet that he could be so crude. He liked to eat barbecued chicken, then have prostitutes suck the sauce off his fingers before going down on him, and he liked to pick the lint between his toes, and he took some pleasure mixed with disgust in walking by a Port-A-Potty near the new construction site at the law school—taking in the smell.

"What's this running for Congress about?" Paul said. "Why are you suddenly running for political office? It seems you, but not quite *you*.

Where's the real fame and glory in it? I thought you liked to play the national gadfly, the outsider and conscience of America. And why'd you announce it all so suddenly, then cut off the press conference?"

"Mystery. It's all about mystery. Don't you see? First I tell them everything, and then I tell them nothing. Familiarity breeds contempt."

"And what about all the people you promised you'd help out?"

"I will. And I want to." Cyrus placed the broad palm of his hand on Paul's thigh and squeezed harder, perhaps, than he realized. A piece of glass separated the back of the limo from the driver. "Do you know what it is to feel you need a new challenge?" Cyrus said. "When I began studying the law, I was sustained by the idea that what I was doing was *just*—what I considered even holy." He attended synagogue on Friday nights and kept the Sabbath. "And I *do* uphold the work of God. But what if God makes his gifts so sound the enemy seems weak? What if the enemy is always slain? Then it makes me think it all comes too easily, and that perhaps I am the anti-God rather than God's tool. Perhaps I'm the serpent . . . So it's only through a new challenge, through a real challenge that I'll be back on the right side. I would run for the Senate or even the presidency, but that challenge cannot be jumped at initially or the wall will go unsurmounted."

"No, I never have that problem," Paul said. He couldn't tell if Cyrus was speaking in this religious mumbo jumbo to scold him or convert him. The only thing he knew was that Cyrus was a hypnotist and a hypocrite. But could he really just leave him characterized as simply as that? As a hypocrite? Hadn't Cyrus won truly landmark cases before the Supreme Court? Hadn't he helped millions?

"I heard about your problem with the tenure committee," Cyrus said.

Years ago, Cyrus had met Chairman Kominski, and—as with anyone he met whom he saw as a potential resource—he'd kept in touch with him all these years. The connection between Kominski and Cyrus was no secret to Paul. It was the reason, most probably, he had initially been hired. Not that Paul hadn't qualified on his own merits for the job. But Paul had come to wonder just how big a role Cyrus had played in helping him get the job. "I'll do my best to convince them to keep you on," Cyrus said. "But you have to learn the power of positive thinking. You have to find your inner strength again. I can bring you to the water, but you have to drink. How hard can it be for you to finish the book? Without some publication, there's little that even *I* can do for you."

There were times, Paul thought, when his brother lapsed into epic thinking. He simply believed in the quest, in being heroic, in conquering, in winning, in justice, in God. It was the key to Cyrus's success in America. He believed in the same optimistic ends as the millions of people who surrounded him. Not that he shared the conservatism of the majority, but he shared the fundamental ends. That's why he'd been able to connect with so many juries. While Paul—what did he believe in? He wasn't sure he believed in anything except for what he found in front of himself at any given moment in time. He was not prone to planning. He liked to wake up in the morning and see where the world would lead him, where he would stumble. He disliked plans more than anything. Even wedding plans. *I believe in fun,* he wanted to say to Cyrus. But he said instead, "You're making me feel embarrassed."

"But before I talk to Kominski," Cyrus said, "I want you to do a favor for me. I want you to promise you'll never speak to the press about our family, or about me. And I want you to talk to Dad about the same thing. It's for your own good, you know." He put his arm around Paul, pulled him tight, and gave him a noogie. Then he fell silent.

Outside the limo, young spring leaves, so bright, were splattered with shadows from the leaves above so that the trees mixed half light, half dark in some kind of Manichaean pattern, the good with the bad. Ahead, they approached a two-story Georgian-style redbrick building with thin, white colonial columns—the museum of the Old North Bridge and of the rest of the Minute Man National Park. At the museum, which stood at the top of Punkatasset Hill on the opposite side of the bridge from where Zoe would be waiting, the minutemen reenactors had gathered and would descend to fight the British.

"I don't want you to talk to Kominski," Paul said. "For once this isn't about you but about me." When he'd entered the limo Paul had thought a drink might actually be nice, but he wanted out of the tiny interior now. The carpeting was so clean a faint odor of ammonia crept into his nostrils. It smelled like Mexicans had vacuumed the car. The drinks bar and the leather interior were all beautiful, shiny and clean. But it was all untouchable and out of reach now. Paul rubbed his hand on the soft leather.

"Suit yourself," Cyrus said. "But if you find yourself floundering later, remember it's easier to resuscitate someone while they still float, before they sink." Cyrus looked directly into Paul's eyes. "You forgot to promise," he said.

"Whatever."

"I mean it," Cyrus said. He told the driver via the intercom to drop Paul off at the roundabout in front of the museum, but too many minutemen were crowded there, forcing the limo to a crawl. Paul unlocked the door and pushed it open while the car was still moving, and the limo came to a sudden stop. "I'll be watching you," Cyrus said. Paul heard him only faintly as he stepped out of the car.

"I have to get back to Zoe," he said to no one in particular. He was late for Zoe. He wanted to find her before she became uncomfortable wondering where he was. He had been late for most things in his life.

A plume of smoke rose from the center of the town of Concord. This was the sign the reenactors had been waiting for. The town of Concord was now officially on fire. In the real battle, nine hundred British were sent west from Boston to take the ammunition supplies of the Colonials at Barrett's farm. Word of the planned raid on the farm was carried by Paul Revere to the minutemen, first at Lexington and then at Concord. The Colonials retreated to Punkatasset Hill, outnumbered. Four hundred Colonials faced the larger British army. (And the British had fourteen thousand troops encamped in forty-seven regiments around Massachusetts, primarily back in Boston.) But the numbers I'm giving, of both the British and the Colonials, played out over the *entire* battle, from the moment the British advanced from Boston in the dead of night to their retreat twenty miles back to Boston the next day. Far fewer fought at the battle of the Old North Bridge. The British lost 140 soldiers over the entire expedition and the Colonials ninety. The key thing to know about the battle of the Old North Bridge is that the Colonials had yet to fire on the king's men. Up until that time, they'd been shot at by the British without returning fire. The battle of the Old North Bridge was the first Colonial resistance to the British where British soldiers were killed. The Brits had the low ground on the battlefield, and they already controlled the bridge. When the Colonials saw Concord burning, they decided to go back to save the village. But to get there they needed to cross the Old North Bridge. Two Concord Colonial companies descended Punkatasset Hill to take on the British. The actual battle took place at 7 A.M., but seven was too early for most tourists, so, although the reenactors would have been glad to get started at that hour, the reenactment didn't take place until eleven. (There was a greater number of drums and fifes at the reenactment, too—perhaps because none of the musicians had to fear for his life anymore. Everyone was using cartridge blanks.) At the actual battle, each Colonial minuteman carried one fowling piece (or musket) and thirty lead balls in paper cartridges filled with powder; each had a bayonet, a hatchet, and a knapsack. (I am giving you all of this information because, like me—the narrator—you probably didn't get these details in junior high. You probably just learned about the defeat of the British at the bridge, or about Paul Revere's ride, without knowing why he was riding anywhere. All that sticks in the mind are lights in a church steeple, "one if by land, and two if by sea," and a man on horseback—who, it turns out, was much older than we are led to believe in school. If you want the ultimate irony, there were no "British vs. Colonials"—everyone in the colonies was British! It was really the British vs. the British. But for the sake of this chapter, I'll keep things the way we're familiar with. You can get this information online. I picked it up online and by visiting the museum.)

Paul Berger hurried down the hill from the museum, along the edge of the field where the reenactment was just starting. He assumed Zoe would be near the bridge, where they had vaguely agreed to meet. If all else failed, he hoped they would hook up after the battle, back at the car. The problem was that hundreds of tourists blocked his way, like spectators at a golf tournament packed around the eighteenth green, so as he rushed toward the bridge, he bumped into one after another. Some told him to watch where he was going. A mother, noticing Paul approach, pulled her two children close in against her thighs. He should have insisted Cyrus drop him off back at the Emerson house, which would have been much closer to Zoe, on the same side of the bridge as her, but it was too late to go back now. Cyrus's limo had long disappeared.

In the distance, sixty yards down the hill, a thick regiment of British soldiers bunched around the other side of the bridge from Paul, and a dozen British stood on the bridge itself. At the edge of the bridge closest to the Colonials and to Paul, two British soldiers pretended to pull up planks from the bridge so that the Colonials wouldn't be able to walk across. Eight British officers stood on the bridge. One placed his hand over his forehead to block the sun to see the Colonials more clearly. Another pulled out a leather-covered telescope to observe the enemy. The swords of the British officers, sheathed in their black covers, bounced at their sides.

The Colonials moved in a blue bulge down the hill, fifers whistling a shrill Yankee-doodle-dandy, the drummers rolling their marching beat in 4/4 time below the piercing flute notes. The booming echoes of the skins of the drums hushed the crowd of onlookers. *I'll have to try that next year,* Paul thought. He had a powerful urge to grab one of the drums and join the group as it moved down the hill. He ran along the edge of the crowd of tourists, trying to keep pace with the quickly advancing Colonials. Where was Zoe? As he dodged the tourists, he looked ahead to the river and scanned the crowd on the opposite side. The water of the river flowed slowly, thick brown with the residue of winter-matted leaves. Plants that looked like rye sprouted along the banks, and a wide crowd of tourists, many with bits of red, white, and blue, the white bright in the brightness of the sun, lined the banks, squinting. There were so many of them, it would be nearly impossible to distinguish Zoe. *But shouldn't it be possible, always, to pick out the person you will marry if you are meant to be together?* Paul thought. It was imperative he should spot her. The Colonials moved closer to the British down the hill. Soon they would be within firing range of the British. The crowd on the opposite bank of the river leaned forward, straining, preparing themselves for the impending battle, their shoulders tense, even the children—everyone sensing war was on the way. Paul pushed through the crowd of tourists faster now, bumping more firmly. He must find Zoe. The drums reverberated, calling each side to battle. There were too many tourists on the other side of the bridge, splayed wide from side to side around the British multitude. A wall of red, white, and blue. A wall of everyone except the one who counted, he thought.

When the drums stopped, the Colonials had massed only twenty yards from the British. And in that moment of silence—when tourists were waiting for the first shot, the musket fire that would be heard around the world, children hushed, the two groups of soldiers separated by only twenty yards of glistening green field moistened by dewdrops evaporating in the sun—Paul finally saw Zoe. She had her purple sunglasses in one hand and her other hand over her eyes, scanning the battlefield. He had picked her out. Not instantly, but he had seen her before she had seen him. It was a good sign, he thought. A good omen for the wedding. And as if he could communicate with her telepathically, she saw him now, too, and waved. She waved hard and then raised her hands into the air next to her shoulders and her eyebrows as if to ask where he had been.

Paul shrugged. He wouldn't tell her about his trip in the limo with Cyrus, the envy he had felt, or how much he loved her. He would just tell her Cyrus had been the man in front of the Emerson house.

The British shot first at the Colonials. A man named Davis was killed on the Colonial side. The man who was supposed to play John Buttrick ordered the Colonials to return fire. "Fire, fellow soldiers," he shouted. "For God's sake, fire!" But there was still some dissent among the minutemen as to who should play John Buttrick, and a second man stood next to the first John Buttrick and called out, "Fire, fellow soldiers, for God's sake, fire!" The first John Buttrick didn't hold a musket. He simply pointed toward the British. But the second took his musket and pointed it at the British side. The first John Buttrick tried to push the second Buttrick's weapon down. "What are you doing?" he demanded. But it was too late, the second John Buttrick, off balance, falling toward the ground and forgetting to withdraw his ramrod after packing in powder, fired.

It took only a fraction of a second for his blackpowder-driven ramrod to fly toward the other side of the river, but the rod went nowhere near the British. It wended wide, fifteen yards to the right, into the crowd of onlookers.

What Paul saw then as he waved back at Zoe was the sudden collapse of Zoe's body. She fell to the ground, and the tourists around her looked puzzled, then screamed. Zoe lay on the bank of the river, bunched in pain. She placed her hand on her lower stomach, just beneath her appendix, near the upper crest of her pelvis. She let out a gut-wrenching cry, and the battle raged on, blue smoke filling the field and the bridge as tourists made space around Zoe. Paul ran toward the river and jumped into the water to get to her. His orange vest was drenched. The brown water was cold, but he paddled as hard as he could to reach her.

CHAPTER 2

The day Zoe and Paul met they found themselves together at a health retreat in Iowa, of all places. The Zaliya Rashna Manapurna meditation center was founded in 1982 by a man from Varanasi, India, who called himself Buffalo Man. (He'd chosen the name in sympathy for the Black Hawk Indians who had lived in Iowa before they were eradicated.) Buffalo Man was skinny, his muscles firm from yoga, and he moved around the meditation center in a saffron-colored dhoti, taking quiet, quick steps, smiling and raising his hands in *namaste* greetings to his students. It was six years before Zoe would be shot at Concord (the date of this chapter is 1998), and she had made a little extra cash on some hot Internet stocks, so she could afford the vacation. She'd heard about the Rashna Retreat—as it was more commonly known— from an actress friend of hers back in L.A., and she'd read about it in *W* magazine. (Zoe lived in Boston now.)

Paul stumbled upon the Rashna Retreat in the late afternoon one day after some summer/time-off-from-school conspiracy research at a gun convention twenty-five miles outside of Iowa City. His research was going full tilt at the time, and he'd already written forty-five pages of a book he had in mind. After three days of interviewing people at the gun show—trying to get personal answers to questions from sweaty, reticent gun dealers reluctant to fill out anonymous questionnaires on how they felt about their sex life—he was exhausted. He'd also been tracking down the latest rumor at the convention about the Black Maltese laser gun, which was, supposedly, under top secret development by the Defense Department and which he was told would bring guns "to a whole new level."

Toward the end of the last day of the show, as gun collectors packed up their booths and weapons, Paul wended his way in the direction of Iowa City. The temperature was a humid 102, and he stopped to pick up a hitchhiker out of sympathy for the scalding heat the man—who was oddly fit and clean for a hitchhiker—must be feeling. The guy said he was headed to the Rashna Retreat and told Paul to just drop him off by the side of the road, next to a bright orange sign with a logo of a woman with hands folded calmly in prayer, the tips of her fingers almost reaching a *bindi* on her forehead. The sign swayed peacefully in the summer wind, beckoning newcomers down a long dirt road leading to the retreat, and Paul's curiosity was piqued. He volunteered to take the man all the way to the front door. Daisies and a field of California poppies lined the road. Paul had heard about the Maharishis of Fairfield, Iowa (kooky, cultish people who called minor levitation "hopping"), but he'd never heard of the Zaliya Rashna Manapurna meditation center. Next thing he knew he met Buffalo Man, an extremely convincing, fast-talking, spiritual guru/businessman, supremely fit and articulate, the type Paul felt was dubiously connected to any spirits yet who seemed to have his shit together and some wisdom to impart, and since Paul was as hot as a banana flambé, and since he knew he didn't really want to spend another night in Iowa City at the Hawkeye Motel (and for this reason he had taken his luggage with him to the last day of the gun show), he accepted an invitation to stay the first night free. Buffalo Man assured him a second and third time there would be no charge for the first night. (After that, he told Paul, he could pay for a week or more of relaxation, meditation, and inner spiritual cleansing by credit card or cash but no checks, and the decision could be made in the morning before checkout.) "What do you have to lose?" he said. "Only your stress." It was an odd parody, Paul thought, of Marx's "You have nothing to lose but your chains." Buffalo Man winked at Paul as if he could read his mind.

At the retreat check-in counter, a woman behind the desk took far longer than she should have. *What is it about New Age and natural herb and homeopathic people that makes them so slow?* Paul thought. He was patient, but twenty-five minutes of waiting for the processing of a simple form? He stared at the diamond stud in her nostril and wondered why they needed his social security number. His weight and eating preferences, and an indication of whether he had any food allergies—OK. But what did they need his SS# for? He parked his Toyota Corolla behind cabin 178. His room was one of the outermost cabins of the retreat complex, and it seemed designed for the summer months, when there was an overflow of spa visitors. The cabin's exterior resembled a tall, round corncrib with chicken wire and corn husks woven into the wire. Was Buffalo Man trying to pack too many people into the meditation center? Was he giving away too many promotionals to attract new customers, trying to reach national guru stardom? Yoga was getting so hot, the last time Paul was at a supermarket he'd seen a pregnant sitcom star posing as a yogi on the cover of *TV Guide.* There was big money to be made in meditation.

Yet once inside the cabin, he dismissed the idea of a scam. The cabin floor, made of smooth, aromatic hardwood that smelled like it had been imported from the rain forests of Burma, and the rich grain of the wood beckoned his feet to shed their stiflingly hot tennis shoes. Most important, some serious insulation separated the outer corn husks from the inner room, and he was bathed in a jet of cool, radiant air-conditioning. He flopped on the bed; or rather, the futon. And although he felt he had outgrown futons (wasn't there a time when most people grew tired of waking up with their face so close to the floor?), it was a surprisingly comfortable mattress fit snugly on a teakwood frame. With his head propped against a firm pillow, he checked out the rest of the room. Across from the bed hung a cloth painting of Ganesh. The elephant god was sky blue, with six arms, and danced playfully in the air above an altar with apples and oranges that someone had arranged in perfect pyramid-shaped offerings to mysterious gods (could they really teach Guatemalan maids to do this in Iowa?). The offering was potentially to Ganesh, but it seemed the retreat was ready to accept the whole pantheon of gods in the universe. Next to the two pyramids of fruit, four small tin cups filled with butterfat candles gently sputtered in the current of the air-conditioning. Paul certainly hadn't felt such comfort under the harsh fluorescent lights of the gun show at the National Guard armory (the fifth biggest show in the country). He closed his eyes and rested.

Later that night, after a dinner of lentil soup mixed with special herbs, including what he took a wild guess might be vanilla—the first course followed by a *bento* box of sushi, and a small bowl of yogurt with cucumbers and mint—he meandered his way to the meditation room, where everyone else was headed. He felt like an initiate drawn into some kind of ritual. The whole place interested him. He'd always wondered what it was like to hang out at an expensive health retreat. He joined the mass of students, who seemed to know in silence, all at once, it was time to gather.

Zoe was already in the meditation room, trying to relax and to concentrate in silence in the central gathering place—a wide-open space for meditation. Her eyes were closed, and when she opened them she saw a chubby twenty-eight-year-old next to her with a Boston Red Sox baseball cap. He was sitting uncomfortably on a purple yoga mat, attempting to fold his pale legs before the evening meditation class would begin. His legs were clearly inflexible, and he let out an embarrassed chuckle and shook his head at his inability to fold them as he thought all yogis should be able to—even a beginner like himself. He wasn't all that good-looking, she thought, but he seemed like a happy Buddha in a Chinese restaurant, although he wasn't *that* fat.

It took Paul a while to figure out the system before sitting down next to Zoe. Actually, he'd sat down beside someone else to start with. As Zoe meditated and warmed up her breathing with her eyes closed, he'd plopped down on the opposite side of the room by a different woman, crashing his body on the polished hardwood floor that looked like it belonged to some kind of martial arts dojo in Japan. He felt like a kid at wrestling camp rather than someone about to get spiritual enlightenment and yogic training. A number of students gave him ugly looks because he didn't have a yoga mat, and they seemed offended he was already sweating onto the hardwood floor. *What kind of sin is that?* he thought. They stopped staring at him, folded their hands in their laps, and concentrated on what, he assumed, must be their mantras. Eventually, he noticed a tall bamboo basket with neatly rolled-up yoga mats in a corner of the room by the door.

Most of the retreat guests had brought their mats to the meditation center from home; the yoga mats in the bamboo basket were thin and marked those who used them as novices. Paul pulled one out of the basket and it unfolded in front of him as he walked. He nearly tripped on its lower lip. The thing must have popped out of his grip since he was sweating; this room was not air-conditioned for some reason. He knew he couldn't go back to where he'd initially sat down since everyone there was giving him a look like he was the devil—a yoga-mat freeloader—and, besides, the room was filling up back there. It was getting too crowded almost everywhere, so he crossed the room to the only area where there was space, and he sat down next to Zoe. He guessed he was supposed to fold his legs Indian-style. That was how you did it, wasn't it? As he tried to force his left foot over his right thigh, Zoe opened her eyes.

What a fucking joke, Paul thought. What am I doing here in the middle of the cornfields of Iowa trying to wrap myself into some kind of butterflied chicken? This whole goddamn room smells like some kind of incense factory mixed with sweat, and I could be back at the Deadwood in downtown Iowa City drinking a brewski or listening to some good fucking jazz. It was the summer season for jazz in Iowa City, and he had caught wind of a good trio in front of a jewelry store downtown the night before. The drummer had been excellent. He had held his beat, anchoring the sound of the bass. Paul drummed his fingers on the yoga mat. Zoe, sitting to his left, much closer to him—or to anyone—than she really wanted to be, asked him if he could stop tapping his fingers.

"Really? Was I tapping my fingers?" Paul said. He was genuinely surprised. "I was thinking about a cold beer. Sorry." He threw his hands, palm forward, into the air. "Honest, the last thing I want to do is ruin anyone's meditation here. Or do you just call it plain yoga?"

"Like plain yogurt?" Zoe said. She thought what he'd said was cute, though ignorant. It was obvious he never looked at health magazines. He had on a pair of white tube socks and jean cutoffs with white threads dangling from the end of his shorts, while everyone else wore Lycra tops and bottoms. His thighs were almost blue, they were so pale, and his shoulders, though broad, lacked muscle. But his eyes were wide, an appealing bright blue mixed with gray, his lids an odd, contrasting pink that heightened their color, so that the blueness of his eyes was poignant, and she had to admit she had a fetish for sex with chubby men or with men who could be playfully naughty and dirty, who could be unself-conscious in bed—as long as they were clean. "As for ruining my meditation," Zoe said. "You haven't ruined anyone's meditation— *yet.* We haven't begun yet. Buffalo Man will be here any minute. He's never late."

Paul studied Zoe's face. Her face was in shadows but alternately cast into relief by bright orange rays of sunset, since they used only natural lighting at the Rashna center (or candlelight, which they counted as natural). Outside, the sun was setting over a Zen rock garden in front of the meditation room and over the cornfield behind it, so that the corn stood in sharp relief as tasseled silhouettes. Paul had left his glasses back in the room, so it was hard to tell if what he was thinking, and what he was trying to determine, was true as he looked at Zoe. "Don't I know you from somewhere?" he finally said.

"Is that the best pickup line you can think of? You know, for a second I thought you were cute. Chubby, but cute. But I guess you're just chubby." She folded her hands in her lap to begin her breathing again.

"How original," Paul said, "to note I have a bit of a weight problem. You must have 20/20 vision. What are you, some kind of sophisticated East Coast bitch who eats bran cereal for breakfast?" Yet he was more interested in finding out if his hunch was right than in getting into a fight. Without his glasses it was hard to see Zoe as accurately as he needed to. He squinted at her. "But, seriously. Weren't you Jessica on *Too Many Lives to Live*?"

"The show was called '*One* Too Many Lives to Live.'"

"OK. But on the promo ads, I think they just called it 'Too Many Lives to Live.' In any case, when I was on tour, I used to watch you on the bus. I thought you played your role with—what should I say?— panache. That show was hilarious."

"Like hilarious—ha-ha?" Zoe said. "It was a soap opera. It wasn't meant to be funny. It was supposed to be tragic, moving."

"I know. But it *was* funny. Campy. Solid. And you did a great job. You played the part with complete earnestness." Even now, she was displaying some of that earnestness. Her brow was tight, her thin, brown eyebrows and forehead clutched in a frown.

"Are you saying I should have played it some other way? I was *good* in that role. And I made good money doing it. So where's the beef?" Zoe's mouth was narrow, and especially narrow in anger, her lips plump, and her teeth perfectly white.

"Who said anything about beef? That's what *I* just said—you were good at it. Jessica was a good role, and you played it really well."

"But you were suggesting, somehow, that earning a buck in a soap opera is unworthy." If he knew anything about the biz, Zoe thought, he'd know you take whatever jobs and money you can get.

"What are you talking about?" Paul leaned his entire body back and put his arms forward like he was pushing against a wall, to the point he nearly fell off his mat. "Whoa! You're reading way too much into this."

"So what are *you*?" Zoe said. "A *musician* on tour?" She knew far too many wannabe musicians, but she was impressed with anyone who could make an actual career out of music. "What is this, a stop in between gigs?"

"*Was*. I *was* a musician. A drummer. Now I'm a teacher. And I think your show had definite quality behind the schlock."

Zoe was taken aback. Not only was he no longer a musician, he was a teacher, and although teachers were OK in principle, fine, not a problem, good for humanity and kids, absolutely essential even, who was he to judge her about her soap opera days? "So what *happened*?" she said. She talked to him as if to a quadriplegic, in a kind voice, slowly. "How'd you wind up a teacher?"

"Well, what *happened* to the role of Jessica?"

"She got terminated. But she shouldn't have been. I'm still an actress." She pulled her thick, chestnut hair back into a ponytail and fastened it with an elastic band, pulling her arms up and around her head in a way that accented the fitness of her narrow chest, long torso, and petite body.

"Well, I'm no longer a musician," Paul said. "Sometimes musicians are eliminated. Forget about what Neil Young says. Rock and roll dies. Fate terminates us. That's the nasty thing, isn't it? The devil is in who pulls the plug. But I've got a good new gig now. I'm working on a book." His final words sounded too loud, even to him. They were less the strong words he intended and felt when speaking about his book-in-progress and more like a tinny, hollow voice in an empty room that sounded especially loud as the other students went silent when into the room came Buffalo Man.

"Most honorable ladies and gentlemen," Buffalo Man said in an Indian accent as he came in. (An Indian-Indian accent, not a Native American one.) He sat facing everyone on a dais in front of the large window. "Have you taken advantage of the palm readings yet? We hope you will enjoy all of our fine facilities over the course of your well-ness stay. As many of you, I am sure, have noticed, here at the Rashna Retreat, we believe in the combination and unity of *all* significant beliefs and cultures of the world. No *one* culture has a lock hold on the truth, beauty, and health. And so, this is why we are offering you the delectable experiences of *three* different kinds of massages—Swedish,

Rolfing, and shiatsu. And this is why you eat *bento* sushi today with dal from my native India—the lentils of which come from my own personal village in the south of India. The yogurt comes from most beautiful wholesome cows of Iowa, and the cucumbers and mint from our own garden here at the Rashna Retreat. So *all* experiences and sources of food and ideas must be ingested if we are to achieve health—even the bad ones—in order that we may know they are bad; and then, like the most beautiful *flute* player who picks only the *right* notes to play, we pick only the *right* sources and we reject the others. So before there is negation, there must be the ingesting of *all* the treats god offers us. Yet then the pit of the mango must be rejected and purged from the system and planted into the ground so that it can grow into a new tree bearing fruit.

"Today, to encourage you to take advantage of our palm readings, we will have a raffle to pick one retreat-student for a reading I will perform *personally*. Naturally, and unfortunately, I am not able to offer this direct glimpse of the future to all of you, but my assistants Jennifer Rashnaji and Bradford Rashnaji will perform the other readings. Your names have already all been entered into the raffle.

"I am encouraging you to take advantage of this reading, not only because of the fun of a raffle, but because it is only by knowing the *future* that we can begin to develop our mental swords to fight our fates. It is only by knowing the future we face that we can begin to define our purpose here in the present." Buffalo Man bobbed his head quickly from side to side in perfect agreement with himself.

"And now, let us work on our breathing and on our yoga." He turned to one of his assistants standing by his side, Jennifer Rashnaji (his assistants were all white), and asked her to turn up the heat for the yoga.

Over the course of the next hour, Buffalo Man put them through various yoga positions. They did the child pose first. The fifty-nine students of the class mounded around the room like ladybugs stuck to the floor, breathing in deeply and then out as hard and as far as they could. With Paul's head down on the floor, battered by the heat—not only did they not air-condition the room, they cranked the thermostat up to 115 degrees—he could barely breathe. He followed the moves as best he could: the cobra, the lion, the table, and even the crow. For a couple of maneuvers he had to hold on to Zoe, and she had to hold him, and he tried not to fall on her in any way, only to follow Buffalo Man's instructions. She was in phenomenal shape, and although they didn't talk to each other, he liked the fact she wouldn't put up with a lame come-on line; for although he hadn't meant to pick her up, hadn't he invaded her privacy when he asked if she was a TV star? The fact she *wasn't* a star anymore was irrelevant. Everyone had a right to their own private space.

It was clear the students in the class were serious about their yoga moves. There was, actually, no bullshit in the class, a surprise to Paul. There was simplicity and beauty in the moves. Yet, although Paul could see the beauty of the positions, they were simply too strenuous for him, and in the heat of the room he nearly passed out. At the end of class he flat out keeled over, and Zoe got him a bottle of water to revive him.

If you (the reader) have ever had your palm read, then you know it's not a thing to be approached without some fear. Paul hadn't come to this conclusion yet, and he had never even thought too much about what it means to have a palm read, because as far as he was concerned, palm reading was something done by ghoulish women wrapped in red, faded shawls, smelling of patchouli, who also read crystal balls at carnival booths or in seedy old brick basements in neighborhoods like Greenwich Village, where gay men might go for a lark, or where hippies might pay for an expert opinion on why nothing was working out in their lives. And did these hippies really need a crystal ball? He had nothing against hippies, but the reason nothing was working in their lives was because they never got their shit together enough to do anything except hang a bunch of potted plants around their rooms and close the shades to block out the bright, harsh light of day. They were lazy. He knew these might be simply ideas inculcated into him by a productive/production-obsessed Anglo-Puritan heritage. After all, he'd encountered plenty of other cultures during his travels around the world. He appreciated relaxation time. He was certainly not driven to endless work. But he believed in work, too, in getting things done, and for this reason he had an aversion to the idea of palm readings, because they seemed to him a fun but delusional waste of time, a pure gimmick, nothing to place any credence in.

Nevertheless, here he was in Buffalo Man's office at eleven o'clock at night, still his first day at the Rashna Retreat, waiting for his turn to have his palm read. He'd been a mess for a while after the yoga class, and he'd retreated to his cabin after thanking Zoe for the water, and around ten o'clock, as he was getting ready for bed, after taking an ice-cold shower, one of Buffalo Man's assistants had knocked on his cabin door and told him he'd been selected for the reading at eleven. Paul talked to the assistant, wrapped in a towel. His whole body was pink from the coolness of the shower, and the sound of crickets played hypnotically in the background. "You know, thanks," Paul said. "I know it's really lucky to have been selected for the reading, but I think I might pass on that one," he told the assistant, Brad Rashnaji.

"Buffalo Man has told me to tell you that you are not the first to be uncomfortable with the idea of a palm reading. He knows you think the idea is fairly foolish and a gimmick, but he insists you come for your reading."

"He told you this just now? By telepathy or something?" It was like a bad C movie. The servant who insists, "My master calls you."

"No, of course not," Brad Rashnaji said. "Telepathy is something that is improbable. Although you never know. Some books call it a seventh sense. I simply mean Buffalo Man has already intuited what your response would be when I told you that you should come for your palm to be read. He said you would say it was a fluke, that you were never lucky and that someone else must have been fated for the reading."

"He came up with that, too?" Paul shook his head to get the water that had settled in his ear to fly out. He banged his temple with the flat of his palm like a coconut, not only to get the water out but because it was a habit when he was confused about a decision. Decisions were tough; multiple options always seemed at hand, all equally good and valid. If he stayed, he would certainly get the good night of rest he needed. The futon was only six steps away, soft and comfortable. And he might even have some fun looking over a few questionnaires from the gun show—a chance to chuckle at the heroic exaggerations the gun dealers indulged in when discussing their sex lives (mixed in, of course, with occasional hints they were a little more doubtful about their sex life than they let on). On the other hand, if he went and had his palm read, Buffalo Man would probably tell him something positive about his future. After all, he was a businessman, right? Keep the customer satisfied. And it would be a good chance to get to know Buffalo Man a little better before leaving in the morning. "What if I take a rain check until tomorrow morning?" Paul said. Maybe he could have his cake and eat it, too. Sleep + palm reading.

"That was the final thing Buffalo Man told me to tell you. Though you may think you can have your cake and eat it, too, there is no way to put off the seriousness of our decisions. While he will not, and cannot, demand you come to your reading, he wishes you to know there may be serious consequences if you delay."

And so, here he was in Buffalo Man's office surrounded by candle-light. He had made the walk to the central building on his own, forty-five minutes after Brad Rashnaji, following a path of neatly raked pebbles all the way to the office. The air was so humid as he walked—it had enveloped Paul's body and the cornfields that lay just along the border of the grounds of the health retreat, and the crickets and insects such as rootworm and cutworm that were cutting at the corn—so that all were unified and connected by the heaviness of the air. He felt instinc-tively the weight of the natural world and the weight of living. Buffalo Man seemed absolutely serious about this. Perhaps not about other things. But he must be serious if he insisted on performing the palm reading at eleven o'clock at night. For there must be other things he would rather be doing at that hour. Like forgetting the retreaters? What did a guru/businessman/spiritualist think about on his time off? Did he miss the people at the retreat? Or did he try to get as far away from them as he could, to a place like Orlando?

"Welcome, welcome again," Buffalo Man said as he arrived at his office. "Have you had a chance to look around? It is important for you to feel comfortable in these surroundings so you will focus on what I am telling you and not on anything else. These objects around us are merely distractions, so please look at them at your leisure and then we will begin."

There was nothing too surprising about the room, though Paul was struck immediately by the number of books, and he was aware of Buffalo Man watching him closely as he walked around the room. Candles and oil lamps provided the only, flickering light and left the room aromatic, smelling like frankincense and myrrh. Rows upon rows of books, tightly pushed together, lined three of the walls, and in the darkness the whole room felt like an Egyptian tomb for a dead king's chief court adviser. The air was musty but holy, and it felt to Paul like generations of secrets were encrypted in the room. The title of a particularly fat book popped out at him: *Shiva: The Destroyer of Worlds.* There was a section of books on organic gardening and also one on chiropractic medicine. A real human spine, from the cerebral cortex down to the coccyx—held together by some glue and clear plastic wire—hung from the center of the ceiling, floating in the air, the white of the bones orange from the candlelight. Most of the room was dark, with shadows filling in the deep corners.

"It feels a little creepy in here," Paul said. "But neat. So neat. In my own work space, I always have papers all over the place."

"That's quite interesting," Buffalo Man said. "You can tell a lot about a person by their work area. So what do you think this room says about me?"

Did he really want an answer? He was probably watching Paul just to get some clues to make his reading more convincing later. Paul would be polite, but he wouldn't give Buffalo Man any information. Let him show his stuff, if he really had any powers. "I don't know," Paul said. "I wouldn't be able to make such a judgment."

"Hmm. That, too, is interesting," Buffalo Man said. "Well, shall we have a seat and begin our concentration together? This is really a two-person thing, you know. You must give your energy to receive energy back. It is like what I am sure you have read about—hypnotism. A person cannot be truly hypnotized unless they are willing to share what is inside of them. Likewise, I cannot *truly* read your palm unless you are willing to believe in the process. Simply try to give up your doubts for fifteen minutes. And as you work with me, I am sure we will get somewhere deeper and more useful than if you resist me."

Buffalo Man directed Paul to a small wooden table by his desk, carved out of sandalwood with the body of Ganesh filigreed into each of the ornate round corners of the table. Every inch of the table was sculpted. The two men sat on carved stools, with red cushions. Buffalo Man took Paul's palms and placed them face up on the table.

"One thing I do not look at is lifelines and that such thing," Buffalo Man said. He dismissed this notion entirely with a quick swipe of his hand. "That is an ancient Gypsy tradition which made its way to Spain via Romania. But to engage in that kind of palmistry you would need to see someone who is familiar with that tradition. I look at the entire palm instead, as I was taught by a teacher in Kashmir." He tapped Paul's palms lightly, warming them up. "So how do you feel? Ready?"

"Skeptical."

"Why skeptical, skeptical, skeptical? Skeptical is all I'm hearing, always, from you."

"I'm not trying to say this to give any offense. I'm just skeptical. I mean, I'd feel just as skeptical of a man in Florida telling me I could catch a big marlin, or if someone called me up and told me I'd won the lottery."

"You see, that is the problem *so many of you* are facing these days. The artificiality of so many things has made you disbelieve even in what is true. So since nothing seems real—even when you have attained all of the possessions you could possibly want—you do not believe you have attained true happiness. For when everything is a chimera, it can never be grasped in the hand. You have gone so far as to doubt even your own authenticity, to doubt whether you yourselves are real. But at some point in your life you must stop chasing after illusions and accept some things as real."

Buffalo Man continued to press Paul's palms. He touched some places firmly and others more gently. He ran his own palm against one of Paul's and looked in the air and concentrated as if he were trying to hear the sound of a mosquito buzzing. He grimaced and touched some more.

"I can see now you are trying to be more cooperative," he said, and he explored around the edge of the palm just beneath the beginning of the index finger, first on the right hand and then on the left. He rubbed and pushed in one spot alone now, and Paul felt a sharp pain, a pressure point that hurt so much as Buffalo Man touched it that he realized he didn't know so much stress could lurk beneath the softness of his pudgy, creamy skin.

"Ouch," Paul said.

"Shh. We are getting somewhere now. You must listen with me." Buffalo Man put his ear down close to the single palm he was rubbing now. He listened to the hand like it was a conch shell that held the deep sounds of the ocean. With his head to the side, looking horizontally away from Paul toward the books on the wall, he began to speak in a more subdued tone like a medium communicating a message from gods somewhere else on the other side of the universe, at the center of the mystery of all being.

"Life," Buffalo Man began, "is a series of concentric circles, radiating outward of each being like the rings of growth on a tree. Each man has one ring for each decade. You are now in the third ring near the end of that ring. In this ring, I can see, you have already begun to give up on your true dream. What was once dearest and nearest to your heart you have now tried to paper over and cover with barbed wire and plywood and chains. The ring is therefore tight and suffocated, but at the end of the ring there appears to be some growth coming, a final warm growing season before the ring terminates. Perhaps, then, you will find your lifelong romantic partner soon. It is quite possible, even, she is here at the retreat, though that is not certain." He pushed his ear directly against the palm of Paul's hand. He listened to one hand and then the other, returning to the original palm. He pressed between the third and fourth metacarpals, and a shooting pain made Paul cry out and nearly fall from his stool. Paul twisted his body away from Buffalo Man, and he felt the need to get up and leave, but Buffalo Man held on to his palm, grasping it, and pulled him back down to his stool.

"Why must I go on?" Paul said.

"Because you want to," Buffalo Man said. "It is the desire of every man to know his fate, even if he does not want to know it."

Buffalo Man did not release the most painful place where his long, thin, bony fingers had been exploring before. He listened closely, again, to the palm. "In the fourth concentric circle of life, near the beginning of the ring, you will lose a brother. This, it is not clear to me, whether it will be a brother of blood or a brotherhood of deep friendship, but it will be lost entirely. No, wait! There are two brothers who will be lost. Each in his own way. One will leave you and another you will leave. This will be an unbearable pain, an agony that will force you to make a great decision you do not want to make . . . I feel also that the love from the third ring, your partner in life, will not reach the end of the fourth ring with you. The fourth ring will be thin and tight. It will not grow far. It will be like the tight ring of a juniper bush. And it will be . . ." Buffalo Man paused; he put his ear directly against the palm and pushed his ear hard against his fingers, which pressed ever more deeply into Paul's palm, nearly crushing him in pain. "And it will be . . ." Buffalo Man's voice continued in a flat tone, "it will be your last ring. From that ring you will cease to be burdened with the trials of life. You will end the cycle of life. What I cannot tell is if you will be reborn, or in what capacity—that is, whether you will be reborn as a dog or a cat or as a sheep or a goat or a cow or a man, or even, perhaps, end the endless birth and rebirth that trouble us all by attaining *moksha.*"

"How can you tell me this?" Paul demanded. "You're sick. A sick man. A sick dude. That's obscene." He attempted to pull his hand away from Buffalo Man's firm grasp, but Buffalo Man wouldn't release his hand, and he was much stronger than Paul. "And what are you talking about in any case, goats and chickens and pigs? You just make this shit up. You're just a speculative con, no better than any of the rest of us."

"Who ever said anything about being better? This is simply what your palm says to me via others who know better. It is not *me* speaking, it is your palm."

"But you're supposed to tell me all sorts of good things, about how rich my fortune might be. Or about how many kids I'll have, and how I'm supposed to be blessed with fortune. Maybe not pure fortune, but mostly fortune."

"And what makes you think that? Because of some cheap fortune cookies made in Taiwan and New Jersey? This is not speculation. This is not tomfoolery. I am not claiming I can tell you the precise nature and timing of these events, but I am telling you they are inevitable. As inevitable as the sun's rising, heating the earth, and causing the moisture of the earth to rise and then fall as rain into the ocean. The rivers flow only one way. To the sea. You cannot force them to go other than the way they will flow."

Paul slumped in his stool, his shoulders bent so far forward he looked like a weeping willow with yellow leaves in the fall. He still didn't believe what the crazy man was saying. But what if it were all true? And why would he lie to him? There was no reason for him to tell him so much bad news. The only good news he'd told him was that he would find someone he loved soon.

"What is the name of the person I will fall in love with?"

"Oh, you think this is some kind of game, don't you? But think about the burden that I, too, face in telling you this news. It is simply what must be told. But there is always a reason for such a telling."

"And what might that be?" said Paul.

"Though there is no way to escape the future planned for us, we can change the way in which we choose to fight that future. If you choose to, now, you can begin a path that will bring you the greatest joy in the time that remains for you. I would suggest you relinquish all of your possessions and go to India and study with the man in Kashmir who has taught me the secret of reading the future."

"Go to the man who taught you how to see how miserable my future will be? Are you kidding?"

"Yes, you must do it if you wish to find any true happiness. Or at least give up all of your possessions. And enter the wilderness naked, until you find your true center. As long as you feel envy, you will never find true peace. As long as you look at the world as a distorted mirror and cannot distinguish what is real from what is false, you will walk in mazes. You will find no true happiness until you remove yourself from everyone who surrounds you, whom you are familiar with. Only then might you seek to attempt to avoid the fate you have been given."

Buffalo Man released Paul's palms and clapped his hands together, bowing his breast to his palms in *namaste* greetings.

"But that's something even you haven't done," Paul said. "There are possessions all over this place. Your whole retreat is an expensive money retreat. Most of the people around here are completely false yogis. What kind of names are Jennifer Rashnaji and Brad Rashnaji? How can you tell me I must do what you don't even come close to doing?"

"That's the dilemma, isn't it? We can know the medicine but find it impossible to swallow." Buffalo Man bowed his head and walked quickly toward the door. "Tomorrow will be a better day. We will meet again tomorrow."

*

Fated to die? Before the age of forty? Most likely even earlier? To lose his two brothers? Paul walked into one of the cornfields next to the retreat. The moon was half full and yellow like the tears of a lion. He had left the retreat behind. The central building of the retreat, a large wooden structure with the check-in desk, dining hall, and meditation center, was empty and hollow as he left the building, the high ceilings cavernous, the heavy wooden beams looming and lit only by a vending machine that sold green tea and mango juice. He was away from all of the buildings now, away from the mowed lawn, away from the cabins that, viewed from the air, formed the shape of the Sanskrit word *om*, away from the pool behind the main building, away from the massage rooms. The cornfield he walked into was the one he had seen earlier, a hundred yards beyond the Zen rock garden. He came up to the edge of the wall of corn, where it met the lawn of the retreat, and the July corn towered over him. He would have to go back to B_____ Community College soon to begin his second year of teaching. Inside the cornfield, the palm-frond-shaped leaves dangled from side to side between pregnant ears on the stalks and drooped beneath the weight of the humidity. He was surrounded by corn, and the leaves rasped his cheeks as he walked. From the moment he entered the corn he lost his orientation. He simply followed the path of a furrow, never straying, walking relentlessly and mechanically at a plodding pace, his feet slowly pounding the moist earth. He had seen a group of Indians at a powwow once, eight men around a drum, each banging a slow death dance, a low lamentation played at a funeral, pounded and pounded as the men all chanted together in high, coyote-like cries, "Ai ai ai ai," "Ai, ai ai." He thought of that rhythm now, that lamentation for defeated warriors, as he walked steadily through the corn. In the indoor tennis court where he saw the powwow dance performed, the chief had explained the Native Americans had played it when the white man had come in his fast choo-choo train, in his Iron Horse that brought soldiers shooting buffaloes out of train windows to starve the Indians and just for fun.

He didn't even know if he believed any of what Buffalo Man had told him. His mind told him Buffalo Man was full of shit; but why, then, did his body feel so heavy, so dejected and weighed down like the corn? And why did he walk away from the retreat following a single row of corn, surrounded by cornstalks that made him feel claustrophobic and that almost guaranteed he would get lost? Was he prepared to spend the night in the cornfield? Now and then a cry of crickets suddenly rose in unison, warning the heat away, warning the producer of the sound of footsteps away. *Every animal,* Paul thought, *lives only to avoid death.* And he had been told his death was appointed, fated, written in the books of the heavens sooner rather than later. So what the fuck was he going to do about it?

He walked on. He had no idea how far from the retreat he was, and in front of him, somewhere not only forward but oddly below, perhaps another fifty yards ahead and down, he heard a whir and grinding of some kind of engine that startled him. The engine whooshed! and moved, zooming like an aural sore through the air and was gone. He continued forward, deep in the corn, and then the corn stopped abruptly at the edge of a sloping precipice, a slanted gash into the earth that led down to a cross-country interstate: I-80. At the edge of the slope, twenty yards above the concrete roadway—which spread in two long bands below in either direction toward what seemed like nowhere—he sat down, and a large semitrailer, an eighteen-wheeler, rushed past, its light bar trailing a white streak that cut into the blackness of the night like a barrage of tracer bullets.

But how exactly would he die? And when? Could he die at this moment, falling down the slope of the ugly, rough, dirt-clod-covered artificial hillside that fell down to the interstate and washed into a concrete rain gully? Could he fall and be hit by an oncoming truck rushing across the nation from California, or returning from its delivery of fruit with a large electric generator to power the baseball lights of a stadium? Or because he was fated to die soon, but in the next decade, did that mean he was invulnerable to death now?

He watched the cars and trucks speed by below him, sometimes a single car, sometimes a group of cars, but even grouped together the cars seemed alone. *Everyone makes his journey to death alone.* The engines of the cars roared; the wind by the side of the road caused tall weeds to sway, gripping forward toward the pavement, trying to break their way into any crack of the concrete. The sheer speed, the pressure of the windshields of the cars and trucks, cut through the muggy air. They would push their way through the ether all the way to their destinations. So would he die unnaturally then? Be cut down by a bullet?

Hit by a train? Or by the propellers of an airplane sucking him into a jet engine? Would he be crushed by the weight of a falling building? Would he fall from the loop of a roller coaster as it reached its zenith? Would he die falling on the tracks of a subway as the train came into the station, or accidentally trip and be electrocuted by the third rail and incinerated to a crisp? He had no idea so many fears lurked within him, just below the surface. He had never had these images before—singly, yes, of course, but never one after the other—a parade of death flashing through his mind at a rate that felt to him like a blind speed. The images flashed one and then another. He saw a red Porsche on a bright blue day, a test car racing around a track in Germany, hugging the curves as it flawlessly maneuvered around one corner and then another at two hundred miles an hour, and then round another corner, until the wheels suddenly slipped out from under the driver, sending the car diagonally, away from the centripetal force that had held it in place so that it hit a side wall and broke into pieces, first a wheel flying off, then blue smoke and a burst of flames, or was it the flames before the smoke, they all seemed to go together in one combustion, and then the front of the car was smashed; the car twirled and hit the side wall again at the end of a turn and, ricocheting, came into the cleanly mowed green lawn at the center of the track, where it ultimately came to a stop. The blueness of the sky shined on, indifferent.

There were pumps keeping patients alive now, respiring while the patients' hearts and lungs could not. There were EKGs monitoring the heartbeats. There were diodes keeping track of the pulse. There were waves of electricity flying along high power lines, into the hospital to deliver power to these patients. And what if the towers failed, somehow fell down? A single tower. Would the patients die? No, a generator would kick in. The power would resume. But even then, the power was precarious. The potential hole exposed momentarily to the engineer responsible for the power system in the hospital.

He, himself, had always tried to go with the rapid flow of everything surrounding him. That was the way he was educated and told he could best breathe and prosper. Though he did his best to seem nonchalant, rebellious; though he had gone the path of a band, at first, as if to say he didn't care about the normal fast path and constructs of engineers and businessmen. Yet hadn't he also tried to take his own part in the rich speed, hoping the band would bring him a piece of the rapid nirvana? Hoping it would give him protection from the pitfalls of bad speed, the possible crash against a wall on the side of a California highway, a crash against the walls of destitution. The balance between good speed and bad was always unstable. And here he was, minutes after having his fortune read, where a stranger had told him such foolish ideas of balance were impossible unless he threw off all of his possessions and went to study with a guru in India. Well that, too, was impossible, wasn't it? He would and could no more go to India and buy into that kind of overly simplistic cure than he could bring back the balance between the good speed and the bad. He felt now he was flying blind. He had been born with so much seemingly endless promise the day men first landed on the moon—July 20, 1969.

From behind him, he heard the rustling of something coming through the corn, moving directly behind and then past, a little further away. In the yellow moonlight he saw a deer step out of the corn, to his right, and perch on the edge of the precipice. Whether it was a male or female he couldn't be sure; but he thought it was a male. The deer had a small rack of thin, pointed horns. It stopped at the edge of the dirt and looked at the traffic below. The eyes of the animal glowed faint amber. It ran quickly down the hill without zigzagging from side to side, stumbling slightly on the looseness of the newly cut dirt, moving powerfully forward. It reached the edge of the concrete and froze. The deer looked up the road, and bright lights of trucks lit up the animal and it stood still. It moved forward, ready to lunge in front of a truck, and then at the sound of a truck's engine, turned quickly backward. It jittered its legs up and down, the white of its tail revealed, the animal stretched as tight as its puckered anus. It seemed to want to cross, and then it turned momentarily away again in fright.

Paul wanted to yell something down at the deer to tell it to get away. He tried to make a sound that would make it aware of the danger it faced. He stood and waved his arms. But the deer looked up the highway into the lights, moving its legs in place, otherwise paralyzed.

He threw a stone at the deer, but he couldn't get it to move. So he went into the corn. He didn't want to see what would happen to the deer. He wouldn't be able to take it if it made the wrong choice and ran onto the road. *What difference does it make if I can save the deer or not?*

he told himself. But it did matter, so he went back to the edge of the highway. And when he got there, he saw the deer was finding another way around his obstacle. It was running to the right, down toward a culvert that ran beneath the highway. It ran into a wide metal pipe and disappeared into a black hole.

Sexually, Paul never hooked up with Zoe at the retreat. They weren't quite compatible yet. But he did run into her the next day by the pool in the early afternoon.

The night before, when he'd found his way back from the cornfield and the highway, he took a cold shower and lay naked on the futon, but he couldn't sleep. Then after many hours of tossing in his sheets and going to the bathroom over and over again to scarcely pee, and pinching his cheeks to reassure himself he was still real, and looking into the mirror, taking some pleasure in the messiness of his hair since it meant he was still himself—that he was still Paul—he curled up on the futon in an awkwardly tight fetal position and conked out. There were no windows in the cabin and no one came to knock on his door. He slept so deeply he drooled. He felt heavy and dull as he pulled his denim shorts on the next day, and without washing his face or combing his hair or shaving, or brushing his teeth, or anything, he lumbered out of the cabin to find some food. He needed food. His belly called for food. He would find food, he told himself, and he pushed open the cabin door. The brightness, a high, light-blue sky littered with streaks of angry, crisscrossing clouds, forced him to blink his eyes unnaturally hard and fast.

Bacon, he thought. Pancakes. Eggs. This is what he wanted, and he stumbled along the raked pebble path that led toward the main building. He hoped he could find the chef, or someone at the retreat who would prepare him some real food, something that didn't taste like it belonged in a boutique. He had no idea where the rear entrance to the kitchen was, but he would find it. He was well aware any direct request to Buffalo Man or to anyone at the front desk for bacon would be rejected.

Near the central building, he pounded his chest and looked directly into the sky. *I'm alive!* he said. He pounded some more. He felt exhausted. Buffalo Man was an SOB, a motherfucker, fucking with his mind. *All*

I need now is to eat some food and get the fuck out of here. Move on. Just move on. It was time to get back to the East Coast. *Forget about it. Forget about it all,* he told himself. But he'd give Buffalo Man a little trick, a little something to remember before he skipped out of the retreat. Revenge is the best medicine. Buffalo Man was peddling crazy palm-reading fear, most likely to try to get him to beg for more teachings and to get him to fork over all his money to pay for those teachings. He would teach Buffalo Man a lesson for fucking with his mind.

From a beach chair beside the edge of the pool, where she was lying back and reading a biography of Andy Warhol (and how he was attached to his mother and how he continued to live with his mother even during his supposedly wild days at The Factory studio in New York), Zoe looked up and saw Paul. He was at the far end of the pool beating his fists against his chest, howling and speaking combatively to the sky. He looked like a homeless Tarzan.

Paul sensed someone was looking at him. He finished his rant and checked to see who was spying on him. He saw it was Zoe and bowed his head. He was about to rush away into the front of the central building to hide, when he had an idea. He made his way to Zoe with one of his tennis shoes untied. The lace flapped against the redwood deck that surrounded the pool. He walked straight up to her and cleared his throat. "Hey, sorry about yesterday," he said. "No hard feelings? No hard feelings intended."

"Apology accepted," Zoe said.

"Good. So I have a question. You've been around here for about a week. How do you get any real grub around here? You know. Bacon. Steak."

"I don't know. You just eat what they serve you. There's no choice. But the food's always good. Don't you like the food?"

"Yeah, it was pretty good last night. But I need a steak. You know what I mean? I'm still alive. I'm turning over a new leaf. I need to feed my growing body."

Zoe pulled her sunglasses off to look at Paul in the flesh. He was pale and pasty. Unshaved. And without his baseball cap, his hair was a disaster. He looked like a lost Tarzan. "No offense, but I don't think a steak is going to cure what's ailing you. Why don't you try a shower and a massage?"

"No time. I'm busting out of here soon. I just need to grab some grub and take care of a little business and I'm out of here."

"Didn't you just get here yesterday?"

"I'm just here for the promotional."

"What promotional?"

"The one-night free deal."

"One night free?"

"Yeah, they're having a promotional where you can stay for one night free and see if you like it here."

"And you're already leaving?"

"I didn't like it here."

"Oh . . . I've never heard anyone talk about that kind of promotional. It must be a new thing. Most people stay for a week or more . . . How'd the palm reading go, in any case? Everyone was talking at breakfast about how lucky you were to win the raffle when you just showed up last night."

"Help me out here, would ya? What's the most disrespectful thing you could do here to really piss everyone off? What's the most disrespectful thing you could do that would piss Buffalo Man off?"

"Kind of a strange question, don't you think? What happened?"

"Nothing. He told me nothing. And that's why I want to get back at him. He said my palm couldn't be read."

"Was it really that bad?"

"He said I had an unreadable palm. That it was too soft and pudgy to be read. That I wasn't cooperating with him mentally and so he had too much interference to get in touch with the spirits."

"Well, then why don't you just forget about it?"

"OK. I will. But what do you think is the worst thing that could be done here?"

"I don't know. But I don't think I want to help you think about it. Why don't you just try to work things out with him?"

"You know what, that's a good idea. I think I'll just go up to him and say, 'You know Buffalo Man, last night when you wouldn't read my palm, that really made me *uncomfortable.* I think it brought forward feelings of *discomfort* in me that I would like to talk to you about. Maybe we could just *dialogue* and work through everything together.'"

"Well, I'm just trying to be helpful."

It was no use, absolutely no use. Why did he find himself having to bicker with her? He had no interest in bickering with her. She was all too appealing to him to bicker with. He should never have even come up to her in the first place. She was right. He should just calm down. He should just find a simple breakfast and leave. "Thanks, I'll catch you later," he said. It was time to hide. It was time to forget the whole place.

He went in to the front desk instead of trying to find the back of the kitchen and spoke with the woman with the diamond nose stud. "Do you think there is somewhere here where I could find a steak or some red meat?" he asked.

"I'm sorry, Mr. Berger, but we don't serve any red meat here. The closest we come is fish."

"Oh, OK. Thanks."

"Did you want to pay for the rest of your week now, then?"

"No, I think I'm just going to stay the one night with the promotional."

"Right. But you see, the promotional requires you to indicate before checkout that you'll be staying only the one night, and it's already two o'clock. In order to stay for only one night, you would have had to check out by twelve."

Paul looked at her incredulously. "Are you kidding me?"

"I'm sorry, Mr. Berger, but it states everything very clearly on the form you filled out yesterday."

"But it's only two o'clock. And I thought I could tell you just now."

"Guests can stay for either a week or two weeks. The two-week plan offers a reduced rate of two thousand dollars per week instead of the twenty-five hundred dollars for the one week."

So what could he do now? How had he come to this exact spot in his life? He was simply doing his research. He was simply trying to do a hitchhiker a favor. He would tell her thank you for informing me, I just need to go to my room to get my credit card. He would control himself. He wouldn't blow up at her. There was nothing she could do, he knew. Nothing at all. She was just a peon. It was Buffalo Man he'd have to talk to, and he was never going to talk to him again.

He went back to his cabin and threw his clothes quickly into his suitcase and threw his suitcase into the back of his car. The only way back to the main road led past the front entrance. He drove slowly by the main building, trying to slink past the front, but Buffalo Man came running out after him. He was running by the side of Paul's car door, and the crank handle wasn't working well, so Paul couldn't close the window.

What would he tell him? "You're a *phony!* Buffalo Man," he shouted. "A crook. I'm going to report you to the Better Business Bureau. A thousand curses upon you, swami."

"Run away if you want to," Buffalo Man said, shaking his head. "But you will see that it will all come to pass unless you purify yourself."

CHAPTER 3

It was the morning of Paul's brother—Andrew's—funeral. There'd been a flurry of preparation for the memorial service at MIT, and all the university officials were glad to "be of assistance," helping out as best they could. The entire country was in mourning, shocked and despondent over the World Trade Center "bombing" that had occurred only a week before. The toppling of the towers, and the attack on the nation's pride, gave university officials an added sense of purpose. Yet in their haste to put the service together, they'd thought about logistics more than aesthetics. The memorial was in Kresge Auditorium, which seated the more than four hundred who jammed the amphitheater in Froot Loop green and purple seats that were a relic of 1950s ideas of modernity: plastic and clashing colors. The seats—backed with itchy polyester fabric—creaked all around Paul, who sat with his family in a row at the front reserved strictly for VIPs, the seats taped off for the governor of Massachusetts and university pooh-bahs. The high ceiling of the auditorium, with its soundproofing panels, was intended to transport piano notes richly to its audience, but as with so many things around the MIT campus, the plan had gone awry, amplifying the audience's noises instead. The voices of students, faculty, and TV journalists clashed in distorted frequencies, jumbling together like ripples from a megaphone traveling underwater in a fishbowl.

Where was Andrew's body? Paul thought. They had yet to find it, as they'd yet to find most of the bodies from his plane that had crashed into the Pentagon, leaving everything smoldering under ash and rubble in the breast of the west wing of the building. From the standpoint of the media, the focus of the story was the Twin Towers, not the crash in Washington, which only magnified Andrew's disappearance. The symbol of money spoke louder than the symbol of government and military power—the Pentagon a mere side note to the great boom and crack of the financial towers. The only real interest in the Pentagon came because everyone wondered just how the fuck a jet could stab itself past whatever wickedly awesome defenses were supposed to have been arrayed around the nation's capital to protect the government from any "evildoers" wanting to destroy the seat of the nation's "great experiment in democracy." Let's face it, Paul thought, after his brother's American Airlines flight 77 Boeing 757 crashed straight through the limestone walls of the Pentagon, sending waves of flames into the air, and ash and debris, and glass, and bodies, and giving filing cabinets a face-lift, it was hard for anyone to take seriously anymore the idea—impregnated in the mind of the American populace during the Cold War—that technology and determination would save us from enemies such as the Russkies or that antimissile defense systems would keep the nerve center of the Stars and Stripes safe forever. Paul had never believed such a shield could work to begin with (he'd never believed in Star Wars), but hadn't he believed the Pentagon was safe? Not the entire nation—but come on, this was the Pentagon! Even in his profound grief, focused on Andrew, the failure of the technological wonder and faith of the nation struck him. How ironic, he thought, that everyone was here at the center of techno-hopefulness and idealism, trying to reassure themselves all was well and still under control.

The noise died down as the crowd waited for the university president to speak, and Paul scraped at a piece of dried chewing gum stuck to his seat. Against his will (since he was intent on shutting out his surroundings to think only about his brother), he noticed graffiti on the seat in front of him that said, "scientists do it better." Then he sat listening to the president of the university describe how "soaring" Andrew's ambitions and dreams had been, how he'd been a model alum of MIT who gave so much to the community when he was a student and who added so much to the community of NASA, too.

What made the words painful and ludicrous to Paul was not that they were untrue. Andrew *had* been all of these things and more, but they were spoken without any heartfelt emotion. They were intoned flatly, without soul, without anger.

The entire problem was symbolized by the setting. Above the president of the university, as he droned on and on, using the event to map out his policy response to the "tragedy" of Sept. 11, a PowerPoint projector beamed NASA's matte white logo and an image of the American flag—the flag twice as large as the NASA logo and bigger than even a car salesman would dare to put on display. The flag dwarfed six potted plants, shivering, evenly spaced apart on stage, wrapped in golden foil. They'd been tied in yellow ribbons, which reminded Paul of Hallmark greeting cards and the first Gulf War. The president spoke from his Formica lectern cast in a faux wood grain—the students beginning to fidget—and he pointed occasionally to an orange space shuttle uniform with an empty helmet and arms and legs drooping on its metal stand, a reminder of Andrew's aspirations during his stint at the Johnson Space Center, in Houston.

And the words of the speech? What wisdom did the president have for Paul? "He was an inspiration to us all," he said. He gave a résumé of Andrew's life, with a couple of anecdotes. He'd met him a couple of times—since Andrew was a top student—and he mentioned those moments, but most of the stories were nuggets a speechwriter had fused together, dug up over three days of fact-finding research, including the time Andrew blew apart a test engine in a vacuum chamber and how he "just kept on working at it until he got the engine right."

"And so, this is the challenge to all of us," the president said. "Not to lose hope. For, as Franklin Delano Roosevelt noted in an equally trying time, 'We have nothing to fear but fear itself.' We must not—and cannot, and will not—give in to those who would destroy our way of life. Instead, we will persevere, providing the tools necessary to fight terrorism as our nation counts on us in this time of challenge. For although MIT is not a training ground for war—not a place for masters of war—it has always helped to guide our nation's policy. MIT will lead the technological path of this nation forward, as it once led our nation to develop the miracle of radar that was so crucial to defeating Nazi Germany."

The speech was entirely unsatisfactory, Paul thought, even if well intended. *Take off your presidential cloak and gown, your university gold medal and staff, your gauzy, cloying words and smell my brother. He's burnt in the wasteland of the Pentagon. Do you have any idea how much better and how much worse he was than what you just said? Why do you have to sanitize death with warm anecdotes and high-minded policy pronouncements that you know have nothing to do with my brother? Beg for your grants from the fucking DOD somewhere else.* The prez told one last "heartwarming" story about Andrew. *I'm not even going to look at him after the speech,* Paul thought. He had never wanted a public funeral. It was Cyrus who'd set up the whole thing, who insisted upon a major event, and after Cyrus hammered out the memorial "concept" with the MIT president, it was utterly out of Paul's hands. Paul's request for a small family gathering, which he was sure Andrew would have wanted, evaporated.

If the president had ever known Andrew, beyond the few times he had met him at some ribbon-cutting-grant-recipient-award ceremony, he might have described Andrew's brief life this way (still in a storybook fashion, but closer to the truth):

When he was young, Andrew played with and put together toy airplanes that flew by remote control. He was short, Jewish, with reddish brown hair and freckles, and his nose was bigger than that of his two brothers, more pronounced in a stereotypically Jewish way, yet less triangular and rounder like a red potato. Of the three boys, he resembled his father the most. The father was a largely bald, strict disciplinarian who shouted, bullied, and noodged the family to agree with him at the dinner table, and while Andrew had a thick pile of hair and was soft-spoken by comparison, both father and son locked themselves in their respective studios to focus intently on their chosen area of expertise. The father spent all his time working in the basement, manipulating plaster for his sculptures, which he would transform into pieces of bronze, as he listened to complex, atonal classical music by Schoenberg and Stravinsky. He refined his sculptures and remolded them until he believed they were masterpieces. Professor Berger, as he was called by his art students (never by his first name), considered most other classical (tonal) music a waste of time, and with respect to nonclassical music, it was simply out of the question, except for some jazz. Andrew listened occasionally to classical music, too, but when he did, he listened to tonal music exclusively, and he preferred bright music with major chords, especially Richard Strauss's *Thus Spake Zarathustra*. (He also liked to go to the Hatch Shell at the Esplanade to catch the Boston Pops playing their show tunes and American favorites such as John Philip Sousa's marches.) But music, for Andrew, was secondary to anything that could be physically constructed. He was most interested in engines and gizmos that could be taken apart and put back together. When he watched ants in an ant farm in second grade, excitement came from observing the ants build their tunnels, not from analyzing their social structure. He was obsessed with model kits. He preferred model historical ships and naval destroyers because they had hundreds of detailed pieces to glue together. At the age of nine, he spent two weeks at the Charlestown Navy Yard, in Boston, making detailed drawings of the USS *Constitution,* a triple-masted frigate with a gigantic oak hull, steel ribs, and fifty-four cannons, that single-handedly destroyed the British Navy in the War of 1812. Then he decided he needed to experience how it felt to be on the ship. So he pestered the night guard to let him onto the frigate.

"Hey kid," the watchman told him after seven days of saying no, "Why don't you just take the daytime tour? It's free."

"For four reasons: First, I already have. Second, 'cause they won't give me enough time to check out the boat. Third, 'cause I've already read everything in the brochures they hand out at the visitor center—and the tour gives the same information. And fourth, because I wanna feel the space of the boat on my own, to imagine what it was like at the battle of 1812."

What could the guard say to that? Well, "No," for another couple of days. But eventually he relented. Andrew looked harmless enough, so the guard told the kid he'd get him on the ship, and he promised to leave him alone on the boat. Of course, he made some effort first to make sure the kid wasn't a pyro or anything. He looked the kid up on police records, and he was clean. And for fifty bucks (the bribe Andrew somehow scraped together) the guard justified the whole thing by vowing to take out the few other sailors at the historical navy base for beers.

When the day finally came, Andrew spent the night on the USS *Constitution,* poring over every part of the ship until he fell asleep at 4 A.M. on the main deck. He'd stepped precariously to the very tip of the prow, up the long needlelike protrusion at the front of the boat, and lain down to look up at the stars. And that was when he decided he wanted to become an astronaut. For although the ship was certainly "cool," well put together and impressive, with his flashlight in hand he'd been able to check out the entire boat in six hours. (In the captain's quarters, at the stern of the ship and below deck, he spent time at the captain's mess table admiring the oak pegs that joined the whole table together as he ate a couple of Hostess Ho Hos.) Whereas *space*. The universe. There was no end to it. No limit to the stars he spent the night looking at as the frigate bobbed gently, oak planks creaking slightly, moored in the black waters of Boston's harbor.

From that night on he began to focus on astronomy. He decorated his bedroom with a mobile of the planetary system and with maps of the moon, and he watched stars through a telescope out his bedroom window. And in the backyard, he built his own, small observatory, an eight-foot-tall domed cylindrical tin-walled chamber that revolved to accommodate his telescope. But he quickly knew his new observatory was insufficient for his studies, and so, when he was thirteen, he volunteered as a research assistant at the Harvard observatory on Garden Street. At seventeen, he was admitted to MIT. (He was two years older than Paul. Paul was the youngest of the family.)

In 1985 Andrew started college, and his thick hair—molded in a mullet—framed his pink skin, accentuating his acne and the wide pores on his face. He grew a fat mustache in the style of Pancho Villa, after reading a book with some references to Villa by Che Guevara, and he thought he looked kind of sexy. He also began to ride around on a black, "classic" motorcycle, a Yamaha. If he'd had the money he would have bought a Harley, but he didn't really care about brand names. What mattered to him was the engine on the bike, and the engine on his bike was pretty good after he souped it up. He had a girlfriend for the first time, then a string of women in college, some who liked to dress Goth. (If he'd been anywhere other than MIT he probably would have come up empty on the girl front, but both sexes were equally desperate at MIT. He'd gone to his high school prom—alone—wearing a tux and a wide, red corsage.) If he thought about his motivations much at all, he figured the reason he went out with women who wore a lot of black was because he liked his women to be independent, individual thinkers who could challenge him and give him enough time alone in the lab. And he liked to kiss them in public because this, too, made him feel sexy. He had no doubt he would be an astronaut one day.

And what did he think about Paul? His little brother. That he was doing his own rock-and-roll thing (which was good), but that Paul wasn't quite as focused as himself or Cyrus, and that his father thought

Paul had bad taste in music and would end up a failure. So he tried to look out for him. He took Paul to baseball games, since his father was oblivious to the importance of the Red Sox and since he dismissed all sports by noting tickets to the games had become too expensive.

Andrew went on to finish his Ph.D. at MIT, studying aerospace engineering, and he got a job with NASA at the Johnson Space Center. He wasn't eager to leave Boston, his friends, or his family, but that was where he had to go if he wanted to become an astronaut.

Before he left town, he took Paul on a glider plane ride over a sandy peninsula that ran eight miles north-south along the coast of Massachusetts. The peninsula was called Plum Island, a national wildlife refuge for birds, composed of dunes and dune grass, scrub oaks, and a wide beach where piping plovers and roseate terns nested. Andrew usually felt ecstatic flying out there because of the mix of dunes and slate-green ocean spreading into the distance below and sky above— each section carving out its niche on the panorama.

The day Paul went with Andrew, a small Cessna tugged them into the air then released the cable, and they floated quietly. Andrew focused on the maneuvers he was making as he circled the glider up, high on a thermal. Then he pushed the glider down in a rapid descent that made Paul feel like he was about to throw up. *Holy mother of God, I seem to be in the vomit comet,* Paul thought. *Why do I put myself through so much torture?* But he knew why he'd come on the trip. Andrew was leaving for the Johnson Space Center the next day, and he'd asked Paul to go for a farewell ride. The small age barrier between them had completely disappeared, and Andrew no longer treated Paul like the youngest. Only Cyrus insisted on treating Paul that way.

Andrew pulled the glider sharply up, into a loop, until they were upside down, and then he held the position.

"If I don't get out of here, I'm gonna toss," Paul said. Andrew didn't seem to be paying attention to him. Strapped into his seat, Paul's head hung toward the ground and his neck banged against the foam rest at the back of his seat. The glider's wings flashed white in the intensity of the sunlight. The world below appeared round in the bubble glass dome that covered the cockpit. Sand formed abstract shapes that intertwined with the ocean and sky, generating an alien landscape. *The genes of our family are also mixed and intertwined but always separate,* Paul thought. He was afraid this was the moment he was going to die. For a while, after his time in Iowa, he'd simply dismissed his encounter with Buffalo Man as one of those moments that carve a tiny eddy separate from the rest of one's life. But slowly he came to feel the psychological presence like a waterfall, and it wasn't possible for him to give up thinking about Buffalo Man's curse, when he and Zoe hooked up in Boston two months after his time at the retreat—which certainly seemed to fulfill the first part of Buffalo Man's prophecy.

Andrew took his hands off the glider flight control and yelled to Paul, "Look Spike, no hands!" (Spike was Paul's nickname.) Paul focused on the back of Andrew's head to avoid throwing up. Andrew's hair was so neatly combed, at the age of thirty-three (the date of this part of the chapter is September 2000), and his hair so faded (all of the red of his youth gone), that the blandness calmed Paul. But Paul could see Andrew's arms stretching toward the ground, touching the bubble of the Plexiglas dome, and this frightened him.

"You have fifteen seconds to promise you won't elope with Zoe, or I'll crash this glider into the ground," Andrew said. "I want to be at any wedding you guys have." It was a strange thing to say, upside down, flying through the air, but in a family of three siblings, all of whom kept their privacy and none who really connected with their father, it wasn't completely out of the blue. Andrew added, "Don't let Cyrus tick you off while I'm in Texas."

"Sure. OK. I promise. Get me the fuck out of here *now.*"

Andrew flipped the glider right side up and pushed it back slowly to earth, landing perfectly on terra firma.

The irony of the marriage comment was that Andrew didn't follow his own advice to get openly married. Two weeks later he began a long series of tests to become an astronaut. At first there were four hundred competing to join the small group selected each year. Then the number was whittled down to a hundred, and he was still in the running. He was assigned to a group meant to design and operate one of the central control panels for astronauts' use up on the International Space Station, and he hit it off with one of the female engineers in his group—who wasn't competing to be an astronaut—and she got pregnant. But everything was OK since they seemed to love each other, though Andrew wasn't ready to get married. They decided to have the baby. In the meantime, he kept working his way through the complex physical and psychological tests to become an astronaut.

And the whole process had become much more difficult, much more precarious when he was informed one day, by a NASA doctor, quietly apart from the others in a white-walled room, that he had only one kidney. The doctor assured him there was no mistake. It was a rare condition, and the reason no one had ever noticed it before was precisely because, without the complex set of tests and without any prior medical condition, or without any surgery or sonogram in the right place, there was no reason he'd have known. He was told the condition wouldn't automatically exclude him from becoming an astronaut—since he was so qualified in all other ways—but no other person in the history of the program had ever been accepted with any comparable defect.

He kept trying to go through the other tests to make it to the next round. Then one evening, he went home and found an envelope from NASA. It contained a curt rejection letter. No reason was given (as I'm told no reason is ever officially given). In secret the doctor told him it was the kidney.

The sadness he felt was so intense he could barely breathe. Yet after discovering he had been rejected, instead of giving up on his lifelong dream, and rather than leaving NASA, he continued to work in the engineering group he had been assigned to. He hoped he might be accepted another year. His girlfriend quit her job to have the baby. (They planned to name the baby—boy or girl—Mercury, after the early space rocket program.) When an emergency arose on the new space station being built, Andrew engineered a solution that allowed two astronauts to complete their mission. He was given an award for the best NASA employee of the year. And then, three weeks later, his plane crashed into the Pentagon.

The ceremony in Kresge Auditorium wound down with a squat organ pumping out a funeral dirge. What Paul needed now was a beer, something less somber and antiseptic than the farce of a procession that had nothing to do with his brother. His brother was about taking apart an amplifier and fixing it with his own set of pliers, about riding his Yamaha in a nerdy imitation of a motorcycle outlaw.

Paul and Zoe walked past Cyrus on the wide, open plaza in front of the auditorium, where Cyrus was speaking to reporters expressing his profound sadness and anger, yet warning of the need to avoid moving too quickly toward enacting new intelligence or wiretapping laws. "I'll be coming out with a comprehensive book soon to explain why terrorism works in a free society," Cyrus said. "And in my book, I'll *also* tell all of us how we should *not* respond to this scum of the earth in such a way that we destroy our fundamental values in this nation or our legal system—which is *exactly* what they want."

"What an absolute nightmare," Paul said to Zoe as they walked toward an MIT parking garage. He was sweating. He couldn't remember the last time he'd worn a suit and tie. After he'd looked through his closet for a suit with no success, Zoe had borrowed one from a friend who was a costume designer. Paul took off his tie and unbuttoned his collar. They were expected at Cyrus's house in an hour, where everyone would gather.

"I don't agree," Zoe said. "If you think about how fast it was put together, it was surprisingly moving. OK, it wasn't moving, but I think it was better than I expected. You're just upset because you're jealous."

"Me? Jealous? What are you talking about? Of what?"

"That Andrew was better than you. That they're all better than you."

"But I've never even *remotely* aspired to be like *any* of them. I mean, what kind of a life is it being an engineer like Andrew? It's not glorious, you know. It's hours of tedious work down there in Texas, of all places, putting together robotics and control panels. Cyrus? He's constantly constipated. And as for my dad, what a living-and-breathing success story. I mean sure, he makes great art, maybe even perfect art. But he refuses to have any contact with the outside world. Nada. Zippo. He just hides in his basement mumbling and grumbling, decrying the fall of the modern world, and every single one of his pieces is done in some classical, figurative tradition that died a hundred years ago with Brancusi."

"Yeah, but then why was the memorial service jam-packed today to absolute capacity with over four hundred people?"

"Why? Because it was natural they should come. And I don't have a problem with why so many showed up at the service. In fact, I'm *glad* so many *did*. Andrew was a part of the MIT community, and he was good at what he did. I'll grant you that. But the reason so many came isn't because of what he *did* and who he *was*. It's because it fits their needs right now. The president of the U. and the Gov. *need* to show and tell everyone they care about what's going on at this time of crisis, and the students *need* to find some place to gather and mourn and make sense of it all. But my shtick, my anger, is simply that I don't think the service was for *Andrew*. It was for politics. It was for a general and diffuse sense of mourning. It was for everyone *but* Andrew. It's about Cyrus and the media."

"Then why'd you come, if you think it's so wrong?"

"I didn't say it was *wrong*. I just said I don't think it's what Andrew would have wanted."

"What Andrew would have wanted, or what *you* would have wanted?"

"Look, we're going in circles here. I tell you what I know, and you tell me why I think I know what I know. But don't you think I might just have a handle on my own feelings? This isn't a case where basic psychology and analysis is going to cure anything. I'm just pissed. Outright pissed. OK? I'm furious. So let's drop the subject and get a drink."

But was Zoe completely wrong? Paul thought. No sooner had he yelled at her than he admitted a lot of what she'd said was true. Of course he was jealous and envious of his brothers. NASA employee of the year! Famous lawyer! He'd seen his brothers on television numerous times. They met with important people. They'd both met with the president of the United States at different White House dinners. They had courtside seats for their favorite basketball teams in Boston and Houston. They were on the A-list, something Paul didn't really care about, but still—there they were; well, Andrew not quite, but close. Cyrus secretly slept with model actresses (which wasn't a secret to Paul) and showed up at movie openings in Cannes and had clinked champagne glasses with Bill Gates in Davos. They never *doubted* themselves. Not for a minute did Andrew doubt he should have the child with his future fiancée. The only reason he didn't marry her right away was because he was too busy working out and studying and pushing himself to become an astronaut. Not for a minute did Cyrus hesitate in any courtroom as he worked over the judge and jurors to support his position. And even when he lost a case, he merely regrouped—labeling the decision a setback for the entire country—and moved on. When Andrew found out he wouldn't become an astronaut, he didn't mope and quit. The next day he showed up at work, on time, determined to prove to NASA a missing kidney that had never been missed before wouldn't be missed in space. Only Paul's father—who'd been categorically sidestepped at a crucial moment in the 60s, after he abandoned his abstract sculpture to return to the figurative form—knew the core of failure, but still he never doubted himself. He made a choice based on a rigid set of principles. He was always certain of his aesthetic judgment.

So where did this constant *doubt* come from that Paul felt was at the root of his envy and jealousy? And how could he get rid of it? Once he, too, had thought he was certain about his drumming and his pursuit of music. But when and how did that certainty vanish? He felt doubt whenever he sat down to try to write his book now. It's not that he wanted *to be* his brothers. He just wanted to have his version of their certainty. *He* wanted his purpose not only to be clear but to be fulfilled without his having to question the validity of his every effort and his every thought and waking move.

And he'd found he was not alone in his feelings of deepening inadequacy and doubt. Why the rise of self-improvement books? Why were they the most popular form of book on the market in the world? And why were sexual aid books the most popular of the how-to books? Why were biographies of heroes like Lincoln and Jefferson and Adams so popular? Even biographies of Hitler were popular. Not out of pity for Hitler's miserable defeat, he thought, but because Hitler was so certain in his hatred. Never mind that he wasn't truly quite as certain outside of his anti-Semitism (with respect to his sexuality, for example). The truth of inadequacy in the hero was not important. What *was* important was that the hero momentarily leaped—avoiding what even he knew was limited in himself, overcoming his doubt. The hero, through his will, gave up fears momentarily, even turning a blind eye to failures.

It didn't matter that the famous basketball player was a former prison inmate with a low IQ. The minute he jumped toward the basket, he overcame his past. It was not perfection that made a hero but rather the will to overcome and ignore any imperfections. Selective blindness and singleness of purpose were essential. And for this reason, Paul had found, gun owners felt most heroic when firing a gun. For a moment, the perfection of the machine overtook any personal failures and doubt. The gun owner became a part of the perfect evolution of scientific human ingenuity. Bang. A progression from the Chinese invention of gunpowder to Smith and Wesson technology. The certainty of the hammer making contact with the cartridge and bullet. This is what Paul, too, wanted. Some certainty. Some freedom from doubt. This is what he hoped to achieve through the back door, not by blinding himself to his failures and inadequacies, because he could not, but by synthesizing in his studies the perfect book about inadequacy through a manifestation of his will.

Isn't this why he and Zoe had ended up together? Failures. Both failures. But they were both still trying to make their hopes tangible and real. Of course, he didn't think of these thoughts all at once, but he had been piecing them together for a while.

When Paul showed up at Cyrus's house, he was well on his way to being drunk—a few shots of JD with more than a couple black-and-tan beer chasers under his belt—and his old Toyota churned up the white gravel of Cyrus's horseshoe-shaped driveway. Quite simply, the house was immense: eight bedrooms with unique wallpaper for each closet, four fireplaces with long brick chimneys that reached forty-five feet up through the mansard roof by the widow's walk (even though the house, landlocked in Cambridge, would never be close enough to see a sailor coming home to port). The four-story house was canary yellow, as if to announce itself to the other neighbors of Avon Hill. But in some kind of afterthought, a realization perhaps that the house might seem ostentatious if openly exposed to the street in New England, a wall of rustic lilac bushes swayed to and fro, obscuring much of the public's view, except what was visible between the white stone pillars placed on either side of the entrance.

The cars in the driveway were a Mercedes SUV, to take the kids to soccer, a BMW Z3 for Cyrus, a Volvo station wagon for his wife, Rebecca (because she found it safer), and a Mini Cooper for when she felt a little sportier. The front lawn—free of dandelions and other imperfections—swept in a neatly mowed and vibrant texture around the house to a wide brick patio and pool with Jacuzzi and a full-scale playground for the youngest daughter (complete with a ten-foot-high jungle gym coated with Acti Guard foam to prevent a hapless child from bumping a precious forehead, a self-raking sandbox, a self-watering slide). In the kitchen—for Cyrus to watch how his legal cases were being received by the public and because he liked WWF wrestling and boxing—a plasma TV screen tilted down just above the breakfast alcove.

"What do you know?" Paul said. He attempted to bump the car door shut with his butt after the door got stuck on his dangling seatbelt, "The place looks like it just got a face-lift." It had been six weeks since he'd been at the house, and the entire estate had been repainted. The car door still wouldn't close. Paul fumbled with the seatbelt, finally throwing the loose strap and metal clip back behind the front seat of the car; then he slammed the door as fast as he could to prevent the belt from somehow escaping. He wiped his sweaty hands on his gray suit pants. The pants were baggy, but at least the length was right. He noticed some of his black shoe polish was rubbing off on the bottom of the cuffs, but he decided to worry about it later. Besides, the black kind of blended in with the gray. He patted around the side pockets of his coat trying to feel if he'd left the car keys in there, and then realized he'd just left them inside the car. What he felt in his pockets instead was a pack of cigarettes that he was eager to smoke. He didn't usually smoke, but whenever he went to a bar, he needed a cig. He decided to wait until he was in the house to light up, however. It wouldn't be polite to come in already smoking, and he didn't intend to offend anyone. Zoe had already told him to behave, and he promised her he would.

Christ, though, he had to pee soon. His bladder was disconcertingly unpredictable. Sometimes he could last a long time—for example, if he just stuck to whiskey or gin. But if he branched out into beer! At least here he had a choice of bathrooms.

Did he blame Cyrus for being so wealthy? he thought, as he looked at the polished brass numbers beside the front door. No, but he did blame him for being an arrogant prick. What kind of person announces on TV he has the answer to every question? What kind of person never says: You know, I'll have to think about that for a minute, I'm just not sure.

In a strange way, it felt like some kind of homecoming going up the steps. Cyrus had never denied his hanging out in the house. He had even given Paul a set of keys—and told him to make himself comfortable whenever he wanted to—but the unspoken reason for giving Paul the keys was that, this way, he could look after the house when they were gone on vacation. And Paul had looked after the house and fed the pets a couple of times when they went down to the Bahamas in the winter. The first time he went to take care of the house, he accidentally tripped off the security alarm. After he phoned the private security service (and somehow convinced them he wasn't a thief calling from the house) and after feeding Cyrus's two dogs—a chocolate lab and an Afghan—he kicked back in the TV room, munching popcorn, watching a Christmas special, and wondered why his brother, who was a devout Jew, had Christmas carol CDs in the entertainment room and why he himself, who didn't believe in god, was watching a Christmas special.

"Behave," Zoe whispered into his ear as they stood before the door; she rang, but it was obvious to him no one was going to come to open the door for him since they were late and since the door was already unlocked for the dozens of guests who were making noise around the house. Paul pushed his way in, barely raising his feet high enough over the entryway to avoid scuffing his black shoes.

He knew as soon as he got into the house it was time to misbehave. Wasn't that what Billie Holiday was really getting at when she sang Fats Waller's "Ain't Misbehavin'"? Behaving didn't make much sense when a woman came up to him with half a carrot stick in her hand and the other half in her mouth, a mess of ground-up orange bits. "Oh, it's just tragic. Tragic what happened to him," she said. With dyed red hair, with loose skin on her neck like the wattle of a turkey, she shook her head and then launched into telling Paul about her own misfortunes and deaths. "Isn't that right, Derek?" she turned to her husband, who was dressed in a tweed coat, "Marty was forty-two when he died and he never knew what hit him." The husband shook his head vaguely and looked away.

The house was one big cocktail party that spread over the large Chinese floral–patterned carpet of the living room, beneath a chandelier, and into the dining room and kitchen. The crowd chattered. The crowd laughed. Cyrus moved around the party, speaking to colleagues. "We just have to do something about these terrorists," one of the more WASPish-looking members of the faculty said, "And if that means we have to kick the Taliban out of Afghanistan, then I say let's get to it."

Paul meandered around the main floor, taking in the sights and sounds, and then he went into one of the bathrooms on the second floor. He closed the heavy oak door behind him and looked down at the toilet bowl, then looked up at the ceiling. "Andrew," he said, and he started to pee into the bowl, spilling a little onto one of his shoes. "I love you man. I'm gonna miss you man." He spilled quite a bit onto a wall, and after shaking his penis to stop, he balled up a bunch of toilet paper and bent over to wipe up the mess. He threw the toilet paper into the bowl and washed his hands, and he thought the floor still smelled, so he balled up another bunch of toilet paper, wetted it with water from the sink, and wiped the floor some more. He threw that toilet paper toward the bowl, but some of the paper missed and stuck to the rim of the seat. So he wadded up some more and wiped up the wet paper and put it all in the bowl. The paper mounded at the bottom of the bowl. Yellow light from an expensive fixture high up in the narrow bathroom illuminated the mound. The bathroom—which had originally been for a maid—was rarely used by anyone in the house, and this was why Paul had gone to it. It was the only unrenovated bathroom in the house. The old porcelain of the toilet was from the thirties. The toilet had a pull chain from a tank high above. Paul pulled the cord, and the toilet rushed with water, flowing up from the bowl, swirling higher and higher, trapped, and he knew right away he had to find a plunger. Water reached the lip of the bowl and began to dribble and splash over the side. He couldn't find a plunger anywhere, and the idea of sticking his hand in the bowl was too disgusting, so he climbed up on the toilet to try to cut off the water in the tank above. The smooth soles of his shoes slipped on the seat, and as he grasped at the tank he pulled the chain, which flushed the toilet again, and he swung back, holding on to the cord, leaning diagonally back, hanging in the air. In a steady whoosh, the water spread over the black and white tiles of the floor, out under the door and onto the carpeting of the hallway.

His gray wool pants were wet, especially around his crotch. He ran with his pants unzipped, trying to close them as he hurried down the steps from the second floor back to the first, trying to find Cyrus.

Rebecca ran into Paul first. "What happened?" she said. "You look like you just saw a ghost."

"The toilet. It's the fucking toilet. That goddamn toilet is plugged."

"Which one?"

"The old one, of course."

"Oh, Jesus. Did you do it?"

"What difference does it make? Someone did."

Rebecca ran upstairs to try to take care of the toilet, and Paul looked around for Zoe. He wanted to grab her and get the hell out of there as fast as he could, but because of the crowd, he hadn't even spoken to his mother or father yet. He would at least have to say hello and goodbye to them before leaving.

Cyrus appeared from what seemed like out of nowhere and tapped Paul on the shoulder. "Jesus," Cyrus said. "Rebecca just told me what happened."

"Told you what happened? How about what's been happening all week?" Paul said.

"Look, if you wanna gripe, come into my office, because we've got a number of very important people here, and we've got Mom and Dad. So if you're gonna spill the beans now and if you're gonna weep and get all babylike, then come into my office."

Paul followed Cyrus back upstairs, to the third floor, where he had his office. Rebecca seemed to have everything under control now with the toilet on the second floor, which meant—from what Paul could see as he looked down the long hallway on his way up the stairs—that she had one of the caterers on his hands and knees, on the watery tiles.

Cyrus shut the study door. The room was heavy, paneled in mahogany with a thick oak desk. Paul had to pretend he had never been in the study before. It was understood to be off-limits.

"So what happened?" Cyrus said.

"Forget about the toilet. What I want to know is what you're going to do to help Maria."

"Maria?" Maria was Andrew's girlfriend/fiancée, the engineer from Mexico. "Nothing, that's what I'm gonna do," Cyrus said.

"But you can't just do nothing. She needs your help."

"Why? She's an engineer."

"Why? The why is obvious. She's nine months pregnant and she gave up her job, temporarily, so she could have Andrew's baby. She doesn't have any dough right now."

"And you believe that sob story? She's a fucking engineer, for crying out loud. She's a professional. She let herself get knocked up, and that's her own fault. Listen, I'm not saying she's not in a tight spot, but I don't see how I have anything to do with it. Andrew never came around telling me he got her pregnant. Did he? And Andrew never came around telling me he had any plans to shack up with her for life. I might add that the last I spoke to Andrew was just minutes before he died, and not once in that whole time did he ever even mention he had fallen in love with any woman named Maria, or that he was going to marry her or have a kid. Don't you find that a little odd? How do I know if this woman is who she claims to be?"

"Oh, give me a break, Cyrus. It's obvious. The reason Andrew never told you about her is because he knew you wouldn't approve of her and you'd just give him shit and tell him to have her get an abortion."

"And isn't that what she should have done? They barely knew each other."

"Barely knew each other? They slept with each other. And they lived together for six months. What more do you need to know?"

"And what if they did?" Cyrus moved closer to Paul's face, until Paul could see the fury in his eyes. His thick-skinned face, leathery from too much time in tanning booths and, when time permitted, from sitting out on the beaches of Cape Cod and the Bahamas, flushed red. "I have absolutely no responsibility for that child. Absolutely none. I was never informed of that child. I never even knew about Maria until you suddenly wanted to invite her to the ceremony—which I might add I'm glad never happened, since it would have absolutely destroyed the purpose of the whole event. And that child will never be a true representation of Andrew's blood."

"You racist son of a bitch."

"Where is the evidence it's Andrew's child? Unless she's willing to undergo some kind of DNA test."

"And if she did?"

"And if she did, it still wouldn't make any difference. While that would prove paternity, it would never prove that I, as an uncle of a bastard, non-Jewish child, would have any responsibility to help out a woman who—given her stature at NASA—can certainly fend for herself. Life has to involve some responsibility, you know. We can't just expect handouts. We can't just expect some deus ex machina to solve everything. Now if I were you, I would change your clothes and go back downstairs and say a quick howdy-do to everyone, and sober up, and go home and sulk by yourself in the corner. This is Andrew's day, and I don't intend to fuck it up with histrionics." Cyrus looked at Paul from his feet up to his face. "You have some shoe polish on the bottom of your pants, in any case," Cyrus said, and he left.

In his heart, Paul had always suspected Cyrus could be like this in meetings with private clients. Who was he kidding? How had Cyrus made it to his position of authority and fame and power? Did he really think he had made it by being warm and cuddly? That he had simply made it to the top of his game by the force of his winning personality? There were some acne scars on Cyrus's face that he'd softened with a dermabrasion rub. It had always been clear he never liked how he looked. Cyrus managed to be at once heavyset and bony. His cheekbones were wide, his eyelids baggy and puffy, his jaw tight. How many times, in private rooms, in legal offices on the top floors of skyscrapers that looked out over Midtown Manhattan or above the catacombs of Wall Street, had he leaned in so close to obstinate clients and enunciated his words so fiercely bits of spit flew from his mouth onto their faces? Yet wasn't the law of the business jungle supposed to be different from the laws of the family? *There is only one code,* Paul thought. *One barbaric code.*

Somewhere in Texas Maria would give birth in less than a month. And Andrew, that dope, had never married her or even bothered to take out any life insurance.

The walls of the house were covered with expensive artwork, oil paintings by Picasso, prints by Chagall, Roman statue heads made of marble, an Andy Warhol painting of Marilyn Monroe, a couple of small prints by Rembrandt. Would he have the guts to steal one of those to give some money to Maria? He looked at a Goya print on one of the walls—a scene of a bullfighter hit by surprise from behind, the bull twisting his horns from left to right up the tight knickers of the unsuspecting torero, the mouths of the crowd open in awe and horror. Paul reached for the print and took it off the wall. He held it, and how difficult would it be to stuff the gilded frame under his shirt and leave? Could it be any harder than ignoring Maria and pretending that he, too, had no responsibility for her? But what about himself? If he really believed so much in helping her out, couldn't he take out a loan? Did he really have the right to ask Cyrus to do what he himself hadn't yet done? He put the print back, and further down the wall, as he followed the surface of the room, thinking, he saw the door to a safe. It was stainless steel and was barely hidden behind an acrylic painting by Keith Haring (signed in the corner of the painting "with thanks" from the artist). The painting was askew. Paul took the canvas down and propped it against the wall. He touched the lock in the center of the safe and found that the door, for some reason, had never been fully shut. Perhaps Cyrus had been using it recently. He opened the safe and saw a pile of papers beneath a manila folder, and when he lifted the folder, he saw there was a neat, crisp stack of stock certificates. He took the certificates and the folder over to Cyrus's desk and sat in his oak chair.

So what have we here? He opened the folder, and it was full of photos of young girls in various naked poses. Some had lipstick and kissed toward the camera while they touched their vaginas. One bent down toward the floor, her behind pointing toward the camera. She held a teddy bear and looked through her legs back at the photographer. The legs of the girls were long and firm and sticklike. Their toes were painted red. Their breasts were barely developed nubs, their nipples still bubble-gum pink. Was it disgusting? A little. Illegal? Definitely, Paul thought, but that made Cyrus no worse than many men. It was something else that caught his eye. He moved the folder to the side of the desk. A handwritten note was attached to the top of the batch of stock certificates.

Hey Zeus! How can I thank you enough for taking care of Fritzy? Now that all the hurdles are gone, we'll come out with the announcement as scheduled on October 31. Put the certificates in your account. Get your broker to short against the shares the day before the announcement. Then buy the shares back when they dip below twenty.

Good dunking to you.

Trotsky

The note was written on Merrill Lynch stationery. Trotsky was the code name they used for one of Cyrus's fellow members of Skull and Bones his senior year in college. Paul had seen the secret black book, once, with the names of the secret society's members and had read through it. Trotsky was Russell L. Altman III. It certainly looked like insider trading info. Paul felt the stack of certificates below the note, between his thumb and forefinger, and the stack was fat, at least an inch thick. He counted out the certificates and tallied up a cool 100,000 shares.

While himself? What was his annual salary at B_____ Community College? Thirty-two thousand a year. He didn't take the stocks, though. Not that he didn't consider taking just one of the certificates, but didn't—and not because he was so sure he was honest, but because he felt certain with his luck he would get caught. And if Buffalo Man was right—that first he was going to meet Zoe, and then one of his brothers was going to die—he wasn't going to allow himself to fulfill the rest of the prophecy. He wasn't going to allow himself to break with Cyrus, to lose his only other brother simply because of some insider trading and kiddie porn.

You're gutless, he told himself as he closed the safe. He put the painting back on the wall, making sure to leave it askew. He lay for a moment on the carpeting in the center of the floor and looked at the blackness of the ceiling, feeling his heart beat beneath the chubby mass of his chest. What leads us to cause so much pain to each other? he wondered. Why must Cain fight Abel?

Coda:

(Does it seem strange Cyrus would be getting such blatant insider trading info from Merrill Lynch? All of my research shows the opposite. During the boom, Merrill Lynch was making illegal analyst recommendations left and right. As for Skull and Bones, I got the info from two roommates who were members, including when I peeked into the little black membership book without their permission.

Two other things I found while researching this chapter: The limestone of the Pentagon all comes from the same quarry in Ellettsville, Indiana. I thought it might be made of granite, but it's not. After 9/11, they used the same quarry for the reconstruction, with 2.7 million pounds of variegated clear limestone, 18,000 square feet cut into seven hundred pieces transported on forty-eight flatbed trucks. The architect of the Kresge Auditorium is Eero Saarinen.)

CHAPTER 4

L.B. (whose full name was Lucky Bunny) was hanging out with Paul at 2 A.M. in their favorite diner in Davis Square. It was about the only thing you could do in Boston late at night because the blue laws made it impossible to drink after 1 and all the bars were closed. Can you believe it? Those Puritans did a voodoo number on the state of Massachusetts. The people of Boston try to compare themselves, sometimes, to the urban jet-setting elite of New York, but you tell me, can a city even attempt to be great if you can't get a drink after one? The stereotype of Bostonians is that they're always bitching, telling you about how bad they have it with the Red Sox (ever since Babe Ruth's curse of the Bambino), or about how shitty the weather is, or that they're snobs—which is the Harvard factor—or that they don't know how to drive, but the real slam is that they're a bunch of subservient *goodniks* who run around taking every chance to tell you about their Revolutionary history while denying themselves a single drop in a bar after 1 A.M. The subway closes at 12:30, part of the grander conspiracy to get everyone home safe and sound, tucked into bed, before they can do anything more than dream about having one too many at the local watering hole. These regulations backfire, of course. Even the cops drink rabidly to get their booze in under the wire. You'll never deny a citizen of Boston a good buzz, but they do it before 1.

So here sat L.B. and Paul in a diner called The Ugly Fitzsimmons, a restaurant that actually had nothing to do with anyone Irish and that was run by a couple of young Jewish Russian émigrés called Boris and Vasily. Boris and Vasily thought an Irish restaurant would be more successful than a Russian diner in Boston—and they were right. They served a breakfast menu all day that included a heaping plate of flap-jacks, biscuits with gravy, grits, home-smoked bacon, and sausage patties that they flipped in their hands back and forth before they lay the meat on the griddle. (They didn't care the distinction between such Southern and Irish food was blurred.) As for their meat, they eschewed, completely, standard packaged sausage patties. "Are you kidding me?" Boris once told Paul. "Give hormone beef to my customers? If I wanted to kill my customers with food, I could have stayed in Russia."

L.B. was no stranger to the immigration tale, either. He was a Jamaican nurse, and he worked with Zoe at Mass General. He'd made his way through the sick labyrinth of our INS (the initial S stands for service?)

by switching to the nursing profession from earlier work as a philosopher in Kingston. (Nurses get green cards easier than philosophers.) Apart from the difficulty of immigrating to the U.S., the problem with being a philosopher in Kingston was that there was no money—no Jamaican Js, as they call their dough—to be made. Because if teachers are paid like crap here, you oughta see how teachers are paid in other countries. (Added to the usual government distrust of teachers, who might be corrupting the youth, there's a vicious circle in those Third World U's: since no one earns any money, the teachers and students are always on strike, and while that makes them feel virtuous it means the local president-of-the-moment, or whoever runs each so-called-republic, turns around then and says to the teachers, "But you guys are never working. So why am I going to pay you?")

To make a long story short, after L.B. got over his youthful days when he thought it might be nice to be a philosopher, he decided it was time to get a job that might feed him. And what better place to go make some money than the land of Uncle Sam? "You see," L.B. said to Zoe and Paul when he first met them a couple of years ago, "to make money you've got to go to where the money is hanging out. 'Cause the only way to make money in some country like Jamaica is to have a scam. I mean, I don't give-a-care what kind of fantabulous stories some rich man from a poor country concocts and tells you 'bout how he made his money *honestly*. If he has a big *pile* of money in his back pocket, and a Doberman guarding the front door, that money he took from the people. There's no such thing as a clean rich man in a poor country."

Vasily came over to the booth where Paul and L.B. were talking and placed a platter of applejack pancakes in front of Paul, bulging with a few extra pieces of bacon. But bacon or no bacon, it wasn't possible for Paul to gain his appetite. He was thinking about Zoe in the hospital hooked up to an IV and a few machines as she attempted to pull her way past what that freak in Concord had done to her with his musket.

"So how was our lady doing today?" L.B. said to Paul.

"Getting better. She's definitely stable now. But you'd never know from the doctors. They give you that look, you know, that says, 'I'd tell you the truth, but then I might get my ass sued.' One of them said today she's in a 'heightened state of stabilized recuperation.'" Paul ran a hand through his twisted hair. He hadn't slept a night since the shooting.

"Ooooh, Ha! That's a good one," L.B. said. "That must have been Dr. Hinkle. You can be sure the English language has reached a cryogenic state with him."

"I've seen so many doctors, I start to forget their names," Paul said. "But it isn't just abstruse language that's his problem. His hair is too neatly combed. His skin's been scrubbed so much it's pink, and he looks like he has a germ phobia. The thing that kills me about most of these doctors is that they seem like the last people who want to get near anyone sick."

"Ain't that the truth! Ain't that a fact," L.B. said. "You see now, the ones who are too clean are the mama's boys who got into the whole profession just for the money. And they don't care a bit for the patients. And it doesn't matter how bland they are, they just have got to buy a red sports car to feel good about choosing a job they never liked. But don't let them even *begin* to fool you. Those are the most miserable doctors, *buying* their trophy wives."

"So if you can't trust the doctors, who are you supposed to trust?" Paul said.

"Well now, don't get me wrong. I'm not implying you can't trust *any* of them. Because there's a lot of them that are pretty good. But you've gotta stay far, far distant from the clean ones."

The thing that was most noticeable about L.B., beyond his tall, big-boned frame, were his hands, which were smooth from wearing surgical gloves all day and from wiping cream on the skin of elderly patients. He had a neat Afro, grown a little longer than most white people would feel comfortable with, that shined deeper than anthracite and that offset his warm, brown, highly animated face. His hands moved through the air, gathering thoughts and articulating points as he spoke, calling forth his words before he sent them off his tongue.

"Now, if I had to make a suggestion to you," said L.B., "any one suggestion, the best doctors are those small, scruffy-looking, old ones from New York who somehow moved their way up through the maze from one of those little city colleges in Brooklyn. Those men, they've got street smarts *and* experience. But if the *truth* be told, it's always the nurses I'm looking at. Don't get me wrong, I'm not saying this 'cause I'm a nurse. I'm just saying the ones who can give the kindness and LOVE are the nurses." He patted his green hospital uniform over his heart. "These doctors, these scientists, the only thing they want us to think about is that healing is taking pills and rewiring the plumbing. But I tell you, I've seen patients come in with the best surgeons in the world—with the *easiest* problems to fix—and without someone taking care of them, they just fall off the planet: dead. And then one of these real brain-stoppers comes in with so many complications he looks like spaghetti before *and after* surgery, but if he's got someone by his side whispering all sorts of goofy encouragement in his ear, the next thing you know he's good enough to walk—you'd think some crazy preacher-man had cast a healing spell on him. 'Course, I don't believe in spells or nothing, but LOVE, LOVE, that's the vital tonic juice that heals all. And I don't care if it *is* a cliché."

"Yeah," Paul said, "but the trouble I'm having with the kisses-and-love healing method is that Zoe blames *me* for taking her off the highway and bringing her to the reenactment. She'll hold my hand for a bit, then pull her fingers away and say, 'If we had just skipped the whole thing. We could have been at the caterers.'"

"But that's the thing, you know," L.B. said. "That's the way Zoe can be. And that's the way anyone can be. It's not uncommon to go through your mind all the could-haves and should-haves."

"Do you think I was wrong to take her to the reenactment?"

L.B. put his finger against his mouth to silence Paul. "Now, how can you be thinking that way?"

"Well maybe I caused it. Played into fate's hands."

"You see! That's just crazy thinking, man. Now you tell me: if you're living in such a way you don't *intend* no harm, then how can you blame yourself for the harm that accidentally comes your way? That's the first rule of Kant's categorical imperative, 'Do unto others as you would do unto yourself.' And you did."

"But I don't know if I *would* have left myself alone. I'm not saying it was the worst thing, but I don't think I should have left her just to talk to Cyrus. I wouldn't have wanted *her* to leave me alone to talk to him. That's what she tells me. And she's right. I shouldn't have left her to go to the river while I went in the limo. Everything would have ended up differently. She has every right to be pissed with me."

"No . . . no,no,no,no,no,no. If you didn't go, you would have been *rude* to Cyrus . . . But you know, man, there's a *purpose* for every *single thing* that happens under the sun. And if you ask me, the *reason* this thing happened was to bring you closer together before the wedding—to make you realize how much you need each other before you tie the knot—to stop your bickering."

"OK, I can see it that way," Paul said. "I can even see it that way—as fate. But if I see it that way, then it's hard not to also see what happened to Zoe as part of Buffalo Man's prophecy. So how can it be meant to be both good and bad? And even if you're right, are you saying we didn't really know how much we need each other already?"

"Well, I'm not saying definitively yes, and I'm not saying absolutely no. But what I *am* saying is that *you're* the one who's been telling me things have been kind of rough between you two lately. So maybe this is the way of making sure everything is patched up and whole before the wedding ceremony."

Hearing it put that way, even if Paul thought it was all too neat and comfortable, he felt the reassurance that can only come from a best friend. So perhaps everything might be all right after all, he tried to convince himself. Life and fate had given Zoe a bullet, and now he and Zoe would melt whatever swords were between them. He had his doubts, as always, but it was possible.

For the first time since he'd come to the diner, he truly noticed his surroundings. Vasily had not only given him a couple of extra pieces of bacon, he'd given him a sausage patty as well. And he'd given him a cup of hot cocoa, too. He downed the cocoa, which Vasily had spiked. Paul looked over at Vasily behind the front counter, next to the register, wiping the countertop, and when Vasily saw Paul, he pointed his finger and thumb cocked like a hammer on a toy gun, and he lowered it and fired.

"Who says hot cocoa is always hot cocoa?" Vasily said and shrugged. "In Russia, we have this saying. OK, we have too many sayings, and I may even have made this one up: 'If cops won't let you drink booze in the open, drink it in secret. And if they forbid you from drinking in secret, hold your nose and make hot cocoa.'"

"Vodka?" Paul pointed to the cup of cocoa.

"What else?" Vasily snapped his towel.

The dining car, empty of other customers, was starting to feel a bit warmer. (Boris and Vasily never skimped on the meat, but they kept the heat down to save on costs.) The booth Paul and L.B. sat in had red vinyl cushions, and Paul lifted his feet, placing them next to L.B. Vasily wandered to the old jukebox in the corner—ducking under the counter to get there—and turned to Paul and L.B. and said, "OK, you choose the music. Russian techno?—Some pretty crazy spacey music a friend of mine developed in the 80s as *samizdat*. This music drove Brezhnev nuts. Hip-hop and gangsta rap?—My current favorite. Old Irish fiddle tunes?—In case a customer walks in and we have to keep up the show this is our theme-song music? Or Yiddish folk songs?— For when the heart burns . . . The folk songs I can do without. But who can say we Jews don't know how to make music of lamentation?"

Paul worked up his appetite enough to finally eat a warm bite of applejack pancakes. The maple syrup, dripping over a scoop of butter and three cakes, was just right. It was one of the reasons he kept coming back to The Ugly Fitzsimmons, even when he wasn't in the mood for the chitchat Vasily insisted on. Something in the Russian soul demanded constant speech and probing, a search for the dregs of every experience. Something in the Russian soul was akin to the heart of a Chicago blues man, the only difference that the blues man sang to acquit himself of what made him feel blue while the Russians wanted or needed to permanently keep what made them feel dark. Yet both found some happiness and solace, or at least the will to live, out of kvetching and crying. Vasily fed a couple dollars of quarters into the jukebox. He pushed the buttons, and after a few seconds of CDs whirring within the brightly colored machine (the original jukebox had been renovated), the song "Matchmaker," from *Fiddler on the Roof,* came forth. The female voice was wan and pleading:

Matchmaker, Matchmaker,
Make me a match.
Find me a find;
Catch me a catch.
Matchmaker, Matchmaker,
Look through your book
And make me a perfect match.

The high tone of a young woman, who Paul imagined with a babushka head wrap begging for a romantic match, could appeal only to women from the 50s who took too much Valium, he thought, or to Jewish housewives in lost outposts of the U.S. (e.g., Wyoming). It certainly wasn't what Paul had expected when Vasily mentioned Yiddish folk music. Had Vasily overheard him talking to L.B. about his troubles with Zoe and decided this was a good tune to encourage them to patch up their romantic problems? Or maybe he'd confused Broadway's version of Yiddish culture with the real thing? The Jews in Russia had been cut off from the rest of the world for so long, Paul thought.

"Ha-ha, just joking," Vasily said. He switched to some genuinely mournful Yiddish music, and Paul leaned back in the thick-padded booth, savoring the thought if not the taste of the pancakes, and he closed his eyes to listen. He saw a man with a wide, gray, scraggly beard that had been pulled by the Cossacks, with a handmade, baggy white cotton shirt covered with mud stains from pushing his wagon, and with a thick yarmulke passed down from generation to generation, belting the music out as if he still lived in the *shtetl*, even as Paul knew the man was probably a professional performer who recorded the tune in some music studio in Moscow. But at least this music *sounded* authentic. Vasily had said, earlier, he didn't want to listen to folk music and that he'd rather listen to hip-hop or gangsta rap, so why had he put it on? As a gesture of support as Paul coped with Zoe's accident? To let him know his suffering would pass, as the suffering of the Jews throughout the ages had waxed and waned? But the truth was the whining and crying *didn't* make him feel better. It made him think of Zoe more. There was little in the sounds of the *shtetl* to generate hope. He opened his eyes and saw L.B. swaying his head gently from side to side, trying to make sense of the music, which was no doubt unfamiliar to him.

When the song ended, he said to L.B., "I think I'm gonna go visit Zoe again. You're headed to work, right? Mind if I come?"

"No, of course not, man. That's a good idea. You can spend the night with Zoe. I'll get you into the building without having to go through all that security."

Paul left as big a tip as he could for Vasily. He might not have made Paul feel better, but he was doing his best. The air was cool as he pushed his way out of the dining car. The sound of Russian techno *samizdat* rattled the stainless steel walls of the diner as he walked with L.B. into the starless, cloudy night.

Normally, in the dead of night, it would have taken only fifteen minutes to drive from Davis Square to Mass General Hospital. Nighttime was Paul's favorite for driving. Not only because there was almost no traffic but because he liked the bright colors of flashing lights, preprogrammed, directing ghosts when there were no cars. There was something funny about traffic lights flashing on and off with no one to stop, yet also reassuring. With the lights came order. With the lights came peace. The lights reflected beautifully on the front window, the few lights from inside the Toyota echoing softly on the interior glass. And in the night Paul's car didn't feel so cheap or dilapidated next to the other cars on the road. If you had asked Paul if he would like a new car, he wouldn't necessarily have said yes, and he wouldn't necessarily have said no, but how could any normal person pass new cars, day after day, and not think a new one would be nice? In general, he disliked the rash of new SUVs on the road, which he considered environmentally ludicrous, but he wasn't like environmentalists who cursed every big car they saw. He liked it that his car was comfortable—that he had made it his own. There was his junk: crushed old paper cups, tattered road maps, Cheetos and other bits of snacks in the carpeting, a few crumpled soda cans, piles of plastic CD cases (usually music most people on the street had never heard of), a few lost and torn pages from student essays he'd read through quickly as he slapped on a grade (and, not too surprisingly, the students never seemed to notice a page or two had come apart from their essays); there were coffee stains on the odd-shaped little mats beneath the seats, since he drank at least six cups a day; and there were a few plastic toys, a GI Joe doll missing his head, and an old figure of Captain America without his shield. Paul had been given these dolls by his friend Ned (he had two friends, L.B. and Ned), who ran a small collectibles store and who gave him the figurines that had been destroyed by clients' careless kids. There were at least a dozen dried-out ballpoint pens stuck in the cracks of the back seat and under the front seats. Every time Paul found one of the pens, he'd toss it in the glove compartment, with the intention of throwing it out later, but he never did, so the glove compartment was a treasure trove of pens that he'd chewed on while thinking, most of them dry.

The other good thing about driving at night, he thought, was that you could drive fast even if you had a crappy engine. Because one of the odd things about the cops of Boston, as far as he could tell, was that, while they would stop you for minor infractions (such as driving through a yellow light just as it turned red, or for not having a valid environmental emissions inspection sticker), if you really broke the law (by playing, for example, your music *really loud* with all your windows down, or driving unbelievably fast, or making a U-turn in a busy intersection), they wouldn't do anything. The cops seemed to give some kind of grudging respect to the most flagrant abusers in the city. Who knows, Paul thought, maybe this was some outgrowth of letting the mob do whatever it wanted in town for so long? The mafia was robbing the town blind of billions of dollars on the Big Dig construction project that was building tunnels throughout the city (while everyone was dutifully slamming back one last shot at 1 A.M.). The bigger the lie, the safer the lie, wasn't that what someone had once said?

So now he drove fast toward Mass General, ignoring the yellow oil light that—for the last few months—had stayed on no matter how many quarts of oil he'd stuck in the engine. He swerved a little around big potholes that cropped up on Beacon Street. There was a persistent clacking sound on both sides of the front of the car that, no matter how hard he'd tried to ignore the last couple of months, wouldn't go away.

"You know," L.B. said as Paul accelerated, "if you were driving in Jamaica, I think everyone would say you're all right. They'd say 'nuff respect."

The traffic light just in front turned solid red and Paul slammed on the brakes. The car screeched and wheels skidded. L.B., thick bodied, his large head perfectly circular like a pumpkin, crouched down and tried to avoid hitting his Afro into the front window.

"Sorry," Paul said.

"That's OK, that's OK," L.B. said, and he leaned gently back into his seat again. He relaxed his shoulders and put on his seatbelt slowly so

Paul wouldn't think too much about his action, and patted his hair to make sure his head was still in place.

When the light turned green, Paul pushed the accelerator all the way to the floor. He was loving the speed. He was loving the cool air of spring blowing around his down vest. In the speed he didn't have to think about Zoe in the hospital. In the speed he felt the beauty of the engine, even the beauty of his old beat-up Toyota Corolla.

"How soon do you have to be at Mass General?" he shouted over the engine. "Do you have time to go for a ride?"

"Well, I've got to be there sooner rather than later, but if we don't go too far . . . there's always time . . ."

The top of the gearshift stick felt well worn and smooth in the palm of Paul's hand. He felt the jerks and little ripples of the gears that made his engine unique. So it wasn't just the speed that mattered but the unique feeling of the speed—the feeling that the speed was his own and no one else's. This is why, he thought, vicarious speed could take a person only so far. He could feel speed just looking at the shiny, thick enamel paint on a bright sports car. If he looked into a club where everyone was dancing, enthralled, he could feel the energy of the crowd. If he watched a band on stage, if he watched the drummer's sticks beating back and forth quickly, he could absorb himself in the energy of the sound. But none of that was the same as *appropriating* the speed, or appropriating the movement, or appropriating the sound. Speed, uninternalized, not made into the unique experience of the person who produces the speed, is not the same as real speed, he thought. *So much effort is going into the speed of artificial reality these days—the speed of what is not actually experienced but is only imagined to be experienced—but that speed can never equal the real thrill of real speed,* Paul thought. *Without my hand actually firmly on the stick shift, without the little jitters of my car, this would all be only a dream.* And no amount of faking the real thing could make it real. He had noticed, for example, in magazines, typography generated by computers that attempted to make headlines look like they had been typed quickly. Some letters were made to appear like the key of a typewriter had only partially struck the page. And this was a perfect simulacrum of the real thing, only it was obviously and instantly false.

It was the real speed he fed off of now. When he came to the Charles River, he turned to the right, away from the hospital just over the Longfellow Bridge, and he rushed along the river on Memorial Drive. There were no stars out; thick clouds hung low in the sky over the river, lit in ghostly flame colors, a pale yellowish brown from the lights of the city. The heavy blanket of clouds pushed down until they nearly struck the tallest skyscrapers. But this was where the greatness of humans could most visibly be seen, Paul thought. The skyscrapers resisted the clouds. The fluorescent lights in the buildings emitted high up the towers as he drove as fast as he could. The lights were reflected and trapped by the clouds, but they also pushed through them. In space, no doubt, the city of Boston glowed even when the clouds were thick. The lights of the nighttime city reflected brightly off the Charles River, swaying in sinusoidal patterns off the water, forming beautiful designs within patterns that changed depending on how you looked at them. Paul drove up the river, then he came to a U-turn and, feeling emboldened and not seeing any traffic, he didn't stop at the red light. He made the turn illegally, rushing through the light, and went back down the river toward the hospital.

"You know, for a while I drove in the ambulances," L.B. said, "when I first came to the hospital. This reminds me of how good those rides were, when we didn't have any patients and we used to ride with the lights still flashing."

Paul nodded. He understood, he hoped, exactly how L.B. felt. It was that level of intimate understanding he wanted with Zoe and with those around him whom he felt he loved. But why was it so hard to feel that synchronicity of thought and experience even with those we see every day? A thin barrier often seemed to creep in, like the space between the photo of someone and who they really were, or their image in the mirror and their flesh. *There is the image, and then what is kept secret behind the image.*

When he made it all the way back to the Longfellow Bridge, he took a quick right, barely slowing at the stop sign. He rushed over the bridge, with its empty subway tracks running in sinister black trails from one end of the long bridge to the other. Then he was forced to go slowly. There was so much construction around the hospital, so many new wings they were building for new patients and so many new parking garages and so many new concrete barriers to prevent terrorism, that he found himself forced to a crawl. The dirt and dust of the construction site covered the car and billowed around him like pollution coming out of a smokestack. He hit the sprayer and washed the front window, streaking the dust in dirty, distorted arcs across the glass. At the entrance to the main parking garage, he looked for the key to the garage that Zoe had given him that would allow him to park free, but he couldn't find it. So he was forced to take a ticket to park his car, and he inched up the parking ramp and searched futilely for a while until he finally found a space on the roof of the garage, where rain might wash his car.

He walked along the roof next to L.B., beneath a light drizzle that had started, still feeling the intimacy with L.B., still feeling faint flickers of what was true, what was fast, what was irreproducible, what was at the origin of all connections, until he heard the sound of gum sticking to his shoes, and when he bent down to scrape his shoe, the last vestiges of the good speed were gone.

Zoe's nearest neighbors were night creatures. The rooms of the patients on her floor huddled together, with walls made of thin cinder blocks, and it wasn't hard to hear the resident freak show even if Zoe did have a private room. To her right was some African-American woman from Dorchester, with milky, unseeing eyes, who masturbated uncontrollably as a result of a major head wound. "Lord Jesus, I'm coming. Yes, sir. I'm coming. Ooh, child. I'm coming." Her son, a preacher, entered and left her room without meeting anyone's eyes, his head held high, trying, Paul guessed, to repress or at least hide his shame. The room to the left wasn't much better: a sixteen-year-old girl who'd been shot by her father accidentally on a bear-hunting trip, and the father (Zack) stood guard in front of her door all night, on a mission to protect her from any pedophiles in the ward. "I've seen those shows on TV," Zack told Paul the first night Zoe was in the hospital. "I know what goes on in these places. And there's no way I'm gonna let some stinking ped-o-phile rape my daughter."

Paul had decided it was best to keep his sunglasses on at all times when talking to Zack, not only so Zack wouldn't feel like Paul was looking at him in any disrespectful way, but also so he would never be able to make a positive ID on him. This was the kind of guy, Paul thought, who might feel pissed off for some unknown reason and then track you down and enter your room in the middle of the night and tell you the reason you'd just been strapped to your bed, tied up in a thick rope, was for your own safety. Someone was always coming to get Zack. But Paul had to admit guys like Zack were some of the most earnest, upstanding kind of people he'd ever met (at gun shows). They didn't make their paranoia up. It was genuine. Their word was their bond. And as long as you could get them to keep their guns in their holsters, they were actually some of the nicest people around.

After Paul had parked the car, and L.B. had got him through the back door past security and said goodbye and went off to work, Paul approached Zoe's room cautiously. He put his sunglasses on at the end of the hallway before nearing Zack. Zack saluted Paul with his legs spread wide, preventing the entry of any "foreign element" into his daughter's room. He had worked out an arrangement with the nurses to permit him to stand this way. At first the nurses told Zack he would have to leave his daughter and let her rest when visiting hours were over, and they told him free entry and exit of her room was essential, but after Zack threatened to take his daughter out of treatment early if they wouldn't protect the sanctity of her childhood—and after they determined he was otherwise harmless, and without a gun—they let him play guard.

"Good to see you again," Zack said. "I didn't expect to see you back here until 0800 hours."

Paul had stayed until 2 A.M. the first two nights Zoe was in the hospital, and then he'd returned at eight in the morning. It was best to let Zack know he was doing a pretty good job of monitoring, though he might try to throw him off a little. "Yeah," said Paul, "I usually *do* come in around 7:30 A.M., but tonight I just couldn't stay away."

"Uh-huh," Zack said. He looked at his Army watch. "I think it was more around 0800, though." He looked up from his watch and changed the subject. "I don't think you want to go in there right now."

"What?" said Paul.

"I said I don't think you want to go in there right now."

"Why's that?"

"A hostile element entered that room about an hour ago, and I never saw him leave."

"I'll be sure to be careful," Paul said.

"You know, ignoring fundamental intelligence has been the central reason for every military fiasco since World War II. That's what happened in the Bay of Pigs my friend, and why the Tet Offensive was so successful for the gooks."

"I promise to be careful," Paul said. He had to admit he felt a little on edge. Zack looked straight ahead, like a special ops Green Beret, ignoring Paul, as if he had now surrendered his right to be protected.

Paul opened the door to Zoe's room and waved quietly goodbye to Zack. He closed the door as softly as he could. The light of the city came faintly through the large window in the room, between metal slats of shades. In some strange way, although he had little patience for survivalists and military reenactors, especially after what had happened in Concord, he had to acknowledge he felt Zoe was safer with Zack next door.

There were few places he disliked more than hospital rooms, but he knew there must be a reason he had come back to the hospital this evening. There was Zoe on the bed, her legs straight in front of her as if she were a corpse in a morgue. She never slept on her back this way; she always slept on her side. But now she lay in tightly wrapped hospital sheets covering her body up to her chin. Her bed was on the left side of the room, the center of all energy in the linoleum-tiled space focused upon her. He had never thought of it before, but the machines existed only for the patient. Without the patient they were useless. In some way, Zoe had regained the center of attention, like an actress spotlighted on stage. So perhaps this wasn't such a horrible state for her after all. Everything in the room pampered her and monitored her, each machine her servant. She was not selfish and snappish in the way of a master, Paul thought, but could he ever live up to her desires and needs?

Wrapped in the sheets, relaxed and luminescent, she looked like a queen bee. Her face, soft, narrow, and with delicately carved features, with large brown eyes closed now, so that her soft eyelashes lay on her cheeks, made him want to come closer to her. Perhaps this was the problem between them. Did she still believe she would be famous someday—that she would actually regain the spotlight she had once briefly had on the soap opera? Such success was something to be mutually hoped for, he agreed, but he wished they both understood that it was unlikely.

"Zoe," he said softly, and he sat down in a hard metal chair, a brown fold-up next to her bed. He didn't want to wake her; yet at the same time, he hoped she would hear his words. "Zoe, I think this is the time for me to come clean about a few things. I'm paralyzed. I've been absolutely paralyzed about the book I've been writing. I haven't written nearly as many chapters as I've been telling you." There was a monitor above her on the wall, a TV screen that showed her pulse, and the pulse didn't seem to be going any faster, so he felt secure now that, although he was voicing his thoughts, Zoe might not be hearing them consciously. "I know I've told you before that I actually *did* get a palm reading that day we met in Iowa, but what I've never told you is that part of what Buffalo Man said was that you would leave me—that our relationship was going to fall apart, or maybe that you would die. And ever since he told me those things, I haven't been able to write. It's ludicrous, I know. Even now, I don't really believe all of what he said. But ever since that day, I haven't been able to. So I think some of the problems between us are due to his crazy curse. And the reason I'm telling you all these things tonight is because I want a clean slate when we get married. I don't want any more big secrets between us. So I'm going to tell you the biggest secrets I have these days." He looked at her face closer and put his ear by the side of her chest to tell if she was breathing faster. But there was no change to the rhythm of her breathing, so he felt calm enough to continue. He leaned back in the chair, and the whole room felt like the dark belly of a whale. Perhaps if he continued with his confession he would be able to liberate himself, to unburden himself, and escape the belly of the beast. He hoped, at least, that by releasing what had been burdening him, he might be able to somehow save Zoe. Maybe his very act of emptying his guts of everything he felt was dirty would make her healthy. It was worth a try, at least, and he already felt lighter from what he had told her so far.

"Zoe, I may never be the man you wanted me to be. I think you started going out with me, and said you'd marry me, because you thought I was some kind of underdog—that I could pull off some last-minute save. I think you've always thought I'm witty and that if I just put my nose to it, I can finish this book and regain some kind of central pride I once had. But what if I just can't do it?" He paused to let his words filter through the empty space of the room. "What if I just don't have it in me?" It was particularly scary to vocalize such a thought. He'd had this thought before, but now he'd spoken it aloud. "Last week, I met with Chairman Kominski, and he says if I can't finish my book in the next couple months, or at least write a significant article, they're going to keep me from getting tenure. Seriously, I'll be kicked out of B_____ C.C. And I don't know what to do about it. I don't see any way out."

He looked at her again for any sign she could hear him, for any stirring, or even for some gasp that might indicate disapproval. But nothing came. So had he really made a confession if she couldn't hear him? If a tree falls in the forest and no one is there to hear, did it really fall? Was this just one more sign of cowardice? Should he wake her? Shake her until she was definitely awake to hear him?

He leaned back in the fold-up chair in the hope of falling asleep. In the morning he would do something about the book. In the morning he would finally make some headway.

But it wasn't possible to fall asleep in the room no matter how tired he felt from having spoken of his fears to Zoe. There were sounds all around him, extremely faint, but sounds that rushed into his ears louder than he felt they ought to. There was, first, the sound of the emptiness of the room itself. The very space and dark void of the room made a sound of oppression, the sound of stillborn air. And he wondered if this nothingness would creep into Zoe's lungs and into his lungs, too. Here he was attached to Zoe in the silence, breathing the same silent air as her, and yet this air seemed to form an empty cocoon between them. If two people were in space, for example, floating in the ether, they would be able to see each other, they might even be within sighting distance, but they would be infinitely kept apart by the vacuum between them. And the crackle of that void seemed all around him in the room. The distance between his body, where he sat on the chair, and Zoe's face, which was only a matter of a few feet away, seemed infinitely distant.

And then there was the sound of the colored lights: green, yellow, and red diodes flickering on the machines just above Zoe. They buzzed slightly. They seemed to possess Zoe, to have more to do with keeping her alive than he did. If L.B. was right, if love was what mattered for healing more than the surgeons and the machines, then why did he feel the machines had the upper hand? These lies everyone went around telling themselves, that their souls mattered the most, that their love was what was strongest, that things should work out simply because that was what was most hoped for, seemed like a cruel joke to him now. Because it didn't seem to matter how much he willed for Zoe to hear him, or for her to give some sign that his confession to her had been an act of love that she had received. Instead, all he heard was the sound of the empty silence of the room and of the lights.

Had there been any signs Zoe was having an affair? Was that what Zack was trying to warn him when he said a foreign intruder had come into the room an hour ago? It was not out of the realm of possibility. He had to admit he'd been absorbed in his work recently, that he had been busy information gathering at AA meetings, and that he had even made a trip to one of the largest publishers of self-improvement books at its headquarters in Emmaus, Pennsylvania. And then, too, he had been spending hours in his office at B_____ Community College, trying to write, to put all his ideas together into some coherent form, but coming up empty. So in all of this, had Zoe perhaps found another man? Some handsome doctor at Mass General who would be much more worthy of the intense romantic passion he sometimes felt flickering in his direction and that he had found himself incapable of reciprocating in those few moments (though, paradoxically, he wanted to have sex)?

Was it a sign of his endless thoughts and of the permutations of his attempts to come up with some explanation for his daily life that made him come up with such melodramatic and baseless suppositions? It was not that Zoe was incapable of an affair—he knew she was not—he even suspected he had found some evidence lately that might support such an idea. But what bothered him was that he was always leaping to such a conclusion before he had any *real* evidence—that he was always leaping to come up with some theory, or some insight, before he knew if the world actually matched his ideas.

Turn off the mind, turn off the mind for just a little bit, he told himself. *Even if your mind runs at full speed, you'll never catch up to Cyrus. He has more talent than you. He and Andrew are simply smarter than you. You have suppositions without evidence, ideas without conclusions, interests without discipline. Just give Zoe a kiss. That will be the best thing you can do now. The very best thing to let her know you have never wanted to hurt her and that you want her to come back to life, to calm you down and to kiss you back and to make you whole again.*

But for some reason he felt that to kiss her without her being awake would be to violate her, and so he only reached out and held her. In the silence of the dark room, he held her smooth hand that lay on top of the tight white sheet. Her hand was warm, not cold as he had feared. Zoe would make it, he thought. They would make it together. A wedding could not heal all, but it was a beginning, the beginning he had finally promised her when she had insisted he finish something for once and that they get married.

It was Thursday, the day he had his morning class. Paul preferred to teach in the afternoon, but Zoe had said it was time for him to get on a normal schedule. He had begun to fall into the trap of waking up at ten after staying up late surfing the Net, looking for interesting bits of information, surfing the endless miles of electronic pages that he thought might lead him to the center, to the spark of the subject matter that would form the kernel of his book. And so this spring term he had signed up to teach an 8:30 A.M. class. That was when she had given him an ultimatum, also, that they finally get married. Six years of cohabitation was enough, she'd said, to finally know if they were right for each other. "I'm not sure, myself, if I know the ultimate answer to that question," Zoe had said to him, "but I know it's time for us to quit futzing around."

In the hospital, when he woke up next to Zoe, Paul thought he would cancel the class, but when he started to tell Zoe he was going to skip it, she told him (of course) not to. "And I don't want to put off the wedding, either," Zoe said.

"Are you sure?" Paul said. "We could put it off for a month or two. Let's wait and see how you feel in a few days."

It was seven o'clock and one of the nurses was knocking to come in. Paul said they could talk about it later. Zoe told the nurse to wait outside for a moment. "No, absolutely not," Zoe said. "We're going to finish something, finally. We're both going to finish it. And I've already spent all the time getting everything set up—the house, the caterer, the dress, the hotel arrangements for the family. Do you have any idea how long it would take to do all of that over again?"

"But you've been shot, Zoe."

"Right. Just above the hip. I'm in pain, but this is all going to heal itself soon. I'll just have to limp to the altar. Are you going to your class?"

"Like I said, I thought I would skip it today," Paul said.

Zoe looked away. "Do whatever you want," she said.

"But you don't mean that," Paul said. "And why should I go to class when you're hurt?"

"Just think of it as me wanting some time alone," Zoe said.

And so here he was on the campus of B_____ Community College for his work. He was already running a little late. On his way out of the hospital, he had seen Zack, who had said to him, "Doing one of those threesome jobs, huh? All I got to say is I never saw that other man come out of the room."

The car had died when Paul was only a few minutes from the campus. He'd been stopped at a traffic light, under a large, metal over-pass that held up the interstate that ran into the center of Boston, and his Corolla had simply refused to go forward. Every light on the dash-board flashed, and then they all went black. "Fucking A," Paul had said. He'd turned the key over and over, but the engine wouldn't start. He had no idea what the problem could be. A line of cars honked behind. "Can't you see I'm just trying to move?" he'd said, and he got out of the car and opened the driver's window and pushed the car to the sidewalk while trying to steer. The right front wheel bumped against the high concrete curb beneath the highway, and a nail seemed to puncture the tire. The car tilted down and forward to the right.

When he came into the classroom, he was sweaty from walking fast to get to the class before all the students left, and sure enough they were gone. He had on the same clothes he'd been wearing the last three days in the hospital. His breath was bad; he had spent the night next to Zoe with his mouth open in a big O after his nose seemed to dry up and clog in the thin air of the hospital. His hair bunched to the left and right like some kind of Chinese engineering student's.

There was no way he could gather the students up now—they had scattered like white noise—and he didn't feel like teaching them in any case. So he kicked his feet up on the seminar table, and he put his head back to sleep, and just as he was about to close his eyes, he saw Cyrus looking in on him, through an oval window into the classroom. He slammed his feet down on the floor and rushed to the door to let him in.

"Nice teaching method," Cyrus said.

"Good one," Paul said. "My car broke down under the overpass as I was coming to school."

"What does that have to do with the class?"

"Everyone was gone when I got here."

"So you were late? That's what I'm saying, you see. How can I help you with your image if you're late? In any case, I went to talk to Kominski this morning and he was gracious, as always, but he said 'no can do.'"

"I thought I asked you not to speak to him."

"Well, sometimes no doesn't mean no. That's the first thing you learn as a lawyer for a defendant. If the defendant says he didn't do something, then maybe he did. And if he says he doesn't want something—like a good lawyer—then maybe he does. Everyone thinks they can defend themselves in court. Just look at the Unabomber or the first World Trade Center bombers in 1993. Every terrorist I've ever met wanted to defend himself."

"Great, but I'm not a terrorist."

"Nobody said you are, but pride seems to get in the way of basic self-defense."

Should he hit Cyrus for his smug self-assurance? Cyrus was a few inches taller than him, and certainly fitter. He worked out on his exercise bicycle and Nautilus set, and since the pool behind his house was heated, even in the winter, and since he had a wave and water-current jet installed to provide resistance, he looked good. Still, a surprise attack might take him down. Paul loved the kung fu movies of Bruce Lee. It was one of the things he was going to discuss in class today. Because one of the key things about Bruce Lee was that he wasn't really supposed to be a tough guy. He didn't go around looking to pick a fight; he simply learned to defend himself as he was picked on. In many ways, Bruce Lee was the common guy's answer to inadequacy. As was Superman, as was the Incredible Hulk: it was essential that the hero be weak first, whether a shy journalist or a wimpy scientist. The comic world was all about the inevitable need of finding a way past the inadequacy.

"I asked Kominski," Cyrus said, "if it wouldn't be possible for some extension, at least through the fall, but he said the rules for tenure must remain consistent within the department. In any case, I suggest you start writing now. And though you didn't hear it from me, if you can't do it yourself, consider a ghostwriter." Cyrus carried a big leather briefcase crammed full of paper: new ideas for his next book, notes for his next class lecture, memoranda to be copied by his secretary (even in the age of the personal computer, he seemed to enjoy giving letters to his secretary to be typed up, and to be fair, he really didn't have the time to deal with all his correspondence). "I've got to get back to the law school," he said. His first-year law class was attended by more than the three hundred who were officially enrolled. Students and visiting scholars crowded the auditorium where he lectured, leaning against the back wall and spilling into the hallway.

When Cyrus was gone, Paul walked around the campus of B_____ Community College. He walked with his clothes loose, his jeans baggy, almost like his students. He walked like a zombie, with no particular goal or place to go. He had heard someone say, once, that a teacher comes to look and act like his students—first-grade teachers like first graders, junior-high teachers like junior-high students, etc. And judging from the one time when he'd gone back to his public elementary school in North Cambridge, there may have been some truth to that. The principal was roaming through the corridors on roller skates, for no apparent reason Paul could make out.

In the central student quad he bought a breakfast burrito and found a bench in the sun. At the top of twenty flagpoles around the semicircular plaza that he had heard was inspired by the United Nations but that looked more like the entrance to a Disney theme park, purple pennant-shaped flags fluttered in the wind, each emblazoned with a fanged wildcat in midpounce—the mascot. The budget for the basketball team was almost as big as for the entire humanities program. The basketball team of B_____ Community College was the best in its division, and many players went on to play D-1. Better than Indiana. Better than Michigan. Better than all those states where basketball was more important than God. The few times Paul had found himself at an academic conference, he had invariably been slapped on the back and chatted up about the team, as though he were personally responsible for or excited by its success. "Tell Jackworth—" they said. And, "Great season!" Jackworth was Coach Jackworth, who kept two pumas in his home that he sometimes brought to the games. (The cats slept on faux leopard-skin pillows and blankets. Paul had seen all of this in the *Boston Globe,* in one of their Boston Personality stories about Coach Jackworth's house.)

About halfway around the concrete plaza, he saw the team's center talking to another student (one of the best guards on the team), and he could overhear the two of them.

"Dude," Guard said. "That paper for American History is gonna be a bitch."

"Don't worry about it," Center said, blowing bubblegum and spinning a basketball in his hand. "Coach said not to worry about it. Says he's gonna get the *tutor* to help us."

"OK, man. That's cool."

So why shouldn't *I* just visit a ghostwriter? Paul thought. If President Reagan could do it, if Hillary Clinton could do it in her memoirs—if none of the lofty speeches were handwritten or even composed by the president of the U.S. anymore (even in a time of war, when statements about the need for common sacrifice and the heroics of firemen were made), if Cyrus had secretaries cooking up personal letters to some of his correspondents, then why not me? The days of Lincoln's handwritten Gettysburg Address are over, Paul thought. *It's the era of the speechwriter. Even Bruce Lee's shouts and cries have to be translated into inadequate subtitles.*

CHAPTER 5

Just outside of Boston, and not too far from Concord, behind a large house once owned by slave masters, and in the garden that belonged to the house—which was a quiet, meditative garden with Greco-Roman statues and a reflecting pool filled with water lilies, and with an occasional frog or two gently ribbitting as if on pastoral serenading cue, and with a garden trellis at the front of the reflecting pool, made of sweet-smelling cedar and covered with vines of wisteria that were still not quite in bloom (though blooms were coming soon)—a crowd of guests waited for the bride (Zoe) to appear. Chairs for the crowd formed two sections, one on either side of the pool, and Paul stood before the audience feeling naked. He felt every guest could see right through his tuxedo, right through the boxers he had bought in Chinatown imprinted with the faces of the world's most significant prophets: Moses, Jesus, the Buddha, Muhammad, Bahā' Allāh, Confucius, the Dalai Lama, etc.

Eight days before the wedding, after visiting Zoe at the hospital on a rainy day when he was nursing an incipient cold, Paul had wandered into Chinatown, where an herbalist gave him some good medicine: dried ginseng tea mixed with other herbs. He was told the herbs in the tea would clear his head, and they did. On his walk through Chinatown, as he looked for an umbrella to keep himself dry, he had also come across a storekeeper who told him about a massage parlor upstairs. The man made it clear the massage was more than just the usual massage; it would be a whole "organ massage, good for liver and penis." For a moment Paul considered the massage. He wasn't sure if it was sexual or not, but it sounded like a one-man bachelor party, and no one had set him up with such a party yet or told him they had plans for one. If Andrew had still been alive, Paul was certain he would have set up a "good time" for him, L.B., Ned, and whoever else might be included in such a fiesta, but with Andrew gone, Cyrus was the only brother left. And as far as counting on friends, L.B. was always up for a party, but he wasn't used to what he considered the formalities of party going in the U.S., the way every party had to be arranged in advance rather than simply spontaneously beginning; and Ned was too absorbed in his store and in his interests (which included aerial snow boarding, skateboarding, and visiting comic book conventions in basements in San Francisco, New York, and Detroit) to think of such a thing.

Consciously, there really wasn't a reason why Paul meandered all the way from Mass General to Chinatown. He simply followed his feet as he thought about Zoe's continued insistence they go ahead with the wedding as scheduled. *So the deed will be done on time.* But semiconsciously—as he wandered first through the Chinatown gate, gilded with yellow paint that was supposed to look like gold and bring good fortune to every poor Joe who passed between the concrete pillars, and then into the herbal medicine store, and then into the store where he was offered but declined the massage (yet found the boxer shorts with the prophets that he was told would also bring him good luck)—he was following a name on a piece of paper he had written down the night before that he'd found at a new dating service Web site called wematchyoudoit.com. He'd been looking at the site because he liked to see the way people sought to do the impossible—to describe in fifty words or less who they were, and what they liked, and what their dreams were for the future, and what they considered the most romantic moment (which would never be the most romantic moment, he thought, because the most romantic moment was when two people were sad together, not happy)—and as he looked at the Web site, with small ads flashing along the left-hand side of the screen, he saw an ad that interested him: "Don't know what to say or how to say it? In need of a Cyrano to give you sweet nothings to whisper? Click here." The link from the ad explained everyone could use a Cyrano de Bergerac. It went on to explain Cyrano was a real man who had lived from 1619 to 1655, that he was a French soldier, a swordsman, and a writer, and that although he was a real romantic, he wasn't particularly good-looking. So Cyrano used his natural ability for language to help good-looking but shy men woo their women. (Like me, maybe you have seen the film *Cyrano,* with Gérard Depardieu. Depardieu does a pretty good job, although he ends up waxing too philosophic in the movie—a sign he's a French actor. For years I've heard about, and even made reference to, Cyrano without having read the original. Cyrano, like so many cultural references, has been separated from his origins. According to the dictionary I just looked him up in, he was the hero of a play written *in verse* by Edmond Rostand. I'm making this reference to Rostand simply to give you the opportunity to go back to the original if you feel like it.) In any case, what the ad on the Internet made clear is that not everyone can find the words to say what they want. It went on to explain the deficiency of greeting cards, which aren't tailored to individuals, and it offered the services of a Modern Day Cyrano to anyone in need. The rest of the cyrano.com Web page gave a link to a personal questionnaire and to a personality test, to be used by The Modern Cyrano to come up with just the right words for the right moment … And in a few minutes, Paul realized this Cyrano might be the person who could write a publishable article for him, or even a book. The advantages were obvious, he felt: this was someone used to plagiarism who didn't care if his words were appropriated by others; someone who was intelligent enough to know who Cyrano de Bergerac was in the first place; someone who dealt with people who felt inadequate all the time; and someone used to being anonymous. The address for The Modern Cyrano gave his location as above a restaurant called The Big Rice Bowl, in Boston's Chinatown.

Paul bought the boxers with the prophets printed on the fabric, and perhaps it was the feeling of so many prophets in his hand, wrapped in a bright pink plastic bag imprinted with the word LUCKY, that led him to search more actively for The Modern Cyrano. After refusing the special massage, he asked the store owner if he could direct him to The Big Rice Bowl. The shopkeeper, a sturdy Chinese man with a crew cut who looked like he belonged on the police force and not in a massage parlor, waved his hand in front of his face, pretending he didn't speak English—although he had just spoken perfectly good English—and said, "Big Rice Bowl? No." The no was emphatic.

Similar inquiries to people on the streets produced similar answers. Even with the address of the restaurant—which Paul looked up in a phone book—he was having trouble finding The Big Rice Bowl. It wasn't just that the street names were hard to follow in this part of town; it was that the old Colonial streets, which had once been cow paths, formed a somewhat impenetrable series of lanes, with old brick buildings where Jewish and Italian garment workers had once plied their trade. Chinese, Filipinos, Vietnamese, and Thais bustled about, but no one seemed to know where The Big Rice Bowl was. (The last time Paul had been to Chinatown was the incident mentioned in the first chapter when he went to pick Cyrus up after Cyrus had gotten drunk in a XXX theater. The red-light district in Boston's Chinatown is almost gone now, part of the gentrification of the area by the powers that be. In its place, the city has built hotels like the new Ritz-Carlton, and the new office for the Registry of Motor Vehicles. Apparently, nothing makes pimps want to flee more than traffic department offices and rich people at the Ritz—who use upscale pimps.)

The rain was coming down hard as Paul walked around Chinatown. He passed the Hong Kong Eatery and China Pearl restaurant and Chow Chow's, but no Big Rice Bowl. He turned left onto a narrow street reeking of rotting cabbage and garbage from a number of restaurants, and twenty yards further, he found himself staring down a dead-end alley cluttered with dumpsters. At the end of the alley stood a small, white building, smudged with the residue of coal, with a large coffee cup on top of the cinder-block storefront, and the name on the coffee cup, which topped what had been a donut stand in the 1950s, read THE BIG RICE BOWL.

Do I dare to go in? Paul thought. His feet answered by shuffling forward. He stood directly in front of the restaurant, peering in, the store inside dark, and despite a WE'RE OPEN sign in the window, there was no one working in the place. But he didn't really need the restaurant. What he needed was The Modern Cyrano's office *above* the restaurant. Yet how could there be an office above the restaurant? The only thing on top of the white hovel was the coffee cup, the size of a small car, with a pair of chopsticks stuck in The Big Rice Bowl. Behind and above the bowl, a redbrick wall with no windows, which was the back of another building facing another street, formed a sheer barrier pointing up to the raining sky. Paul stood in the dead-end alleyway, with dumpsters on both sides. The wall of brick above The Big Rice Bowl offered no hint of how to find The Modern Cyrano. *This is the problem,* he thought, *with taking ads from a dating service Web site seriously.* Why would The Modern Cyrano give a real address? Would he want to be bothered by his forlorn and estranged customers? The whole point of The Modern Cyrano was anonymity. So, of course, The Modern Cyrano wouldn't give his real address. He probably laughed knowing that, occasionally, someone like Paul tried to find his way to The Big Rice Bowl. And he probably laughed, too, Paul thought, at the idea the person looking at the blank brick wall—like the wall in Melville's "Bartleby the Scrivener"—would seek to form some symbolic meaning out of such an alleyway, in the same way readers of Fitzgerald's *The Great Gatsby* were pushed to read so much meaning into the symbolic eyeglasses that looked out over the Valley of Ashes. What Paul thought was that he could choose to read some symbolic meaning into his position right now—stuck in the dead-end alleyway, with a coffee cup turned into a new rice-bowl-symbol that might indicate rejuvenation but that instead seemed to augur decay—but wouldn't that all just be too simple? Because, after all, the complexity of life couldn't be reduced to a symbol. Anger, defeat, whatever he might be feeling now was much more complex than any symbol.

(A more realistic portrayal of this moment might leave him simply stuck in the alleyway, crying, turning around in defeat, but this isn't a moment of realism. Or at least not of the kind of realism we are used to.) So it might seem too magical, but from one of the dumpsters behind Paul he heard a loud bang as a metal door hit the empty garbage container, and he noticed a man coming out of the doorway, and he ran up to the door and caught it before it shut. The Asian man who came out ran on his way as Paul called after him to ask if he knew anything about The Modern Cyrano. Paul went into the building and looked for a list of the tenants, but there was no list. There was only a row of beat-up metal post office boxes with illegible Chinese characters. The narrow entryway was made of grime-worn linoleum, and he looked up a tightly wound metal staircase at least six stories high. There were two doors to each floor, and after going up to the two on the first floor, with no sign of The Modern Cyrano, he headed up to the next floor.

But what am I doing here? Paul thought. *This is pathetic. This is desperate. There is academic writing, writing that the academy will accept, and then popular writing.* And the two rarely mixed. Or at least only at the highest level, when academics who had long been established were allowed to be incomprehensible to the public—as with Einstein—or, occasionally, when a professor simply felt he could no longer live in the ivory tower anymore and that he should communicate with the educated masses—as with Camille Paglia or Cornel West in *The New Yorker* or *Harper's*. And weren't these popularizers of complex thoughts instantly shot at and labeled as soft? Labeled as media sluts? Wasn't their scholarship instantly questioned? So how could he get a man like The Modern Cyrano to even begin to fake an academic article? And perhaps this pointed to the real problem for himself, he thought. Did he really know how to write a proper academic article? Did he really have the proper training, or the ability to obfuscate, and have the tone of certainty and of authority to write an essay that would be well received? Received at all? Sadly, he felt, while almost every professor ran around telling his students to write clearly and with genuine and interesting arguments, very few of the articles he ever read in academic journals were clear or worth reading. The possibility of converting his own thoughts and feelings into academic jargon sickened him. This was, he thought, one reason why he was stuck at B_____ Community College. It was the reason he had only a master's degree and not a Ph.D. After his band fell apart, he needed a job, and he'd had enough interest in scholarly work to move his way quickly through an Am. Stud. master's program—especially because at his State U. there was no requirement for any written thesis. So he was unfully trained and he was unwilling to write academic jargon. And then (with Cyrus's help?) he'd received the job at B_____ Community College from Chairman Kominski. So perhaps coming to The Modern Cyrano was nothing new, perhaps he had always been coasting along as a fake.

But he wasn't an outright fake yet. Was he? Before Buffalo Man had struck the fear of death and abandonment into him, he'd been going along at full speed writing his book. And he had plenty of research. So he could still leave this building and never find The Modern Cyrano. Couldn't he? Yet every time he sat down at his computer to write, his typing lasted the length of a page and then fell silent. He deleted whatever he had written. Nothing was ever good enough; nothing ever expressed the complexity and insight of what he truly wanted to say. He wanted to express what it felt like to be alive now, in this moment, when so many good people, he felt, had lost their faith in themselves, when so many people found themselves impotent, drinking, bored, abused in their jobs, belittled, uncertain about their neighbor, uncertain if they shared anything in common with their neighbor, wondering if a bullet was going to come from out of nowhere, wondering why they disliked the politicians but why they kept reelecting the same politicians, wondering why they were too fat, or too ugly, or too thin, or too tall, or too short, or had the wrong hair color, wondering why they had so many headaches, wondering why they couldn't believe in god anymore, wondering why they woke up each morning and wished they hadn't, wondering why they weren't good enough to be famous, wondering why even vacation had to be so boring. He had seen these people around him every day, in the supermarkets, on the subway, in his classrooms. And while he realized they were also happy, that their loathing was mixed with joy, that their sadness was mixed with love, and lust, too, and while he was leery of anyone's saying that this time was different and worse—for hadn't there always been bad mixed in with the good?—while he resisted the notion that modern anomie might indicate a greater sadness, or that urbanization and the speed of daily life, or that advertisements were crushing them all—what he wanted to know was: what was the kernel of this unhappiness in himself and in the people around him? WHY DID HE FEEL LIKE SHIT AND SUCH A LOSER? Was it simply biological? Or an eternal curse from a freak named Buffalo Man? And what could he do to ameliorate this problem for himself and for those around him? What went beyond the questions to solutions?

And since he found it impossible to write the appropriate article and book about this topic, he hoped The Modern Cyrano might be able to help him. If nothing else, even if The Modern Cyrano wouldn't or couldn't write for him, at least he might have some insight into the answers.

When he reached the top floor of the building, he found a door unlike all the others. Whereas the others had been metal covered with worn, gray enamel, with Chinese names written beneath the glass-eye peepholes, this door had a painting of a 17th Century man with a goatee and a sword in his hand, and a big nose (of course) and a flourishing aristocratic hat with a brilliant white feather, and at the top of the door in bright red letters was written THE NOSE KNOWS!

Paul knocked on the door, feeling odd as his knuckles rapped on the face of Cyrano. It seemed somehow that he might cause harm to someone by knocking on the image of a man, so he made only one solid knock.

He waited a few seconds, heard a metal bolt unlock, and then a chain removed. An eye peered at him through the peephole before these other sounds were made, and then the door swung all the way open to reveal a young man, with a goatee, dressed in a costume just like the one in the painting on the door. The man in front of him wore red tights, and he had wooden shoes with brass buckles that looked like they had come from some costume room at a theater. His shirtsleeves, of blanched white linen that still bore traces of natural brown, were puffy, as if he wore loose-fitting clothes to engage in the sword fights of pirates. His eyes were lined in black, which made them seem unnaturally wide and added a look of exuberant authority to his face. He lifted his broad-brimmed, floppy felt hat, with its long white plume, off of his head, swept it in front of his face and body as he made a bow, and dropped his head. "The Modern Cyrano," he announced. "Purveyor of fine words and word entreaties at your service. Come in, come in," he said.

"Actually, I'm not sure this is going to work," Paul said, taking one look at the man bowing in front of him. "I'm in need of an unusual request. I think I should probably be going now."

"Forsooth! But where would you be going? If you've made it all the way to this apartment, then you must be desperate. The only place left from here is down the path to debauchery."

"Maybe, but maybe not. I have a feeling I made a mistake in coming here. I think I'm just gonna go now." Paul pulled his Red Sox cap firmly down over his eyes, until the wet on the cap dripped onto his shoes.

"Love will never be conquered this way, with such uncertainty," The Modern Cyrano said.

"Right. Or maybe. But this isn't a problem of love."

"Oh," The Modern Cyrano said. "Well why didn't you say so before?" He spoke these last words in a normal voice. He threw his hat onto the floor. "In the past," The Modern Cyrano said, "I've found this costume does wonders with the most confused clients. Romantically confused, that is. I don't get many people who actually come here in person. Most just use the Web site, but when they do, they expect the whole nine yards. If I just speak to them normally dressed, I lose some authority. I've found there's never a hitch if I act the part. So what are you here for? Paying client, or are you another reporter who wants to do a human interest story?"

It seemed Paul's whole purpose in coming had shifted. Whereas he had come to get The Modern Cyrano's help, it now seemed to him that

The Modern Cyrano was some form of a failure. What could be more of a failure than a businessman dressed in a theater costume trying to please pathetic customers who came to his door seeking words of romance? There was almost no chance this man could help him now. If anything, the only value the guy in front of him—dressed in tights—might have was as a subject for his own writing. Somewhere near the end of his book on inadequacy, for example, he might have a whole chapter on failed Internet business dreamers, people who had hoped to make a fortune selling their wares on the Internet, only to find the boom had turned to bust. This is why he decided to stay rather than do what he knew he *should*—which was to leave. But what kept him in the apartment/office in Chinatown was also his feeling that everyone had a story to tell if given a chance. He wanted to learn The Modern Cyrano's story. And perhaps in his failed way The Modern Cyrano might still have some words of useful advice to give him. Because if "misery loves company," this could be taken two ways: the usual way—that bitter people like others to suffer with them—or a second way, that when one is miserable, the company of others who are miserable might be true company, true love.

For the most part, the room Paul entered looked like a college dorm in an old industrial loft. It was not too wide or deep, but it was high and had a pressed-tin ceiling in an elaborate Victorian pattern that indicated it had been built with some care and money. An old white marble fireplace, with roughed-up, chipped stone and with a mantle covered with the wax remains of candles, took up most of the wall to Paul's left. The wood floors were gray from wear and had bits of sand in the cracks between the boards. A heap of dirty laundry lay in the center of the room in front of a bed with unmade sheets, and to the right a desk assembled from sawhorses and a plywood tabletop was covered with piles of disordered papers. A wide computer screen flashed metallic gray light into the otherwise dark room, and a box with flashing red lights that looked like a computer server was crammed beneath the desk.

"Have a seat," The Modern Cyrano said. He pointed to an Aeron swivel chair in front of the computer. Paul sat in the chair and wondered where The Modern Cyrano would sit since there were no other chairs. The Modern Cyrano sat on the bed, and Paul swiveled his back to the computer, looking at The Modern Cyrano, whose face was lit up from the glow of the monitor.

"Nice place," Paul said, pointing at the decoration on the ceiling and the fireplace.

"This was the back room where the managers had an office when the whole building was a clothing factory," The Modern Cyrano said. "From what I understand, the tin was imported from Italy."

"How do you know?"

"I did some digging. One of the old janitors in the Dunkin' Donuts around the corner says he remembers what the building was like before the area became Chinatown. He said his grandfather was one of the managers of this building, and they had the same tin pattern in their home."

"So are you a history buff?" Paul brightened a bit. Perhaps The Modern Cyrano might be of some use after all.

"Not really. The causality of events is useful, of course, and the saying that history repeats itself may also be true, but it never repeats itself predictably. That is, one can predict the likely outcome but not when an event will begin or end. I may be certain, for example, that the stock market will crash as it did in 1929. And it may well in fact crash—just look at what happened to the NASDAQ—but not when I think it's going to crash. And so while it may be of some use to know what is coming, if you can't figure out *when* it is coming, your information is as good as useless. And then there is another problem with history. When the past points to future problems, no one wants to hear about the past. In general, the power of history, I think, lies in its stories. If the story is good, the history is interesting. If the story is dull, then who cares how significant the actual events may have been? That's why we read biographies most."

Paul was surprised at the depth of this answer. He threw all his fears about what he might be able to get from The Modern Cyrano out the proverbial window and placed himself fully into the conversation.

"So why do you think how-to and self-improvement books are even more popular than biographies?" he asked. "At least by sales."

"Because they offer the greatest story of all. The story of oneself. The *evolving* story of oneself. In any good story, there has to be some kind of moral choice. Taken one step further, the how-to book is part of our moral choice about ourselves. If we choose to exercise and to eat less, for example, then we choose to be good and successful in some way. If we fail to exercise or to eat less, even after reading the how-to diet book, then we have chosen to be bad and to fail. The how-to book is an essential way of making our moral choices clearer. It is part of forming our stories of ourselves. And what we most want to engage in is a story about ourselves, especially about our potential success. Why do you think Kodak snapshots and digital cameras are such an important part of our daily life?"

Paul shrugged.

"Because they document and enshrine our story. Each photo album tells our story. Each photograph concretizes our story as we wish to be seen. Fiction is just a poor man's cousin to the photo album. Fiction gives us the story of others, so that we can look at ourselves. Sometimes we're interested in these stories because they're about characters *unlike* us. Those stories help us define ourselves as sane when others are not, or let us know that we are not the dreaded 'other.' But usually we like our characters or protagonists to be a more heroic version of ourselves, or at least to have those qualities we consider heroic. That's why Charles Dickens's protagonists, like David Copperfield, are always so good. Best sellers have clearly defined good and evil characters."

"So if you have the role of stories all figured out," Paul said, "why don't you just write a heroic best seller or come up with a better way to create personal photo albums over the Internet instead of running a small Web site selling language?"

"Because it's one thing to understand a subject matter and another to infuse it with the intangible—to give a story life. A good story requires credibility, which I find I can't write in fiction or express in any photograph. But the one area where I know I *can* create this heroic and successful sense of life is in romantic expression. I'm a good lover. You see my bed here . . ." He patted the bed. "It's not just unmade because I'm lazy—although I admit I don't like to make my bed. It's unmade because I'm always using it to make love. I'm a seducer. And part of the thrill of seduction is overcoming resistance. I want to see how I can get attractive women—or men—to come to my apartment in an alleyway in Chinatown. And by extension, it's a thrill for me to get two relative strangers over the Internet to fall in love, or at least into bed. Just think of the difficulty! To lure someone just with flirtation, and especially words, all the way down this alleyway with its rotten-smelling dumpsters and then to convince them to keep going up all those flights of stairs, or to cause someone who I've never even met over the Internet to succeed in seducing their partner. It's not as easy as you might think. You yourself were about to turn around when you knocked on the door, even though you wanted to come here badly enough to find out where a crazy restaurant like The Big Rice Bowl is and where a man with a ridiculously jingly name like 'The Modern Cyrano' lives." He pointed to the door to indicate the place where he had lured Paul.

"So is it all just a game for you?" Paul asked.

"Everything in life is easier if no emotions are involved." He stood up from his bed and turned from Paul.

"But what if emotions *are* involved?"

"As in what?" The Modern Cyrano spoke to the fireplace while picking at the wax on the mantelpiece.

"As in a book I'm trying to write, and as in a woman I'm about to marry."

"Let's take them one at a time." The Modern Cyrano sat back on the bed. "And here I have to warn you I expect some form of payment at the end." He put his hand out palm up to indicate he would prefer to take payment now.

"How much?"

"A hundred."

"OK. But first we talk." Paul had no intention of paying him yet. The Modern Cyrano was twenty-eight, maybe thirty at the outside. He had the same know-it-all-ism that Paul knew Cyrus had at that age. But wasn't the first lesson of adulthood the forced realization that one really knew nothing? That all facile answers were meaningless? Wasn't that the basic thread that ran through all of Socrates' writing? And the reason, in fact, for the Socratic method? Questions should be asked knowing that no answer will be final. So what made him think he could get any final answers from The Modern Cyrano here? "The problem with my book," Paul said, "is that I have writer's block. And maybe the reason I have writer's block is because I feel too emotional

116

about the book. If I could just be cold and clinical like you, then I could write my ideas down right away. But I'm writing about feelings of inadequacy, and I find the subject is too large and important to be limited or delineated. And I find that if I write this book in a way that is not successful in its aim, then I, too, will be unsuccessful." He looked down at his worn-out tennis shoes.

"Well that's simple enough, then. You suffer from writer's block because you fear failure. You fear your book won't be well received. This is really no different than the romantic suitor who is petrified. The reason most people can't be successful at attracting someone else is *not* because they are incapable of attracting that other person but because they fear they will be rejected. If you thought your book would be well received, then you would be able to write it."

"Exactly," Paul said. He looked plaintively at The Modern Cyrano. "So how do you do something you fear you cannot do?"

"Well, the hard way, of course, is to develop the skills to do something. And the easier way is to hire someone to do it for you. All of us want, in a way, what we can't have. Why do you think white boys listen to hip-hop in the suburbs? They fear they're wimpy and boring so they buy the hipness of others through the music. And old men who fear impotency buy little blue pills. What I offer, for example, is the chance for someone to buy their way past their fears."

"That's what I've been considering myself," Paul said. "Maybe I could hire someone like you to write an academic article, or a book, for me. I'm up for tenure in a couple of months, and if I don't have something published by then, in a good journal, I'll lose my job."

"Sure, you could do that. I'm not certain I would be able to write exactly what you want. But I could work on that. But then you have to realize this is simply an avoidance of the fear. It's no different from buying Viagra—it gets rid of the impotence but never really cures the feeling you can't get it up on your own. If you choose to have me, or someone like me, write an academic article for you—well, it could work. But the price isn't only the money but a deepening sense of failure and fear. Of course, I'll be glad to do whatever you want if the price is right, but I just want you to know the full cost. Maybe you want to think about it for a while?"

Paul swiveled back and forth. He tapped his right leg up and down.

"Maybe," Paul said. "Maybe I should think about it for a while. But I don't think I have a while to spare. I need it all now. Preferably before I get married to Zoe, my fiancée, in about a week. If this isn't all settled, I'm going to be a disaster in bed on our wedding night . . . I'm not sure having you write for me would be such a blow to my ego, either. Let's take this fear thing you've mentioned. On the one hand, it *might* be a fear of failure that's preventing me from finishing the book, or I might just be too emotionally involved in the whole project, but there's another element, too. This guru, a guy in Iowa who runs a crackpot health retreat, read my fortune and said all sorts of horrible things were going to happen to me—and a lot of those crazy things have come true. So I'm not sure that *I'm* the one who's really responsible for this writer's block. I think a lot of my problems and fears may just come from him. And in a way, if you can write this article for me and finish everything up, then I can keep my job, keep my fiancée, and basically tell that guru in Iowa to fuck off. See, I've thought about this idea of having you write something for me, and I think if you do it, the curse from this guru will be short-circuited somehow. This whole thing has become ridiculous to the point that here I am trying to ask someone like you to write an academic paper for me. But the way I feel right now, you're my only option."

"So you want to take the easy way out?"

"Yeah."

"Suit yourself." The Modern Cyrano took a yellow legal pad off his desk and scribbled something. His handwriting was surprisingly neat, Paul thought.

"When can you get started?" Paul said.

"When can you get me the money?"

"How much?" Paul wondered if the last check he had written had bounced. The cost of the wedding was mounting.

"How long is the project going to be? Normally, I charge a buck a word."

"Let's start with a thirty-page article. Ideally, in a week, although if it takes a month, that will be OK. But I can't pay you a buck a word. That would bust me clean out."

"How about $5,000, then? Half price."

"If it gets published, OK. If not, I can only give you a couple grand." This seemed a good way to stall.

"All right. But I'll need full payment of the two thousand before I even start to write." The Modern Cyrano gave Paul a look that let him know "the Doctor" would be "out" unless the money was in.

"I'll pay you when I bring you my notes and research material. I'll drop everything off tomorrow after I teach." He thought he could come up with some money excuse later.

"Where do you teach?" The Modern Cyrano said.

"I'd rather not tell you."

"I graduated from Columbia seven years ago," The Modern Cyrano said.

"That was when I showed up where I'm teaching now," Paul said. Seven years seemed like ancient history to him, another era when he'd first walked into the department and discovered he and Chairman Kominski liked the same chewing gum.

"What department do you teach in?"

"Am. Stud."

The Modern Cyrano nodded, as if he knew the type. "I double majored in theater and economics," he said.

Paul stayed fifteen more minutes, describing his rough ideas for the essay to The Modern Cyrano. When he was done, The Modern Cyrano showed him to the door and bowed with too much of a flourish. As he bowed, Paul was struck by just how perfect The Modern Cyrano's nose was—an aquiline WASP nose, an elegant, unobtrusive nose—and by just how handsome he was. He seemed the very opposite of the real Cyrano, not only physically but also, Paul realized, emotionally, for he appeared to have no true love. His words, unlike Cyrano's to Roxanne, would never be used to woo his *own* love. The pure challenge of seducing people to his room for a quick fuck didn't count. The Modern Cyrano was a player, not a lover, no matter what he said.

So then have I made a Faustian bargain? Paul thought. But the words *arrangeable, manageable, doable,* and *can do it* went through his mind. He walked down the tightly wound metal staircase, whistling, and when he reached the bottom and kicked open the door—because he didn't want to touch the sticky doorknob—he walked out the alleyway, and, as if on autopilot, made the turns necessary to bring him back to the Chinatown gate. In his hand was the pink bag with the word LUCKY written all over it, which wrapped his underwear with the prophets.

Lucky indeed, he thought. So it really wasn't that hard after all, was it? With one visit to a brutally honest and admittedly intelligent twenty-eight-year-old—The Modern Cyrano had solved all of his problems. Hadn't he? As they said during the Internet bubble, "The Net changes everything. The Net brings success." He was at least on his way to a better trajectory. First things first: he would secure his tenure and please Zoe, then he would prove to Cyrus he was better than he thought, then he'd go back to Buffalo Man to tell him his ridiculous curse had no hold on him anymore. He felt—as a hard raindrop dripped through a hole in his umbrella—that he simply had to rearrange the order in which the dominoes were falling. Push them back, and begin anew. Change the circles of growth from the way Buffalo Man had predicted. What if it did seem a bit Faustian? It was also pragmatic. Sensible. Necessary. Inevitable. Cyrus was right, of course. Cyrus was always right. This was the way the world worked. Pragmatism must win out. He would be pragmatic. He would look out for number one.

(I intended to start this last section returning to the wedding scene hinted at in the beginning of this chapter. Only I'm not going to, because after sidetracking into Paul's visit to Chinatown, it would make this chapter too long. There's a lot that will happen in the wedding scene. And I feel a little rusty after putting this chapter aside for five weeks. Why five weeks? I procrastinated, applied for some writing grants, became a wreck and I went to San Francisco—from Boston—to see my wife, who's been working there for a while. She works for Forbes, a company with the unenviable motto the "Capitalist Tool." She's been working for them for three years now against her will—during this recession that the government calls a recovery—ever since the small company she used to work for was bought out by Forbes. Despite their luxurious reputation, Forbes is cheap, so they don't worry too much about separating husbands and wives. After a while, I couldn't take it anymore—I don't function well or write well without Laura—so I went out to see her in San Francisco, and this chapter has probably suffered in its ending and length because of the delay.)

CHAPTER 6

The day Paul's band broke up, Paul smelled of bubble bath. The band (which I will call simply I.C.N., for Incomprehensible Cool Name) had been on tour for eight months promoting their fourth CD. For the most part they toured the U.S., but the rep from the recording company, named Chad, insisted they do a few concerts in Belgium, Switzerland, Liechtenstein, and Andorra. It seemed that the band, according to computer models, was most likely to increase their following in the smaller countries of the European continent. Likewise, the band tended to tour smaller cities in the U.S.—Indianapolis rather than Chicago, Boise instead of Denver, Santa Barbara and San Jose instead of L.A. Occasionally they hit a bigger zone like Detroit or Philadelphia.

"What we're looking for is a geographical niche," Chad had said when he informed the band of his plan for the tour. He'd been imposed on the band after they finally got a contract with a big record label for this fourth CD, and one of the conditions in the fine print was that their old manager, their friend Max, had to be booted. "We're not only going to have a musical niche," Chad said, "our band is going to use regional supra-cross-germinating music zones. The computer models from our marketing department have told us this is going to create a grassroots megaband. I.C.N. is going to hit the audience from two sides—from above, with the hippest ads you've ever seen—and from below, from the little people of America, pining away in their stinky rooms for a new sound." Chad had never managed a band before. He had a newly minted M.B.A., which was good enough for the record label.

Paul felt Chad was bullshit, but a record deal with a major label (according to the band's lead singer, Melvin Watson), after a number of close calls where the band had gotten stuck paying for "power lunches" with small-time music executives, had to be accepted. Paul almost quit when Chad came on board and presented the new music strategy.

The day Paul nearly bolted, I.C.N. was practicing in Melvin's base-ment. Paul was perched on his drummer's stool, eyes closed, slack-jawed, lips moving in time to the sound of the bass as he reached quickly back and forth to beat the drums and the percussion. He was in his trance, moving with the music, bobbing with it again and again, feeling the unity of the band's sound. His short blond hair pinched together from drips of sweat pearling down from under his baseball cap (which sported a tractor company logo), and he was so absorbed in the music that when the jam ended and Melvin insisted they had to accept Chad, Paul came out of his reverie and said simply, "Um, I don't think so."

The other members looked at Paul in utter silence. Jeff, the bass player, considered seriously what Paul had said; you could tell by the way he stood with his bass guitar resting limply against his crotch he wasn't ready to move on to the next song. T.J., who played rhythm guitar, finally said, "I think you're right, Paul. I mean, part of me thinks you're right. But me and Marlene [his wife], we've been waiting too long for this kinda bump up, ya know what I mean? So I think we gotta do it. We gotta keep him."

Melvin pointed his mic at Paul like it was a scepter and a laser gun all in one. "Blam!" he said. "You had to do it, didn't you Paul? You had to say what everyone thinks. But we've already signed. We're in this shit together. And Chad stays—he's the nephew of the CEO of the company."

So Chad, who wore silk leopard-skin patterned button-down shirts and a ponytail, who was far too skinny to ever lift any sound equipment, who showed up one day with a temporary tattoo of Ronald Reagan on his neck, and who liked mixed drinks with maraschino cherries, was the boss of the whole eight-month tour. He was twenty-seven and he could barely grow a beard. And he kept saying things out loud like, "Everyone OK with their drug supply? Anyone need more drugs? If you don't tell me now, I can't get it from the record label's usual supplier."

They stayed in fairly classy hotels—Sheratons and Hiltons, an occasional Four Seasons, and in Vegas at the Mandalay Bay Resort. The days of sleeping on the floors of friends' apartments with dirty shag carpeting, and cheap motels, and then HoJos, were over. Paul felt the beauty of America was that you always knew exactly where your place was on the hierarchy by your type of hotel. *All are created equal and endowed with equal rights? What a bunch of bull-shitty caca.*

Melvin decided that if they were going to be a real band, they had to trash a number of hotels during the tour. In Birmingham, Alabama, on Valentine's Day, after having sex with three African-American women simultaneously—who followed him from a concert—Melvin called a white priest in the local phone book, told the man of God his father was dying in the hotel room, posed naked with the three women around him when the priest entered, and then defecated on his bed in front of the priest. Then he wrote with smeared feces on the wall "Melvin loves the Three Negresses." Chad said that as long as Melvin stayed within the usual parameters of the expected overflow costs of hotel-room destruction, such behavior was OK with him, but that if Melvin wanted to start breaking guitars and things, that would definitely *not* be OK because there was no budget for "musical instrumentation destruction" on his Excel spreadsheet. "No Jimi Hendrix maneuvers are allowed on this tour," he said.

Amazingly enough, CD sales rose solidly during the first six months of the tour, according to Chad. The sound of the band was tight enough. The bus would roll into a city, and twenty- and thirty-somethings, driving by in their cars, would honk. A few would meet them as they got off the bus at their hotel. Most of the fans talked to Melvin. He'd taken to wearing pink fur coats with fringe foxtails, emblazoned with the words SAVE THE PLANET written graffiti-style on his back. He also had a pair of black jeans made that he planned to wear onstage that had see-through plastic pockets. Chad insisted Melvin wear under-wear with the see-through costume, but otherwise he said it fit into the record label's "promotional dress code."

"What is this, some kind of naked purgatory?" Melvin said. "Fruit of the Loom is OK but not bare butt cheeks? If I can't show it all, people are gonna think I'm some kind of mama's boy. I'm not gonna wear no stinkin' underwear onstage." Chad decided if word ever got up to company headquarters, he would simply plead the Fifth—nudity, he knew, was good for sales.

Toward the middle of the tour, the band even had an extended inter-view on MTV, for twenty minutes. MTV wanted to profile just Melvin, but the entire band went on to make witty jokes, to pretend they didn't care about the interview, and to tell the interviewer they didn't know where they were headed musically—they were just enjoying making decent sound and having fun on the road. The interviewer leaned back with laughter and said, "But isn't your manager Chad Langley? What's it like having the nephew of the CEO of BRL [Big Record Label] chap-eroning you?"

The members of the group didn't know what to reply—at least all the members except Paul, who usually kept quiet during the interviews except to interject occasional one-liners. Paul said, "It's been hell. Chad's set up a schedule for when each of us can go to the bathroom on the tour bus. He's an inefficient efficiency-freak. I can't speak for the others, but I never let him tell me what to do."

Melvin leaned in front of Paul and added, "But seriously. It's been a great opportunity to have Chad manage I.C.N. I think he's doing a great job."

On the morning of the last day of the tour, Paul woke up on the floor of his bedroom, at home instead of in a hotel, in his still-small apartment in Somerville not more than a mile from where he'd grown up in North Cambridge. His chubby, round face, highlighted by sunlight at ten o'clock, shined so bright his head looked like a blotchy pink balloon against the blue shag carpeting of his floor. *What am I doing on the carpet?* he wondered. Had he grown so used to the hard recliner seats on the tour bus that his body craved the ground? Was he still so drunk from the night before he didn't know when he'd made the move down from his bed? His bed still had the comforter on it that he'd used since he was a kid. It was covered with NFL helmets of the big teams of the 70s: the Cowboys, Redskins, and Steelers. His brother Andrew had given the comforter to him for one of the Christmas celebrations his mother liked to have—even though she'd converted to Judaism—and that his father deemed an irrelevant, Jew-hating practice. "The only reason Christians celebrate Christmas is to spend money they don't have and to rub it in they think the Jews killed Christ," his father liked to say. "The truth is," he added, "I don't think they even know why they celebrate Christmas. They just do it because it's a tradition—like sheep." Andrew had given Paul the comforter, in any case, and said he thought it would be good for Paul, because any kid who couldn't act like he really cared about football would continue to get beaten up on the playground. It wasn't enough to be a drum player to ward off accusations of being a wimp, Andrew said (at least not at Paul's age then of eleven). What Paul had always liked about the helmets on the comforter was that they twirled in the air at different angles, with no particular direction, and they were flat and iconographic, smoothing out the harsh roundness of real helmets, promising a world where dreams could be stamped on fabric. This wasn't the kind of analysis, of course, he made when he was young, but it was what his eyes seemed to know instinctively—that in reduction and iconography and oversimplification there was comfort.

He lay naked, apart from his comforter, on the bumpy shag floor which felt all too hard, all too three-dimensional. But otherwise, the three-dimensional reality of experience and of the light coming through the windows was all good for him now, he thought. Even in his hangover, he'd triumphed. They'd completed the eight-month tour—except for the last concert, which would come later that night. The bright spring light filtering into his eyeballs let him know the birds were coming north soon. *What can I afford? Not much yet.* But soon, when the next CD came out—which they would start working on after the tour ended (Chad had it all scheduled)—he might be able to buy an apartment. For the moment, money from the tour covered only the cost of the tour, Chad said. Yet it wouldn't be long before he would be able to switch homes, to build a new nest as the winter ended. He'd buy a house with two floors, or at least with a big enough studio where he could play his drums. He wanted a place where he could play his music loud without bothering anyone. *Maybe I'll go downtown and buy a new shearling coat to wear to the concert,* he thought. The final concert would be held in his favorite theater, the Orpheum.

He got up slowly and looked at the long, thin mirror nailed to his bedroom door, which he had found outside on the street—the majority of his furniture he'd discovered on the curbs of Somerville and Cambridge on garbage day (there was good garbage in Cambridge)—and for once, as he looked at his naked body, with his pale, wide thighs and protruding, round belly, he didn't mind the fat so much. *Am I fat? Yes. But no one cares, if you've got money and you've been on TV.* Even if he was thirty pounds overweight, his arms were in great condition after the tour. His upper body was fit, even if his lower body wasn't. He felt the best he had in years.

To keep the feeling and speed and rhythm of the tour going, he decided to take a bubble bath. It was a habit he'd formed while on

tour. Many of the hotel rooms had different kinds of bubble bath—
"lavender," "sea spray," "fresh spring," and "summer's breeze"—and
when none of the other band members were looking, he tried one of
the packets and fell into an addiction. His favorite bathtub had been
in Liechtenstein. That country seemed to have inordinately large bathtubs and toiletries as a means of overcompensation, going out of its
way to make a statement that although it was small, it would make up
for everything with luxury. *This is what happens to a country when it's a
giant bank that eats too many sausages,* Paul had thought while bathing
happily in Vaduz.

Now, sitting in his tub in Somerville, surrounded by bubbles, Paul
closed his eyes and felt the whoosh of speed. He saw flocks of mergan-
sers and Canada geese flying in military squadrons, a lead goose, head
bent forward, slicing through the air, flapping its wings as it cut through
the clear blue sky of spring, the other birds all following in a V-shaped
pattern, the wings beating in unison, fluttering through the coldness.
The birds flew directly overhead as Paul stood by a lake, craning his
head backward until he nearly fell into the water, and then, fast and
low the birds moved on. But not before a man with a rifle next to him
pointed his long barrel up into the air and shot the lead bird down.
The sound of the recoil of the gun. A quick pop. And then the bird fell.
The other birds paused in the air, wondering perhaps if they should
fall, too, and follow their leader downward; then the birds squawked
and reared back, hovered, and stumbled, a few gray feathers falling off
their suddenly arrested wings, and then a new leader emerged and the
birds continued on even faster now, knowing that speed was their only
safeguard. This was not what Paul had expected, the sudden shift, the
sudden break, especially in his bubble bath, but he chose to see strength
in the persistence of the birds, their determination to continue despite
the violence that had interrupted their flight.

And soon he had other, more pleasant visions as he slid further into
the tub, his chin bearded with foam. He saw gold coins pouring swiftly
out of clay amphorae held aloft by Nubian slaves, cascading over a
beautiful woman who looked like Cleopatra. The princess—before she
had become the queen and lover to Marc Antony, when she was still
in her early ascendancy—might have felt pain as the gold coins fell
heavily one and then another over her body, but she seemed not to

flinch, smiling all the while instead, her full lips parted in an expression of smug satisfaction as the gold flowed over and around her body, until she was covered in a mound that rose to a pointy pinnacle over her back, the coins so thick around and surrounding her that Paul wondered how she could breathe.

The whoosh of the coins rippled, one cool golden stream, just like the harvest of rich wheat flowing through the combines of Kansas into loading trucks, or like the white gold Paul had sniffed on tour, lapping up cocaine into his nostrils. The feeling was golden. The feeling was not slow. The feeling was one of bubbles growing and expanding, but never popping. Only percolating and tapping in a wonderful ecstasy of sensual pleasures, bubbles all around him now as he lay in his bathtub in Somerville.

This is the fucking life, Paul thought. *This is the cleanliness and clean feeling of an asshole wiped clean by bubble baths.* He was, he felt, on the cusp of arrival. Just like in those movies as the plane comes in to the gate, and the debonair man dressed in a crisp blue suit with expensive British tailoring waltzes into the airport, looks at his expensive watch, and knows that his car, his sports car, is waiting outside, ready to be handed off to him, so that he can go driving through the countryside at high speed, in a convertible, in a silver sports car, with the leaves swaying in a blind blur behind him as he heads off on a road that can lead only to danger, which he will escape, and to a beautiful model waiting for him at the end of it all at a small château. French food. Wine. No, none of that pretentious shit. He would arrive at the castle and leap up the steps and find his own drums set up in the center of the castle. He would be the only member of the band, in the tall open stone entryway of the seventeenth-century castle, no sign of a butler at first, until he would begin to play, echoing, crashing his drums, wailing, releasing everything, all of his energy in a fury, and the butler would come and stand next to him, finally, with a silver platter and serve him, and smile and say, "Sir, would you like your four o'clock tea?"

When the bubbles had slowly dissipated, Paul stood up from the bath refreshed, not minding the harshness of the towel as he wiped his body. He was going to have soft towels soon. The band, he felt, was on the verge of making it. He decided to visit his mom and dad later in the afternoon. It was time to show them the new Paul.

"Hi Mom," he called her fifteen minutes later. "I was thinking of coming over to the house . . . It's not a good time? . . .Well, how about just for thirty minutes. Thirty minutes around four o'clock. You're coming to the concert, right? OK, OK. I got it."

So he would meet them at three instead of four. That was what would work best for them. They might make it to the concert. They might not. She was preparing for an exhibit of her paintings.

Who knows more about music than Ned? Paul thought. Really no one, if we were talking about music trivia—knowing all the members of a band, or knowing musical influences. About how to play music, that was something else. About how to play music, Paul felt he himself wasn't great but he was good, certainly better than Ned. But around Ned, Paul felt not only he knew almost nothing about music, he felt reinvigorated by music because Ned loved it so much. He wanted to be with Ned before the last concert, so after his bubble bath, he went to Ned's store.

Paul flipped through a collection of vinyl for sale to the left of the door to the store as you came in—the door was covered with fliers for underground concerts, underground films, and a promo for The Vapids, a new cleaning crew of lesbians who promised to make your house as clean and vapid as "our lives and the lives of our customers." "We are empty," their flier said, "just like you. And we will empty all of the garbage in your home."

"What's up with those chicks?" Paul asked Ned, as Ned priced a Japanese tin robot and put a sticker on it. There were only two other men in the store, so it was OK to engage in guy talk.

"Dunno, really," Ned said. "I usually avoid such nihilistic 'garbage,' unless people are willing to be truly suicidal, but I've heard from various customers their vacuuming is excellent. A true sign of manic depression, if you ask me. I think one of the women was high on her lithium and she offered me fifty bucks to put up the flier, so I said sure."

"Fifty bucks?"

"Yeah. Business is 'out-fucking-standing,' she said. She was running around with a 1200-watt vacuum cleaner on her way to one of her customers. She said she's even thinking of buying a condo in Cambridge." Which was no small thing given how expensive real estate was. Ned and Paul liked to call Cambridge the place where yuppie babies need never scrape their knees.

Cambridge was nothing like North Cambridge, where they'd grown up. (The way you knew you had entered North Cambridge was to look to see where the chain-link fences in the front yards cropped up and the dilapidated old houses leaned toward the old doughnut shops on Mass. Ave.) But even North Cambridge was getting a face-lift now—just as, Paul realized, I.C.N. was putting a new face on himself. It seemed the two were changing in tandem. Lofts were being renovated. Natural ice cream shops were becoming the norm, with logos of fresh, organic milking cows. North Cambridge was becoming hip, and Ned's business was finally coming into vogue. When he was a little kid, Ned's basement was covered with comic books and toys that no one else cared much about at the time. But now, in 1996, his store was small but thriving. Anything that could be labeled as exclusive, anything that could be labeled as different, was in. Collectibles were a sign of the times, and Ned offered his small piece of individualism, like tattoos from a tattoo parlor. Ned's store sold mint-condition rarities that could be found almost nowhere else in America—not even on eBay—a mixture of rare Japanese and American pop culture dolls, albums for connoisseurs, a few comic books (not the kind that attracted acne-faced teenagers; these were adult comics for adult collectors who might spend more on a comic book than on an expensive designer chair). Ned's store was filled with first-run movie and band posters, with a large chunk of them from countries like Slovenia and Slovakia.

"How about closing up early and taking a walk around with me?" Paul said.

"Just leave?" Ned said. "I knew it. I knew this whole tour would go to your head. I knew you would think you're a big fucking rocker now. You're gonna be just like the others. I can see it. I can sniff it."

"Sniff it?" said Paul.

"No calls for six months. No sign of you anywhere. Not even a—'hey dude, I'm sorry I'm on the road, but the tour is going real hot-diggity-dog.'"

"Nah," Paul said. "You know it ain't like that."

"I bet you're already having dreams about hot naked chicks going out with you, covered in jewels and lamé dresses and all that tacky crap. You probably imagine yourself in some kind of castle wailing your heart out on some drum set with some butler serving you expensive food. Or driving around in a silver sports car and shit like that."

Paul's shoulders drooped. "Is it that obvious?" he said.

"Yeah, man. And what's that bubble bath smell all over you? Dreams of the big time?"

Well, he'd had some of those dreams lately, hadn't he? And so what of it? It was true. Walking around the old neighborhood, it had seemed less depressing this morning; it had felt different. Whereas before the tour he'd walked into the local Italian deli wondering if he would eat pasta or pasta again tonight or pasta, now he bought one of those expensive panettone cakes that he used to watch dangling from the ceiling. And for once he hadn't sensed people were looking at him thinking, Who's that short, pale, chubby weirdo wearing an orange down vest? Yeah, he'd gone into the deli and paid for everything with a fifty, that's right. So what of it? On the way to Ned's, he'd walked by his old elementary school where he and Ned used to hang out, separate from most of the other kids, where they used to play stickball. He had even gone in for the first time in years because he wanted to see the principal. He hadn't given a fuck about Mr. Dickel in those days—moving around on his roller skates through the halls and trying to molest little girls—but now he wanted to go back and see him just to let drop during conversation that he'd been on tour, that he had just been on MTV. So why not feel good? Why not finally feel his back muscles straighten and feel his posture improve because the weight of others' disapproval was no longer pressing on him? This is what fame, even a taste of fame, could give, he knew. Even if his band wasn't really a great band. Even if Melvin was a bit of a phony. *Are we great? No. But we're pretty good,* Paul thought. *Better than pretty good. High average, which is more than most can say.* And when the lights came up onstage and they came out, and the crowds cheered—expecting to be entertained—and when he held his drumsticks, and when he swiveled on his drummer's stool, and when they could give that entertainment for an hour and a half and occasionally even beyond their set (that is, beyond the obligatory encores that were not really encores but embedded in the plan Chad gave them), he was pumped up, he was larger than his body, he was . . . well, even Paul knew the rhetoric flying through his brain was getting beyond what might be tolerable for others.

"Listen, man," Ned said, "I'll go out with you on one condition. That you at least take off those designer sunglasses and put some dirt on your nails. That bubble bath, or whatever it is, is making your nails too shiny."

But did his parents notice anything about his aura when he went to see them later, at three o'clock, after hanging out with Ned?

The house that Paul had grown up in was eerily silent when he came over the porch and in through the back door. It was the silence of the books of his father's library, and the silence of the collection of hundreds of CDs of classical music that his father kept in the library. The house smelled faintly of leftovers. His father liked to cook, but he always cooked too much of one dish, a single, heaping mound that seemed to grow and grow because he was often thinking about his latest statue, or talking endlessly, talking and talking, telling Paul what to think. Telling Paul he knew nothing. Nothing. Why didn't he read more? Why didn't he display greater insight? Get your head out of your goo-goo-ga-ga-bang-bang-bong-bong and think seriously for a second. "Look at Andrew, look at Cyrus," he would say, "they're gonna make piles of money. Just piles. And what are you gonna do?" His father had a thick Brooklyn accent. He was bald in the front and center, and he let the rest of his hair, which had once been obsidian and which was now gray, puff in flying buttresses circumscribing his head. His ears pointed forward, flapping for all to see; yet they seemed clogged, incapable of hearing. The silence of the house meant either his father was teaching—which was improbable on a Saturday—or that he was in his basement working on his statues.

From the back door and through the kitchen, which had been renovated over the years—since his parents had bought the house cheap in their early artist days—Paul made his way into the living room, with its worn-out Oriental rug. *Even you I might be able to please now,* he thought. But when he stopped to consider the nature of his success, it seemed unlikely. "I don't need the world," his father had said once, "the world needs me. Fuck the world." After his father had broken with abstraction, he'd been instantly rejected from the art world, losing his budding prominence. And even the oddball critics who admired his statues considered him a strange perfectionist, a backward-looking man who'd had "so much talent" but who refused to "add anything new." "Does the world really need another Michelangelo?" a leading critic had written in the *New York Times* in the 60s, after his father had made his shift from abstract art. So he made sculptures in his basement without an audience, pouring plaster, pouring lead, and pouring bronze for no one but himself.

His mother, who always ended up in bitching fests with his father (they bounced trivial complaints back and forth like Ping-Pong balls, rhythmically, elegantly, as if they were part and parcel of the art scene and of the common New York culture they had grown up in), didn't dare to disagree with his father artistically. Soon after his father moved back to figurative sculptures, she moved back to figurative painting.

"Hi Paul," she screamed from her studio down to him. "Hi super-chunky-munchkin! I can hear you coming in," her voice trailed out her studio door. "Don't forget to take off your shoes, honey. I vacuumed earlier today. Sherry Cherrymore [her gallery owner in New York] is coming over later tonight, and they're coming to pick up the last two paintings in an hour."

Paul grabbed a cookie from the kitchen on his way up to her studio. His father's studio had been set up in the house first, and only now did she finally have her own space instead of commuting to the studio at the college where she taught art. When Paul came into the new studio—a large, square room with a high ceiling and two skylights that flushed the light gray mistiness of clouds since the weather had changed from the promising blue of the morning—he found her in front of a rectangular still life of a cantaloupe surrounded by other fruit on a silver dish. The cantaloupe was cut open to reveal moist, ripe seeds, the flesh of the fruit opened into a dark and inviting interior. "What do you think?" his mother said. "Am I good or am I good? This is the most sexual, most gorgeous painting. Just look at that fruit. It's so hot even Dante would give up his Beatrice for a night with that fruit."

Paul munched on his cookie. Standing in his mother's studio, he knew it was useless to complain she had forgotten about his concert.

"Do you have any idea, Paul, who is going to be considered the greatest painter of this era?" she asked between putting the tiniest dabs of paint on the last of the still life. "Odd Nerdrum is good. And let me tell you, it certainly isn't going to be Cy Twombly or Basquiat—ach! I feel like puking just saying their names. That stuff is crap. Crap, crap, crap. Temporal. Base. Flimsy. It's worse than Roy Lichtenstein. It's junk. That's all it is, junk."

But he would remind her in any case. "Mom, you didn't forget about my concert at the Orpheum tonight, did you?"

She stood a little back from her canvas.

And it was true her paintings were exquisite even if no different, as far as Paul could tell, from the classical paintings of yore. She had theories about how the cuts in the fruit of her still lifes were different from the cuts in the fruit of paintings of the past; how they were so much more aggressive, how they showed females were empowered now in the way the fruit indicated the *vagina dentata*—the tooth of the vagina— that gave modern women power. (Or as she liked to say, women had always had the power of sex, only they'd had no other power. Now, sexual power was more pungent because it could be used simply for aesthetic reasons and not solely to manipulate. She had fantasies that her classical paintings were in tune with Madonna's popular appeal on the music charts. "I love Madonna," she would exclaim. "I love her because she's so strong and sexual.")

Paul stood looking flat, he thought, in the misty gray light that poured heavily through the skylights in the ceiling. His jeans fell like heavy drapery over his body, clinging to him without definition—his body the opposite of the bright, curved orange melon in his mother's painting—flat, flowing opaquely over his body down to his dusty and worn tennis shoes. He felt he was receding into the unfinished plaster of his mother's unfinished studio. The wall behind him was gray with Sheetrock, not plastered over yet. The air smelled of turpentine and oils, which masked his very presence.

"Listen honey, I know it's bad timing, but what's done is done. This is the only day Sherry could come up from New York to talk to me.

It sucks. It stinks. I know, but that's it. You'll just have to give us a recording of the latest album."

She stood in front of her painting admiring her work, gazing at it, looking at her reflection in the black background of the painting.

"And Dad?" Paul said.

"You know how he feels about that kind of music you play. I'm sorry, but he wasn't going to go in any case."

Paul shoved the rest of the cookie into his mouth.

"It's going to be me," his mother said. "When all's said and done, it's going to be me."

The lights on the marquee shined, welcoming home I.C.N., and Melvin tried to move his way down the aisle of the tour bus, past seats cluttered with guitars, as three women, one in front and two behind, clutched at his chest, his nipples, his back, his sunglasses, his black jean jacket, which had a new logo aphorism for this last concert: "I Am Just a Rock Sex Symbol. Rock Me." He kissed the woman in front; he walked forward while twisting his body back to kiss the two women behind. "Always make sure you've got three women with you," he said between kisses, speaking, Paul thought, directly to him. He stopped for a second, pulled his lips away from a small-breasted, dyed blonde—Melvin was insatiable, and had no type: anyone would do—and sniffed the air. With a puzzled look he said, "Paul, are you switching your bubble bath on the last concert? I thought you would stick to lavender tonight. Really thought you would."

Paul blushed. So Melvin had known all along. Probably since Liechtenstein. *But who cares? I smell "Bronx raw sewage delicious" tonight,* he thought. That was the name on the golden wrapping paper of the beauty product he had bought at Neiman Marcus a couple of hours ago. After Ned had told him to get rid of the earlier smell, he had gone for a makeover. He smelled bad now—expensively bad. The brand was called Garbage, and according to the saleswoman at Neiman Marcus, it was the latest, most popular scent. So he was ready to jam now. He was ready to drum. He felt like hugging and tackling everyone around him like a football player. He felt like taking off his shirt, putting on a fishnet cap, dropping his jeans down low, and screaming naked with a pistol in his hand. "This stuff makes you feel like a gangster," he said aloud to no one in particular.

Chad was next to him on the bus, typing on his handheld database. He always seemed busy trying to keep statistics and things—though once, when Paul had been behind Chad as he seemed to be working, he saw Chad was really playing a computer game. "What 'stuff' makes you feel like a gangster?" Chad said. "You aren't taking gifts from rival record labels? Are you? You know that's strictly forbidden in the contract. Don't you? Only *we* can bribe you." Chad put his handheld into his silk leopard-skin front pocket. "All right," he said, "Listen up guys. We're going to have a series of photographers waiting in the lobby entrance to take a few shots for articles tomorrow. So please try to cooperate, OK? Paul, that means especially you. And T.J., no strumming on your guitar or running away to be with Marlene, all right? Just try to hold off on missing Marlene for a few minutes. I think that does it, minus the usual caveat that I hope you've all already put in your requests for your drugs."

It was dark, seven o'clock, and the concert doors would open in half an hour. A hundred people loitered in front of the theater, a number of fans looking intently at the bus, trying to catch a glimpse of anyone within. *We must look like shadows,* Paul thought. The ability to be seen was not a two-way street: the rich, the famous, the powerful could always see out, the rest wondered who lay behind the screen. It felt good to be unseen for once. Paul put on his sunglasses, and the tinted lights—running in quick blinking patterns along the outside of the bus as he stepped out into the brisk air of the night—looked even more beautiful, a rush of color delight. He moved with the band as a single jostling unit, bouncing coolly, fast but slow at the same time, Melvin radiating energy in the lead, people gathering around them, the presence of bodies that protected them that wanted them clustering around them. Melvin paused to sign a few autographs; Chad tried to push them forward faster, but Melvin insisted on taking time with his public, and as the others in the band looked coolly and dimly out to nowhere in particular that Paul could tell, he turned his gaze up to the marquee and saw the name of the band in lights like an icon, like the needle of the Empire State Building, chiseled in black and white sign lettering radiating energy, a sense of permanence, into the night. He had heard of Buddhists who made sand paintings so intricately with colored bits of sand, piece by piece, grain by grain, who when the sand painting was done, simply gathered their painting up and tossed it into water to emphasize the impermanence of life on earth; and he could respect that feeling in the core of his body, since he felt all was impermanent—yet he was no Buddhist; even knowing that the letters of the band's name would come down tomorrow, it was precisely the feeling, precisely the appearance of temporary permanence and solidity and of having mattered that so deeply touched his inner core.

He knew he might even tire of going from concert to concert on the next CD tour. He had already seen the cost of repetition and felt the blur of one place into the next. But in this sign, at this moment, he felt only the positive force of the speed of the lights.

And then the band was inside the theater and the sounds of the fans and of the traffic outside were gone. Only the whir of cameras: a clicking, a clicking.

There were six photographers and one print reporter. "Do you have anything you want to say?" the reporter asked Melvin.

"Yeah, I just want to thank all our fans at home for making this such a successful tour and for making this such a great homecoming."

Fifteen minutes before the band was supposed to go on stage, Paul sat in a barber's chair next to Melvin, his face rubbed and slathered by a makeup artist. He was thinking about whether Cyrus would come, about whether Andrew would be able to get him to, as he had assured Paul over the phone. *He has to come,* Paul thought. *Cyrus owes me at least this.* Cyrus had had the bigger bed in the bedroom they'd shared growing up until he'd left for college. His trophy case and other possessions, such as his law books, left no place for Paul to put up any of his own stuff. *I can't believe it if they don't come,* Paul thought of his parents. But he knew Cyrus was likely to be a no-show as well. Cyrus had told Andrew he was busy. He was working on some case in

Washington, and he might be having dinner with the president. "Look, if it's a choice between the White House and bad music, where do you think I'm gonna be?" Cyrus had told Andrew.

Paul looked at his reflection in the mirror as the makeup artist finished with the eyeliner. His skin looked awkwardly orange from the Pantone stick that would make him seem tan under the lights. But what caught his eye were two men running behind him. *Did I just see what I saw?* What he thought he saw was Chad being chased by a man reaching for his collar, who looked like the CEO of BRL records (Chad's uncle).

The commotion was all the more unusual because T.J. was sitting quietly on a psychedelic paisley-patterned couch behind Paul, making out with Marlene, when Chad came streaking by. Paul heard a screech, the sound of feet abruptly stopping against the linoleum floor, and the next thing he saw in the mirror was Chad flying headfirst onto the couch, sandwiching T.J. between Chad and Marlene, followed by Langley—the CEO of BRL—falling onto Chad so that a giant club sandwich was made out of Langley, Chad, T.J., and Marlene.

"What the fuck?" Melvin shouted. "What the fuck is going on here?"

Chad pursed his lips and motioned to shut up.

"No, I won't shut up," Melvin said. "Who the fuck is this?" He pointed at Langley, who was choking Chad now. The old man, with neatly combed-over gray hair, a square head as solid as an anvil, the ruddy nose and cheeks of a drinker, with a blue blazer and gold buttons that had anchors on them as if he were about to sail on a yacht as the captain of a Bahamian boat, lifted Chad off of T.J. and said to Chad, "*You* shut up." He turned to Melvin and said, "And you, if you have any idea what's good for you, you'll just go out there and finish your last stinking concert." Chad didn't resist anymore. He walked with his head bent over, like a trapped animal with a noose around his neck, the strands of his skinny ponytail drooping against the will of his hair-care products, under the hand of his uncle in defeated, flaccid obeisance. The two men left the backstage area quickly.

"Do you know who that was?" T.J. said to Melvin. "I can't believe you yelled at him. That was Langley. That's Langley. Chad's uncle. The CEO of BRL. We're finished, man."

"Oh, Jesus," Melvin said. "I didn't know. I didn't know. What should I do?"

This was the only time Paul had ever heard Melvin ask someone else for advice.

"I'll just go tell him I'm sorry," Melvin said. "Where is he? I'll just go out there and tell him I'm sorry." He started to hurry after Langley. It looked like he would be willing to kiss Langley's shoes if necessary. But it was unlikely such a small indiscretion would lead to the end of the band, Paul thought, and Jeff said the same thing to Melvin.

"Come on," Jeff said. "Just forget about it. It's some kind of family problem. Don't you ever have any family problems? Just let 'em work it out themselves." Jeff had his bass guitar on, and he moved his fingers quickly up to the high point of the frets to emphasize his fingering prowess meant what he had just said was for real. Melvin looked at Jeff's fingering. He moved toward the door to go after Langley. He stopped and looked at Jeff's fingering again.

Was this a bad sign, with Melvin so indecisive? Paul thought. He had never seen Melvin this way before. But then everything changed when the backstage manager came to tell T.J., Melvin, and Jeff they had to give up their instruments to be connected onstage for a final sound check. The group moved into the smooth rhythm of preparing to go out. Melvin started jogging in place, then sprinting in place, boxing the air like he was some kind of lightweight champ. Paul held his sticks and beat them rapidly on the makeup counter, next to the blush that had been placed on his cheeks earlier to overcome his normal pallor. He beat against the Formica countertop; he tapped ever so lightly against the mirror, watching the tips of his sticks move back and forth against their image in the glass as he made sure he didn't beat too hard to leave any mark. He heard the sound of fans screaming for the band to come out, the voices of the audience muffled behind the backstage door, yet not so muffled he couldn't hear the guitars receiving their final tests by the sound engineers.

And then they were on their way to the stage, sauntering as a unit again with Melvin in the lead, Melvin beating his fists against the cinder-block walls at the back of the theater as they moved into place near the double metal doors that would open out to the crowd. *I think he's gonna be here,* Paul thought. The white, pink, and sky blue lights, all fusing into one, were hot and pierced his eyes like an atomic cloud as he moved onto the stage and sat testing the drums. It was from the back that he loved to play, not clearly seen by the audience but crucial, he felt, to the band. Without the drummer—without the beat less seen but most heard—a band was nothing, Paul always felt. He didn't begrudge Melvin getting all the kudos, all the obvious praise. He knew Melvin wrote most of the songs. But without the drummer, where would they be? And as he tested the drums, he looked up from his drum set into the crowd and up to the balcony, and at the center front of the balcony, he saw Cyrus with Andrew looking down at him. Cyrus looked admittedly bored, completely out of place with a wool sweater in a hot theater, apparently occupied checking out some young women below rather than looking to see what the crowd was making noise about as the band came out and began to play. Paul had time to look out into the crowd because the song started with T.J.'s playing a long lead-in.

Watch me now, Paul thought. *Watch me Cyrus, 'cause I'm gonna run circles around your punk lawyerly ass tonight.* He twirled his drumsticks back and forth in his hands like tiny pencils. He wailed on his drums, feeling the transcendent power of the gods of music. Was it any wonder, Paul had thought before, that the Japanese and Africans and other believers of animistic religions thought that wood had power, that giant trees had power, that those trees, or parts of them, hollowed out and beaten upon, releasing the spirit within the wood, brought one closer to the center of what was universally understood to be god? There was nothing more mystical than drumming, he felt, nothing that could explain why the beating of a drum made him want to cry or to laugh, that made the audience want to stand up and bump and groove. If god was what was unexplainable, then why look out to the cosmos for the infinite? In the microcosm, in the inexplicable hum and moan and vibration of the skin of the drum, in the inexplicable wonder and ecstasy of resonance was the infinite, too.

And so he tapped into that resonance, that speed, that hum, that moan, that soft tapping, that wild sound that had made its way into the consciousness of each civilization, from the Australian Aborigines to the Greeks, lending his love of the sound to Melvin.

Yet was love alone enough? Could the love that Paul felt for the drums mean that they must obey his command beautifully? Near the end of the concert he had his drum solo. All eyes looked at him, and he played fairly well. He started slow, he played the percussion, he moved from snare to bass, from electronic drums to the real, pounding his feet. He lost himself in the echo and the rhythm. But it was when he looked up at Cyrus for a moment, as Paul's hair flicked sweat up into the air, that he realized mere love is not enough. You can love something and not be fully proficient at it. The mere fact he had even noticed Cyrus looking down at him, looking at him not with complete indifference but with a smirk on his face—which seemed to imply, Yes, you have made it partway to excellence but not all the way—let Paul know Cyrus was right. It was not that he couldn't fall into a state of subconscious playing, but that even when he played subconsciously, the notes came out only as good, not as perfect. A gap always remained; the chasm between the one who "can do" and the one who only comes close to doing. Paul finished his drum solo, and he felt the stare of Cyrus claiming his infinitely greater perfection from above. *Why was he meant to be what he is when he was born, whereas I was not?* Paul thought. *Why was he given the gift of perfect ability without even paying for it?*

And the news about Chad? What had he done that caused his own tormentor—Langley, the CEO of BRL—to torment him?

When the concert was done, the last encore played, the band gathered together in the dressing room. Marlene ran up to T.J. and gave him a kiss that dissolved into an interwrapping of the two as she pulled him back toward the paisley-patterned couch. It was just the four members of the band with Marlene in the back room for a moment as they savored the end of the tour. Melvin grabbed Paul around his neck and grabbed Jeff, too, around his arm—who resisted at first because he wasn't used to being touched. Jeff usually used his bass as a form of a shield, even when he did close grinding guitar duets with T.J. or Melvin. But for once, even Jeff let down his resistance. "Come over here," Melvin said to T.J., and Marlene reluctantly let him go. The four men, the four of them huddled together, with Melvin's arms around Paul and Jeff reaching around even to T.J. on the other side of the foursome. "I love you guys," Melvin said. "That was the fucking best we've ever played."

And it was the best, Paul thought, even if it would never really be good enough.

So here's the story of what Chad had done: He'd run a huge deficit on the tour. They'd lost close to a million on the trip. There never were any computer models. He had used all that lingo to make them think he knew what he was doing. It wasn't *all* a scam. The band actually had been selling a fair number of CDs and T-shirts, at least for the first three months of the tour. But after that, the CD sales started going down pretty sharply. When they did the interview on MTV, Chad had showed it to his uncle and Langley had assumed the tour was doing well. But the whole thing was a financial disaster. So even though they *had* been able to fill up the Orpheum, and some of the other venues, the simple fact of the matter was the band wasn't selling enough CDs. Chad hid the losses with the help of a few accounting guys. "Don't worry, it'll be a tax loss," he later told his uncle. And although you'd expect a band to lose money on their first big tour, and even though you'd expect a company to know they'd have to sink some money into a band before they could start making money back, that was the last album I.C.N. ever made.

CHAPTER 7

What I have as I write this novel are often doubts. This is not the first time I have sat down to write a novel. I have two sitting in a drawer, as writers like to say euphemistically (they're really on some old computer disks). The first novel I wrote was a completely hopeless attempt when I was nineteen. I wrote that book in Jamaica, with the help of a small grant, while working on a farm run by a fifty-year-old man from the U.S. who knew nothing about farming. That man, Jake Kreutzer, was a big-shouldered guy who played football at the University of Vermont in his younger, glory days. Then he went into a period of hippie pot smoking that led him to Jamaica. Clearly, his life wasn't going anywhere as far as American success stories are concerned, but given his good build and fairly handsome features—he looked, in some ways, like he could be a movie star—he finally saved his ass by marrying a wealthy woman from New York whose father had made money owning a chain of supermarkets. From that day forward Jake lived a fairly luxurious life, moving between his wife's apartments in New York and London and occasionally down to her place in Montego Bay, Jamaica. He knew he was dependent on her (and she was one of those neurotic psychologists living off her family money), and maybe because he was drawn to having affairs, he eventually separated from her. By that time they'd had a child—a daughter who they both spoiled tremendously, as far as I could tell—so, although Jake had no means of supporting himself, he still had a way to live off his wife. He was that rare guy everyone is secretly a little envious of even though he's pathetic: a deadbeat dad who receives alimony from his wife.

When I was writing in Jamaica, I ended up somehow on this small "herb farm" that Jake was running. I put the herb farm in quotations, not because he was growing pot or other drugs (although he smoked a lot of ganja and hired prostitutes), but because the farm was hopelessly run-down. When Jake's ex-wife came from the U.S. to Jamaica, he'd pop into her house, ostensibly to visit his daughter, and steal something (a TV, say, or a cordless phone). These are the kinds of people you meet when you're trying to get into the writing biz. You meet them because you're trying to get some favor (in this case, I was trying to get an inexpensive place to write on his farm).

I think I put this story in because it's a story about how eager I was to make it then. I wanted to become like Ernest Hemingway.

I thought all I had to do was find someplace where I could write every morning, in a setting fairly "exotic," and I would just churn out some really good book. I did get a draft of a novel done. But the writing in it was horrible—overwritten and sappy. I didn't know anything about the craft of writing then (how to make a scene and action clear). So the question is, Now that I've been writing for fifteen years, since I went to Jamaica, can I finally pull it off? I've published one short book of stories, but I don't feel those stories express much of what I want to say or who I am. This is the first book that might come close to communicating honestly and directly what is in my heart.

With that little opening (which might seem confectionery sweet but is as honestly written as I can) I think I'm ready to start this seventh chapter.

So where is our hero? Well, he was up much of the night before his wedding day. At 5 A.M., Zoe was still asleep, though not completely, because she could hear Paul in the next room sitting on their old couch (which they'd found left on the street by some old Cambridge woman who'd used it on her sunporch). Zoe was not the kind of person to pick things up off the street. She liked to primp, to buy dozens of facial creams and delicate soaps. The bathroom of their apartment—a condo that cost more than they could afford, bought with the one-time windfall Zoe had received from her brief soap opera days—was full of these creams. Other than the couch that Zoe had given in to after Paul's pleas, the entire apartment was designed by Zoe with feminine taste. There was a framed print of the child-book character Eloise dressed in pink, holding a bouquet of daisies and sniffing the flowers. There was a drawing and mixed-media collage of James Dean done by a friend of Zoe's from L.A., in a fashion-sketch style with bits of dry palm fronds, and the way Dean was portrayed (like a hunk instead of a tough guy) made it clear the art was intended for women or gay men who felt the same way. In the kitchen, green, handblown drinking glasses with bubbles filled one of the cupboards. The idea, Zoe felt, was these glasses were a little funky, a little retro, colorful and fun, what she considered good taste. In the bedroom, she'd insisted long ago Paul throw out his comforter with the NFL helmets, and in its place there was an immaculate down comforter with a light-blue duvet cover. The bed, a big wooden four-poster, elevated the mattress high to let everyone know this was the nest for the family to come; it suggested the primacy of the bed and the primacy with which Zoe had selected it. The walls of the bedroom were painted "robin eggshell" blue. The wicker night tables on both sides of the bed gave the feeling one had ended up in a B & B.

As Zoe slept, released from the hospital recently, Paul propped his knees on the small couch (which Zoe allowed him to keep only because she said it was well made), and he looked out their apartment complex to a quiet side street four stories below. The thing that held his attention was an emergency-colored orange pickup truck owned by the city of Cambridge with a flashing light bar on top. The pickup was moving slowly down the side street letting out a fog, a bilious, noxious trail that fell in thick heaviness around the road, creeping off the flatbed like a ghost. *So this is how they do it,* Paul thought. *They poison us all to kill the mosquitoes.* The newspapers had been full of stories about the West Nile virus infecting birds, feeding on them and then infecting humans, who sometimes died. The true menace wasn't nearly as big as the headlines made it sound, Paul believed. After all, as far as he could tell, only twenty people had died in the entire New York–New England corridor since the virus was discovered a few years ago. It seemed absurd to fumigate and poison everyone to save a few. But who knew just how bad the virus really was? Was it an epidemic about to explode, as doctors announced regularly on the radio? Or just a tiny problem, something to be aware of but inconsequential? Like so many problems, he felt, he didn't know what the scale was anymore or what to make of it. If these problems were as large as they were portrayed, then certainly his *own* problems were trivial. But were these problems as big as constantly told? Or perhaps they were even worse? And where did that leave *him*? In a world of wars in Iraq and Afghanistan, what difference or significance did his small problems—with respect to his inability to get tenure and whatever doubts he might have about the viability of his marriage to Zoe, or about Cyrus and Buffalo Man—have? *Yet the problems in the news are just that—news—*he thought. *They scare me, they fill me with dread, but my problems are MY problems. And my problems matter, too, even if they'll never make the headlines.* Because the thing the pickup truck below made clear is that when something is actually concrete and real before one's eyes, then the headline ceases to be a headline. The truck below had converted the news to reality. *It is not that we should think globally and act locally,* he thought, *it is that we should act within the sphere in front of us, in the sphere of our own life, which is real.*

And what was most real to him now was not just the pickup rolling slowly like a hearse below his window, spilling clouds of death over all creatures, but the reality of the small sculpture he'd stolen from Cyrus's house.

The theft had taken place a few days ago, after he'd rummaged through boxes of notes in his cramped office at B_____ Community College to give some highlights to The Modern Cyrano to work with. He'd left the office and caught a bus that dropped him off half a mile from Cyrus's house. The screech of public transport was never heard from within the walls of Cyrus's mansion, not even if you went up to the widow's walk. The closest sound to a public bus was lawn mowers pushed by Mexican gardeners. Paul went by bus because his Corolla still wasn't working; it was in the shop (being slowly fixed by his Portuguese mechanic, who asked him if he'd ever considered selling the car for scrap). *But if I sell the car, then I'll never quite feel the speed of driving the same way again,* he'd thought when he refused his mechanic's hint.

Money, money, money, that's what he needed. The car. The wedding. Although the wedding wasn't the root of their problems, was it? *I mean,* he thought as he took the bus, *even though I make just a few bucks at B_____ Community College, and even though Zoe's a nurse, we ought to have some money saved up, shouldn't we?* The press was full of stories about how in demand nurses were. So Zoe's salary wasn't that bad. L.B. certainly seemed to manage. He even sent some money back, occasionally, to his family in Jamaica. (Although he also had a habit, Paul noticed, of leaving the bill when they went to a restaurant—left in that casual way that suggested: Look, man, we both know I'm from one of the "easy islands" where money shouldn't be anything, so don't worry about it, just pay the bill.) L.B. saved some, even if he relied frequently on the kindness of others. (He liked all-you-can-eat barbecue specials.) So why were they so hard up for money? Paul thought. Because it seeped out of their pockets; because Zoe liked to go out to dinner all the time; because Zoe liked expensive clothes; because she needed to belong to a massage and wellness center on top of a health club; because Zoe said all these things were necessary to maintain and preserve herself, not only for her emotional state (since she liked to look in the mirror) but for her acting career. She made almost nothing when she got parts in the local theaters—not because the theater companies paid shit but because she almost never got a lead role. It had been five years since her last big part, a time when Paul had thought her career might in fact revive (or even really *begin,* given that her only other claim to fame was the soap opera). Zoe spent money, and Paul knew, despite his protests, that he loved her in part because she did. Unlike him, she took care of her body; unlike him, she was physically admired. He loved the bright red lipstick she wore, her high cheekbones, and the clarity of her large brown eyes. And it all seemed smart to him (though dumb at the same time) that she had yet to give in to the forces of decay that surrounded them. She still had her dreams and plans that—(though it might take some time)—she'd get one more shot at a good role, or that even playing smaller parts, someone would see her on stage and think she had the perfect face for a movie. Proof of the viability of such a plan was clear: a friend of hers, an actress in Boston hitting middle age, too, had been tapped by Woody Allen when he'd been munching peanuts in one of the local theaters. He'd had one of his neurotic moments of self-proclaimed brilliance and known the woman on stage had to be in his next movie. That was the kind of thing, out of thin air, that Zoe believed could happen to her. "I know, I know," she told Paul a month ago, when he said it was good she had high hopes but that he hoped she wouldn't be crushed if they never materialized. "But that's what I *want* to believe. And if I want to, what's the problem? *Wishing* makes it so. Or only wishing makes it so. Your problem, Paul, is that you've become schlumpy. You've gone from a grunge, cool professor to a dwindling has-been. You're funny, so why don't you let your humor show? You're smart, so why don't you let your intelligence show? You've got to give up living in the shadow of things. Andrew's never coming back. And Cyrus is always going to exist on a different plane. But if you put your mind to it, you could finish your book, and I think it could be brilliant. But you've got to find your compass again. You seem to have lost the reason why you started your book in the first place. Not to be a symbol of inadequacy, but to find the path out of inadequacy."

Yet could such a path be found? Or could such easy advice be given to anyone effectively? When he'd begun reading how-to books, he thought they might provide such a path and that he might not only be able to come up with some analysis of why these books were so popular, or what their typical mechanism for conning their readers was, but also, in the hope that somewhere, planted cryptically inside these books, he might find an elixir, a central idea that would not only help himself but to heal America, too. The vague plan for his book was a bit ludicrous, he knew: after providing amusing case studies of various inadequate individuals and their phobias, and how they were archetypes throughout American history, and after analyzing the efforts of the broader culture to overcome these phobias and problems (Horatio Alger, Dale Carnegie, etc.), he hoped to drop his own pebble of healing, his own discovered wisdom—to send ripples into the current of the American psyche, hoping that if even only one individual picked up his book and found it useful, then that person would not only be connected to him but might pass on the meaning, or path, found in his book to another, and in this way the book might slowly creep as a stream of hope through the veins of America.

But the veins felt so clogged as he took the bus to Cyrus's house to steal something to pay The Modern Cyrano to write an article for him. For even if The Modern Cyrano *could* write an article that would be published and that would allow him to keep his job, without the feeling of his *own* words, would this article ever connect with another reader, and would it ever truly be able to ripple outward? He had read once E. M. Forster's epigraph to his novel *Howard's End:* "Only connect." And if The Modern Cyrano wrote on his behalf, then who the hell was he connecting with? With no one. Connecting only with his career. Connecting only with his failure mirrored back. But he'd hire The Modern Cyrano in any case in the hope that if he could just make it over this hump, he would move beyond his fears and this obstacle. Whether Buffalo Man was to blame or not he *was* cursed, he thought on the bus to Cyrus's house. And he would end the curse. He would regain the pride he'd felt until Cyrus looked down at him while he played his drums at the Orpheum.

It was fitting that he should steal from Cyrus, he thought as he walked from the bus and the diesel smell into the perfumed enchanted "forest" of Cambridge's mansions. True, he could go to a bank and take out a loan against Zoe's apartment (although the title was in her name). Also true he could probably scrounge up some money another way. He might even be able to beg from Cyrus, allowing that Cyrus would press him endlessly to confess what he needed the money for. If he told him the truth, Cyrus wouldn't scold him, he'd simply do worse: look at him and shake his head, as if to say, "I'll help you out because you're blood, but not because I think you have any promise. Now go away." Yet rather than say this, Cyrus would let the weight of his silent disapproval and of his shaking head plant the unspoken words in Paul. Cyrus was the master of the silent treatment. He could stare down a bulldog. Paul saw him do it once: bring the dog from growling, hind-quarters scraping, until it sniffed his shoe gently and licked his toe, and whimpered at his feet.

In a message on Paul's answering machine, Cyrus had let Paul know, the day before, he would be in Vegas for a conference and he was going to take Rebecca and the kids. "Swing by and check out the house while I'm gone," he'd said.

The yellow mansion glowed in the setting sun, as Paul approached, heavy with the weight of Cyrus the way a pyramid in Egypt must have looked to the slaves who had built it. And the idea that came to Paul quickly was that he should bury his notes beneath the shrubs and wood chips that were meant to scare away weeds and vermin, before he entered the house, on the odd chance someone might come up to him—the maid who cleaned or even Cyrus if he hadn't really gone to Vegas. *If he sees these notes, he'll just laugh outright at me,* Paul thought. He'd never told Cyrus exactly what his book was about, and Cyrus had never asked. Cyrus had told Paul the quality of the content of his first book didn't matter; all that mattered was that it should be on a sexy topic and be successful. If Cyrus saw Paul's notes, he'd howl with laughter. He liked to laugh, but only at others, or if at himself only when the joke was the kind that faulted him for being an overachiever.

Paul buried his notes and looked around the house's front. There was the Mini Cooper, the Mercedes SUV, and the two other cars. He schlepped up the mansion's high steps through the entryway, and meandered through the large living room with its immense Chinese, floral-patterned carpet and headed into the kitchen. He thought if he found enough goodies in the fridge—always full to the brim with soft drinks and candy bars, leftover pizza, and half-drunk bottles of expensive wine—he might decide not to take something from Cyrus.

What has changed since before? he thought as he stood in the large kitchen, with the plasma TV screen, trying to figure out what food to take, staring into the fridge. The day of Andrew's funeral he'd been certain he couldn't steal from Cyrus to give money to Maria for her baby. (She had ended up more or less OK after all, just as Cyrus had predicted. She had struggled. Yet, according to Maria, having to raise the baby all by herself made her more determined and ingenious. "Like they say," she told Paul, "necessity is the mother of all invention, and I never could have stood taking any money from Cyrus, in any case.") What had changed was simply the passage of time. Then, he had believed losing his relationship with Cyrus would be a sign Buffalo Man's prophecy was true—with the inevitability he would die at a young age, somewhere in the "fourth ring" of his life.

But he wanted some kind of solace, to not hold his tongue anymore, to not bow any longer completely to Cyrus. *So what should I steal?* he thought. Should he go for one of the most valuable paintings? The Warhol, the Chagall, the Picasso, the Rembrandt? Too impossible to get rid of. He walked around in the fast-approaching darkness of nightfall, and decided on a small pre-Columbian statue. Also difficult to sell, but compact, unlikely to be immediately missed, something that could be blamed on one of the maids, the kind of art Rebecca never missed since she wasn't interested in art for its aesthetic value but only for its monetary and conversational value. (Although anything stolen from Cyrus would eventually be noticed. He loved his art almost as much as successful legal cases. And he felt he deserved his art and that the beauty and perfection of it mirrored his success at his lawyerly craft.)

What Paul took, finally, was a small figure of a woman suckling a child. The statue felt hot in his hand, although he knew it was cool. Stabbing his brother—even with a pin—made the statue hot like blood, the way Brutus must have felt when he stabbed Caesar. Before Paul committed the crime, he'd been certain he would need to rush out of the house before he could actually bring himself to steal something. But he felt a warm glow instead, like hot spit, and he went into the TV room and watched a game show. The host of the show looked a bit like Cyrus: curly hair that fell in neat studio-combed locks, tall, a fine gray suit, charming—millions of viewers locked in to the banter. Paul sucked on one of the candies Rebecca left in various bowls around the house. He hid the statue between two large cushions and leaned back on the couch with his feet on the coffee table, faintly aware of the wood-chip residue from the garden he was leaving on the furniture. He imitated the gestures of the host; smiled like the host, laughed with the host. One of the guests spun a big wheel around and around, and when the wheel stopped, it fell on a space with a number too low for the contestant to continue. The host smiled, telling the audience not to go away, they would be right back. The host's assistants—blondes with blow-dried hair and manicured nails—held the arm of the contestant in euphoric support, supposedly, but really more like cops dragging him off stage. The host turned to the last remaining contestant and crowned him the winner. Paul spit on the TV and left the spit to ooze down the face of the host. When it reached the bottom of the screen, he hurried down to the kitchen, nearly tripping on the Oriental carpet stair runner, and pulled down sheets and sheets of paper towel, and ran back upstairs and wiped the screen clean. *Leave the statue. Put it back.* But Zoe was still in the hospital; he had time to do what he needed, and he took it. He hurried outside with the figurine stuffed into one of his pockets and went to the shrub where he'd left his notes and dug them up.

All of this he reflected back upon as he kneeled on the couch in the living room while looking down four stories at the orange pickup as it sprayed a fine, misty cloud of death. Should he feel guilty? He did, somewhat. But he'd sold the statue to an art dealer near Harvard Square already and paid The Modern Cyrano when he gave him his notes—at least the initial two grand he'd promised. He didn't have the article, yet; even The Modern Cyrano couldn't work that fast, it turned out.

Meanwhile, Zoe lay half-awake, half-asleep in bed, aware of Paul's kneeling in the other room as she thought about the classes she was taking without his knowledge. They were sex-therapy classes. She'd been shy at first about showing her body to the group. Now she masturbated using some of the visualization techniques taught in the course, imagining the class instructor gently touching her breasts and back, as they all touched each other in the class in a large circle; imagining she was relaxed, imagining she was making love on an island beach; hearing the instructor, who told the men to squeeze their penises at the base to prolong their erections and for the women to learn how to rub the upper inside of their vaginas to stimulate not only the clitoris but the surrounding wall, until she came, fitfully, then happily.

The guests had been arriving for over half an hour. The underwear with the prophets was a little tight, and Paul kept trying to pull it away from his critical frontal infrastructure without anyone seeing, which wasn't so easy with a tux that was too tight as well. The man at the tuxedo store claimed Paul had specifically ordered this smaller size, or that Zoe had ordered the tux this way on his behalf to avoid him looking too baggy and short on his wedding day.

"Are you fucking kidding me?" Paul told the man when he went to pick up his tux while Zoe went with one of her sisters to get her hair done up. "Zoe would never have done that. This tux is gonna make me look like a sausage from Liechtenstein. And I can tell you those sausages are based on the lederhosen the bankers wear over there. You've gotta get me the next size up."

"No can do," the Serbian owner of the store said. He was a refugee of the Bosnian war—trying to avoid being prosecuted for war crimes— and he'd decided to seek safety in the lion's den of the U.S.; he figured that if he could get U.S. citizenship, he could avoid the international criminal court since the U.S. didn't believe in it. "We don't actually own the tuxes we rent," he said. "We rent them from somewhere else. Actually, I get them sent to me from my cousin back in Serbia."

"So what am I going to do?" Paul said.

The wedding was set to begin in six hours.

"Well, I can give you a much bigger tux and we can tighten it up with safety pins and extra cummerbunds. Or you can keep what you call a sausage—and sausages are delicious, you know. I miss the Serbian sausages."

Eventually they settled on the sausage tux because Paul looked like a meatball with loose pieces of spaghetti around his waist when he put on the other suit.

Later, at the wedding, he got kind of used to the tux, including the way it pulled on his crotch, making his socks show a little too high—when Melvin Watson, the former lead singer of I.C.N., gave the whole look his seal of approval. "Pretty fuckin' cool, Paul," Melvin said, fingering the fringe of the tux. "No ball and chain for you, man. Looks like you told your bride you're gonna keep your own style."

Melvin was one of the many guests who'd parked their cars beneath a broad beech tree by the stone gate to the estate. There was every kind of car you could imagine under that tree. From the shade of the tree, a long grass field, neatly mowed, rolled gently up and down, lending the feeling of a country manor in England as it rolled all the way to the top of a hill where Paul stood on the second floor of the Codman House (a mansion built in 1740), looking down at the guests as they came to the outdoor wedding area. There was L.B. There was Ned (his best man). There were the members of I.C.N., who he hadn't seen for years. There were his now-divorced parents (their marriage hadn't lasted after Andrew's death), and his parents' friends, including artists from New York and their friends from Boston from the more than thirty years they had lived in North Cambridge. There were Zoe's six brothers and sisters and her uncles and aunts, her mother, but not her father, because he was already dead. (Zoe was the baby of the family, and her father had always tried to give her whatever would please her.) There was Chairman Kominski with a few other colleagues. Paul spent almost no time with them outside work, but Cyrus had suggested at the last minute he invite them all in case they had any say about his tenure, which Paul did (though more out of courtesy than any desire to follow what Cyrus had told him). There was The Modern Cyrano, who claimed he needed to go to the wedding to get a better sense of who Paul was in order to write the article for him. ("To have the right voice for another," he said, "to give them words, you have to know what a person is made of so you can see where the mental block for them comes from.") The Modern Cyrano wore sunglasses and a plain brown suit. He was strictly incognito, doing research. And there was Zack, the paramilitary guy from the hospital. He'd invited himself after he'd heard Zoe was getting married from one of the nurses. And what could Paul say to a survivalist who pushed his beer belly into his chest and breathed down at him as he said he'd be there early to set up security? Besides, security couldn't be a bad thing, could it? (It might keep away the press following Cyrus everywhere since he'd declared his campaign.) A hundred and fifty people meandered up the long lawn, the whites of tuxedo shirts shining against black jackets. Zoe had written in the invitations the wedding would be formal. The women came in flower-patterned dresses, holding clutch purses, thankful for the bright sun that made it easier to show off their bare shoulders in the crisp air of spring this second of May.

There were a number of guests Paul didn't recognize—it was a given, he thought; weddings grow out of control of the bride and groom to include extras. But one of them (who might be a freeloader? there must be stranger things than wedding crashers who just want good booze and food) appeared more foreign than the others. A tall, sturdy man with a face that protruded like a boxer dog's, who was too tan for this time of year unless he lived in Hawaii or had his own tanning bed—dressed in a flower shirt, curly hair sun bleached, body muscular like a surfer's—came into the house (where no other guests went except to the bathroom). He seemed to know directly where he wanted to go, because he went upstairs and entered the room where Paul was pacing alone, looking out the window down at the guests.

"Hi . . . Paul?" the man said, and he put his hand out to shake. "Great to meet you. I've heard a lot about you from Zoe."

From Zoe? *Who the hell is he?* "Are you a cousin?" Paul said, and he shook hands automatically. If he could, he'd like to ask Zoe who a lot of these guests were, but she was on the opposite end of the mansion getting dressed in the master bedroom with her bridesmaids.

"A cousin?" The guy chuckled. He had a corduroy baseball cap, weathered from sea spray, tightly secured over his smooth locks. "No, I'm no cousin. Though, if you believe in extended spiritual love, then I guess I might be. No, but listen man, I'm not trying to threaten you in any way, I'm just a good friend of Zoe's." He gave Paul a wink, as if they were all surfer buddies who'd been in 'Nam together and who were about to go out and catch a wave. He patted Paul on the back—a gesture that felt too intimate—which caused Paul to lean forward a bit from the strength of the guy's arm.

"Listen, you ever hear about rhino powder?" the guy said.

"About what?" said Paul.

"You know, rhino powder. Especially rhino powder mixed with bear testicles." The man wrapped his long, muscular, hairy arm—strong from swimming in triathlons and steering helicopters—around Paul, and he whispered the words again directly into his ear: rhino powder. Paul shook his head. "Well that's great then, 'cause I've got an important gift to give you. These are pure, time-tested aphrodisiacs. I know that may sound a little goofy, or even like a bunch of bull to you. Heck, I was even pretty skeptical myself the first time I tried them. But these are gifts from this little guy who's a significant medicine man on the big island of Hawaii. They're a gift from the great god of love who dwells high up in the volcanoes. So I thought, as a little token of my appreciation for Zoe, and with best wishes for the two of you, I'd give you this tube of rhino pills mixed with bear testicle powder."

Where was Zack when you needed true security? But the guy didn't look too dangerous. With his corduroy baseball cap with the logo of a popular Hawaiian surf shop (not to be confused with the more obscure logos Paul wore), the guy looked like a forty-five-year-old frat boy, happy, tan, fit, and ready to participate in any athletic adventure, a positive member of society who wished only to spread happiness and warmth and cheer—and, apparently, virility—to the world.

"Listen," the guy said, "the last thing I want to do is put any stress on you, Paul. No stress, no way, no how. That's the motto at my school. Or, at least, not unless you're trying to test yourself. And I'm getting the feeling this is a whole new world for you that would probably be best approached at a later time. So for now I'm just going to leave this little gift and tell you you've got one hell of a sexy wife. Zoe's fantastic. The guys at the school all agree. And if you ever want to—after this wedding is over, after things calm down a bit—I'd be more than happy to set up a whole set of visualizations *together* for you and Zoe. 'Cause that's what I think you need, Paul, to solidify things between the two of you. But in the meantime, listen, hang-ten man, and try these pills tonight if you want to. Or better yet, take one of them now to get ready for later. 'Cause it can take a little while to kick in."

Was this dude handsome or what? Paul had to admit he was smooth. Tall and standing over Paul like a palm tree protecting a young monkey, he put his arm around Paul's shoulder, hugged him affectionately, and gave Paul the tube of pills. He wrapped him like a blanket and shook his hand again in an effusive way; then he was gone. Paul had imagined many things would surprise him on his wedding day, but this definitely topped even the Serbian tux man. He looked at the pills in the clear tube, dark brown that glowed more golden in the soothing light of the late afternoon.

Could this all really be happening to him? And what had the guy meant when he said Zoe was "one hell of a sexy wife"? How would he know? What school was he talking about? The school of rhino aphrodisiacs? Or was this the guy from those therapy classes she'd been hiding from him? The last thirteen days he'd been wondering whether he and Zoe were actually meant for each other, or whether anyone was meant for the other in marriage. Could he truly trust Zoe? He'd come across a piece of paper right after she went into the hospital, stuck in the bottom of her drawer beneath her clean white underwear, which she loved to bleach free of stains and which he loved to take out and smell, taking in the scent of her. While gathering clothes for Zoe in the hospital, the paper—a schedule for a series of "sex-therapy classes"— had tumbled out. He'd felt, ever since then, he should confront her. He wanted to know before they got married whether she really wanted HIM, whether she was really happy with him or whether she'd been seeing someone else. And the only thing that kept him from asking was a profound feeling that if he did, he didn't want the real answer, and he hoped, also, if Zoe had something to tell him, she'd do it on her own. *Have I been a fuckup in bed, too?* he'd wondered when he first saw the sheet with the schedule for classes. There was no address on the paper or way of knowing where she went for the course. Now, it seemed, he'd met the instructor of her class.

He swallowed two pills with a bottle of water the guy also left; it was a brand that claimed to be from Tahiti, called Elixir. The fine print on the back of the plastic container said the water was bottled in New Jersey.

Like minutemen behind a stone farm field fence jockeying for position, hustling, crouching on their knees, peeking over the lip of the stone wall that hid them from their enemy, photographers from the national and local press corps thrust their telephoto lenses toward Cyrus as his limo cut up the long, stone driveway toward the eighteenth-century mansion. The car kicked up pebbles of granite and winter's dust into the air. Cyrus was late; the wedding was scheduled to begin fifteen minutes ago. Beams of glinting light reflected from the lenses, beautiful colors of tangerine, wild raspberry, and desert reds and browns, cutting through the chill air, reflecting back toward the object of their desire from the heavy metallic cameras that fired and clicked to suck up a moment in time, to steal a flash of Cyrus heading toward his brother's wedding. The winter dust hung in the air from the violence with which the limo had approached, and Cyrus didn't make any effort to jump out quickly. He waited in the car for whatever might make his tux dirty to fall by the wayside as the few other stragglers who knew they were late for the ceremony hurried up the hill by foot toward the garden in back of the mansion where the delayed wedding was about to begin. At Cyrus's own events—lectures at the law school and the Kennedy School, trials, meetings with sports heroes and movie stars, and with the president of the United States—he was always on time. For family birthday parties, concerts, art openings, weddings, and funerals he was late.

No other car drove up the driveway that arced up to the mansion. It was forbidden by the historical preservation society that rented the place. A sign clearly indicated all cars should park by the gate beneath the beech tree in the "event parking" area. Only "service vehicles" were permitted closer, and even then only to the carriage house. But on Cyrus's orders his driver had ignored the sign, heading straight to the mansion, and for this reason Zack hustled his beer-belly-army-fatigue-covered body up to the limo to check out who was failing to obey clear civilian orders.

It looked to Paul, from where he waited for Cyrus—knowing he couldn't begin his wedding without him, having already delayed the wedding, and trying one last time to get a little more space between his crotch and tux as he peered out the handmade glass windows of the estate to the limo where dust was settling—that Zack might run straight into the car as he charged, like Teddy Roosevelt (supposedly) ran sword thrust forward up San Juan Hill. As in the best silent movies, Paul could hear through the glass Zack harrumphing, cursing at loose-cannon civilians who chose to disobey orders. Zack had a long way to go, running after the limo from over by the cars where he'd been making sure they were all properly parked.

For Zack, the problem with civilians wasn't just that they were often willfully greedy and stupid; it was that they were so oblivious—so unobservant of their surroundings. They not only failed to see when they took up an extra parking space, they had no sixth sense for danger. If it weren't for him chasing the limo, for example, who would guarantee there wasn't some kind of crazy suicide bomber driving the vehicle? A sleeper-cell Al Qaeda operative? Security was something civilians took for granted. They woke up only when it was gone, whereas the key to safety, Zack knew, was preemptive strikes.

The mansion Paul was ensconced in, and that Zack seemed so eager to defend, was hardly the kind of property, Paul thought, Zack would be eager to give his life for. It was hardly the Stars and Stripes of liberty for the common man; if anything, the mansion probably had belonged to a member of the Whig Party who denied the whole idea of democratic rule. The three-story house was imposing, with Ionic columns at the entryway and along the side porch. The benches on the porch, made of wrought iron shaped like swans, must have cost a fortune in an era when a dozen dollars meant something. Wide black shutters (a reminder the rich could always shut out the light of day)—so large they would take the heaving of a maid to close and open them—wrapped each window like a lid on a treasure chest. Above the limo—which Cyrus had still not exited—a balcony on top of the roof for cool summer parties crowned the house with a wooden balustrade painted picket-fence white that shined in whiteness as if God had personally blessed the Codmans and as if to remind everyone below that, unless they were a friend of the Codmans', they would never rise up to the heights of such leisure and glory.

So it all seemed fairly odd to Paul that Zack was so eager to defend the security and rules and regulations of the Codman House. What difference did it really make if Cyrus's limo rushed up to the mansion? What difference could it possibly make to Zack? (The only thing important to Paul was that Cyrus was late again and that he'd shown his usual indifference to the needs and expectations of others.) Why would Zack, an avowed libertarian who seemed to hate the moneyed class, run so hard to defend the rules of this wealthy mansion? At best, as far as Paul could guess, Zack believed in loyalty. But the question to ask was, What was he loyal to? (because he himself might not know).

But it seemed what Zack was loyal to, Paul thought, was simply Paul and Zoe. At a time of difficulty in his life, when his daughter was in the hospital, he and Zoe had been nearby, and both of them had been friendly enough to Zack—to the extent Zoe had any contact with him. So it must have been that Zack was simply loyal to those for whom he felt comfort. Yet then, maybe it wasn't that at all, Paul thought; maybe he was simply loyal to the chase, to the hunt, and like a guard dog, he chased after cars, and Cyrus's vehicle had entered the compound.

This last idea seemed to make the most sense as Zack made his final, long-running approach to Cyrus. At last—now that the dust had settled, and now that the chauffeur had opened the door for Rebecca and the kids, and now that the chauffeur had come over to Cyrus's side and opened the door and stood by the door, holding the tip of the door like the doorman at the Ritz, waiting for the honored guest to step out— Cyrus edged slowly out into the front receiving area of the mansion, the sound of his heels pressing into the granite pebbles, which even Paul could hear from his second-floor room through the windows, as if Cyrus were claiming the whole area around the mansion as his own. It was this feeling more than any that made Cyrus seem taller than he was, Paul thought: the sense that wherever he went he was the proprietor. Paul had read once in a magazine the key to being a cowboy in the Marlboro ads, for the models who worked for Philip Morris, was to gaze over the huge spreads of Western land before them as if they simply owned it all. They needed to look as if the ends of the earth belonged to them. Cyrus adopted the same attitude. His surroundings were his own. The Codman mansion above him was instantly his own. The long granite driveway beneath his feet was his, too.

Yet the downside to such a way of thinking, Paul realized as he watched Zack run full speed like a kamikaze toward Cyrus, was that it offered almost no sense of vulnerability. Because when Cyrus stepped out of the limo and rose to his full height in front of the chauffeur, in front of the mansion—indicating by the way he paid no attention to the driver as he turned toward Rebecca and the kids and told them to follow that he belonged in his surroundings—he made the mistake of being totally unaware of Zack.

Cyrus turned his back on Zack and headed to the Italianate garden where the wedding would be held. Zack ran up the long curve of the driveway toward Cyrus, yelling, "Hey you! You. Yeah, you."

Cyrus looked behind at a full two hundred pounds running in paramilitary gear at him. He didn't break his gait. He'd been through enough protesters—people throwing pies at politicians beside him at the Davos conference in Switzerland, people calling him "a fucking Jew!" people calling him "a traitor" who loved "niggers," people calling him a shill for the tobacco companies—that he simply nodded his head at the chauffeur to let him know he should put a stop to this unknown attacking militant. "Direct confrontation only feeds the beast," Cyrus had told Paul once as to why he never responded to threats other than to point calmly and firmly at the person the police should arrest when such threats were illegal. "The press will make mincemeat of you if you let them catch you fighting someone. They'll choose the photo that makes you look as if you've lost, even if you beat the other guy up. The best bloody nose is the one you give your opponent in the courts and in the court of public opinion. Never let the tabloids get any shitty photos of you."

So the only photos the press behind the stone wall would be able to print the next day would be of Zack running after Cyrus, being fended off by the chauffeur. MYSTERY MAN ATTACKS CONGRESSIONAL CANDI-DATE would be the headline. Huffing, puffing, telling the chauffeur off, Zack said, "Nobody has the right to be above the rules here."

"Hey, listen, listen, this doesn't concern you, OK buddy?" the chauffeur said. "This is a private wedding."

"Right, this is a private wedding," Zack said, "and *I'm* the one providing security."

But it seemed Cyrus had written his own rules, once again. He had come to the wedding late, inevitably and knowingly, Paul thought.

Perhaps it isn't quite so surprising what Zack did, then, during the wedding if we keep in mind his sense of shame at being fended off by the chauffeur and more or less ignored by Cyrus. For the moment, as the wedding was about to begin, Zack retreated like a wounded dog to the bushes around the Italianate garden to set up a new observation post. He placed himself, with his military dog tag, belly down on the ground under a hedgerow of yellow flowering bushes that radiated spring with delirious balls of yellow, like bright, round smiley faces, along the far side of the wedding area. The bushes were elevated above an intimate, tranquil, rectangular garden that formed a peaceful theater where the wedding guests had gathered, and from this more elevated position, Zack looked down, monitoring the whole wedding.

Let's just say it hadn't been easy to select who would perform the wedding ceremony, or even what kind of ceremony to have. At times, Zoe felt they should write their own vows. Wasn't that the new thing to do? "I mean, come on," Zoe had said, "the Bible was just written by a bunch of old white men with long gray beards living in caves by a Dead Sea. How frickin' romantic and inspirational could that be?" Surely, they could come up with some better vows and sayings of their own. Paul agreed. (Not about the uselessness of the Bible; he was an atheist, but he could certainly see poetry in many parts of the Bible. So could Zoe, but not for the purposes of a wedding, she said.) So for a couple of weeks, they were going to be the scribes of their own ceremony and vows. But where to turn to for inspiration? Well, poetry, right? Zoe had said. Until she and Paul reflected on the number of weddings they'd been to where people got up and read "meaningful" poems by true romantics such as Rainer Maria Rilke. And the problem with these moments of poetry was that they were so god-awfully unpoetic. Could a poem ever be more mangled than at a wedding or a funeral? OK, so they wouldn't steal poetry directly for their ceremony.

Of course, they could also simply pledge love and faith to each other and all other good things in their own words, they thought. That was good enough for Paul. Because in the end, marriage vows are only as meaningful as the people who speak them. A vow rooted in tradition spoken without having been internalized wasn't really much of a vow. So Paul told Zoe he'd be glad for them to write their own vows. But then Zoe suggested a smorgasbord of vows: a dash of Buddhist blessings, some from an animistic tradition, and why not even a great vow she had read in a lifestyle magazine about cannibals who pledged not to eat each other or any relatives? Zoe was kidding, of course, but the whole thing weighed on her. In the end, fearing the old, dead, and stodgy, yet uncertain of what should actually be in a wedding if not something rooted in tradition, she decided—and Paul was willing to do whatever she decided—they should have both a rabbi and a priest marry them.

This would be inclusive, yet bending of the rules enough to satisfy the side of her that needed to bend the rules. And it would solve the none-too-hidden fears of their families that each was marrying someone from a different tradition.

Paul's parents had already dealt with the mixed-religion question at their own wedding. The solution for them had been for Paul's mother to convert to Judaism. But it didn't seem that had worked too well, since none of Paul's grandparents had spoken to his parents for years after their wedding. Cyrus categorically told Paul he was making a mistake marrying anyone who was not an M.O.T. (member of the tribe). "Listen, I'm telling you," Cyrus had said, "think what you want, but one day you'll wake up and she'll be screaming at you, calling you a dirty Jew."

For Zoe, who was only nominally Catholic, having a rabbi and a priest seemed a way to fend off whatever fears seemed to lurk in her family that she was marrying a "dirty Jew."

What they ended up with, then, was a rabbi and a priest.

You didn't need the binoculars Zack was looking through to see the mustache on the rabbi-ette. She was short, no higher than five feet, and her hair rose in some kind of 1970s feminist statement, a high-heaping, enveloping mound, a bush of curls that let it be known she was most comfortable in Birkenstocks with further body hair growing profusely on her pale legs and under her arms. Was this really the solution? Paul thought as he stood before her, waiting for Zoe to appear. Could it really have been the only solution? The problem with finding any other rabbi was that none of the "boys" would perform a mixed marriage. Jews were fleeing from their religion so fast these days—getting on the A train to marrying goyim—that rabbis were trying to stem the tide by making sure only circumcised men married circumcised women. If you wanted Christian or Buddhist or especially Muslim pussy, tough luck, you better look elsewhere. Only this rabbi-ette from Brooklyn was willing to hook up such a depraved pair. The rabbi-ette's lofty 'fro made her look oddly shorter rather than tall, and this shortness was exacerbated by a loose-fitting, formless garb made of natural cotton and hemp. She stood in front of the wedding party next to a scrawny priest as pale as the winter of New England who smiled broadly, welcoming his flock-of-the-moment, a flock like the other flocks he saw week in and week out and that he was happy to bless for the right amount of money, or just happy to bless because "gosh darn it" he was happy. He smiled and smiled, nodding at the large collection of people in front of him as if he knew some of them, when he knew none. "Oh, it is a wonderful day for a wedding," he said. Oh, all days were wonderful days for a wedding. A few large cavity-fillings made of silver, and his yellow teeth, drew even more attention to his smile. *Why do priests always have such poor dental work?* Paul thought. Given that Jesuits could solve the most intractable problems of philosophy and that monks had kept alive the ideas of the Greeks, Egyptians, and Romans in illuminated texts for centuries in the monasteries of Europe, why didn't they ever put some of that ingenuity into avoiding cavities? But the cavities seemed to confirm, Paul guessed, that all truly were sinners in the minds of the priests: everyone had something delicious they were addicted to—chocolate, pizza, money, sex, boys, young girls. There was nothing truer, Paul thought, than the poor dental work of a priest.

When he stopped looking at these minutiae, and stopped taking in his surroundings—the daffodils, the red tulips bordering two raked paths that led up to the trellis at the front of the garden where he and Zoe would be married; the cool trickling of water out of a clay statue face of one of the Bacchae spouting gently into the crisp air; the Greek amphorae; the gentle ribbitting of frogs in the long pool with water lilies, coming out of their winter slumber to embrace the new life of spring—Paul thought that more than anything this was *his* wedding, his and Zoe's alone, not pertaining to anyone else. That a wedding is a communal act he was not only well aware of, he was glad his whole family was present—even Cyrus. But it was their *own* in that no one else could claim the love he and Zoe would profess to each other now. All the people gathered together to show their love and support could never make or destroy a marriage, contrary to what he'd heard priests and ministers and rabbis say at so many other weddings. Love was sealed, hermetically, between two people, if it was love. Love was joined by the two and could only be separated by the two. And after all the doubts he might have had about whether he and Zoe were meant for each other, he felt all that mattered was that he was willing to *give* his love. He would simply *give* his love and hope to receive it back from Zoe in all the years to come. And so, although he wore the underwear with the prophets meant to bring him luck, he no longer thought of their luck at this moment. It was he and Zoe who would have to make their marriage work. No outsider could make it work or fail. And he was ready to do more, to do all he could to try to understand the mysteries of the person he was marrying, which were not really mysteries but instead gaps between one individual and another.

The sight of Zoe walking down the aisle was strange even to Paul. He hadn't expected to see her so much more beautiful than he usually regarded her. It didn't matter at all she was limping and relying somewhat on the support of her mother to bring her to the central place beneath the wedding trellis in front of the rabbi and priest. If a bride was said to radiate, she was radiating. She walked toward the front of the audience slowly, giving little hints to one person or another that she saw them, taking in the eyes of the crowd and giving back her love and appreciation.

Paul stood next to Zoe, who went bug-eyed momentarily when she saw how tight his tux was. He shrugged to let her know there was nothing he could do about it. And he felt, for perhaps the first time, beautiful himself as he stood next to her.

It was during the second part of the ceremony, after the rabbi-ette had warned that their decision to have a mixed marriage would be difficult, and after the priest told them how joyful it was that God had brought the two of them together, that the usual question was posed before the actual exchange of rings. "And so, if there is any reason why God should not join these two delightful young people together, let him speak now or forever hold his peace." The priest looked to his notes to continue to the next order of business. It was the second wedding of the day for him, the second where he'd brought his intimate love and understanding of God to a new couple, and if he could finish quickly enough, he might be able to get in a few holes of golf before the sun completely set. (Paul and Zoe had met him once, a few weeks ago, to give a few particulars about their names and how they'd come to know each other.)

The audience looked at the priest, waiting for him to continue, as he did, but he was interrupted by a man with a beer belly dressed in Army fatigues who dropped down heavily from yellow flowering bushes into the tranquil spring garden.

The plants and dirt that had surrounded Zack beneath the bushes, and that now clung to his Army fatigues, made him look all the more like a survivalist. Military field binoculars dangled from the back of his neck; cartridges latched onto his regulation military belt; boots tied crisply protected his feet; a bowie knife in his hand pointed forward toward the guy with the Hawaiian shirt who had visited Paul in the mansion before. "That man! Him!" Zack said. "I've seen 'em together in *compromising* situations at the hospital three or four times." He pointed his knife over at Zoe. "This is a basic compromise not only of the teachings of the Lord but of basic operational planning. Hanky-panky before the wedding WILL COMPROMISE your mission, make no mistake about it . . . Now, I'm not saying this wedding MUST be stopped. Everyone's got to make his *own* decision. It's a free country, after all. But if THIS MISSION's going to continue, then FULL OPERATIONAL problems and violations of basic procedures prior to engagement MUST, I repeat, MUST be fully evaluated. 'Cause what I'm seeing today—" Zack pointed at Cyrus, "—is a lot of disregard for BASIC OPERATIONAL PROCEDURES. And any engagement entered into on false premises will lead to false security."

So was this the truth? What had really happened? That Zoe had been having an affair with the guy in the Hawaiian shirt? That he was more than a sex-therapy instructor? That he was actually doing her?

Zoe pointed at Zack and yelled, "Who is this nut? Someone get rid of him. Someone get rid of him *now. You're* a fucking liar! This guy's crazy." She went into some kind of theatrical lines, "*For what you have wrought your eyes shall be turned to brine.*" The audience stopped rustling their programs. Even the frogs knew it was time to be silent. Ned jumped down from the trellis area to run over to silence Zack. Paul never knew Ned had this kind of physical strength in him, but it seemed the days of skateboarding and telling cops to fuck off had given him proper training for playing a wedding bouncer. Ned wrestled with the bowie knife, lurching to the right, the left, then the right. It didn't seem Zack had any intention of harming anyone, but he had no apparent intention of giving his weapon up or recanting his accusation and slinking away. In the middle of this, as most kept their eyes on the ongoing match between Ned and Zack, Zoe left the garden as quickly as she could hobble, and Paul went after her, feeling on the one hand that he wanted to give her his hand to help her and, on the other, that if everything Zack had said was true—and even if it wasn't—he'd just been humiliated in front of everyone he'd ever known.

They were inside the mansion now, in the master bedroom, where a large scenic painting—of the sun rising gently over the Atlantic with a sailboat calmly moored in Boston Harbor, rays of orange heat-kissing light opening up the day—dominated the room over the master's bed. Zoe flopped on the bed with her face down, the folds of her carefully pressed cream-colored wedding dress bent in odd directions.

"Zoe," Paul said quietly, not wanting to go too close for fear he might make her cry more sharply, "Do you want me to come closer, or to go, or stay?"

She continued crying with her face buried in the covers and reached above to pull the cover of the bed down so she could bury herself deeper in the sheets and pillows. There were still combs in the room used earlier to recomb her hair. There were still a few fallen rose petals from her wedding bouquet on the floor. And, since she wouldn't tell him whether she wanted him to stay or leave, Paul stood frozen halfway between the door and the bed, until he couldn't wait any longer, and he moved slowly up to Zoe and sat on the bed. What he wanted to ask was whether anything Zack had said had any truth. He knew Zack was a crazy survivalist prone to his limited, paranoid way of seeing and, like everyone, limited to seeing only what he wanted to see. Maybe the guy in the Hawaiian shirt had simply come into the room one or two times to say hello to Zoe in the hospital? Zack had warned that one time, for example, there was someone in the hospital room with Zoe when there had been nothing but silence and the noise of the lights on the machines that monitored Zoe. So it was more than likely Zack had simply made up some ludicrous claim. Yet if this were the case, then why had Zoe run into the mansion? If this were the case, wouldn't she have just waited for Ned to subdue Zack, for the calamity to die down, and then they could have continued with the wedding?

He wanted to reach out to Zoe to touch her hand and comfort her. But if he did, he was sure she would push his hand away, either in anger or shame.

"Zoe," he said, "What should we do now?"

"He's lying," she said.

"OK, he's lying, but then why are you in here?"

"Because he only came to see me a few times in the hospital, and we didn't do anything then. He just came to try to cheer me up."

"In the middle of the night? I was there most of the day. Who is he?"

"I can't tell you. We're sworn to secrecy in the class."

"Well, if it's all so secret, then why did he come up to me earlier and give me some aphrodisiac?"

"You already know him? You've known all this time and you never asked me about him?"

"No, I just figured it all out today. I found a piece of paper in your drawer when I brought you clothes in the hospital, and it was a schedule that said 'sex-therapy classes' on it. Then this guy showed up today out of the blue and told me I should take some aphrodisiac."

"It was just practice, you see? I was just practicing so our love life would get better. We make sex like we're not in love, Paul. Like we're not even meant to be together."

"And do you believe that?"

"Sometimes . . . Sometimes I've thought it. Sometimes I feel we should be making love at least as well as others, and I'm not sure we do. I think our sex life could be better."

Paul looked down at his belly beneath his wedding tux. It's not that he was so fat, but clearly he was out of shape. But who was she to be telling him to get his act together? Didn't she have enough problems of her own? Her unwillingness to recognize she would never be costar-ring in a soap opera again.

"So that's why I went to this therapy class," Zoe said. "And I know you'll think that Tom—the guy out there—is just a flake. You'll think he's just some kind of guy who looks like he's in a fraternity, or some kind of surfer dude. But he really wants the best for all of us in the class, and I think he's getting me back in touch with the sexuality that's been trapped inside of me. You see? Because I feel so sexual inside." She pointed to her breasts, then down to her vagina. "I feel so sexy, Paul. And sometimes I think you don't even see how sexy I am. Or if you did, I think you'd get yourself in better shape . . . So yes, I did sleep with him a couple of times, but it wasn't about him. See? It was just about reconnecting with the sexual side that's inside my body. And the only reason I did it is in the hope you and I can benefit from this together. Because if I can rediscover my libido, then I think we can reignite our libido together."

"So are you telling me you still love me?" Paul said.

"I'm certainly not telling you all this because I don't love you." She pulled Paul close to her on the bed. She rubbed her hands through his short hair and took off his glasses and kissed him, gently at first, slowly, running her hands along his closed eyelids, then across his forehead and down around his mouth. She undid the buttons on his tuxedo shirt, told him it was funny his tux pants and top were too tight. When she opened his fly, she was surprised to see the boxers with the prophets, but she didn't stop digging further, until they reached the point where the prophets did bring good luck, Paul using all his energy, his renewed energy to make love, so that for the first time in years and years the bed in the historical Codman mansion rocked back and forth with the sound of lovemaking.

An hour later most of the guests had left. Zoe's mom and others in the family came and knocked on the door to see what was happening in the bedroom. Promises that Zack had been sent away were made. The rabbi-ette even came to the door and suggested that if women in the 70s could make it past the humiliations of people like Richard Nixon and had the strength to burn their bras, Zoe could find the strength to do "whatever you want to do, honey." The priest had skipped out long before to get in his golf swings. But the rabbi-ette stuck around for a while outside.

Paul and Zoe eventually came out, and with forty or fifty people sipping champagne—Cyrus's idea of how to keep them busy, even though he'd already left himself—there was some of the original audience to watch them get married.

Yet on the couch in their apartment later that night, after they had tried to make love again as well as they had in the Codman House, but with less success—Paul's head full of champagne, looking out the window at another emergency truck coming a second day down the alleyway spraying chemicals to kill the West Nile virus—Paul thought: Have I chosen wisely? Have *we* chosen wisely? In his heart he believed Zoe *did* love him. He believed her when she told him she was simply taking the classes to improve their sex life. He understood why she had to keep the class a secret from him. But if she felt the need to keep that a secret for so long, and if she had married him, then hadn't they actually already separated even if they were coming back together? And once separated, could they ever really be rejoined? What did marriage mean after unfaithfulness? And if he had already been separated from Zoe, then wasn't Buffalo Man's prophecy right, that he had lost her and that he would be separated from his last brother, and that he would die in the fourth ring of his life—which was now? He felt the speed of questions fly through his brain like shards of light moving through the ether of the cosmos. He saw the truck below let out extra chemicals, an extra powerful burst of mist into the air. The lights of the truck sped up; the truck rushed down the alleyway with the lights of the emergency bar spinning around and around in an orange miasma diffused by the chemical cloud, as the pickup ran a red light at the end of the road.

CHAPTER 8

"The key thing," Dr. Wurstheimer said to Paul in his lab at the Worland Institute, "is to stop feeling your problems come from without—that your problems are *external* to yourself. You, for example, have determined all of your problems are rooted in the outside world. The fear of death we have been talking about the last hour is really a claim some *other* man has cursed you. It is a claim this man has some kind of magical power over you. And wouldn't that be nice and convenient for you? Because believing in his prophecy makes you think your antagonist is without. Or when you blame your famous brother for making you feel insignificant, that's just the same thing. But the problem, in the modern era, is never really without. It is always within. Your problems are not really external, they are internal. To heal yourself, you must transform yourself. To transform yourself you must accept that *you* are your own antagonist."

As Dr. Wurstheimer spoke, Paul lay on his back on one of the conference tables in Dr. Wurstheimer's lab. The second-floor room was dim, lit only by the lights of various aquariums; pink and blue hues from fluorescent fish tank bulbs made Paul look like a cadaver. Dr. Wurstheimer was seventy-six, a psychologist and Nobel laureate who'd won his prize for studying the nervous systems of fish and how they relate to their learning capacities. During his analysis of Paul, he moved around the lab dropping fish food into the various large tanks.

"Up to a point, I can accept what you're saying," Paul said. "But isn't the prophecy a real problem? So far, the trajectory of my life has followed the path of the predictions. And isn't my brother's fame and success a big part of what's eating me up inside? So why do you say the modern problem is within?"

"Because, what is your capacity to change the outside world?" Dr. Wurstheimer said. "Can you get rid of whatever curse this man whom you call 'Buffalo Man' has given you? And even if you were to go back to Iowa, could you make him take back his predictions? Or can you suddenly make your brother Cyrus into some kind of failure instead of one of the most famous lawyers in America? These things are not only unlikely—even if you could, they wouldn't get at the reason for why these external facts hold *significance* for you. The particular reason for why a person fixates on a particular *external* problem has everything to do with what is *within* them."

"So what do you suggest I do?" said Paul. "I can barely sleep these days."

"Transform yourself. Regenerate yourself. Stop being so jealous and try to find accomplishments in smaller things. Begin with small changes. Strive for what you can attain. Give up your anger at the world. You've been trying to make the leap to success all at once with your book. Make small things, a very small sailboat, for example, and sail it in the water behind us."

All of this was easy for a Nobel Prize winner to say. How hard could it be for a successful man to give out advice? A successful man could take his analysis of his problems and implement his solutions, and he could easily exhort another to do the same. But the real problem, Paul felt, for "modern man," and certainly for himself, was not to find the advice or to analyze what the problem was, or to realize that the antagonist was within rather than without, but to implement the solution. *The problem for modern man is not that we don't know our problems but that we don't know how to implement the cure,* he thought as Dr. Wurstheimer kept moving around him, first feeding the fish and then cleaning the tanks.

A half hour later, Paul was back at his job, which he'd had since late July, after the tenure committee at B_____ Community College voted him down for continuation in the Am. Stud. Department. He'd been working at the Worland Institute for almost two months now, as one of the two night security guards. Not long after he arrived at the institute, and after he'd expressed an interest in one of the fish in Dr. Wurstheimer's lab (a large, all-white goldfish named James Brown), he and Dr. Wurstheimer had begun speaking together at least once a week, and often every night.

"Begin with small changes," Dr. Wurstheimer had said, and in some ways the change in career *was* a change that was pleasing. The Worland Institute, which lay along the bank of the Charles River in Cambridge, near MIT, was the brainchild of a famous inventor who'd made piles of money in the 50s. The idea behind the institute was that there should be a place for brilliant scientists to gather free from the hassles of the outside world. All scientist-members were supported directly by the institute; they didn't have to waste their time applying for grants. They had their own labs, with as much space as they required. And as far as was humanly possible, the institute shut out the outside world and relied upon its internal resources. The Worland Institute made its furniture and prepared its own food; it provided its own drinking water drawn from the Charles and filtered internally. The institute—a large brick building built like an anonymous post office, with no windows facing out to the busy road in front of the building, as if passersby might contaminate it—had windows only on the side of the building that faced the river. In the center of the building, the upper floors looked down an indoor atrium at a large Japanese garden, complete with stone lanterns, moss, bamboo, trickling streams, and mini waterfalls. The scientists walked around this indoor garden on the ground floor whenever they needed a more communal space, and the bamboo trees, which reached up to skylights at the top level, gave the feeling the very air of the institute could be generated from these trees and stored within. The only view—of the Charles River—was more like a landscape painting of the Longfellow Bridge, gracefully arcing over the river in its nineteenth-century glory, than a vista to the real world outside.

Paul's sense of time was transformed working at the institute. There were no clocks, and none of the scientists and researchers seemed to care what time of day they came or went. A few were night owls. They came around the same time as Paul, at seven in the evening, and he was no longer surprised when he bumped into one of them as they walked through the Japanese garden, moving up and down over little stone bridges and through the grove of bamboo, lost in thought so deep they nearly walked into him or even off the path into one of the streams or corner waterfalls.

Other than these occasional encounters in the garden, and at the second-floor greenhouse cafeteria, the scientists rarely left their labs. So it was great, Paul felt, to walk through the institute: solitary, not bound to any social interaction, free to spend his time thinking and walking and generally enveloped in the quiet of the building.

His favorite place to hang out was on the roof, which he could justify going up to in order to see if anyone was putting together some kind of plan for a break-in or to see where some of the local high school kids had spray-painted graffiti. Whether the students made graffiti or not he didn't really care, but whenever he saw some, he was required to report it, and the graffiti was instantly sandblasted off. In front of the building on the side of the institute that faced the road, there were a large number of cameras monitoring at all times.

Paul would stand up on the roof, on the smooth tar paper that spread in a wide plane in front of him, next to immense heat-exhaust and intake pipes for the air-conditioning, and he would feel he was enlarged standing on top of such a large building. What he would sense was an odd, pleasurable mix of floating—high up, taking in the sun as it went down, enjoying the vista of the Charles River and being as elevated as the commuter trains that moved over the bridge—and, at the same time, being tethered to something bigger than himself. The building was massive, the inside was calm, and although he knew he was inadequately trained to be a night guard (he had lied about having this kind of job before), the fact that he could show up at work every day and that no breach of security would take place made him feel he was part of the successful guarantee of the tranquility of the world-famous institute.

The willingness of Dr. Wurstheimer to let him in his lab and Dr. Wurstheimer's desire to talk to him were also comforting. At night, sometimes, after Dr. Wurstheimer had left, Paul would watch the white goldfish James Brown (as large as a carp) respond to the music he was being trained with. The experiment was to prove fish could distinguish between various subtle forms of music and that they could be trained to engage accurately in differentiation. James Brown was made to listen alternately to Delta blues and Chicago blues and sometimes, as a foil, to Jimi Hendrix. When he correctly identified the music, by bumping his head into a metal bar within the proper time parameter, he was given an extra fish pellet. "From little things like this with fish, we can learn big things about how our body is set up to learn," Dr. Wurstheimer had told Paul. Paul simply liked to watch the graceful movement of the fish as it twirled, making moves of chasing its tail, turning in circles and circles, in silent, sweeping movements of quiet, slow speed to the sound of a blues guitar. It seemed that the fish, far more important than identifying the difference between Delta and Chicago blues, had found a way to combine the big with the little, the bigness of its innate instinct to move any which way with the small choreographed beauty of controlled movement and velocity.

*

At 8:43 P.M., September 24 (2004), L.B. showed up in front of the institute. A security camera whirred into place, adjusted itself downward
as it zoomed in on the approaching suspect, and beamed a high-res
image back to the central control booth near the front of the building.
All guests were monitored closely. When they entered and left they not
only had to pass through a metal detector to ensure they weren't taking
in or out any unauthorized equipment, they also had to pass through
a machine that tested for any contaminants that could harm the highly
controlled environment of the institute.

There were so few visitors and scientists, two men were deemed
capable of providing total security. One was always supposed to be
in the control booth by the front entrance, where an array of eight
black-and-white TVs rotated images from around the building. The
booth had a thick glass wall that allowed each person to be seen as they
went through the various front-entrance detectors. The guard with
Paul on the night shift was a cousin of L.B.'s who L.B. had managed to
score a visa for. His name was Delray Johnson Bunny, and since Delray
thought the gig at Worland was pretty sweet, he'd told L.B. about an
opening for a second guard, and L.B. set up Paul with the position.

Some nights, after Paul did his duty walking around the institute
checking for any anomalies, he would come back to the central booth
and hang out with Delray, and they would listen to baseball games on
the radio. Other nights, Paul would just hang out in some of the labs.

On this night, Paul was in the booth with Delray when L.B. came
through the security check, and L.B. and Delray joked in the big booth
about some of their cousins back home in Jamaica: Bunny Jr., Tick Eye,
Cat Eye, and Tiffany.

"Damn, that Tiffany," Delray said to L.B. "Now she is *one* cousin I
wish wasn't a cousin . . . 'Cause if you ask me—see?—why should the
good Lord keep the best fruit forbidden from the family?"

"Good question. Good question," L.B. said. "But I thought you were
supposed to be studying during the day before coming to this job. And
all I hear you talking about is *bumba clot* [pussy]."

"I don't know, man," Delray said, "it's just hard to study sometimes
. . .You know what I mean?" Delray turned to Paul for support. Paul
didn't gesture yes, and he didn't gesture no. He knew what Delray was
saying, but he also knew L.B. was trying to get him to study more to

complete his college degree within the time frame of his F1 visa so he could land a more permanent job in the U.S. with an H1, and then turn his H1 into a green card. L.B. kibitzed with Delray for the usual chunk of time (L.B. had once told Paul the only thing more offensive than failing to take time to talk to cousins was failing to listen to your mother), and then he and Paul retreated to the auditorium of the institute, where they liked to watch DVDs.

"So what's up, cop?" L.B. said to Paul.

"Please—call me Sheriff Berger," Paul said. "It's a strange thing, you know, there are so few Jewish cops. You always hear about all the Jews as teachers, or lawyers, or doctors, or businessmen, or whatever. But I feel so comfortable here. I think I was meant to spend my days in a place like Worland."

"I hear you, man," L.B. said. "I hear you. Delray says this job is a piece of cake. But you're gonna get bored here, man. I mean, no offense—'cause you know I set you up with this job, and I think it's a good break for you while you gather your thoughts after what happened at the college—but a job that's beneath you, that's never challenging you in the places where you need to be challenged, that's not going to hold your attention and growth too long."

"What makes you say that?" said Paul. "Maybe this is where my potential is really at, and I should just accept it."

"You see these hands?" said L.B. "You see how smooth they are from wiping the bottoms of all those geriatrics? Now, I'm not saying I'm bitter or anything being a nurse. 'Cause I'm not. I'm not bitter about any single thing. You see? But if you asked me if I like my job working as a nurse at night, I'd tell you you're on crack. 'Cause there ain't no one who's meant to be a college professor or a philosopher who's gonna be happy as a nurse. You understand me? I mean, look at Zoe. She doesn't mind being a nurse 'cause it pays the bills for her to do her thing in the theater at night. And even if she doesn't get any lead roles, that's OK. That's OK. See? 'Cause she's using the one job to keep doing the other. And that's what Delray's got to do. And that's what *you've* got to do, too. See? What I'm saying, man, is that you've got to keep writing your book even if you don't have the goal of tenure pushing you forward. Hell, it might even be easier now that you *don't* have that albatross of a tenure committee looking over your shoulder."

Paul didn't say anything. He didn't feel like talking about his book. He'd let the whole thing flounder the last couple of months. He took a cigarette out (he'd started to smoke Marlboros recently, often on the roof as he watched the commuter trains running back and forth from Cambridge to Boston over the Charles), and he offered a cig to L.B. There were signs all over the institute prohibiting smoking. A five o'clock shadow—that looked odd on a face as baby-skin smooth as Paul's—sprouted nevertheless. L.B., who didn't want to make anyone too uncomfortable for too long, decided to ignore the warning signs and he took a cig and smoked it with Paul.

The two of them sat in the back row of the auditorium like schoolboys playing hooky. In expectation of L.B.'s visit, Paul had set up the DVD player with a film about surfers who just had to catch the biggest, sickest waves on the planet. On the big screen, they watched guys get pulled by a Sea-Doo in front of some killer waves as high as sixty feet tall off the coast of San Diego and ride them from the peak, where there was surf spray and foam, until the waves came crashing down. They watched the Gen X surfers defy gravity as they pushed their squat legs against the water, riding the tubes all the way to nirvana.

It seemed to Paul (even after noting how inarticulate most of the surfers were—capable only of saying things like, "More than catching a wave, surfing is just about having fun, you know?") that these surfer-bums had somehow found the key to success. So what was it? Was it their devotion to *one* cause, to one activity? Was it their willingness to take the risk of defying the cultural conventions of what a productive citizen was supposed to be by throwing themselves wholeheartedly into hedonistic pleasure? Was it their happiness and love of an activity that led to great ability?

Yes, it was all of these things of course. But he'd known just as many others who were equally devoted to one cause and activity, who were equally willing to take risks, who found equal pleasure, but who never measured up in the eyes of those who surrounded them. (He, for example, had tried to tell Chairman Kominski, just before the tenure committee voted him down, that he had all these qualities.) But the one quality he seemed to lack was the *ability* to write.

By the end of the movie, Paul had finished smoking his first pack and he was onto his second. He flipped off the DVD after the credits ran through. (He liked to watch credits all the way to the end. He felt, even if he couldn't read the names of those at the bottom as they whirred up the screen, that each of them should be acknowledged.) And in the process of flicking off the DVD, one of the major cable TV broadcasters came on. It was a 24-hour news channel (CNN), and on the big screen—an immaculate flat panel that was remote-controlled, that could be lowered and raised smoothly for the Nobel Prize winners and for the other leading scientists, magnificent enough in size to equal the burnished wood paneling of the auditorium—he saw the face of his brother Cyrus. His face was worn-out, craggy, deprived of sleep in a way it rarely appeared. A voice delivered the news over images of Cyrus being relentlessly trailed by a camera: "A new poll in Massachusetts reveals defense lawyer Cyrus Berger is slipping behind in his race for the 9th Congressional District. After an early surge, many have questioned his commitment to fighting crime . . . Allegations have surfaced Berger is close to 'a bevy' of controversial former clients." The screen cut to one of Cyrus's recent defendants, Lamont Jackson, an African-American NBA star accused of rape. The voice continued: "A spokesman for the Republican Party called Berger unfit to serve and suggested that, if he's elected, Berger will encourage a crime wave that will hit not only Massachusetts but the nation."

The central allegations against Cyrus were that he would: let black prisoners out of jail (since he claimed they were imprisoned disproportionately), work to oppose the death penalty, and force the country to put aside the president's hoped-for national amendment against gay marriage.

"Can you believe it?" L.B. said. "That's how they do it, isn't it? They take a man's strengths and try to say he doesn't even have them. I mean, look at what they're trying to do to that man Kerry. They've got people thinking his Vietnam War medals are some kind of sin. But then, when one of those politicians actually *does* something wrong, they look the other way. I mean, if you want to say something nasty about Cyrus, there's plenty of nasty things to say about him. So why do they have to take his strengths and make them so dirty?"

It was true, Paul thought. He could barely recognize his brother as he was portrayed on TV. The image blared to the nation was like a photo negative. Black had become white and white black. And the blackest things were never reported—not only the kiddie porn Paul had found that one time in Cyrus's office at his house or the illegal stock trades based on insider information, but what Paul had seen three months ago:

On a hot night in early July he'd gone to the Harvard Law School to pick up a letter of recommendation from Cyrus for the security guard job. Cyrus had told him he'd leave it on his desk, typed up by his secretary. Paul was supposed to pick up the letter the day before he actually went, but he'd become late and put it off. It was 10 P.M. (he was out for a walk after he'd fought with Zoe about what he was going to do with himself in the future), and although he hadn't planned to go to Cyrus's office—since he only intended to walk around Cambridge smelling flowers—his feet led him to Cyrus's building.

The postmodern building with a large Roman arched doorway seemed to Paul designed not only to proclaim the supremacy of those who worked within, it seemed to intentionally make the viewer feel small. The uppermost edge of the five-story building jutted out a canopy of steel—rust-weathered brown—crowning the tower. The scale was all wrong, he thought. The building was too high at street level and too imposing on top. It was as if the architect hated any sense of community, as if he wanted to claim himself above those who would wish to socialize on any communal scale.

The heavy front doors, fifteen feet tall, were still open at this late time of night because of a computer center in the basement, where a lone grad student toiled to fix glitches. The other doors were locked.

On the top floor, where Cyrus had his office, Paul reached the outer door to the reception area, where two secretaries and three students worked for Cyrus during the day. He used a credit card to open the door. (It was surprising how lax security was in these university settings.) From the reception area it was a few quick steps to Cyrus's office. Cyrus rarely worked at the law school, since he was on the road so much he preferred to work out of his large study at home. The office at Harvard was primarily for show, when he received important guests or did a TV interview and he needed the presence of his library and the authority of Harvard to lend power to his words.

Paul went to Cyrus's office and opened the door to find the letter. What he saw *in flagrante delicto* was Cyrus: his back to the door, suit jacket on, pants around his feet, his pale white ass pushing forward toward his desk as he was "doing" some young woman. Her feet, with shoes still on, were high in the air. She had her butt on the edge of the desk and her legs wrapped around his body. His hands were on her breasts, beneath the thin, transparent dress fabric, and he was thrusting hard. Her eyes were closed and long neatly combed dark brown hair fell behind her as she lifted her jaw—a smooth, pale, youthfully taut face, bright-lipsticked mouth parted halfway in a smile between pleasure and a painful grimace.

"Fuck me," she said. "Yes, fuck me. Fuck me, Cyrus." Like in porno movies, there didn't seem much conviction in her tone.

Paul didn't stay to look further. From what he could make out of the young woman's face in the moonlight coming through large office windows, she was a grad student of Cyrus's whom Paul had seen once, with a name he'd forgotten . . .

After extinguishing his last cigarette in the auditorium of the Worland Institute, Paul looked around to make sure he'd left no trace of his smoking and he spritzed a little Light Fresh Scent into the air.

Did Paul ever expect to be kidnapped? No. The key to a kidnapping, of course, is that it should be involuntary. Otherwise, it's a scam. Yet in some weird way, he wasn't as surprised as you might think when the event happened. Along with the calm of working at the Worland Institute, part of what he liked about being a security guard was the feeling at some unknown time an adventure would befall him. He'd taken the job knowing explicitly it was unsafe. Although he knew he was hiding from the world at Worland, he wasn't like some literary janitor working the night shift cleaning toilets just to pay the bills. There was a part of him—as he made the rounds and watched James Brown chasing his tail in his tank—that precisely hoped something exciting would happen; a burglary, for example, where he might be the hero capturing the criminal. Or maybe he would just watch the criminal, too afraid to make an actual bust, relying instead on calling in extra cop support before the criminal could be apprehended. Or maybe someone, some French industrial spy, for example, or the CIA or some other govt. agency would find a reason to come into the Worland Institute to find out the secret goings-on of the solipsistic place. It's not as if there was a lack of research with value at the institute for all sorts of "evildoers." One of the scientists had stopped a particle of light from moving, stone-cold dead. Another was splitting subatoms. It was certainly possible future energy, new fuel-cell technology, or the seeds of a new bomb were in the process of being discovered. The desire to break into the building could come from many, many sources. And the only reason the lab was protected, really, was because the institute was so incognito—without even a sign on the outside of the structure—that few knew enough to consider the building a place of significance. The Worland Institute was something far different from what the mundane outside of the building made it seem.

The attack began with music, loud, full of trumpets, full of trombones, flutes, and cascading snare drums. "Hail to the Chief"—that old chestnut escorting every president as he walks down the red carpet doing his best to look like a commander in chief (bordered by those dopey, thick, iron-necked Marines) next to every Tom, Dick, and Harry leader of the world who will support the good ol' U.S. of A.—blared through hundreds of speakers to every cranny of the institute. The sound system had been set up in the 50s to give public service warnings, when everyone feared Commie attacks. The music was the summa of all "Hail to the Chiefs." It was simply spectacular, like fireworks going off, as if the Pope and the leader of China and the top Russky and even the crown prince of Saudi Arabia (who had all of the real goodies these days) had all come and bowed at once to the greatness of America.

Poor Delray. He was toast first. The kidnappers came straight through the front door. (Why does everyone think an intruder is always going to come from the roof or someplace exotic?) Of course it would be nice, for dramatic effect, if they did. But these guys just popped the front door open, smashed all the metal detectors, and before Delray could even think of using his gun—which he'd barely ever fired, except when visiting some friends in the ghettos of Kingston—he was hog-tied like in a Western movie.

Paul was casually doing his rounds with L.B. when the attack began, swapping stories, using an electronic wand to check in to each of the various labs. (It was an odd quirk of inefficiency that although he had to check in to each lab over the course of the night, there was no time limit for his movements. Hence, he could take four-hour smoking breaks on the roof. He theorized the gizmo that monitored him must have been designed and built in Puerto Vallarta.)

As the music clicked on, Paul figured Delray must be going crazy studying for his first tests of the semester. *Maybe he's trying to block out his cousin Tiffany?* he thought. Something must have sent him over the edge. The only place to make an announcement or play music was in the central control booth, and if the music was meant to be distracting, it was working.

Paul had just reached Dr. Wurstheimer's lab when the music came on, and James Brown—the fish—was making the strangest movement listening to "Hail to the Chief." It's not that he was dead. That was clear because his mouth was still twitching, gulping for air, but the King of Funk had gone straight up, vertical, as if the rhythm of "Hail to the Chief" had overwhelmed his programmed funk-response mechanism system.

Are there fish earplugs? Paul wondered. The music pointed out the problem with attempting to shut out the outside world entirely. Because if such a sound as "Hail to the Chief" could make its way into a place as isolated as the Worland Institute, then no place was safe. And if a fish like James Brown was trained to experience only one kind of music, then when another form of music intruded, the whole peace and calm and intuition process and knowledge the fish had developed were worthless. So what was the implication for himself, Paul thought, since he'd escaped to the institute after failing to get tenure?

"Hold on a sec," Paul said to L.B., "wait here, and I'll go see what's up with Delray." But L.B. refused. The two walked, hands over ears, out of Dr. Wurstheimer's lab along the second-floor walkway over the Japanese garden. Paul looked for Delray. He couldn't wait to get the music off. The only good thing was all the scientists were gone for some reason this evening. *What nobody knows about isn't a problem,* he thought. Once Delray turned the music off, everything would be all right—assuming James Brown wasn't dead.

The five men attacking Paul had code names. One was called The Worm Tickler, another Never Too Many Flowers, a third The Honorable Chipmunk, the fourth Cedar Tree (C.T. for short), and the last, the designated "violent man" in the movie and media material, was named Bark (like bark on a tree). Bark was a very dark, black man, who strived throughout to maintain an appropriate scowl (it was a role he'd been told in acting school all black men should be prepared to perform). The five kidnappers were dressed in stretch-tight green leotards, leafs sewn on for camouflage, and the bodysuits covered everything except their faces. The men ran with rope and equipment around their shoulders for rappelling and carried, attached to heavy-duty nylon belts: plastic handcuffs (made from recyclable material), small Maglite flashlights, avalanche security flares, pouches with all-natural PowerBar snacks, and the requisite (regrettably inorganic) lights and cameras to complete the shoot at hand.

The reason some of the equipment was regrettably inorganic was because The Honorable Chipmunk, who was directing the production fresh out of NYU film school, believed it was essential to have authenticity. "You don't think Cecil B. DeMille used faux stone tablets when he made *The Ten Commandments,* do you?" he told The Worm Tickler when they were buying equipment to make the movie and advertisements. "No way man, anything ON-SCREEN has got to be real. Which is why we're going to shoot real film. None of that video crap. I told Cyrus he either pays for a real production, with real high quality, and the best version of Final Cut Pro software for editing, or I'm out of the project."

The camera shot for the opening sequence of scene 2 (the capture and kidnapping of Paul) was taken from below. The lead camera was set in the Japanese garden, pointing toward the balcony where Paul and L.B. hurried toward the elevator to go find Delray. The Honorable C had to decide quickly where to take the shot from; he knew a bit about the layout of the institute, but not much since there was little in the way of public records. But he knew there was a central atrium with a balcony, and so he sent the four kidnappers up to a place high enough to unfurl their sign and then rappel down to Paul.

The guys up top were good. Flower and Worm rushed out of the elevator—a stainless steel, fluorescent interior that shined unnaturally like the inside of a bank—and black commando hats stretched over their faces so only their eyes could be seen. They ran with Uzis, carefully covering each other, each protected at all times by his brother, until they reached the edge of the highest balcony. The Honorable C motioned with one hand, as he zoomed in doing camera work with the other, and squinted through the lens while the two men let fly a neatly designed banner that announced GREENPLANET.COM had come to spark global change.

From where Paul ran on the second-floor balcony to get Delray, he couldn't see the banner yet, but he could see The Honorable C with his camera setup below, and he yelled, "You! Hey you! Yeah, you. What the fuck do you think you're doing?" The strength of his voice surprised Paul. He wasn't the kind of person to yell at anyone before understanding what was up. But with the loud music, and the sudden intruder—who looked harmless enough with his camera yet who was still an intruder—he felt his animalistic side, which so rarely came forward, burst out.

And that was exactly the look The Honorable C had been hoping for. He cut away from the banner above and zoomed in on Paul's face. The look of fear, of anger and savagery, was perfect. He pointed a spotlight at Paul, and the light made it nearly impossible for Paul to see down into the atrium. The bright rays, like a police car searchlight, hit directly into his eyes, burning his retinas.

Flower and Worm hitched their ropes to the balustrade quickly, tested them for weight, and then leaned off the top balcony into the atrium, ready to drop further at the Honorable C's command.

"Give me your gun," L.B. said to Paul.

Paul fumbled, trying to get the damn thing out.

"Come on. Faster," L.B. said.

"I'm trying. I'm trying."

But next thing Paul knew, it was too late. Flower, Worm, Bark, and C.T. rappelled down in one smooth, long shot. The Honorable

C followed them as they flew through the air like cascading water. "Hail to the Chief" had been replaced now with some kind of hip-hop that was giving the guys extra energy for their rappelling moves. The Honorable C told his crew before not to worry about the sound during the invasion. He would overlay the crying of whales in the deep ocean wilderness on the final cut. "Hail to the Chief" was simply to announce to the world a great new director was in the process of being born—like the music in Coppola's *Apocalypse Now* as the swarm of helicopters maneuvered over the wasteland of Vietnam. The music was to pump them up, to get into the groove.

By the time Paul got his gun out of his holster, L.B. was leaning out over the balcony yelling at the Honorable C, "Hey man. Let's be reasonable, no?" A pair of army boots kicked L.B. in the face, and he stumbled backward. It was Bark kicking. This was even better than what The Honorable C had hoped for. It was black-on-black violence. The best kind. He'd thought only Paul would be present, but between the footage of Delray getting his ass tied up in the central control booth (scene 1) and now L.B. getting it in the face from Bark, he had everything he needed to convince the world these kidnappers meant business.

L.B. could never have been subdued so quickly without Mace. He tore at his face, his eyes burning, as he fell to the ground . . .

The thing about Bark was that he wasn't a natural at committing violence. He had grown up in a nice, middle-class neighborhood, and his mom always took him to church on Sundays. Yet The Honorable C had insisted he practice and get his role down to be the lead kidnapper. Now that he'd conked out L.B., he turned his full force to Paul.

"Don't move, or I'll shoot," said Paul.

Bark hesitated.

"Don't worry about him," The Honorable C yelled up. "He'll never shoot. It's too scary if you've never done it before. Cyrus tells me he's harmless."

Worm and Flower, two actors looking to be stuntmen some day, told Bark to hurry it up. "Come on," said Flower. "Nigger, do your Nigger Pow, or whitey's gonna have to take over." Flower hung in the air from his rope, two stories above the camera below, and shouted down to The Honorable C, "I told you environmental terrorists shouldn't be led by a black dude. Who's ever heard of a black environmentalist?"

"Just keep your eye on the 'victim,'" The Honorable C said.

And true enough, Paul never pulled the trigger. But was it because he was scared? Because he didn't have the guts? Or was it because he couldn't believe what he thought he had heard, that Cyrus had something to do with the whole thing. What did they mean when they said Cyrus told them he was "harmless"? What did he have to do with any of this?

In preparation for the attack, Bark had practiced moving stealthily through the forests of New England, trying to get the slinking gait of a practiced environmental terrorist moving like a man connected to the deepest roots of the ways of nature. But The Honorable C had told him he would also have to subdue Paul, and for this he reverted back to his acting class, when he had pretended once, with a teacher who believed in Stanislavsky, to be Bruce Lee. So the Nigger Pow looked more like a Karate Kick than any kind of slugged black fist.

"Good. Good," the Honorable C shouted from below. "But don't hurt him yet too badly. We're gonna take a break and get some close-ups of all the horrible things they're doing in this institute."

The rest of the footage included shots of particle accelerators and other nefarious equipment. The highlight came with an interview of Paul in Dr. Wurstheimer's lab.

A close-up of Paul revealed two ingrown holes in his left ear where he'd had earrings when he was playing with I.C.N. The shot was meant to prove the victim was who they claimed he was. (Paul told them he didn't otherwise have any birthmarks on his body that were identifiable.) The camera pulled out from his ear to show his entire head against the aquarium, where James Brown was seen struggling for breath next to him, still unrecuperated from the musical assault.

A boom mic was on now for the interview, and the music was turned off in the building. The Honorable C set up especially bright lights in Dr. Wurstheimer's lab, so Paul looked like he was in a police lineup, dazed and unable to see all the men who were looking at him. His hands were handcuffed behind and he sat in a chair with his feet tied, the cool glass of the aquarium the only thing that gave him any comfort.

Just cooperate, Paul thought. *If you cooperate, they won't hurt L.B. anymore and they'll leave Delray alone.* That was the way to do it, wasn't it? To distract them with himself so they would leave the others OK.

The interrogation questions were asked by the Honorable C, off-camera. Bark was left on-camera to point a gun at Paul. "Just leave me alone," Paul begged. "Just please, leave me alone." Paul sweated.

The Honorable C began the interview: "Isn't it true you torture animals in this place?" The camera zoomed in on James Brown. "Isn't it true there are nuclear experiments in this place that could lead to the destruction of humanity?" The camera zoomed in on Paul's eyes, which were now teary.

"Listen, I don't know what you're talking about," Paul said. "I don't have anything to do with this—" He tried to look around Dr. Wurstheimer's lab, but his movement was limited by the rope around his chest, strapped to the chair, and by the sharp, sturdy fingers Bark kept pressing into his neck.

"So do you deny the presence of animal research in this building?"

"No," Paul said. "But James Brown is just a fish."

"And what about the monkey research on the fourth floor? Or all the research in this place that leads to global warming?"

"As far as I understand," said Paul, "they're working to end global warming here by finding alternative fuel sources."

"As far as you understand . . ." Bark mocked, his voice falling into some kind of Nazi accent. The accent came to him unexpectedly, from some other recess of his acting-school training. "When all else fails," his acting coach had told him once, "a well-done Nazi accent will always provide certainty a character is truly evil and will convince an audience, even while providing some comic relief."

But Bark didn't have the chance to go fully into this new voice because an alarm went off suddenly in the building.

"What the fuck is going on here?" The Honorable C said. "Worm, I thought you told me you had Delray turn off all the alarms first."

"I did," said Worm.

"Flower, go check what's happening in the front booth."

And it seemed, when Flower got there, Delray had somehow worked his way up from the floor—though he was completely tied with ropes and gagged—and punched the alarm system.

Flower kicked Delray and turned the alarm off. But it was clear it was too late to stay now. "Let's get the fuck out of here," The Honorable C shouted. "Good work everyone. It's a wrap."

Now that the police could be coming, they went up to the roof and rappelled down the back of the building, where no one would be looking. They lowered Paul's body quickly, his head banging occasionally against a brick wall. Paul could hear the sound of the commuter train running over the Charles River across the Longfellow Bridge, and for the first time it was no longer comforting; it sounded like he was attached to the tracks.

CHAPTER 9

Like a good ecoterrorist in his camp, The Honorable C—real name Chuck—sat on a dirt pile cross-legged, with an M16 on his lap, sporting a Che Guevara green beret and camouflage fatigues as he spoke into the camera. His chin pointed up as he grasped for words of inspiration to bestow on his followers. "The history of the world," he paused, reflecting upon that long history, face contorted now in sadness and revenge, "is one big systematic raping of the earth by us humans. Do we intend to fuck the earth up so badly? Not necessarily. But the capitalist system we've attached ourselves to—that we tacitly support each and every time we go to the supermarket—is the rapist. Have you ever truly listened to the jackhammers of construction men as they build the foundation of a building? Have you ever really listened to it as they plunge their shovels into the bedrock of the earth? Let me tell you, you can hear the earth cry. Thousands—no, millions—of years of the evolution of the earth are destroyed all at once. It's not just the tree on the surface that's uprooted, but the whole fucking bedrock."

The entire catechism, on-camera of course, was taking place in a field that had once been a garbage dump and that was now covered with loose, brown dirt rising and falling in the most unnatural man-made bulldozed hillocks. Weeds and brambles grew on the plowed-over dirt, in haphazard clumps like tufts of chemotherapied hair, wherever a few seeds had managed to attach. The cables of a high-tension power line ran over the dirt, cutting a path from tower to tower in a linear buzzing shot that spread a halo of radiation below the towers, killing the few remnants of dying vegetation further.

For the past week or so, the ecoterrorist kidnappers had kept Paul in this camp by day, where they slept in camouflaged tepees near highway 2. Paul had no idea where he was because he was always blindfolded whenever they took him somewhere. What he knew was that he was too far from anyone to be seen or heard. On the first night, when they brought him to the camp—just as they were about to shove him into a tepee—he shouted as loud as he could, begging for help. But no answer came except the faint roar of traffic in the distance.

Yet in this scar of the earth, where the camp lay and where he cried out to any human who might listen, he was close to the "nature" Americans across the country and people around the world admired. The blotted piece of carved-up dirt was less than a mile from Walden Pond. It wasn't far from the parking lot where thousands of tourists flocked to pay the entrance fee to a Ranger Ricky to park in the crowded lot before heading past a reconstructed cabin that Henry David Thoreau was supposed to have lived in. The real cabin was on the other side of the lake, where only the foundation remained—left in a small pile of rocks, curtained off with a metal chain to protect the hallowed ground. Paul had seen the reconstructed cabin by the parking lot before. When he saw it, he'd looked in admiration, believing it to be the real thing. He found it comforting a man could live so sparely in his tiny cabin, which couldn't have been much bigger than eight feet by ten. Yes, he knew Thoreau wasn't as independent as he claimed in his book *Walden* (after all, Thoreau left his bean patch regularly to eat at his mother's house a couple of miles away in Concord). Still, the cabin had impressed him because it was a place where such genius of writing had been inspired. The very sparseness of the cabin—a bed, simple iron stove, and straw-backed chair—implied the discipline of Thoreau's writing. It wasn't the simplicity of an antimaterialistic life that impressed Paul, it was the beauty of Thoreau's language and the rigor as he churned out his book and converted an entire nation into believers that beauty should be revered, that the earth was God's temple, and that man should live unshackled from the dirt and poverty of his own constructions, free in his human spirit. Looking at Thoreau's cabin, he felt he was seeing the original soul that had tried to heal his nation's soul. When he found out later—as he walked around Walden—that the cabin by the parking lot was *not* Thoreau's real cabin, he was disappointed for sure. But did it really matter if everyone failed to see his real home? In a way, all that was irrelevant, he'd thought, as long as people were inspired when they saw the sparse, reconstructed cabin. The idea of living simply, contemplatively, in harmony with nature in that cabin was enough, even if Thoreau had never quite been there. It was an ideal to strive toward, Paul had thought. And in some ways, as he looked at the real ruins of the cabin on the other side of the lake later, he thought it was appropriate the remnants of the real cabin were hidden. If left next to the parking lot, they might be stolen, kicked, graffitied, taken as souvenirs, whatever.

And yet, that day when he'd gone to Walden with Zoe, she'd told him, "I think it's disgusting they pretend it's his cabin when it's not.

It's like some kind of embalmment." The words lingered in his ears as he walked through the parking lot by the cabin, hearing cars pulling in and out at the peak of summer as parents tried to control their kids by telling them they'd have to be good if they wanted ice cream from the truck at the end of the lot.

Near to Walden, then, Paul was close to Nature, but he didn't know it in the ecoterrorist training camp.

The last week had fallen into a routine that exhausted him, leaving him unable to sleep even when he desperately wanted to. During the day he was forced to stay cooped up in the camouflage tepees. In the evening he was allowed out—always under surveillance and with shackling—to have some dinner, which consisted of either home-made beef jerky or tofu curry over brown rice. After this mundane meal (The Honorable C pointed out it was the end of September, so no fresh spring green vegetables would be eaten by any real ecoterrorists living off the land), Paul was allowed to watch the guys train with crossbows, aiming at target silhouettes of deer, rabbits, bears, and capitalist men and women. Sometimes they filmed their training. Others, they gagged Paul and shot footage of him attempting to spit out the gag. The Honorable C took to spending much of his time on-camera rather than off. "I agree," he'd told Flower one day, "realistically, Bark isn't going to do too well on the authenticity front as head ecoterrorist. So I'll have to change my role from a cameo to chief public educator . . . I don't think this'll be a problem, though. If you look at all the Woody Allen films, he's always on-camera somewhere."

What made Paul so tired, however, wasn't all this training in the camp. It was the regular nighttime excursions. In the first "eco-resistance," which Paul would call an act of sabotage, they drove to the Boston suburb of Medford (a bland part of town attached to one of the exits off I-93, where gas stations and Dunkin' Donuts enliven the overpasses and middle-class Italians think plastic squirrels, Virgin Marys, and cheap wrought-iron trellises are signs of beauty). Paul had no idea where he was on any of the excursions because (as mentioned before) he was always blindfolded. It wasn't until he got to the actual "site of resistance and liberation" that the mask was taken off.

The whole idea for the "liberation activities" had come to The Honorable C during his pre–film and kidnapping advertisement campaign research. He'd clicked on a few ecoterrorist Web sites that explained how to spike redwoods in California to save the giant masters from the rabid chain saws of modern-day woodsmen. Now that oxen and axes were no longer the tools of the trade for the new Paul Bunyans; now that they moved into the forests with machines that looked like rocket launchers and that grabbed the trees to haul them away; and now that a large tree could be cut to build the main bar counter for a "Wild West" theme park in New York City, the Web sites explained it was time to fight back. Less than one-tenth of 1 percent of the wild forest—or old growth—was left. All that could be found anywhere else was the puny residue of mighty giants that were replanted occasionally. What we were left with, the Web sites said, were the ghostly remnants of a once-diverse forest. If you were a flying squirrel or a spotted owl, good luck. Your days were numbered. As the giant trees were cut, the whole forest ecosystem was dying. From the death of small things— spiders that once grew in webs that had enmeshed the branches of cedar trees and redwoods—larger things died. Big insects could no longer feed off the small moths that made their nests in the bark. Birds, in turn, couldn't eat the larger insects. And eventually, animals at the top of the food chain, such as spotted owls and mountain lions, could be sighted almost nowhere except feeding off the garbage dumps of those who had built their new mansion developments on the edge of our national forests.

On some of the Web sites there were detailed plans for how to build a pipe bomb, how to pour the proper amount of sugar into the gas tank of a bulldozer, or how to make a letter bomb to send to an intransigent congressman or to an unscrupulous corporate chemist. But if you were unable to make such violent contributions to the future generations of the natural world—and to the very survival of humankind—or unfor- tunate enough to live in one of those already uninhabitable zones on the East Coast, you could take matters into your own hands in a more local form of sabotage.

And so, within the first two days of being kidnapped, Paul was pushed into an old forest green VW bus, along with the rest of the ecoterrorist film crew, and taken blindfolded to the Sav-Mor storage facility. It took them a while to find the place. Although Paul couldn't see anything as the van drove around and around, he could hear:

"How could you have fucked up so much getting the map off MapQuest?" The Honorable C said to C.T.

"What are you talking about?" said C.T. "I typed in the address just as you gave it to me. It's not my fault."

"Well then, whose is it?" Bark said, putting on his trademark growl. He was doing his best to get into the good graces of The Honorable C again so he could get more on-camera time.

Should I resist, try to make a break for it now? Paul thought. Ever since his kidnapping, he'd been trying to think of the best way to get out of his situation unharmed. The first 48 hours, which he could only guess at because he had no access to a watch—as far as he could reason in his initial state of shock, shackled by the handcuffs cutting into his flesh because the kidnappers hadn't taken into account his wrists might not be as narrow as those of a trimmer environmentalist—his sense was the best way to stay alive was to be cooperative. Yet, perhaps, it was time to make a break for it now, as he listened to the bickering between C.T. and The Honorable C. Because how competent could these guys really be if they couldn't even find the place they were headed to? Yet mixed with these initial thoughts of bravery were sounds Paul was becoming more attuned to with his eyes covered with the thick blindfold. He could hear the metal clanking of gun against gun in the back of the van and ammunition cartridges in a metal army case. Years ago, he had actually admired these sounds when he went to the gun shows in Iowa, doing his sexual-confidence research. Then, the sound of guns clicking, cartridge slots opening, pieces being oiled, and springs calibrated had filled him with a sense of wonderment at the mastery of gunsmiths and awe at the machines humans had developed that could so accurately send a piece of metal flying faster than sound to its intended target. Although he'd felt no spiritual connection with the gun owners in those shows, he'd understood their love of the machines they carried. But part of owning those guns, he'd understood in Iowa, was that there was a code to using them wisely. Sure, many didn't. But those who told stories about the battles of Iwo Jima, which they read about in history books, or about being at Khe Sanh—who thought the *concept* of America still stood for something even though they had doubts about liberals trying to take the whole goddamn place over, stripping them of their love of country (liberals like the fucking porker

Hillary Clinton, who was just a fascist Commie pig as far as they were concerned)—still believed in some code with those machines. It was as if, despite their twisted brains, they understood the vast power of the tools they had been given.

But what about the nutty, so-called "ecoterrorists" he was with in the back of this van that kept moving here and there, like a rat caught in a maze, toward the Sav-Mor storage facility? Although Paul recognized the sound of the ammo in the back of the VW and could even hear crossbows banging one against the other, which he'd also seen in Iowa, he knew these "ecoterrorists" were ignorant of the code of these machines; and it was as obvious as hell they had nothing to do with real environmentalists. So who the fuck were they? What were they doing with him? And shouldn't he just make a break for it whenever he got to where they were taking him?

Yet, when they finally pulled into the Sav-Mor storage warehouse, slowing from the blind speed Paul had felt once more as they hightailed it on the interstate from the ecoterrorist camp in Concord near Walden to Medford, he felt less certain about whether he should immediately resist.

The Honorable C told Bark to remove Paul's blindfold, and the heavy cloth was taken off. A camera pushed close to Paul's face as he attempted to adjust to the flashes of fluorescent light reflecting off the camera lens. The source of the light was the Sav-Mor sign: white, large, with big red letters lighting up the name of the repository. Sav-Mor! it said. And in smaller letters, in a sweeping cursive worthy of a nun's handwriting, "We treat your important possessions right! At the right price!"

For a sign promising such loving attention, once inside Paul felt he had never seen a lonelier place. The building cried out with abandoned possessions put in a permanent nursing home, not even allowed to die in a garbage dump. The empty hallways with numbered doors receded to focal points like the arteries of the human consumption machine. This was where the residue of weekly shopping went. This was where faux, high-end wood bed frames, made of chewed-up wood-particle scraps—never even cherished once taken out of the bright lights of the shop—sulked in terminal pain. Most of the objects in storage were oddly loved and hated at the same time, Paul thought: loved enough to not be thrown out entirely, hated enough to be forced out of mind. The objects—leftover plastic furniture, bookshelves, toys, beds, and hobby equipment such as photo enlargers that no one used in the digital era—were wedged into three different cubicle sizes. Like meals sold in fast-food chains, there was no small size, only what Sav-Mor called value, extravalue, and supervalue.

There was more than enough time to look at the place as The Honorable C walked through the warehouse, searching for the perfect spot to carry out his act of planned revolutionary, on-film, nature-liberating sabotage.

Once he found the right place, The Honorable C moved most of the film equipment onto one of the large dollies stacked in a neat pile at the entrance to the facility. When Paul saw the fifty flatbed dollies, made of heavy-duty plastic with large caster wheels, he found it hard to believe so many customers could be in the facility at once that all the dollies could be needed. But two big drink-vending machines by the entrance confirmed the place must be busy, particularly on weekends. That was when families came, fathers with sons, teaching their boys how to be useful and to be a man by helping to carry heavy objects from the truck to the family storage receptacle. *These storage facilities are more intimate places for us and our possessions than our graves*, Paul thought. *Hidden, but more vital. A place of security, where permanency can be found.* In these places of limbo, there was no death, only row after row of permanent repositories of trust where eternity might be found—a place where sadness and guilt toward the people who had given presents, whose gifts were now being placed out of the house, or toward a possession no longer wanted, could be obliterated softly away.

In this warehouse, which spread wider than a football field, with three floors connected by heavy-duty elevators, The Honorable C decided to make his ecoterrorist mark. Now that they were back to committing violence, he was willing to give Bark more screen time. He handed him a big sledgehammer, and—though it would have been easier to break the padlocks on the units with a wire cutter—Bark dramatically smashed the big locks off the storage doors.

Within such a giant facility this act of terrorism was too small to matter in any way, Paul thought as he watched the entire event, forced to stand next to Bark like a prop. There was no way to beat the storage facility at its game. *There will always be more space in which to place things than any kind of terrorist can ever destroy.* But the effectiveness of breaking open three garage doors was still real, Paul guessed, because for a moment what was destroyed wasn't primarily the objects in the facility but the curtain that *hid* the objects. Walking through the neat corridors what was essential was that an appearance of cleanliness and order should be maintained. Even if everyone knew behind each door there was chaos, the key to the facility was knowing each warehouse was linear, neatly padlocked, well kept up with regular fumigation visits to ensure the death and destruction of any animal intruders. So once the doors of the storage facility were torn open, they left exposed the true chaos of jumbled belongings. They revealed the possessions of a storage locker like a cheap whore's lingerie. After Bark ripped open a few of the storage cubicles and scattered the possessions into the waterproof corridors of the Sav-Mor facility—tossing the objects with abandon as Paul was forced to look on and to be in the camera next to him—the effect was to leave a ruptured zit on the otherwise clean face of the facility.

"Throw some of those things with a little more violence, would you?" The Honorable C said to Bark. "C.T., go in there and help him some . . . OK, one more take." He let the camera roll, and Bark and C.T. lifted an empty sky blue baby pool and tossed it into the air, then let fly a lawn mower and a golf bag full of half-rusted metal clubs.

The trip to Sav-Mor had been only the first of half a dozen such nature liberations.

The sun was setting on this seventh or eighth day of Paul's captivity. He wasn't sure of the day as he watched the bright orange orb sink behind the electric towers. The high-tension wires cut in sharp black lines as night began to fall.

Seated beside Paul—(as mentioned at the beginning of this chapter, since it's time now to return to that scene)—The Honorable C continued his manifesto on the raping of the earth by construction workers. It was a long, rambling speech starting with mention of the Roman copper mines, where Barabbas—the thief spared from the cross by Jesus—was forced as a slave to dig into the earth to build opulence for his masters. Then the speech moved through the era when the British cut the tall forests of New England to use pine trees as single masts for their trade ships. The Honorable C progressed through the oil trade, not only in Texas but the impending move to open the Arctic National Wildlife Refuge to modern drilling.

Before reaching this point in his speech, in which he emphasized ideas by raising his M16 (as if, Paul thought, he had watched the tapes of Osama bin Laden carefully), he peppered famous sayings in from pioneers of the environmental movement. He made references to John Muir, Henry David Thoreau, Ralph Waldo Emerson, Walt Whitman, David Brower and his sea-kayaking hippie son Kenneth Brower. These were the spiritualists who'd saved the Grand Canyon and Yosemite from being turned into dammed bathtubs and who inspired Teddy Roosevelt to set aside most of the other famous national parks the U.S. still had. The Honorable C even threw in a few words from Edward Abbey, a sometimes goofy writer (as in his book *The Monkey Wrench Gang*) who occasionally wrote beautiful prose about Utah and the juniper desert out there but whose writing was overrated in Paul's opinion. Nevertheless, making a reference to Abbey was probably a smart move, he thought. Abbey might be an obscure writer to the general public, but he was a guy who would resonate well with all the environmentalists out there. And no matter what, quoting these guys like scripture was certainly worth The Honorable C's effort. Because if there was one thing Osama bin Laden had taught the world of terrorists, when you're engaged in a dubious and criminal activity, try to find someone who has better ideas than your own to convince the public and your followers (e.g., Muhammad in the Koran).

Paul was planning to add a chapter to his book on failure titled "The Environmental Movement," in which he intended to explore how the right wing had managed to tarnish it to the point it seemed destined to lie, like a heap of dried-out tofu parched in the desert sun.

Dubious extremists or not, he had thought quite a bit, after the death of his brother Andrew, about why terrorists seemed to be so popular in the U.S. even while they were loathed. Call it the Jesse James effect, he'd concluded. Few would ever stand up for a guy like Jesse, and certainly even fewer still for a hideous man like bin Laden, who had shown almost no value for life, but the will of Americans to be untethered and free in the midst of so many daily restrictions—parking signs telling everyone where to park, and laws prohibiting kissing in public or saying on TV any of the profanities that everyone normally said—had led the citizenry, Paul theorized, to love anyone who would dare to play the outlaw. For this very reason, he had begun to feel some comfort being involved in this kidnapping, while at the same time feeling the whole thing was a farce. He was now with the outlaws. He was now with the bad guys, who were free, even if their constant filmmaking made it clear they were something significantly less than real outlaws, and even if he still wanted to escape.

With his hands handcuffed behind his back and a fly buzzing around his head—one of the last insects of fall now that it was cranberry-picking season—Paul noticed The Honorable C straighten his beret before he let fly his list of demands:

"We make, therefore, these four demands. First, we call on Cyrus Berger to deposit ten million dollars—I repeat, TEN MILLION DOLLARS—into the accounts of Greenplanet.com. And if he says he doesn't have the money, remind him he's one of the best lawyers in the country. Second, we demand an immediate cessation to the use of all hydrocarbon fuels. Third, we call for the immediate end of all nuclear power. And fourth, we call for the liberation of all domestic pets, which are used simply for entertainment purposes. Those of you who claim you love your pet so much you would die without it, just look into the mirror and ask yourself: Does your pet know you are looking into a mirror? Is your pet a human being? No, your pet is not, so let your pet free."

It was, in short, Paul thought, a sometimes touching speech full of well-intended rambling and extreme demands and contradictions as sharp as the oddity that while these "ecoterrorists" practiced with their crossbows firing at silhouettes of capitalists, they also fired at images of bears and deer and wild poultry and they wanted to abandon pets. So what was Paul to make of his strange surroundings and of his strange kidnappers since they had taken him from the Worland Institute? Were they filmmakers or environmentalists? Were they environmentalists or survivalists? Did they have any real plan to get the money and other demands they'd just made to the world, or were they simply out for publicity? Trying to size up his captors over the last seven or eight days, he'd felt they were bluffing him; yet even knowing they seemed involved in some odd media project for which he was simply an actor and a prop—a representative hostage—the sharp and consistent pressing of the handcuffs into his wrists reminded him there *was* an element of reality to the whole adventure. He wasn't on some movie set with Jesse James. This wasn't a Western. And if Buffalo Man was right about his prophecy (as he seemed to be in all ways, so far), then perhaps this was just the ludicrous way he was fated to die in the middle of the fourth ring of his life.

So why didn't Paul get tenure? If even I, as the narrator, am a little skeptical about all these unusual events and people whom the character Paul is meeting, well then at least I want to get the whole story. There are too many significant gaps so far. I still don't know what happened between the wedding and this kidnapping. Did Zoe leave Paul completely when he lost his job at B_____ Community College? And whatever happened to The Modern Cyrano, who was supposed to save Paul in some kind of Faustian bargain from losing his job?

Well, the Zoe part I'll have to get to in another chapter, but before I continue with the ecoterrorist kidnapping, I want to go back to the events surrounding Paul when he was fired from his teaching gig. Part of the reason for going back is because, while Paul certainly felt more comfortable when he was at the Worland Institute, he could never give up the feeling he was stabbed, that the entire world was laughing at him—all of the senior professors and even the normally staid Chairman Kominski—chuckling and slapping each other on the back as they walked out of the room where Paul had the final tenure inquisition. They seemed to Paul to be telling each other they were brothers who would back each other up, that their own prospects for financial security were more sound with his elimination, and that there were more scraps for the rest of them as the budget at B_____ Community College was cut further and further.

So here's what happened with The Modern Cyrano:

"OK—it's clear that much of what you lack is focus and discipline," The Modern Cyrano said to Paul. "Take your plan to do a chapter on the history of the failure of the modern environmental movement at the end of your book. That's enough for an entire dissertation. And who wants to learn about so much failure in any case? That's the problem with not only most lovers who fail at romance, but with most academics. They accentuate the negative. They tell sob stories. They focus only on the warts. I mean, how many bald men have I seen on a date patting the top of their head nervously? Or shifting their fat ass in a chair back and forth, wiggling like a kid? Focus. Narrow, and accentuate the positive. The positive might grate against most academic journals, but a narrow topic will do them just fine. And since you're on a tight schedule, I think a bit of gendered Americana will have a better chance of slipping in. I suggest the title 'From Failure to Success: How Jackie Kennedy Raised the Hopes and Spirits of the American Housewife.' That's why we're here—" The Modern Cyrano pointed at the exhibit and sale of Jackie Kennedy memorabilia in the atrium of the Kennedy Library.

This part of the library had a towering glass ceiling that allowed the viewer to believe the soul of John F. Kennedy was rising literally at that very moment into the heavens of Boston. Looking at the glass, Paul felt the building was an experiment in deification. The floor was of black stone, to impart a sense of permanent gravitas. The sky above felt intended not only to give the feeling of a cathedral and of Kennedy's soul zooming into the heavens, but also seemed to fuse Kennedy with the space program he'd pushed so hard for. The only thing keeping the glass walls together was a latticework of triangular metal tubing that looked like the structure of the International Space Station. Both of Paul's brothers enjoyed going to the library: Andrew because it reminded him of his quest to be an astronaut, and Cyrus because, as he'd once pointed out to Paul, he was greatly influenced by Kennedy's book *Profiles in Courage,* in which Kennedy wrote about the strength of leaders who took unpopular yet wise decisions. Kennedy had won a Pulitzer for that book, at a young age, and the fame of it along with the none-too-subtle money from his father propelled him forward.

Only one of the objects at this Jackie Kennedy fundraiser was, in fact, her own prize possession. After all, the library could hardly keep its reputation if it sold all its goodies. So the place was filled, instead, with Jackie Kennedy favorites. On sale in one booth were black Chanel sunglasses. Another sold hair bands wrapping in half-moon halos, from the early 60s. Travel booths promised Jackie Kennedy–style trips to Switzerland and Cambodia if anyone felt like mixing Jackie's good sense of charity with moments of astute art observation at Angkor Wat.

There were Jackie Kennedy sets of china, which Paul noticed were being made in China, and white Nehru coats for sale, for when Jackie made her famous visit to India. There were model kits of the Jacqueline Bouvier mansion—a reminder Jackie had always come from wealth and that she had always been classy. There were crystal perfume spritzer bottles and black and white, long-tailed tuxedos, for those who wanted to dress like Jack when he'd danced and danced with Jackie after his inauguration. There were horse whips and felt riding hats and a few leather bridles with JBK engraved on the bits. And not surprising to Paul, one of the biggest sections was the Cape Cod zone, where seashells with pictures of John-John beachcombing and of Jackie sailing with Jack were for sale. The only major thing missing, Paul thought, was all the conspiracy material. Where were the copies of the Warren Commission Report that Jackie must have cried over? And where were the replicas of her black veil that she had worn as a widow, stoically, in the famous promenade as the body of her husband was carried down Pennsylvania Avenue by a train of horses while John-John and Caroline stood at attention?

The Modern Cyrano moved slowly through all the booths with Paul; they paused at the one true item from the library being auctioned off. Then they stepped outside, and Paul looked at the waves of the Atlantic coming toward them on this bright day in May—white-capped and frothy, a warm wind blowing toward shore as if they were captains at the prow of a ship—the USS Kennedy library behind them.

"So what you're saying," said Paul, "is that if I want to keep my job and get an article published quickly, I should write about redemption and the overcoming of failure?"

"Right," The Modern Cyrano said. "Of course, I'll do all the writing. I happen to be a big Jackie O fan; I just love her clothes. And underneath all her dreaminess, she was really very calculating—a tiger in regal clothing. I often think of her when I write love notes for women. In any case, I'm well up on her past. So no need for you to do any research for the piece. And that's what you're paying me for, isn't it?"

"But I don't think I ever would have come around to wanting to write about Jackie O on my own," said Paul. "She just strikes me as kind of vapid, you know what I mean?"

"Suit yourself," The Modern Cyrano said. "But she's an icon, and America loves her. She's riches to riches. And because of all of Jack's affairs and his young death, she's also rags to riches. She confirms not only the rich suffer, too, but that somewhere up there, someone is living a great life on the Onassis cruise boat. And what really makes her inimitable is that she makes the small feel like they can be someone."

"You mean a kind of how-to person incarnate?" Paul said.

"Exactly," The Modern Cyrano said. "She's someone everyone can aspire to. Americans are much more interested in role models to follow than tales of woe. That's why we leave all those brooding thinkers and novels to the Europeans. *Profiles in Courage* is more our thing. And for good reason, too. It works."

But it didn't work. No one wanted the piece. Part of the problem might have been The Modern Cyrano promised to write the article with Paul's original voice in mind. So the whole thing felt pretty sarcastic—an odd mix that seemed both to laud Jackie O and make fun of her at the same time. And then there was the problem that The Modern Cyrano submitted the article online rather than on paper to the list of journals Paul had given him. Even though the world lived in the digital era, online submissions were out of fashion. When Paul discovered The Modern Cyrano had made this gaffe, he sent the article out again in paper form. But that made him look too eager, sending out twice for consideration. And even if everything had gone right, the truth was all the time had run out before any proper reply.

Did Paul simply leave it at that? No. Even while with The Modern Cyrano at the Kennedy Library, he didn't tell him he was attempting to continue writing his book again, trying to finish a new chapter before the tenure-committee meeting. If he could just get a chapter done on his own that he really believed in, he felt certain a string of chapters would follow. This was his hope as he stayed up late each night in his office at B_____ C.C., attempting to put all his thoughts together. He would begin, and begin again, deleting every phrase. His voice on the page was drier than confetti, more parched than the deepest Sahara. And at these moments, he would feel the weight of the prophecy of Buffalo Man creep up on him, the hopelessness and despair, his fate of an early death, and the fate of all men to fail to ever achieve any real permanence in the grand scheme of things. *Nothing is permanent. Nothing at all,* he would tell himself. His mind kept whirring, imagining the staccato shout of gunfire, the quiet death of men on the battlefield, and he listened to the sobbing of his frozen-up soul.

So when the day of the tenure-committee meeting came, Chairman Kominski pulled Paul aside before the meeting and told him the prospects didn't look good. Paul sat in a concrete bunker they called the faculty meeting room. B_____ C.C. was designed in the 60s to be riot-proof. The students could burn the whole place in anger. Now that it was the new millennium—and people were angry still but quiet in their anger, only willing, Paul thought, to let their frustration simmer and buzz, because they didn't believe any change was possible—there seemed no function to the concrete roof beams of the building.

"We wish you the best in your future endeavors," Chairman Kominski wrapped up the meeting. "And we thank you for all the service you've given the department."

There is a pond, a couple miles from Walden, called Sandy Pond, that most New Englanders and Bostonians don't know about. Some know of it because of a museum of modern art at one end of the lake called the DeCordova. The DeCordova is one of those odd contemporary museums that try to be open to the general public and exclusive at the same time. The exclusivity is evident in the shape of the building. It looks like a castle with round watchtowers and has a high patio on the back that lends the feeling of some kind of rampart, a wall that has to be scaled in order to access the supposed "treasures" of art inside. At the same time, the museum is one of those institutions that want to let you know just how good art is for you. (I call this the vitamin approach to art.) And because art is so good for you, the museum claims to want to bring it to the masses. If you go to the DeCordova museum, then, one of the things you'll find is a side building for public art classes. (Which, of course, are too expensive for most students who really need art outreach. And how is the public, other than the rich who live in Concord and Lincoln, supposed to get all the way out to the museum for these regular art classes, in any case?) There's a gift shop in the same side building to remind you that you, too, can own art. Art is accessible. Art is fun. Art is bright-colored creations you can buy for around $200, or even less, in the shop. Some of this "art" is made in the classes by students; the other by local artists not famous enough to sell for very much. What is unstated in the gift shop is that all the art is fairly crappy. Because if it were any good, everyone in the shop knows they wouldn't be able to afford it. The gift shop is to let you know art is accessible and available but not available at the same time. The real art is in the museum, locked up.

The grounds of the DeCordova reveal the same tension. The museum sits on top of a hill, and all along the hill there are statues that are modern for the public to walk through, which means first and foremost the statues are large and that most do not have a figurative form. Many are towering Pisas made of thrown-out garbage, bright-orange plastic plates. Or some take normally small objects, like a baby pacifier, and make them big. One of the central ideas behind bad modern art is that if you take something small and make it huge, then it must be good. Sometimes this works, don't get me wrong. But usually it looks like you're staring at a giant pacifier.

The grounds of the museum are therefore public but still private. Everyone can walk around the statues, even for free, without paying admission into the building, but without studying a lot of art, most people can't enjoy what they're looking at. They have no idea what traditions are being broken. For those who've had the time and fortune to travel to places like Italy to see Michelangelo's statues, they can understand how this art is a response to the traps and strengths of figurative art.

All this is a long-winded way of bringing us to Sandy Pond, which I was once told by a very interesting coworker—who loved to champion the rights of smokers—is the lake where Thoreau really liked to hang out more than at Walden.

And it was to this pond that Paul was now headed.

Late on a beautiful Indian-summer night, when the air was blowing hot then slightly cool through the trees and over the statues, a VW bus pulled into the entrance. The hill up to the museum parking lot was steep, curving sharply to the right, and The Honorable C almost stalled, failing to get down quickly enough to a low gear. The engine made a grinding noise; the old bus halted and then lurched forward suddenly as the new, low gear finally connected. One of the tires went off the road and the bus nearly struck a statue of the head of the Buddha (twelve feet tall, made of rusted steel). If anyone else had been driving, The Honorable C would have chewed him out, but this was a trip with just The Honorable C and Paul.

The truth was, the Honorable C was getting pretty tired of being with his entire cast and crew all the time. It was exhausting to have to always bark out orders to Bark. It wasn't easy being an auteur and the head of a large media campaign. The smell of garbage, or the imagined smell of it beneath their ecoterrorist camp, was also starting to get to him. What he needed was some R & R; and since Paul seemed smarter than the rest of the cast, and a pretty mellow guy who so far hadn't tried to escape—minus some initial howling when they first got to the camp—The Honorable C decided it was time for a one-on-one walk in the woods with him.

The Honorable C parked at the end of the lot at the base of the DeCordova museum, by the edge of the woods, and let Paul out. Paul's legs were stiff as he stood on the pavement. He still hadn't become used to the packed dirt and cramped tepee of the ecoterrorist camp. The Honorable C took Paul's blindfold off and left his handcuffs on and walked to the edge of the lot, where the forest began, and pulled out a hiking map. When he flashed his Maglite on the map, Paul saw it was a guide to the various paths around the lake. At the top it said "DeCordova Museum—Sandy Pond."

So here I am, Paul thought. For the first time in over a week, he knew his exact location, and it was strange how important it felt to be able to know his position on a map. To see the words of a place he recognized meant he wasn't obliterated. He was still within the bounds of familiar territory. He could still make a break for it, knowing generally where he was in relation to his home. A map was more than a map; it wasn't merely a guide to other destinations and a marking of territory, it was a reminder how close or far a person was from everyone and everything they loved. Looking at it, even briefly, he knew how far he was from Zoe and Ned and L.B. The chance to run away from this odd kidnapping was clear to him, and his spirits lifted as The Honorable C told him he should walk in front, entering the dark forest that would take him further from the museum which he knew could bring him safety. Because certainly there must be a guard to protect all the art in the museum. *Right?* So all he had to do was somehow overcome The Honorable C on their walk and then run back to the museum. Or, since he'd walked on the paths with Zoe a few times before—when she got it into her head it was time to go out of Boston to visit the country to see horses, beauty, and the houses of rich people and to fantasize about what it would be like to live in the country—he knew there were houses not more than a half mile away that he could run to. These were the homes of occasional joggers, with their golden retrievers, who he had seen whenever he'd walked around Sandy Pond with Zoe. And there was another reason he knew the pond. For a while, Zoe had considered the DeCordova a good wedding place for them, until she decided there was nothing really classy about being married next to statues of balls made of jumbled wire. The idea of an avant-garde wedding had appealed to Zoe, at first, as something out of the ordinary, but in the end, she realized she wanted what she envisioned as a more "romantic" wedding in a traditional wedding space.

The day of their wedding felt far behind now, much further than Paul could have imagined, so quickly. *How does love fall apart so fast?* He still had hopes he and Zoe could patch things up, but ever since he lost his job at B_____ Community College, he'd felt Zoe's only contact with him was giving him advice. "Why can't you finish your book, in any case, and apply for some other teaching job?" she'd tell him. Or, "It's time for you to get your shit together Paul. You've been coasting. You've been using Buffalo Man's prophecy as some kind of crutch for doing nothing. But I simply don't think he has that kind of real predictive power. You know what I mean? I mean—the spa was great—their whole health regimen was great. But that was a different era, during the boom times, when we all thought Internet money grew on trees. Now we know better. Hype is hype, and I think he just hyped you up. Like you said, he was probably just trying to get your money."

Paul hoped, and assumed, Zoe was looking for him all the time he'd been kidnapped. A couple of weeks before he was taken from Worland, she'd told Paul in the middle of the night to move out from their apartment and said that time apart might do him good for focusing his mind. "Maybe if you fear you'll really lose me, then you'll get your act together," she'd told him. And so he'd spent the two weeks before his kidnapping sleeping on Ned's couch in Somerville. It was a scratchy old couch that Ned had kept for years after he'd inherited it from some underground-music lover. The couch should have been incentive enough, Paul thought, to begin writing his book again and searching for a new teaching job. But instead, he found himself lying on Ned's couch in the afternoons, trying to sleep as sunlight came through the dirty windows, until it was time to suit up in his security outfit to head to Worland. What does a thirty-five-year-old (by this time, at the end of summer, he had hit the big 3-5) who's failed in a rock band and failed at plagiarizing, and who finds it impossible to write but who likes to think of himself as a teacher—but who doesn't really want to teach—and who has two famous brothers, one who's dead and another who's insulting, do to regain his sense of self-worth and pride?

What he does is he lies, Paul thought. He lies and he lies and he lies. For this reason, he hadn't even told L.B.—that night of the kidnapping—that things had gotten so bad with Zoe she had kicked him out of the house. Instead, he told himself things would work their way out, somehow; that in talking to Dr. Wurstheimer, something would eventually click; that by watching the white goldfish James Brown, something—some kind of answer to his state of paralysis—would be found. He envied that fish, because James Brown knew exactly what he was supposed to do. He was constantly trained and told precisely what to do. If only we could all be given some kind of Pavlovian training for life, he'd thought as he'd looked at the fish. Someone to ring the bell for us and tell us how to proceed.

But there was no bell. Only the random stream of events that came at him from the left and right, from out of nowhere, pushing at him in his depressed slumber.

The Honorable C told Paul to walk into the dark forest, which opened up like a crypt by the side of the DeCordova parking lot, and Paul obeyed.

If he could howl now, howl out in anguish, howl out without cynicism, Paul felt he would howl. The usual humor that protected him from sadness wasn't working now as he walked through the woods with The Honorable C. It wasn't the talk between them that made him want to howl. Some of their conversation had been OK. They hadn't talked too much at first as they made their way down a hill from the parking lot. In those first few minutes in the woods, Paul stumbled on the exposed roots and uneven rocks of the path. It was a night with a clear sky, and with plenty of stars, all of which might have promised some kind of freedom, a signal to follow like a slave running away to the North on the Underground Railroad, guided by the North Star and the moss on the backs of trees. It must have been much scarier for those slaves, however, than usually imagined, much less of a wondrous bound for freedom, Paul could tell, because when you are under a canopy of trees, you cannot really see the stars. The slipperiness of the path was made even slicker by the first dead leaves of the fall. The leaves hadn't decomposed yet, so they retained a waxy feeling under his feet. *The first leaves are in limbo,* Paul thought, *as I'm in limbo tonight.* Still, stumbling on the dirt and rocks and leaves woke him up like a traveler late at night who slaps his own face. This was his chance to take his freedom into his hands, to outwit fate. If he could escape from The Honorable C and from the kidnappers unharmed, then wouldn't this be, potentially, some kind of exorcism of the curse Buffalo Man had given him? If nothing else, he would have his liberty back, and a renewed sense that liberty was worth something.

How fast can I really run, though? Paul wondered, feeling the weight of his tummy. Even with the limited meals of tofu and beef jerky, he was still soft around the middle. A week of kidnapping wouldn't change that, and since he was forced to spend most of his day in the tepee with the others, watching them play cards, he was also soft and stiff.

Eventually, after they made it down to the lake, which the path followed the rest of the way, he worried less about whether he could run faster than The Honorable C. He focused on the wide openness of the lake, a flat mirror that reflected a placid surface up to the shining stars and the moon. The only sound at first other than the wind blowing through the trees was an occasional small animal poking through the dirt. Paul would hear a rustling; the animals were unidentifiable. The ways of nature seemed as impenetrable as the ways of man. Hidden foragers, hidden journeys seemed to preoccupy both, only hinted at by the faint sounds of people and animals working. But then, in the distance and on the smooth surface of the lake, coming from out of nowhere suddenly, he heard a group of honking Canada geese. Once he arrived at the edge of the water, he saw there were hundreds of geese taking off and landing in the calm of the night. It wasn't easy for them to take off or land. In both directions they came and went, and they did their work with a natural grace, but it wasn't easy. The birds had to flap and flap to go up and push the air and water behind them, running at full speed, running on faith as fast as they could power themselves before they were able to finally lift up, only to have to flap and flap more, to keep flapping for miles until they could eventually reach a warmer climate in the south for the winter. Likewise, the landings. The animals twisted to the right and left, honking to attempt to clear some landing area, trying not to hit any of the other birds that wanted simply to be comfortable on the lake; and even when the geese touched down, they had to brake with all their might to avoid flipping head over heels.

After The Honorable C and Paul walked halfway around the lake, The Honorable C told Paul to cut left, down a different path that was darker than the lake, through some bushes that felt like nettles because they scraped along Paul's arms. Eventually they curved back to a small old brick building along the lake. The hut was an abandoned place for water pumps for the town of Lincoln. The lake still served as the primary water source for the town, and so mixed with trees of "beauty" at the pond, there were regular metal signs tacked onto the trees that warned swimming in the lake was forbidden to protect the water source. Here and there metal chain-link fences kept joggers and walkers on the paths through the woods. Although the place looked natural, it was no longer really so, Paul thought. It was no wonder the geese made so much noise as they landed and took off. They faced a constant battle not only against the forces of gravity but against the people who would destroy their few remaining watering holes.

The cabin, which no longer had pumps, had become a shelter for occasional beer drinkers who came to the lake. The concrete floor was broken into cracked chunks; beer bottles littered it, and the interior smelled of urine.

The Honorable C looked into the hut to see if it was a place they could hang out, but when he smelled the urine, he told Paul to move forward to a concrete ledge carved out of the woods that overlooked the lake.

So why don't I just get behind and push him off the concrete into the water? Paul thought. Yet could he really endanger The Honorable C's life that way? This was no ordinary kidnapping. Minus the pain of his hand-cuffed wrists, it was clear there wasn't any real danger to him—other than the potential of an accident with all the weapons of his captors.

It was time to find out what this whole scheme was about. Until now, Paul had chosen only to observe and not to ask too many questions for fear he might set off Bark or one of the other kidnappers.

"Can I ask you a question?" Paul said, and he sat on the edge of the concrete facing the lake Thoreau had once liked to bathe in, where bathing was no longer permitted. "Is this all just about the money? To try to squeeze Cyrus out of some money during his campaign? Because I don't think he'll give it to you." He thought maybe if he could be honest with The Honorable C, this would convince him the kidnapping had to end and that it was futile. This was his best way of trying to escape, he felt. Not to run and to outfight The Honorable C, because there was little chance he could do so handcuffed and in his generally out-of-shape state, but rather to convince him the only way out of this whole experience—whatever it was—was simply to let him go free with a promise there would be no retribution, no attempt on Paul's part to press charges. A quid pro quo: you let me go, I let you go. It's what the geese had been telling him, he felt—make way for each other taking off and landing.

"I'm amazed," The Honorable C said, "at how long you've lasted before asking this. But you've been even more compliant than Cyrus told me to expect."

"You know Cyrus?"

"He told me I was supposed to clue you in a long time ago so you wouldn't get too nervous, but for the sake of the entire documentary, I felt the need to hold off."

"What does Cyrus care about a documentary of me hanging out with what—to be honest—doesn't really seem like a bunch of real terrorists?"

"He doesn't. Of course he doesn't care about the documentary part of this all. He doesn't even know I'm *making* a documentary. All he knows is we've arranged for you to be kidnapped by some ecoterrorists and we've provided him with video footage of a badass black dude taking you. And so far it all seems to be working."

"What do you mean?"

"Well, when Cyrus's polls started sinking because everyone thought he was too much of a lefty who was going to treat black people and homosexuals semidecently, he realized he'd have to do something to bring in votes from the right. He knew he was going to have to shift his image. That's when he came to me, and I promised him a successful media campaign that would bring him victory."

"So I'm just a tool for his fucking victory?"

"No, not a tool—a victim of rampant black crime and the excesses of terrorists and the environmental movement in general. The environmental movement is trying to extort Cyrus. They're demanding TEN fucking million dollars, which is a lot of cash for a movement with as wimpy a name as Greenplanet.com. I mean, these guys aren't even an established movement like Greenpeace. So here they are, not only asking for TEN million dollars, and making outrageous claims for the end of hydrocarbon use, but they have YOU kidnapped. And guess what Cyrus does? Does he cave in to these madmen? Does he give in to their crime spree to save his brother? Hell no. He makes public speeches telling these environmental fucks to go to hell. 'Cause he's not some kind of wimp who will just give in to a bleeding heart cause. Even when the life of his brother is on the line. He'll stand tough against crime on principle. He's a crime fighter. He's a terrorist fighter. He's got the balls it takes to take on the most heinous elements of society."

"But isn't that a kind of ridiculous plan for a lefty congressional district in New England?" said Paul. "I mean that might be some kind of a good strategy in Texas, but what makes you think it will work up here?"

"Not at all. Not at all. That's one of the biggest myths around. Because, secretly, everyone's afraid of environmental EXTREMISTS. I mean, sure, a lot of people love going to buy organic food at the supermarket, and they like taking nice walks in the woods, and they want their national parks, but as soon as some freaks start telling you that you should go back to a pretechnological state of farming or hunting-and-gathering to prevent global warming, even the lefties panic. Everyone loves to hate the EXTREMISTS. Very few want to be at the edge of the herd."

And now, in the distance, over the sound of geese landing and taking off, louder than the sound of their wings flapping to freedom, Paul could hear a lone coyote howl. It was the sound of solitude. It was the sound of complete abandonment. He had no idea coyotes could survive this far East in the few patches of woods left between the criss-crossing roads that ran through New England. How dare his brother do this to him. How dare he. But hadn't Paul been somewhat complicit letting himself last this long with these "ecoterrorists"? he wondered. Why hadn't he fled all along? Was it mere laziness, or curiosity? Was it that he had no direction anymore ever since Zoe had thrown him out of the house? (Which seemed only to further fulfill the prophecy of Buffalo Man that he was doomed?) How dare his brother use him only to push forward his fame. Paul began to howl and howl, howling as loudly as he could, pointing out his chest and raising his head to the moon in the way he imagined the coyote was howling now, placing his voice in sync with the animal.

"Shut up," The Honorable C said. "Or someone will hear us."

But Paul wouldn't shut up. He howled and howled. He puckered his lips toward the moon and felt a oneness in his soul with the running coyote that never got to rest as it tried to regain its old familiar ground. He stood on the edge of the crumbling concrete and flapped his arms like the geese, looking at the moon, pretending he could lift off into the sky.

"Shut up," The Honorable C said again, and with Paul's eyes closed, The Honorable C strangled Paul until he was silent.

CHAPTER 10

Did he want revenge? Of course. But how should he do it? Paul thought. And against whom? If he somehow conceived of a way to approximate the abuse he was taking from Cyrus, and if he carried out that plan against him, then wouldn't that simply fulfill the break in his relationship with his brother that Buffalo Man had always predicted?—the break that would lead to his death. Then what about revenge against his kidnappers? But were they the cause of his kidnapping? How much could he honestly punish The Honorable C, who seemed to Paul an overly eager filmmaker who had simply gotten out of hand with ideas of a reality TV-style documentary while earning big bucks making a tough-on-crime, anti-ecoterrorist political campaign for his brother? The Honorable C wasn't the prime mover behind his problems. Only Cyrus had the selfishness to cook up a plot to kidnap his brother for fame and victory, as if Paul were cattle, meat to be chewed to the marrow of the bone, a TV prop to suit his ends. Cyrus was the one he needed revenge against more than anyone. R-E-V-E-N-G-E! He thought about these things almost constantly, especially in the new place he was being held kidnapped—where the next scene takes place.

"Do you want some tea?" said Bal. (Bal was short for Iqbal.) "Or a copy of the newspaper? They keep delivering all the papers and magazines."

These last words Bal said with a hint of disbelief, Paul thought, as if someone, somewhere, long ago should have cancelled at least some of the subscriptions. Paul was in the suburban Boston office of *Rake-It-In* magazine, and the only person who still worked in the office was the security guard—Bal. Bal was an immigrant from Pakistan in his late fifties, and in many ways it seemed degrading, to Paul, that a man with such proper posture and so polite should have to pretend his lifelong ambition was to watch over the possessions of an abandoned office.

But the office hadn't always been abandoned. Judging by all the blown-up cover reproductions of *Rake-It-In* that glistened like fluorescent ads in an airport—of supermodels shopping, riding in Beemers, or just holding fistfuls of money—Paul figured the office must have been a place humming with activity once, busy welcoming multibillionaire entrepreneurs. During the Boomtime, being the reception man who greeted all those people as they came out of the elevator—as Bal did then along with his other, security functions—might have been a job more worthy of his helpful, cheerful solicitude.

And then, really, the security job was a way of survival for Bal, Paul realized. Bal had seen all the changes to the area around Route 128 and survived with a job throughout, even after all the New Economy kids had come and gone. He'd even survived all the interrogation sweeps by the FBI of Pakistanis after September 11th. "Before this confluence of buildings was built, there used to be a drive-in movie theater here," Bal had told Paul a couple weeks ago, when Paul was first delivered to his latest holding pen. "I was the projectionist," he said. "I could do the job pretty well, you know, because I had always liked the movies in Lahore. And it wasn't all that hard, really, even though I didn't get too much sleep. It was a good job. But this is a good job, too."

The drive-in had been close to Route 128, and in the place where the theater once stood a complete transformation had occurred. Now the buildings of a mini Silicon Valley replaced the projection booth and the scattered speakers of the car lot. From out of those ruins came the neatly planned buildings of The Future. The roads in this part of suburbia were wide, with freshly poured concrete and neatly formed curbs that swept gently off the highways. The big median separating the two directions of traffic to the complex had been planted in the late 90s with luxurious trees. Flowers were placed in tiny circles at the base of the trees and cedar wood chips everywhere else to keep out any weed intruders. The lawns and shrubs around the complex, which had grown so fast during the hi-tech boom of the 90s, had all the makings of instant luxury—because they required poor immigrants to maintain them and because the plants hadn't grown there naturally over time but were placed in the ground all at once to complete the rendering of an architectural drawing.

There were bike paths around the building where Paul was captive, and also little bridges over man-made creeks (that filled up with water only when it rained hard). Behind the ten-story building where Paul was being kept, a man-made lake looked like the center of a new golf course. Yet, despite all this effort to give a homey feeling—so employees in this new hi-tech zone might want to go for a bike ride or stroll around their place of employment—the giant parking lot in the middle of the development made it clear no one lived close enough to ever bike to this place. During the Boomtime of the late 90s, the area had grown on cheap land so rapidly nobody lived nearby. The employees came in their cars from downtown Boston or from homes nestled in "historic" New England; so you were much more likely to see a bunch of men in chino pants sitting on benches during their lunch break than anyone biking.

But the boom of the 90s was over now. The enormous parking lot—still fresh with neatly arranged crisp white lines marking spaces for a couple thousand cars, still with newly planted trees growing with metal poles holding the trees as they attempted to break into soil far from the nursery where they'd grown up—formed a wide plane of near emptiness now. Where once there had been a hard time finding a parking space, now there were a hundred cars at most in a day. The feeling of emptiness was made even greater because cars continued to park next to each other in some kind of congregation, as if the drivers wished to pretend the sense of community that had resided within the buildings was still functioning.

"There used to be Bar-B-Qs here," Bal said, pointing from the penthouse of the building where Paul was held, down to the parking lot.

On Fridays during the Boomtime, after the stock market had closed at new highs (the stocks of many small-tech companies in the building complex up by 15-20 or even 100 percent in a single day), the barbecue grills were out in force, sending the smoke of premium beef up into the air. People threw Frisbees. People leaned against their new cars and snarfed down hamburgers with all the fixings. People talked about taking trips to Argentina to go rock climbing and grueling, but fun, trips to subsidiaries in Bangkok, and the whole parking lot felt like a picnic, with endless wine and beer and fast cars and new toys—such as Windsurfers.

But the boom had ended long ago. It was now late October 2004, and Paul's neck hurt from sleeping on top of a desk in one of the abandoned offices. He thanked Bal for his offer of tea; Bal certainly wasn't supposed to be treating him so well. (C.T.—who had worked in this enormous office space during the Boomtime and who had suggested the place as a refuge—had told Bal to treat Paul decently but not to give him any favors.) Bal had other ideas. He would come and ask Paul if he was comfortable enough.

Paul looked at the front page of the newspaper Bal had just put down in front of him, and he saw a photo of a dead child hit by a stray bomb in Iraq. "Do you ever wish for revenge?" said Paul. "Against the U.S. military and the president."

Bal shook his head. "No, no revenge. Only peace. What good is all this: you kill my brother, I kill yours? What those men did on September 11th was wrong. It was simply wrong. And so are these bombs in Iraq. Revenge makes the heart feel warm, but it hardly solves the problem."

"So what solves the problem?"

"To act rightly oneself. That's all that God or anyone else can expect a person to do."

Bal wouldn't stick around for long. It was in his nature to be present and then gone, like a waiter in a fine restaurant. After he gave Paul tea and offered him the paper, he disappeared, and Paul padded around the wide-open former office of *Rake-It-In* magazine.

The problem for the magazine was that they still had two years of their lease before they could give the place up. They rented the space for $50,000 a month, and they'd sunk a million into making the office luxurious enough to receive the young entrepreneurs of the "New Economy," but without the advertising from now-defunct tech companies, it was no longer worth keeping the office open. Whatever journalism and other business functions remained had been cut back to just the New York office. In Boston only space was left, and Bal—the sole remaining employee, who had once greeted visitors and who policed the cavernous office now—protected the few valuables that remained. If the Boomtime ever came back, he would ensure all the cubicles were still waiting for new employees. And there was one object of value still left in the office: in the reception area, paneled with teak, and with a cool stainless-steel desk that implied the speed of money and the precision of computers, there was a bright-orange Harley-Davidson gleaming in all its chrome beauty. The motorcycle was a reminder of the good speed that could be had with money, of the Boomtime that had vanished.

The way Paul had arrived at this place, where the light was too fluo-rescent after living outside in the ecoterrorist camp, was by the VW bus. One night, The Honorable C came into the tepee where Paul slept. Bark, C.T., and Flower were playing cards. "Change of location," The

Honorable C told everyone. "Cyrus has given me a heads-up the cops might be catching on to where we're hanging out, and it's time to add some spice to this reality documentary. We need more tension. More conflict. A pursuit. A change of location. My film-school teacher used to tell me if the plot isn't building, it's dying. We're going to flee, but where to I haven't figured out yet."

Initially, The Honorable C thought a trip to Maine or New Hampshire, to spend some time sabotaging amusement parks and ski areas and then adulating nature in one of the national parks like Acadia—which afforded a wonderful view of peregrine falcons from the parking lot on top of Cadillac Mountain—might be just the thing. All this could be done while outfoxing the cops.

But once they were on the road, C.T. suggested his old workplace, where he'd had an up-and-coming position in the Internet Media Division (IMD) of *Rake-It-In*. He'd worked on live Webcasts, with interviews of rich CEOs and features on expensive restaurants in Boston for the Living section of the Web version of the mag. Not too many people watched the Webcasts, but it was undeniably growing then, doubling from a thousand viewers to two thousand and then doubling again.

"From what I understand, the place is completely abandoned now except the old security guard, Bal," C.T. told The Honorable C.

The Honorable C rejected the idea out of hand. Even in an abandoned building, another person in on the kidnapping might blow their whole cover. But C.T. promised Bal was an extremely nonjudgmental and welcoming person. The reason Bal had survived through all the changes along Route 128, and made it through to the other side of the Boomtime, was because he just went with the flow. "He's got that gift that immigrants have of adapting," C.T. said. "Besides, he's a Paki—they interrogated him extensively after September 11th, and if he brings any of us to the cops, he's just bringing himself back to the FBI. He's a security guard who can't bring anyone in, for his own security." After a lot of convincing, with C.T. persuading The Honorable C any commercially successful film should have more than one kidnapping to keep the plot going, and that, therefore, they would need more space for such a kidnapping, The Honorable C gave in. "And one other thing," said C.T., "for the purpose of keeping Cyrus's campaign going, all the equipment for the Webcasts should still be there. It'll be easier to send footage to the press that way than from the tapes we've been dropping off at the mailbox at Walden."

A storm was coming, and then it arrived. The winds blew strong around the modern glass fortress where Paul looked out the windows, watching trees stretch every which way with few roots to rely upon. There'd been reports of unusual weather rising around the tiny globe. Down in Antarctica, large chunks of ice were wrenching free from the stone that normally anchored the ice to its master. Pieces the size of Rhode Island were falling off as rays of the sun broke through the ozoneless barrier of the sky. It was two days before the election, and a hurricane was headed in a curveball that had never been seen from the Pacific toward El Salvador. The banana trees of El Salvador would collapse. And now another storm came from the north, whereas nor'easters usually came from the south. The weather of the world was changing poles, and outside Paul's window, the sky screamed as missiles of rain lodged in the crying ground of whatever wilderness remained. What have we done? Paul thought. Fucked it all up. While his kidnappers played at making environmentalists seem like fools. The earth too hot. Then cool elsewhere. Presidents denying global warming. Satellites broadcasting the weather. People unconcerned in the cool shelters of their homes and with more sunscreen doses put on daily.

Despite the rain, The Honorable C, C.T., and Flower were getting suited up in their green attack uniforms again, and they told Paul to hurry putting his blindfold on or they'd be forced to do it more brutally. Paul looked at the sky once more and before the cloth was placed fully over his eyes, he saw bolts of lightning hit toward the ground more ferociously than Zeus was supposed to have capacity. In the distance, next to the artificial lake that dominated the landscape, lightning struck the tower of a high-tension line that swept along following the path of Route 128. A flash of blue sizzle; the current was absorbed by the tower, and the construction of man seemed more powerful than nature. Not even a flicker in the building. Paul put on the blindfold. He rode the elevator down with the kidnappers—feeling a slight pause that made him wonder if there wasn't a small effect from the lightning after all, a small surge that showed the system was not invulnerable—and on the ground floor the door bing!ed open, and he was pushed out into the giant parking lot, unable to see, only capable of feeling the stinging rain as it fell over his light jacket.

It was Sunday evening—the election would be Tuesday—so for the first time the kidnappers must have felt it was quiet enough they could take Paul out before complete darkness. With the storm drenching them, there was no need to fear anyone being out and about. The wet poured into his shoes and inside his shirt collar.

Why have I let things get this far? he thought. *If I had more courage, I would have fought back ages ago(?)* He used a question mark because he didn't know. It was said, according to the Stockholm syndrome, that those who were kidnapped came around to the idea eventually the cause of their kidnappers is somehow just. But he wasn't sure the syndrome arose from anything more than inertia of the will to survive mixed with the innate weakness of most people. One of the lies, he thought, that led to the feelings of failure that raged through the country was that everyone was meant to believe success and courage were the norm. There were daily accounts of firemen running into buildings to save small children, of people surviving avalanches and riding out storms on sailboats. This was the news that was supposed to give humanity its purpose: a striving, an ever-marching movement forward, as society built bridges to a place higher, more distant and stronger over the rainbow. But the odd thing was, while human beings prided themselves for this courage and made it the focus of their stories, how rarely, they knew in their hearts, this condition really must be. For otherwise, why bother with all these stories pronouncing our courage? Paul thought. No, the natural state of man wasn't the person who escapes from the concentration camp of the Holocaust alive—fighting to get an extra scrap of bread and to live like Elie Wiesel. The natural state of man was to be average. So while Paul felt there were elements of courage within him, those elements were no more than average. He was an average person. Special perhaps in his powers to see, he thought, but not in his powers to do.

So here he was, simply trying not to get wet as they pushed him through the cold sheets of mind-tingling rain. Once in the van, the door slammed shut and he was guarded by Bark on one side and C.T.

on the other. The tires slipped momentarily from the wet, and then the old windshield wipers—man's feeble effort to beat off nature—kicked in, flip-flapping.

From then on, Paul was more disoriented than usual because of the sound of traffic next to him. The rain turned him around; he felt the tires accelerate, stop and start again, over and over, then roll along an interstate, and the next thing he knew the van was hydroplaning, the wheels of the old bus slipping ever so perceptibly, moving sideways, at great speed in a way that could be sensed only with a blindfold on. Was this the moment of his death, then? This now? The van hydroplaning off Route 128 as it curved around the outer boundary of Boston and crashed into a wall of barren slate? The rain echoed off the cliffs of dynamited rock beside the road, then was muffled by the interstate pavement sucking in the sound that had spit out from the tires of the van. The van rolled on.

So it wasn't with a bang or a whimper that the world would end but with a neutrality, a numbing sound of repetition, drops banging against the roof of a van, an unintended storm marching back against human beings who didn't question why it had come, so unusually, even when they had made it come by their own global warming.

How could he stand up to Cyrus, then? So void of his courage. So filled with the neutrality of the culture that surrounded him.

Once they were near Cyrus's house, the remains of Halloween pumpkins littered the front porches of the mansions of Avon Hill. Many of the homes were decorated with hundreds of dollars of ghosts, goblins, and witches. Strands of sprayed Styrofoam, meant to create scary spider webs, hung from the restored woodwork of the Victorian houses. Cardboard cutouts of bats, taped to the broad windows of the mansions, drooped listlessly, no longer tethered to the make-believe of the day before. Even the youngest children, who had walked safely with their parents from one mansion to another asking for piles of candy, as they listened to their parents chitchat about their upcoming winter vacations and warnings not to overindulge in candy, knew the bats were no more dangerous than any of the other decorations their parents had bought at the mall. In the well-manicured lawns of Avon Hill, the rotting pumpkins after Halloween behaved. Like pumpkins everywhere, they decayed, so that the ghoulish features of the carved-out lanterns were accentuated by the rotting flesh of the squash, but they seemed to do so gracefully, more slowly, like some kind of fading movie star. The pumpkins were bought in high-end supermarkets, where they glistened organically, or were bought during day trips to the countryside, and so these pumpkins bore no resemblance to the mass-produced pumpkins trucked in from the fields of the Midwest, which rotted quickly, just as the flesh of peaches trucked in from California to the East Coast went from rock to mush within days of being brought home from the store.

Cyrus's wife, Rebecca, had decorated the house appropriately with dozens of bats, goblins, and witches and had even posted two full-size blown-up skeletons in the front driveway. She was gone from the house now and had taken the kids to one of the numerous activities they were engaged in: violin lessons, tae kwan do, computer courses, debate clubs, etc. The Honorable C called Cyrus on his cell phone as they drove through the storm, and apparently received the all clear.

When the van door opened, Paul knew exactly where he was—not because of any conversation he'd overheard (he could barely make out who The Honorable C was talking to in the rain) but because he smelled the territory of his brother like a subordinate dog smelling the ground of its superior. Ever since he was a boy, he could remember smelling Cyrus before he even came within sight. Paul felt and smelled the weight of Cyrus, and as he stepped out of the van, he smelled the wet wood chips of Cyrus's lawn where he'd once buried the notes for his book when he went to steal the pre-Columbian statue to pay off The Modern Cyrano for his help—which had seemed so promising at the time, worth even robbing his brother for.

Bark, C.T., and the Honorable C pulled Paul, running up the steps. They hurried past a ghoulish pumpkin grinning, with teeth that looked cleaned by a dentist, and pushed Paul quickly up to the front door. Cyrus opened the door slowly. The Honorable C gave him a look of exasperation to let him know he could be cavalier and domineering with others but not with him. "Close the door, quick," The Honorable C said to Bark and C.T. "They could be monitoring the place. And guard the door in case anyone tries to break in."

Cyrus let out a heavy, sweet smell mixed with a strong acid like a muskrat or a skunk, and Paul was tempted to lunge at him, to snarl and bite back, to fall on the ground gnawing his shins; but with his hands restrained and face blindfolded, he continued to stand. He knew the only way to win against Cyrus was never to flinch, never to show any emotion, never to let him see he had caused anger. To show emotion to Cyrus was always to let him know his bait had worked, that he had succeeded once again. His strategy in the courtroom was to incite anger, an outburst that made his opponent seem unreasonable, which then justified his own deathly stabs back.

"We have some things we need to talk to you about," The Honorable C said.

"And you couldn't do it some more secretive way?" Cyrus said. "You had to just barge in here?"

"You haven't been responding to my recent messages."

"The campaign is in its final stages," said Cyrus. He moved to the living room, beneath the high golden chandelier, to the large leather chairs and couch that looked like the kind found in a Harvard alumni club where billiard rooms and cigars were the norm. The heavy furniture was planted firmly, powerfully, in control of its surroundings like a famous lawyer in a courtroom.

"Have a seat," Cyrus said.

The Honorable C removed Paul's blindfold, and Paul looked at Cyrus to see what his first reaction would be, if Cyrus would show any shame, but the look as Cyrus stared straight at Paul was one of complete certainty without guilt.

The Honorable C sat on the couch. Bark and C.T. guarded the door, on the far side of the house from the living room, and Paul and Cyrus faced each other mano a mano, two fighters in a ring. Paul remained handcuffed.

"Did it ever occur to you there are limits?" Paul said. His wet, dirty blond hair was greasy from weeks without a shower, and it was ragged in an uncut shape.

"Limits are for people unwilling to know what it takes to win. I'm a winner," said Cyrus. "And when I do what it takes to win, I bring glory not only to myself, and to our whole family, I act for a greater good. You tell me, can a virtuous loser shape the Supreme Court? Can a virtuous loser change the laws of the land? Can a virtuous loser talk only about the means and not the ends? The great mistake of most academic lawyers is that they focus only on the process, only on the purity of justice. They write arguments of crystalline purity for colleagues who live lives of piety. They write about justice in a world that doesn't give a crap about their justice. Well, I'm not going to settle just for words. The one who shapes the debate is *always* the winner. The lawyer who pins his opponent is the one who sets the precedent. What is right or wrong is always debatable, and therefore to enact your position of justice, you must gain authority first."

"And so that justifies kidnapping your brother?" said Paul. He wet his thick lips. Despite the rain, he felt parched in Cyrus's presence, dry like a bag of dust.

"Generally, no. Generally, I would have to agree kidnapping one's brother violates some kind of higher code—some code of religious or biblical justice that is taboo. But let's face it, Paul, what were you doing that was so important before you were kidnapped? You were lost and wallowing in self-pity, playing the role of some kind of security guard. You were running around believing some man named Buffalo Man had put a curse on you that's given you writer's block. You failed to get tenure at a community college that only demanded one significant article out of you. And you'd even fallen so low as to rob one of my pre-Columbian statues and to walk in on me in my office when I was having sex with a grad student. I mean, don't you think I have cameras in this place to protect this mansion? Don't you think I knew you walked in on me? Whatever minimal harm I may have done to you over the last few weeks has been a gift. This is your wake-up call, Paul. This is the bell of reality, Paul. Hello. It's time to get your head out of your dreamworld. The world owes you nothing, Paul. I owe you nothing. And if this is what it takes to win an election— If hiring a bunch of basically incompetent kidnappers is what it takes so that the people of this congressional district will feel safe in their homes, and certain that I won't be soft on crime and niggers, or homos, and that I'll fight for their security against terrorists, then so be it. Because once I'm elected, they'll be happy with whatever I do, and they'll go back to watching the Pats and the Sox on TV. And that's how real justice gets done."

Was his brother a purist or a relativist, then, after all? Paul wondered. He was certainly an absolutist. Absolute in his belief that whatever he wanted to do was A-OK. Relative in that it was fine for him to have flaws because he was famous—while Paul wasn't. A purist in that he claimed to be the sole person to know how to accomplish anything. He was a relatively pure asshole, then, Paul thought. Whereas Paul, what was he? He had to admit that—even if a self-serving justification for Cyrus's own despicableness—Cyrus's critique of himself wasn't wholly unfounded. What was he? Where was his substance? Why had he allowed himself, a person of intelligence, to fall to the level of a failed academic? Had he simply become a sarcastic observer of the world who saw only hypocrisy and who used his wit to find the holes in the world around him, rather than to see the buds of goodness, too? Was he simply a carper, a destroyer rather than someone who could appreciate what it takes to make the world grow? Had the relativism and neutrality of his time left him only to drift in a sea of rampant cynicism, or even worse, nihilism? Where could he find happiness and success, some kind of constructive offering to give the world?

Cyrus's critique was, in its own, self-serving way, devastating. But it was just that. Another form of self-serving words. No better, Paul thought, than his own failures, even if it would lead to Cyrus's election. And yet it *would* lead to Cyrus's election. That was what made it all so disgusting and yet enviously admirable at the same time. Throughout Paul's ordeal, since he had been kidnapped, he had to admit there was an element in him that admired his brother's audacity even as he felt disgust.

"You're an asshole," Paul said to Cyrus, and he spit at Cyrus's feet.

"Good," Cyrus said. "Now you're showing at least a little strength. But not nearly enough, I have to say."

The Honorable C, who sat quietly on the heavy couch throughout their encounter, cleared his throat.

"What is it?" Cyrus said dismissively.

"What it is," The Honorable C said, dressed in his ecoterrorist suit, feeling the can of Mace attached to the hip belt on his side, "is that you're significantly behind on your payments to the ecoterrorist mob. You were supposed to have that second hundred grand to us a week ago. You missed the drop-off."

"That's it?" Cyrus laughed. "That's why you risked blowing your cover, coming into the heart of Cambridge just to tell me you want your money?"

"Well, can you think of a better reason?"

"You'll get your cash soon enough. After you deliver all the way to the end zone. You'll get your money, and the bonus, too, if everything works out on Election Day."

"And if it doesn't?"

Cyrus shrugged.

"Just remember we have your brother as a hostage," The Honorable C said.

"Right. But I'm sure you're smart enough not to do anything. And what are you going to do, in any case? Run to the cops and tell them everything? You'd be an accessory to a crime."

"Come on. Let's go," The Honorable C said to Paul. "I guess you're going to have to be a real hostage now."

"See. What are you bitching about?" Cyrus said to Paul. "They're obviously harmless. He's a film student, for crying out loud. How badly off can you be?"

The commando raid was in progress. Bark, C.T., and the boys scaled the Somerville Hospital, climbed down the roof exit, and descended to the fifth floor, where Zoe was taking care of a drunk Vietnam vet shouting obscenities. It was the time of night when it could be either dead quiet in the hospital or when the demons inside the patients came out. Zoe was calm with the veteran, named Walter Dividus. "I don't blame you," said Zoe. "Really I don't, Walter, but you gotta keep it down so the others can get their shut-eye. Know what I'm saying?"

"They kicked me out of the fucking VA, man," said Walter. "I mean, after killing gook after gook, they kicked me outta the VA. And I've done it, too. Killed me scaaaads of gooks."

Zoe directed Walter back into his room. The only other guy in the room with four beds was Zack, the old soldier of fortune and bear hunter who had basically ruined Zoe's wedding. Ever since Paul was kidnapped, things had gotten so out of hand, Zoe had even relented to Zack's free security services. The press had found out somehow she worked at Mass General. They'd followed her when she went in and out of the hospital, asking for comments how she felt about the kidnapping of her husband. And since she'd been having a strained relationship, at best, with Paul before he was taken, and since she felt it was none of their business in any case, she finally sought a temporary transfer to an out-of-the-way hospital where the press wouldn't pursue her. "I agree," her boss had said. "It's not exactly the best publicity for MGH." She was in the "SOMERVILLE HO" now.

Bark had never lived near a ghetto. Yet because he was more attuned than most to seeing the influence of black culture on white America, he'd been the first to point out the odd signage on the outside of the hospital as they climbed to the top to break in to kidnap Zoe. "Did you see that sign?" he said. He laughed and shook his head while hanging in the air from his climbing rope. "Look at what those stupid white folks are doing now," he told Flower. "I mean, I know they're trying to attract clients. But reverting to hip-hop language for prostitutes to try to get hospital customers— Damn. Those whiteys won't stop at anything."

Sure enough, the main hospital sign, in an area that was primarily an enclave of middle-class Italian Americans and Irish, said SOMER-VILLE HO. It wasn't some kind of temporary error. The thing had been left that way for years.

Paul, too, had noticed the sign when he'd lived near the hospital in his days with I.C.N., when he'd believed he was going to make it to the big time. He could only theorize that the sign, high up on the hospital, was a symbol of the blindness of routine. How many people actually noticed that something on the sign wasn't quite right? How many read the full word "Hospital" out of habit, even when that word was no longer there? Or maybe it was just that the hospital didn't have enough money to fix it. (Yet, how expensive could it be?) Or maybe it was just a small sense of pleasure that something was unfixed. Maybe everyone wanted the sign unfixed. Or, possibly—and this is what Paul finally settled on as his best theory—the guy who was responsible for the entire building never went out to the side. So unless the adminis-trator who ran the whole building was willing to take the energy to walk down and to the side (and there was no entrance there), then he would never see that his hospital had taken on the look of a Sex Motel.

Whatever the cause, Flower, C.T., Bark, and The Honorable C had penetrated the Somerville Ho. It was 2 A.M., after they'd driven to Cambridge to tell Cyrus it was time for him to come up with the other half of the dough. Things were all going according to plan. The Honorable C had spent the last couple weeks preparing this second kidnapping, ever since he'd hit on the scheme as the best way to get a climactic punch to his reality-TV film documentary—and when he realized it was just the kind of event that would outrage the public to the point they would all vote for Cyrus out of sympathy for his tough-on-crime, tough-on-ecoterrorism stance.

The Honorable C filmed his men running in "action mode" down a long, linoleum-tiled corridor toward Zoe's ward. The hallway was empty; it was a perfect shot of his actors running hell-bent to their next hostage. The terrorists receded into the distance with new martial arts toys—nunchakus made of ebony—bouncing against their sides. "I got them off this survivalist Web site in Oregon," The Honorable C told the crew. "Apparently you can use these things to kill squirrels if you need meat."

The ecoterrorists reached the end of the corridor, where the long hallway with fluorescent lights came to a T, and two ran to the right and one to the left, just as The Honorable C had instructed. "If one group is delayed then the other can proceed," he said. "Besides, it makes for a better action shot watching you guys split up." The key was to come at Zoe from both sides to avoid any escape. The whole place was set up with a maze of rectangles so that all patients and doctors could move freely throughout the building.

As soon as the kidnappers broke to each side, The Honorable C panned to a biohazard sign just next to him. It was bright yellow, with an elaborate symbol that looked like the flailing tail of a scorpion, and the word BIOHAZARD warned all intruders to keep out and all janitors to have on their work gloves as they removed the garbage, until they tossed it into a big dumpster in the basement.

Later, in one of his kidnapping lectures on the need for environmental reform, The Honorable C would point out that using the word BIOHAZARD made it sound as if it was the natural, biological world that was dangerous, when it was really the things human beings made out of organic material, as they twisted everything into new combinations, that was the threat. He would also note that if this garbage was so dangerous it needed to be incinerated, then why were we allowing it to be made in the first place?

Once Zoe got Walter into the room with Zack, the two of them swapped stories about their days in 'Nam. Zoe heard Walter tell Zack about his time up at Khe Sanh, and then he added, "And now they tell me I'm just *lying* about my PTSD. And they kick me out of the fucking VA when my leg is broken. The same thing's gonna happen to those boys coming back from Iraq." Zack came out of the room and asked Zoe suddenly, "You OK? They here? Is anyone here?"

"What are you talking about, Zack?" said Zoe. Zack was convinced the ecoterrorists were going to come and get her. The trouble with these vets, Zoe thought, is that after serving on the front lines, they were so goddamn paranoid.

Zack looked behind the nursing station where Zoe was working alone, monitoring the vital signs of various patients on her computer. He looked under her desk and down both corridors. He sniffed the air, trying to tell if any prey was near. And when he was satisfied, he went back to Walter's room to trade more stories.

A few minutes later, the ecoterrorist squad showed up. Zoe kicked and tried to scream, and was generally harder than Paul to control when he'd been taken hostage at Worland, but the shock of bear Mace to the face stunned her enough to make the task easy.

And Zack? Some sixth sense gave him the feeling Zoe was in trouble. He ran out from Walter's room and saw Zoe gone from her station. He knew she wasn't in the bathroom, because she had dropped some pills for a patient on the floor. Zack sniffed down one corridor, then along another. *There are four of them,* he thought. The fluorescent lights burned wearily down the long corridors as he ran toward the emergency exit that led up to the roof. It took him a while to run with the weight of his beer belly impeding his progress, but he made it onto the roof just in time to see a dark green VW bus hightailing it out of the place toward somewhere unknown in the night. The sign of the Somerville Ho buzzed quietly, precariously, almost seductively beside him.

Late the next night, when the stars powerfully pushed light through the earth's diminishing ether of ozone, shining brilliantly in a way stars do not often get to do in the cloudy area around Boston, Paul and Zoe stood on the top of a bird-watching tower with their hands handcuffed behind them to the railing. They saw the flashing lights of a FedEx plane coming in for a landing at Hanscom airport, tracing an incoming flight path over the most important National Wildlife Refuge in the Concord and Boston area. Before the screaming jet approached, there had been only natural sounds in the refuge—cold wind blowing through the dried-out reeds of cattails, and of the last geese taking off and landing, making their way south for the winter. The time for the escape of the birds was nearly gone, and many of them refused to spend a full night of rest. The whining jets encouraged the birds to leave sooner, and a flock of geese rose in fright, flapping with all their might, attempting to clear the far-off, high treetops at the end of the marsh that lay in front of Paul and Zoe. The Honorable C, C.T., and Flower were in the process of documenting the regularity of flights that had begun coming to the Hanscom airfield recently, as growth in the air package delivery business turned the old airfield into a major commercial flight center. During the day, small, private jets of executives like Bill Gates glided over this marsh that had been one of the most important duck-hunting grounds in Colonial times.

Now the marsh was protected—a fiberglass sign put up by the National Wildlife Refuge told all the visitors in a big educational placard next to the refuge parking lot. Wooden bird huts, like small hotels, had been constructed for great blue herons to perch on and to nest. This was one of the last patches of wilderness where migrating birds of all sorts could land in the area. Bark had already been sent to spray-paint the visitor bathrooms: "No more potty breaks in the marsh," he scribbled on the walls of the toilet huts. He painted on the mirrors inside the bathrooms, but they were made of vandalism-proof stainless steel.

The Honorable C tilted his camera at the sky, filming the armada of planes as they came in one after another toward Hanscom Field. He was on the ground at the edge of the parking lot, pointing his camera first at the marsh and then at the sky; and since Bark, C.T., and Flower were busy and no one else was nearby, The Honorable C instructed Paul and Zoe to be handcuffed to the top of the bird-watching tower, where he could keep a lookout on them at all times. For added security, he sent Bal up to chaperone the two of them.

"Could you give us some privacy?" Zoe said to Bal.

"Most definitely," said Bal. "It is certainly not my intention to be of any annoyance. But I also cannot anger these men, or they'll send me back to the FBI." He walked down one level of the tower, which looked like a lookout for a park ranger watching for fires, and focused on the wildlife around him, attempting to give the reunited couple their privacy.

Zoe said, "Well, now you're famous, Paul. Isn't it ironic? I.C.N. almost got you there, but then it didn't. And I've certainly never gotten there acting. But you're famous now. Everyone sees you on the news every night. They see a photo of you next to some crazy ecoterrorists. Then they see a calendar telling them how many days it's been since you were taken hostage. And then, usually, they get some follow-up interview with the police saying they're doing everything they can to find you and that they've got some good leads. But they never seem to be able to find you. People are kind of impressed, I've gotta say, with the ability of these ecoterrorists to keep eluding the cops. And then Cyrus comes on at one of his campaign events, and he promises to get you released, but not by giving in to a single demand of the terrorists, only by standing up to them and being tough."

"I'm sorry," said Paul. "Really, I am. I'm sorry for getting you all involved in this."

"Good. I'm glad you're sorry. But not because you got me into this. I don't really see how you got me into this directly. But indirectly, what have you been doing hanging out with these hacks? I mean, I'm not accusing you of looking enthusiastic in all the footage they've shown of you, with the destruction of supermarkets and storage facilities and everything. But you just don't seem to be resisting. You know what I mean? Look at these guys. They're amateurs. It shouldn't be so hard to break away."

"So are you saying I'm letting myself be voluntarily kidnapped?" Paul said. "Are you saying I've just been sitting on my fat ass with these people? Look at me! Look at this," he tried to point to his ragged and greasy hair. "Look at my clothes." He tried to point down to his jeans, covered with dirt. "You're saying that I've been sitting on my fat ass while I've been kidnapped?"

Zoe bit her pretty lower lip. Her hair was up in a ponytail. She had insisted to The Honorable C that he let her feel comfortable, and Bal had helped her put her hair into whatever shape she desired. "What I'm saying Paul is that things don't just happen. People let things happen to them. We are not just victims of circumstance. And some day, when you finally get through all the excuses for why you weren't able to finish your book, and when you think about why you even wanted to devote so many years to writing a book about feelings of failure, you'll see that you aren't the victim of your brother or of some guy named Buffalo Man, you're a victim of yourself."

"And you have life all figured out, then, Zoe? Why hasn't your acting career ever taken off? Are you a victim of laziness, too, or did you just not have the talent? What would you have done differently these last few weeks if you'd been kidnapped? Go ahead. Shout out. Shout out as loud as you can to the wilderness. It's not so easy. You'll see. I screamed my head off all I could when I first got to the place where they kept me."

"I don't know why I never quite made it," Zoe said. "But it wasn't for a lack of trying. I've yet to give up on the world, Paul. The world will meet me halfway someday. It's up to me to make it happen. Who knows, maybe in some perverse way this kidnapping will be the trick I need to get some attention."

"So does that mean you're not going to try to escape?"

"I'm going to wait to see what happens. I'm going to get what I can out of this for *me*. I'm tired of waiting, Paul. I'm tired of waiting for my day in the sun. Stranger things have happened. Who was Patty Hearst before she was kidnapped? A nobody. Who was Charles Manson before he killed a bunch of people? Stranger things have happened to give a person their lucky break."

"And you think it's lucky to be famous for being someone who was kidnapped or as a mass murderer? Who cares if you get fame that way? I never joined I.C.N. to be famous. OK, I hoped that I'd be famous. But that wasn't why I joined the band. I joined because I wanted to make some good sound. I wanted others to dig the sound of my drumming and the sound of our music. But then I just realized I was never really good enough for us to be anything more than a Top 40 alternative band opening up for better acts. Sometimes you just aren't born with the goods. That's what Buffalo Man's prophecy really means. It means not only that everything is happening literally according to the way he said it would—first my hooking up with you, and then one brother dying, and then the two of us splitting up, and then my other brother breaking away from me—it means sometimes we're born with misfortune. Maybe you and I have just been born misfortunate."

"And you believe that?" said Zoe.

"Well, how else can you explain that scientists can predict the exact time when two planets will align? And the exact time when an eclipse will occur. And the exact amount of years it will take for light from the stars to reach the earth. The universe is full of cycles, Zoe. It's an endless grouping of waves of predictable and unpredictable cycles. And it doesn't take someone of religion to see that our choices are limited by fate. Do I believe in fate? Theoretically, no, but it certainly seems to be happening according to the way Buffalo Man predicted."

In the distance, the planes were coming in one after the other, faster and faster, bringing in an astonishing number of packages, swooping low over the marsh of Concord that was half-drained in the fall to prevent an exotic species of Chinese carp that had already worked its way up the Concord River from leaping into the marsh. But then, Paul thought, looking at the lights of the planes flashing and blinking like warnings from a lighthouse at the edge of the sea: If all is fate, then was it inevitable that these planes should have been developed? Was it inevitable that men and women should have discovered all the tools that led up to this plane, at this point, screaming with its jet engines across the sky, scattering the geese into the night looking further south with their weary wings for another watering hole to rest in? Was it inevitable that the atomic bomb was dropped on the citizens of Hiroshima and Nagasaki? Was it inevitable that lasers were now being launched into the sky to weaponize space? Where within all of the atoms colliding and moving forward and backward, bumping into each other in a seemingly ineluctable progression of blind colliding speed, full of cycles and crashes, was an individual supposed to find the strength to carve out his own human destiny?

And what he wanted to do now was to reach for Zoe's hand, to attempt to reconnect to her, to find some shared warmth. He reached with his handcuffed hands toward her. But his fingers, halted by the cutting of the barrier, couldn't quite reach Zoe and she stared out blankly, high up in the cold air from the highest platform of the tower, looking out at the traffic coming into the runway.

CHAPTER 11

Do you remember the hostage crisis in Iran and how it played out with the election of Ronald Reagan's first term? I don't, exactly. The details are pretty fuzzy now. I was just a boy when day after day they flashed hostages up on TV, looking haggard, slumped on the floor of the U.S. embassy, guarded by smiling revolutionaries waving machine guns in the air, wearing radical Islamic headbands. Other than feeling something had gone terribly wrong, I remember a cover of *Newsweek* after Jimmy Carter sent some Army helicopters to rescue all the hostages. The helicopters blew down in a sandstorm (or somehow their mission failed; I need to look up the exact cause on the Net). The big news just after Election Day 1980, therefore, was that the whole group was suddenly freed—after more than a year of Carter trying to get them released—the day Reagan was inaugurated. In contrast to the outgoing president, Reagan looked like a hero. It seemed that, because he had been elected as a cowboy-hat-wearing, tough-talking leader against the Soviets and Iranians, the hostages were released. Later we found out Reagan sold weapons illegally to Iran. He traded with the enemy. But all that info came out *after* Inauguration Day. All that mattered was that a rabbit had suddenly been pulled out of the hat, and the U.S. embassy hostages, who looked so unshaved, blindfolded, and fearful, were free. A secret trade with the enemy or not, everyone was feeling good and patriotic on Inauguration Day as the embassy heroes of Iran came home.

In a way, the same thing happened to Paul. He was freed on Election Day 2004, after the votes came in and Cyrus won his tough-on-terrorism, tough-on-crime election by a fairly comfortable margin.

Paul didn't know the outcome when he was placed in the VW bus for one more ride in the ecoterrorist mobile. For old times' sake, Flower, C.T., The Honorable C, and Bark blindfolded Paul. Ever since they'd returned from the bird-watching tower the night before, Paul had been separated from Zoe, so he had no idea what her condition was or where she was being held captive. The only info he could get out of The Honorable C was a promise she was fine, and in a secret moment Bal assured Paul of the same, but otherwise their lips were sealed.

An hour before his release, The Honorable C told Bal to go to the office where Paul slept each night to cut his hair and make him look more presentable. "I want him to look like he's going to the Oscars," he said in front of Paul.

"I'll try to make you look glamorous," said Bal.

It was funny, Paul thought. Now that the movie was over, they were trying to make him look like a movie star. But was this any different really than what they did to the real movie stars as they got ready for Oscar night? For weeks the Hollywood actors turned into the characters they were performing; they plumped up if they were playing a fat suburban American husband. They tried to look wasted if they were a murderer. They chopped their hair into a mangled mess if they were playing trailer-park trash. And then, on Oscar night, they primped and preened into an unnatural state of glamorous ecstasy.

Bal did his best to prepare Paul for the secret upcoming event. He accomplished little more than a perfect bowl cut that made Paul look like he belonged to some British band of the early 60s. It had been a long time since Paul had looked this unfashionable. Touching his cropped hair, he sensed something wasn't quite right, especially since Bal giggled. "I don't know if my wife would approve of this haircut," said Bal, "but I've done my best. Honestly, Mr. Paul." Occasionally, when Bal wanted to be more generous than usual, out of some kind of holdover from the colonial days in Pakistan, he would call Paul: Mr. Paul.

"Thanks," said Paul. "I'm sure it's your best." There wasn't a mirror. In any case, he was simply glad to have it short. It was amazing how good fresh-cut hair felt after weeks of tangled strands with occasional mud and twigs.

"Can I have a baseball cap?" Paul asked The Honorable C. "With a logo of *Rake-It-In* mag if you've got one."

"No can do," The Honorable C said. "Once we get to our destination, there will be a shitload of lights and cameras, and any kind of cap will block your face in shadows. Hats are good for only one thing—when you want to create a shifty, pensive mood, like in those film noirs. But this is your turn to come out of the shadows."

The Honorable C blindfolded Paul, and the entire entourage took him out of the office of *Rake-It-In* and down the elevator that bing!ed with one last chime like a game-show winner, and then they were in the van, whizzing through the cold, crisp residue of the rainstorm of a couple days ago.

The VW roamed through the crowded streets of downtown Boston, following Colonial cow paths of the early city, until finally they found the basketball arena. Paul was dropped off in the main alleyway behind the Fleet Center and his blindfold was removed. He was told by The Honorable C to walk straight a few yards and to enter the building through a delivery door. From then on, he'd be escorted by a "Pakistani-looking" man to his "final destination."

Sensing his freedom, Paul might have run as fast as he could, but after weeks of captivity and following orders (to avoid occasional slaps and to make his life easier), he didn't resist his captors. The VW idled next to him; The Honorable C filmed the scene while the rest of the ecoterrorist boys watched and waited for Paul to enter the door as commanded. Paul slumped his shoulders, standing exhausted in the alleyway. He smelled beer residue, pretzels, french fries, and hamburgers, and a couple rats scampered side to side, trying to avoid the CO_2 fumes of the VW that rose as blue smoke in the night. It was amazing, Paul thought, the van had never been pulled over by a cop for being such an environmentally unsound 1970s vehicle. Looking at the rats, he thought the animals were the truest sign of what the future nature of the earth would become. To avoid their sharp teeth, he proceeded as quickly as possible, following the command of his captors. He was too weary to flee, and he was curious what his purpose would be now that he was being sent to a new location.

Once he opened the metal delivery door, he found himself in a bright kitchen with clanking plates and a dozen assistant-chefs in aprons, covered with blood and with the remains of food, rushing from one area to another gathering ingredients, chopping, and bringing plates of foie gras and portobello mushrooms to other chefs who scooped up the livers and tossed them into pans to be sautéed. The smell of such rich food intoxicated Paul. He walked up to one of the plates on a tray waiting to be brought out to guests in the private sports boxes above, and with bare hands, he picked up some of the foie gras and sucked the tasty meat. *It's a cliché*, he thought, *but it's only when you have back what you have lost that you realize how much you lost.* He licked his fingers and started in on another plate. "Hey, what the fuck do you think you're doing?" one of the cooks said. "That's for the VIPs."

"It's OK. I know him," a Pakistani-looking man calmed the chef down. He came quickly up to Paul and told him to cut it out in a whisper. "I'm Bal's cousin," he said. "It's time. Come with me." They walked to the back of the kitchen, where food supplies were kept in large, stainless steel fridges packed with goodies for the patrons of the private skyboxes. Bal's cousin was dressed in a tux, with a starched white shirt and bow tie. He led Paul to a service elevator. No one else was with them on the ride up.

"What's going to happen to me?" said Paul.

"I don't know," the cousin spoke with a Boston accent; he'd lost his Pakistani accent years ago. "Bal simply told me to take care of you. He told me to bring you upstairs and have you wait until a man named Cyrus calls you forth, and he told me to tell you you'll be reunited with your lovely wife, Zoe, soon. Other than that, he said he couldn't give more details—so I won't know anything if the FBI comes my way again. Do you know what they did to us after September 11th? . . . After I take you into the arena, I'll have to leave you alone to wait for Cyrus, to protect my security."

"Your security?" said Paul. "*I'm* the hostage. Aren't you supposed to be focusing on me? And if it's so unsafe for you, then why are they using you as the intermediary?"

"Apparently there are some tough new security measures into and out of this event. The only way to get around them is by taking the back elevator through the kitchen."

"No offense," said Paul, "but they think it's safer to have a man from Pakistan escort a wanted person who's been kidnapped through the most obvious elevator in the back kitchen?"

"Given the current high-level, code-red antiterrorist standard of this building—ever since the Democratic convention this summer—it seemed the only way. It's crazy, I know, but it takes a Pakistani food worker to break legally into the system." The cousin winked.

And so, Paul made it into the 2004 Election Night "Making America Safe Again" victory party. Well, almost victory. The Democratic candidate, John Kerry, had lost to the tough-talking Bush, who promised even more security than the security-promising Democrats. Cyrus and most of the other Democrats in Massachusetts had won, however.

(If it seems like I'm picking on the Democrats, just imagine what a field day I could have had if I'd made the Republicans the sponsors of the ecoterrorist kidnappers. Believe me, this isn't about one party or another. But if I'd made Cyrus a Republican, you, as the reader, might just have written such practices off to the Republican side. In any case, I hope blind partisanship won't turn off any readers. And for the record, other than when I strayed to Ralph Nader in the 1996 election, I hold my nose every couple of years and vote as a Democrat.)

The Fleet Center is home to the Boston Celtics, and with a gaudy leprechaun logo that looks like an alcoholic thief, the fans of the Celtics clap their hands as they listen to pumped-up baseball organ music transplanted to basketball games to hype the crowd up during dull moments. The fans watch the game on a giant, four-sided cube TV, taking in the light diodes that flash and flash with the action or inaction. The fans look to the TV to see what's really happening, as if the JumboTron score is more real than the score they can see with their own eyes as the players do their moves and sweep poetically to the basket in front of them. The JumboTron is everything. It is the place where graphics dance. Without the JumboTron, the professional experience of watching the game as a spectator might die.

But the Fleet Center is not always in the throes of some Celtics game. Like most arenas, it plays a dual function. With a light-show conversion, it's altered into a dark theater for hip-hop and rock concerts. The arena is a space for people to come together to momentarily feel they have shared the same experience. It's a place to feel warm together. A place to scream together. Yet the high ceiling, which blows air in and out to regulate the temperature of the place, and which pushes down on the spectators as if a leaden cloud of concrete, always threatens to absorb the sound of the crowd and to leave the spectators feeling alone. For this reason, the JumboTron is so vital. It's an object in the center that all spectators can look to, at once. Even when the noise of the crowd is dissipated by the immensity of the stadium, the JumboTron keeps everyone moving together on the same page, at the same moment, aware of either the same score, or the same replay, or the same close-up of the lips of the rock or hip-hop performer on stage.

Paul couldn't miss the JumboTron, therefore, when he was finally brought into the Fleet Center. And it was only when he saw the screen flashing a red, white, and blue American flag solemnly in the dark amphitheater—where dozens of round tables for political donors had been set up below—that he knew where he was. *So this is it,* he thought, *the main event.* He felt the energy of expectancy, the same way he used to feel with the crowd waiting for I.C.N. to come onstage. Was it possible that all these people could really be waiting for him? That he could be a main event again? Only now, as he saw the image of the American flag waving in full Technicolor on the gigantic JumboTron, did he fully absorb what Zoe had said the other day, and completely appreciate that he might have been transformed from himself as an individual into a symbol of something greater for the culture surrounding him. Was he the collective victim, then? Just as his brother Andrew and the other victims of September 11th had been more than three years ago? There were those like Cyrus, Paul thought, who delighted in feeding off the need of the culture to concoct such heroes and to find such leaders. Paul himself knew he'd wanted, when he was with I.C.N., to tap into the collective consciousness and energy, and to lead in some way the taste and feelings of his country or the people who surrounded him. But that wasn't the same thing, he felt—as he looked at the flag of the United States waving on the JumboTron. He didn't want to be the repository of the heroic triumphing over the fears of terrorism of his citizens. He didn't want to be unveiled as someone who had been saved by Cyrus's tough talk against a bunch of clownish ecoterrorists.

And yet, whether he desired such an outcome or not, the minute he was brought forth into the arena that spread below him, Paul knew a symbolic person could no more choose their symbolic role than they could choose success or failure. Had he, or anyone else who felt they had failed to reach their dreams, or who had failed to have the capacity to reach their dreams, ever wished for life to take its regrettable and self-effacing (in the sense of self-erasing) course or trajectory? Never. So in the same way, when he was brought into the arena and when he cast his eyes down at Cyrus—up on the central podium lauding his victory and proclaiming the great things he intended to do for the people of Massachusetts—Paul knew he couldn't escape the title of "hero" that was about to be branded on him. He looked around to see where Bal's cousin had gone, and he'd disappeared. Paul moved forward in the dark, watching his brother under the spotlights of the Victory Night production. His brother looked directly at Paul on the other side of the stadium. Cyrus quieted the crowd of onlookers cheering his victory. The supporters—shouting and clapping—waved signs with his name on them and hooted into the air, and the JumboTron echoed their sounds and flashed with the face of Cyrus. They followed his gesture to quiet down and sat in their seats, where they were eating a victory night meal. And when they all sat at the tables of starched white linen—which held real silverware, guaranteeing their campaign donations were worth the influence they'd hoped for when they had given their money—Paul saw Zoe seated near the podium.

She was dressed not like someone who had been at the bird-watching tower with him just the night before. She was dressed like a beautiful actress ready to receive her own Academy Award. Her red lipstick accentuated the beauty of her lips. Her hair was pulled back to show off the finesse of her chin. Her brown eyes glistened like those of a famous TV actress who had finally risen above the soap operas to speak to her fans. She was seated beside Cyrus.

A spotlight fixed suddenly on Paul, as bright and piercing as the searchlight of a country for some hope, and then Paul, though blinded yet again, focused on what he could hear, and he heard a gasp, the words of Cyrus announcing his saved brother, and then the roar of those who wished to turn him into an icon, the screams and shouts of supporters.

Paul's face was projected on the JumboTron as large as any professional basketball player's after he's scored the last-second winning shot. He twisted his neck, trying to see through the blinding lights, which felt like a band of cellophane wrapping him in a trap. But he didn't flee. Following the voice of his brother, which called him down the stairs of the arena and across the tables of the campaign contributors, dressed in black and white tuxedos, and then across the red, white, and blue floor covered with stars and stripes, he moved feeling no longer fully in possession of his body.

When he finally made it through the crowd of well-wishers reaching forward to touch him like he was some kind of Jesus resurrected from the dead, he found his way up to the podium. Zoe gave him a kiss that felt warmer than he'd felt in months. She smiled and looked into his eyes, as the heat of the lights sprayed down on them, and stared at him deeply with what seemed to Paul a warning not to tell the truth about his kidnapping experience.

So what should I do now? he thought. *Is this the moment to spill the beans? Is this the moment when I should tell the audience clapping and screaming beneath me, wild with enthusiasm for my courage and tenacity in the face of horrible ecoterrorist kidnappers, that it was all a hoax?* But the choice didn't feel like a choice. Beneath the lights, he couldn't think clearly, and certainly he couldn't choose. What was he to do as Zoe looked at him, not begging for anything but linking her fate to his and commanding him to think about their future together if ever there was to be a future?

Cyrus slapped Paul on the back and introduced him as "my little brother, who has made me so proud these last few weeks."

It was a moment of only lights, only the brightness that seemed to replace the darkness of the blindfold that had covered his eyes before. The TV cameras zoomed in on Paul's face. The crowd, after screaming their support for Paul, hushed in a moment of expectancy to see what he would have to say. But there was nothing he *could* say other than, "Thank you." "Thank you." "Thank you." "Thank you," he repeated into the cameras. He felt his life was no longer his own. He chose at that moment not to choose whether to expose Cyrus or to ridicule his lie, because in the brightness of the lights, with the cameras looking on, there was no freedom to make such a choice.

* * *

Eight months later, July 4, 2005, was Paul's revenge day. He didn't like to use the word *"revenge"* because it sounded so petty, like someone who's come unhinged, and he felt it was more the word of a Greek tragedy than a comedy, and he felt his life was more comedic than tragic. Call it his "hoped-for chance to get a bit even," then. And it wasn't really about getting even, Paul thought, it was about finally setting the record straight. For a while people had come up to him and asked for his heroic autograph even while he could barely make a dime because he was unemployed and slept on his friend Ned's couch. (Zoe had made it clear he wasn't welcome back at their house.) The strangeness of guys in pickup trucks and NASCAR dads occasionally stopping to tell him how great it was he showed those ecoterrorists just where they could shove themselves slowly became more normal, as did the initial sight of people pointing at him from a distance when he walked through downtown Boston—especially when he was near the swan boats paddling along the man-made lake at the center of the Boston Public Garden. Was it simply that families out on a relaxing day had time as they meandered through the park to notice an obscure casualty of modern ecoterrorism? Or was it that in the back of their minds, as they watched squirrels munching on leftover remains of tortilla chips and ice cream cones, they recalled there had been ecoterrorists who once threatened the peace of normal life? In the back of their psyches, Paul thought, they feared the manicured beauty of the downtown public garden would be replaced by wilderness if the ecoterrorists had their way. Whatever the reason, people pointed at him when he walked through the garden.

But Paul's fame had diminished almost to zero the last eight months, and few approached anymore; most seemed to forget why they even recognized him. He had heard more than a couple parents, pushing kids in their SUV-size strollers past him, say, "Who is that guy? I know I've seen him somewhere, but I forget what it was all about." Others remembered vaguely and told each other, "He's the brother of Cyrus Berger—that guy taken hostage by the ecoterrorists—and Berger wouldn't give 'em the money. He held out until they were forced to release him."

It wasn't the rush of media attention and then the slow slide into obscurity, however, that led Paul to this day of revenge. His desire for getting even had nothing to do with being a failure while Cyrus's fame continued to grow. It was more the feeling that time had passed and Cyrus could get away with his pathetically obvious and manipulative scam. The dupe had worked. Cyrus was in Congress, on TV most nights, building up fame and talking already about a potential run for the Senate. TV pundits noted he was one of the few nonactor celebs who had been able to take his fame from "real life"—as a lawyer—and transfer it to the political realm. There were plenty of actors like Reagan and Schwarzenegger who had made the transition, but how many famous lawyers had done the same? Cyrus was a natural, the critics said, and on Sunday mornings he appeared on the national political talk-show circuit to bash his opponents and call for more of whatever he believed in. So he had gotten away with using Paul, he felt.

Paul had tried to finally get the discipline and focus in his life that The Modern Cyrano and Zoe had told him he needed. He'd started taking aikido classes, for a few weeks during the coldest months of the winter, but he wasn't able to keep going. He started to spend afternoons in the Boston Public Library, trying to focus on just the first chapter of his intended book. He had gone back to the theme of the origin and history of "how-to" books. But as he sat in the high-ceilinged reading room of the library, with its inspirational neoclassical statues of great American thinkers, his mind wandered to the many obscure encyclopedias and dictionaries in the room. He picked up a volume on the history of the development of small mining towns in Colorado and discovered that Guggenheim, who had poured all his money via his descendants into art, had made his loot by cornering the gold market in the town of Leadville. And what he noticed in these books and anecdotes was that there was always a simple explanation given for "success"—perseverance. But where was the explanation for failure? Failure seemed to have thousands of origins. And could there really be such an asymmetrical explanation for success and failure?

Precisely what led him back to The Honorable C, then—whether it was his renewed inability to finish his book, or a desire to correct Cyrus's lie, or simply time to get even—wasn't quite clear to Paul, but he traced his way back to his former hostage keeper eventually. The instigator of the search might have been Ned. Hanging out with Ned one afternoon, in his store full of obscure rock posters and statues of Japanese action figures, Ned suggested: "Listen, if I was still under the fucking spell of a guy named Buffalo Man, I would either go kick his ass back in Iowa—which is what I think you should have done a long time ago—or I'd find the last person who did voodoo on me and set things straight."

He found his way back finally to The Honorable C and Bal by asking a couple of Pakistani food vendors if they knew a guy who fit his description, and once he connected back with Bal—who was so happy to see him—he was able to steer in the direction of The Honorable C.

For safety's sake, so no one would associate them, The Honorable C had insisted they meet on a farm outside the town of Lincoln, near the Codman residence, where Paul and Zoe married. The farm was about twenty miles outside Boston, and inside a dusty barn an old fridge sold prepackaged frozen organic beef and also free-range eggs. It was a pay-as-you-take system, with a box for customers to leave money. Other than the fridge, the barn was empty, and it seemed its only purpose was to let people walk around feeling nostalgic for the days when the barn had been filled with hay. The Honorable C and Paul parked their cars in the lot by the barn. They met inside by the fridge full of eggs—exactly where Paul had been instructed—then they walked out to the co-op vegetable gardens, where urban farmers from Boston came to till the land.

It was a bright blue day as they walked past the last of the small animal pens where a couple of goats named Daisy and Buster munched on organic food pellets. (The farm was a well-known petting zoo.)

The Honorable C wore a Dolce e Gabbana getup, far removed from his green ecoterrorist uniform. He had on a bright white shirt with a wide-open collar that revealed his chest hair had been waxed off. His body was evenly tanned, his bell-bottom jeans immaculately ironed, and he was wearing black-rimmed sunglasses with the gold D and G logo on the side.

"Nice to hear from you, Paul," The Honorable C said. "So what's cooking?"

"Nothing much. Just some aikido and things. I'm back to working on my book."

"Good. Good. So how's it coming?"

"I've decided to go back to the first chapter to focus on just the origin and development of how-to books."

During the kidnapping, they'd talked a bit about the book; but not too much, so The Honorable C had no way of understanding this was potentially a major improvement.

"And you?" said Paul. "How's it going for you?"

"Not too bad, though Cyrus never made the final payment, of course. I had a feeling he'd flake in the end. He cooked up some excuse about us violating some subsection of one of our contractual requirements. In any case, for the most part things are going pretty well. Although the problem is, I can't really claim any credit yet for Cyrus's campaign given the sensitive nature of the thing—so I haven't quite reaped the financial rewards of the whole project yet."

Paul looked ahead at the gardeners clipping flowers in June and tying up the stalks of tomato plants. He'd tried growing tomatoes a couple times in New England, but with the cold, short growing season, it wasn't easy—though some people always seemed to have a green thumb. This was the moment of conversation he'd been waiting for the last few days and dreaming of in bed.

"Well, let's go public, then," said Paul.

"What do you mean?" The Honorable C said.

"Let's tell everyone the truth about the campaign."

"What for?"

"Easy. For me, let's call it some kind of purification, getting rid of a lie. It might just put some genie back in its bottle and save me."

"And for me?" The Honorable C said.

Paul didn't respond at first. He watched the gardeners pulling weeds, eliminating the bad from the good. He knew The Honorable C would see the obvious benefits soon.

"Oh, I get it," The Honorable C finally said. "A chance to finish my reality TV documentary with a bang instead of a whimper."

"Right," said Paul. "I've been thinking the only reason you haven't shown your documentary yet is that the ending was kind of wimpy: me up on stage thanking everyone for treating me like a hero upon my release from my hostage ordeal. It wasn't exactly inspirational. Especially if you have to compete with *War of the Worlds*."

"No, it wasn't exactly climactic," The Honorable C said, and he took his sunglasses off to show Paul just how disappointed he'd been with his final performance at the Fleet Center. "I had hoped for one of two different kinds of ending—either you exposing Cyrus in front of everyone, or at least weeping emotionally that the whole ordeal was over. But instead you just seemed to look into the cameras as if they were blinding you. In some kind of daze. I had someone inside the arena, of course, to get final footage. What are you proposing, then?"

Walking around the farm and petting zoo, Paul didn't know exactly what he was proposing. All he had in mind was a vague idea of telling the truth about what happened during his kidnapping. The truth might be just what he needed to exorcise Buffalo Man's curse and get even with Cyrus. But by July 4, after a good deal of input from The Honorable C, the plan was set.

Most tourists who come to Boston find themselves, eventually, following a red painted line on the ground that bobs and weaves from Revolutionary War-era monument to monument. They pass the cemetery that holds the graves of Sam Adams and Paul Revere; the line takes them past the Bunker Hill memorial, where the Colonials first united as a regular army to fight the British. It passes Faneuil Hall, where the colonists debated how to fight for their independence, and it certainly takes everyone to the Old South Meeting House, home of the Boston Tea Party. The Old South Meeting House is a beautiful tall redbrick church with a slate-colored spire and was the highest building of its time. It must have made the colonists feel like their city of Boston was a special place, a great new center in the New World. Colonists met in the Old South church to discuss just about everything—grazing rights—or to listen to ministers preach, and eventually, after the British had raised taxes on tea without the consent of the governed, Sam Adams and his friends dressed up like Indians and whooped and hollered from the top balcony, pretending to be belligerent Red-faces, and in this disguise, they went down to the main harbor to dump a large new shipment of tea that the British government said couldn't be sold without paying the tax. What we're all taught in school is that the interesting thing about this tea party is that the colonists were finally fed up and taking action against their oppressors. But the interesting question might be why the colonists felt it was necessary to dress up like Indians to rebel against the king? Everyone present in the Old South Meeting House knew who these rebels were. Did the rebels really think their war paint and feathers, or whatever they were wearing to be "Indian," hid them?

261

Or did they really think their community was so large that people wouldn't know who they were? What I'm suggesting is not that they were cowards—it's plausible to believe a little safety and security was provided by the costumes—but it seems what they were recognizing is that an unvarnished, unhidden act of rebellion is much harder than a revolutionary initially thinks. What begins with great certainty on the part of a revolutionary mixes eventually with all the fears of taking action. And the Indian costume of the rebels at the Boston Tea Party reveals that even if the cause of a rebel is just, even if outsiders support it, the very act of breaking the rules of a society makes a rebel suspect. The rebel is always engaged in some act of sin, and he's certainly resisted by the majority until a tipping point is reached, a critical mass where open revolution is joined by the masses.

Today the Old South Meeting House is anything but a place for revolutionary beginnings. Tourists wander through information displays. They glance up at the balcony where the fake Indians yelled out against the king. They are warned not to touch anything by the park rangers on duty, who try not to fall asleep as hordes of tourists move through the building and then go back on their way, following the thick red line to the next important historic location.

Down the street from the Old South Meeting House a couple of blocks is one of the major Boston shopping areas. Historic buildings mix in with the new. Shoe stores, with row after row of shoes made in China, mix with the more historic Filene's Basement, which has just merged with Macy's. There's an old clock on Filene's, with Roman numerals encased in a patinated copper shell. Beneath the clock that chimes each hour, hundreds of mostly African-American shoppers make their way from one store selling Nikes, big gold chains, and music to another. Of course, there are white people shopping in the area, too, but because the Orange Line of the subway, which runs through the racially segregated area of Roxbury, stops right near Downtown Crossing and Filene's, most of the shoppers aren't white. Teens skip school and hang out in the shopping area near the Old South Meeting House. Others walk around with boom boxes. And a couple of guys beg for spare change.

In the middle of all this activity, near a Burger King and Wendy's, there's a food court where workers who don't have enough money to go on a power lunch grab a quick bite in one of the dozen restaurants where patrons eat cafeteria-style at small tables with swivel chairs attached so no one can steal a chair. The lighting is always dim, and in front of a few of the fast-food joints, a hired helper gives out free samples of chicken teriyaki or New Orleans bourbon chicken, or some other kind of chicken, to entice each customer.

This isn't normally a place for press conferences. Many of the customers of the food court are men who look like they've never exercised and don't get much sex play from their wives, and who wear cell phones on plastic clip-ons over pleated polyester pants.

This is the food court The Honorable C chose for the climactic moment of his film. Here was the place where ecoterrorists could most cringe: neon lights cramming every inch with signs seducing customers; Styrofoam containers for each meal; Chinese food court vendors dressed in vaguely Japanese kimonos, wearing disposable white paper hats shaped 1950s-style. The animal meat in the place has been terrorized—pressed into chicken McNuggets.

"With the McDonald's we'll accomplish two things at once," The Honorable C told Paul after he cooked up the plan. "First, it has the obvious horrific environmental connotation. But more importantly, for our final scene, it's a great place for you to go postal. You always hear about shootings and guys going loco at a Mickey D's."

Paul was early for "the final event." The action wasn't supposed to begin for another fifteen minutes, so he sat at one of the food court tables, where The Honorable C directed him. The place was more crowded than he'd expected. Thousands of people had come to town to celebrate July 4 in the nation's historic capital. The Boston fireworks would be televised around the country later in the evening, as viewers watched the Boston Pops in white tuxedos play Broadway show tunes and Tchaikovsky's *1812 Overture* as rockets kissed the sky. And of those thousands who would watch the fireworks later, a couple hundred patriots had found their way to the food court to load up before heading to the esplanade along the Charles River.

Feeling the worn-out Formica bottom of a swivel chair—wiggling back and forth, side to side—Paul thought not only of all the patrons who had killed time over a fifteen-minute lunch break, he thought how lucky he would be to unburden himself soon of the lie he'd been holding in for the better part of eight months. He smiled and waved at the camera across the food court. The Honorable C shouldered the camera himself, unwilling to take any chances on this final shot. Paul opened and closed his palms and felt as light as bubbles coming out of the top of a soda can. He thought all those TV reports about how sad and conflicted a man felt just before committing a crime—going postal in a bank or in the office of some hi-tech company after being laid off—was all bunk. The thing about the news reports was that they always tried to make the audience feel the gunner or "nut" felt remorse for what they did. But why would a nut feel remorse in the act of getting revenge? That was just some crap the TV shows implied to prevent everyone from going out and getting a gun and taking out all the people who had pissed them off and fucked up their lives. NO, there was no hesitation to the person taking revenge. The stations liked to say the gunner "hesitated" or that he was "sweating" or that he was "crying." Closer to the truth, Paul felt, was that anyone doing something audacious to get back at those who had jerked them around felt liberated.

Therefore, whereas on a normal day in such a food court Paul might feel some disgust, he swiveled back and forth playfully in his cramped chair waving at the camera. The Honorable C lowered his hand, apparently to tell Paul to tone his movements down. Paul stuck his tongue out at The Honorable C. He felt the gun in his pocket and jiggled the smooth stock of the revolver, and it felt as smooth as it had in practice. Over at the Indian food booth, he heard a woman tell the owner she was allergic to spice, and she asked if he had anything that would be OK for someone allergic to wheat, milk, and also chicken. By the Greek food stand—with a large poster of a greasy gyro placed over the Acropolis—an overweight patron asked for twice the creamy garlic sauce on his shawarma. At the McDonald's he saw a customer order four cheeseburgers. "You know why I order the small, regular cheeseburgers?" he heard the customer say. "Because if you add up the weight of four of 'em, it's the same as a Quarter Pounder, only it's fifty cents less. It's all marketing, you know what I mean?" The teen behind the counter wiped the sweat off the acne on her face. She bent over to count the change her cash register had informed her of and nodded vaguely she had heard the calculations of the wise multi-cheeseburger patron.

It was ten minutes to 1 P.M. now and Paul sat and watched as other TV cameras came into the food court to set up for the press event. A few food patrons pointed at the cameras out of interest, but nothing was happening yet. The only thing of real interest was the extra lights. Then a couple men in suits, members of the mayor's office, put up a banner GOING THE EXTRA MILE. For the most part, it was a slow news day: the few Boston news helicopters flew over the esplanade along the Charles River, estimating the number of patriotic picnickers and sunbathers in the park. Paul had seen the helicopters on his way to the food court, hovering with fast-talking traffic and weather reporters who hoped to graduate to becoming DJs on big-time rock stations someday.

Compared to the reporters floating in the sky, it looked even less appealing to be a reporter cooped up in the food court on July 4, Paul thought, rather than hanging out with a bunch of friends at a barbecue, sipping beers. But this was just the price to pay to work one's way up to the top.

In a few minutes, Cyrus would arrive along with the mayor, and then the whole plan would kick into gear. Paul looked over at The Honorable C and gave him a sarcastic thumbs-up. The Honorable C pretended not to see Paul, and he zoomed in and out on the GOING THE EXTRA MILE banner to be sure he had just the right focal point for the event.

Only now was the woman who was allergic to everything deciding what she could finally eat. The plump man who'd ordered the shawarma with extra cream sauce had already sat down, slurped an extra-tall Coke, finished his shawarma, and was headed downstairs to the bathroom.

The savvy-cheeseburger patron was done with burger number three and jingled the remaining change in his pocket.

"You got any change, man?" a homeless dude, smelling like he'd been sleeping for days in his urine, asked Paul. Paul reached instinctively into his pocket where the gun was waiting. He felt the hot metal, and without any change, he told the homeless guy, "I'm sorry, man. I don't even have my wallet on me today." What he wanted to add was that the guy should stick around a few minutes and he might see some fireworks.

At the Subway sandwich shop, a little beyond the Indian stand, Paul could hear a patron asking if the baloney on the sub was really as good for the heart as all the ads on TV said. "I don't know," the food server said. "But if they're saying it on the ads, then I gotta believe it's true. You know what I mean?"

All this talk of food was making him hungry, and he thought of going to the Mickey D's to order a Big Mac—though he felt it was never big enough; he preferred the Burger King Whopper—yet as he stood up to get some food The Honorable C lowered his hand to tell him to sit down.

An advance man tested a microphone in front of the GOING THE EXTRA MILE banner, and then the mayor of Boston showed up with Cyrus walking beside him. Four TV cameras were lined up in front of the banner, and The Honorable C had set up his camera on a tripod next to the journalists. He wore a press badge that dangled around his neck, like the others, and no one seemed to pay him any attention.

"Thank you for coming," the mayor said, opening his arms in a welcoming gesture toward all patrons of the food court, who only now began to pay more attention to the event in progress. "Today we are here to celebrate the Ten Millionth Meal served at this food court. As all of you know, providing healthy, satisfying meals and a rich diversity of food has always been a part of the development plan of this city. And I think there could be no finer place to celebrate such a milestone than at this food court, which really has brought so much vitality to this downtown area. July 4th has always been a celebration of the great spirit of entrepreneurialism that helped our Founding Fathers develop this great country. And one thing our Founding Fathers also had in spades was generosity. So today, on behalf of the city of Boston, I want to thank Mike Magliozzi, the owner of this special food court, for not only keeping such a clean and well-run place for the citizens of Boston to eat in, but also for his generous donation of the thousand McDonald's Kids Meals that will be handed out to the citizens of Boston on the esplanade today as we get ready for the hell of a good—I mean heck of a good—fireworks show we're gonna see tonight." He paused and turned to Cyrus, standing by his side. "Cyrus, do you have anything you'd like to add before we walk over to the esplanade?"

A few patrons clapped as the mayor finished his comments. The shawarma eater emerged from downstairs, wiping his hands on his shorts. The vegan and irritable bowel syndrome lady had picked through the first part of her white rice. The Subway customer was licking the last of the extra mayo on his low-calorie baloney sandwich.

It is time, Paul thought. *Time for the truth to be told.* It was time for a new Boston Tea Party. From within his pocket—the one that didn't hold the gun—he pulled out some greasepaint and as quickly, yet as precisely, as he could he drew red, white, and blue lines across his face in the way he thought an Indian chief might draw war paint. From a plastic bag next to his feet he pulled out an Indian headdress that looked more appropriately Sioux than anything belonging to the Algonquin or other nearby Indians of New England. The thing was, the costume store sold only one kind of Indian costume. How then, had the "Indians" at the Boston Tea Party dressed up for their revolution? Paul had thought earlier. There were no Plains Indians around New England, and so there was doubtfully any long Indian headdress for Sam Adams and his followers to wear as they whooped and hollered. Had they simply run around with tomahawks trying to look menacing as they imitated the many stories of Indian rapes and kidnappings that so titillated the colonists? Paul had been puzzled, when he'd been in the costume store in Chinatown, as he'd tried to imagine just what a real Native American costume from Boston should look like. But the truth was, with no more Indians around to meet new Pilgrims, with Indians only running casinos these days in the few plots of land that still remained for them anywhere nearby, he had to just wing it on the costume front. And so, as Cyrus came to the fore to add a few comments, he was suddenly interrupted by a fairly short round man dressed in a Sioux costume with red, white, and blue war paint on his cheeks and a long red, white, and blue headdress of dyed eagle feathers that went from the tip of his Indian-chief head gracefully down (in an arc put together by Chinese workers) to the floor.

With a move as quick as he could muster, Paul jumped onto the smooth bottom of the swivel chair that had caressed so many fat asses in the food court, and he hoisted himself up onto the table itself. He was hollering up and down. He was whooping like a Native American. He was yelling out that he was bringing a new Boston Tea Party. He shouted out whoops of "pow wow wow wow, pow wow wow wow."

The mayor looked to his aides to see if this was all part of the planned festivities. Cyrus continued with his comments, paying no attention to the whooping. He'd learned long ago to ignore the pink elephant in the room in any political situation. The aides looked at the manager of the food court, but the manager didn't seem to know anything. And still Paul was hollering and moving his legs up and down, his feet jingling with the sound of a few bells he'd sewn on some moccasins that he'd also bought at the costume store.

"Would the gentleman please sit down?" Cyrus finally said when it became apparent he couldn't simply continue to ignore this Native American. "Would the gentleman sit *down*. I want to assure everyone here that I support the rights of Native Americans, too, but this is simply not the time for a protest of this nature."

But Paul had made a choice, he knew. He was in the act of making a choice. And could a choice be stopped once the process had begun? The way he saw the choice was whether he could continue to allow others to determine his fate or not. How long had he let himself feel like shit because his brother was simply better than him at everything he did? How long was he going to feel his brother Andrew's death had been appropriated by Cyrus? How long was he going to let himself feel his parents favored Cyrus's brilliance over his own mixed abilities? How long was he going to fear toppling, or inhibiting in any way, his brother's fame because in the process of tainting that fame, he might limit his own residual worth? How long could he put up with being abused by others, such as his brother's KIDNAPPING of him simply for a selfish, expedient end? His brother wasn't the first to abuse him, he felt. He had been the fat one when he was a kid. He had been taunted then. He had felt the failure of I.C.N. and he felt this failure—this near success that had turned to dust—nearly every day since the band had gone under. He had felt the abuse of failing to get tenure at a lowly community college. He had felt the condescension of his brother as he told him he owed his very job to him at that college. He had felt Zoe's telling him he was jealous of his brothers. How long could a person simmer with all this abuse and not take any action? He was a victim, he thought, THE victim.

And yet, at the same time, the choice he was making as he whooped and hollered, he felt, was also a choice to put the blame on his brother when surely he deserved more than a bit of the blame for his life himself. Could he merely blame his family, his culture, or Buffalo Man for the trajectory of his life? Could such an easy way out, and the lure of victimization, absolve him of his inner faults, foibles, and failures? Could he really place his inability to be a great musician or his inability to overcome his writer's block at the feet of his brother and those who surrounded him? Then how to cope with the pain of failure and with the weight of simply living? he wondered.

So what he was choosing, or what he was in the act of choosing, might be cowardly, he felt, simply placing the blame on another. And yet, what he wanted to believe he was choosing—as he moved his legs up and down rapidly in a powwow movement—was to no longer live with any doubts or hesitation or lies. When he was kidnapped by The Honorable C, he had cried into the wilderness next to the tepee and he had shouted, but he had never fully demanded his freedom. Well, that had changed now. He was demanding his freedom. He was in the process of exposing a lie.

Paul pulled out his gun and shot six quick loud bullets into the ceiling, just to be sure he had everyone's attention. The patrons all, finally, put down the remains of their fast food. The food court was silent. The neon lights burned on brightly, yet even the light seemed to bend and hold quietly for Paul to speak. If the saying goes you could hear a pin drop, it was now silent enough to hear this Native American talk.

"How dare you try to tell us— How dare you try to tell ME when it's OK for me to speak and when I should shut up," Paul said, and he waved his gun in the air. "I'm sick and tired of your usurpation of my liberty! Do the words 'give me liberty or give me death' mean anything to you? Do they mean anything to anyone anymore? Kidnapping me! This man," Paul said, pointing at Cyrus, "kidnapped his own brother. He kidnapped me just so he could seem tough on crime, tough on ecoterrorists, and now look at what he's getting away with."

He was ready to go much further in his speech; he was ready to give full details of what Cyrus had done to him over the years, and especially during the kidnapping, but by this time, as the initial shock of the gunshots had worn off, the mayor's security guards tackled Paul. They tore off his Indian headdress as The Honorable C filmed the whole event.

You might expect an event with as much gunslinging as this would lead to widespread investigations of whether Paul's allegation of being kidnapped by his brother was true. Certainly footage of Paul shooting in the air and whooping and hollering was on all the TV newscasts that night—cut between the fireworks and the Russian *1812 Overture*. But other than being portrayed as the ranting of a disgruntled brother who had become traumatized by the events of his kidnapping eight months before, no one believed for a moment, or even really heard further about, Paul's charges against his brother once the truth was brought into the open.

Coda: When I began this chapter, it was the day Michael Jackson was acquitted of the charges of getting a young boy drunk and sexually molesting him. Twenty-two hundred journalists—2200!—camped out in front of his courthouse to beam the verdict to the world. There was a hush when it was announced a verdict was ready. Hundreds of fans waited nervously, waving signs in Jackson's defense. A few others tried to shout the fans down—pure guardians against rape and pedophilia and anyone who is "weird." Then the verdict was announced. Jackson was found innocent. The fans went wild. The prosecutor and all those who were sure MJ was guilty were pissed. An uproar. An event on TV. All the talking heads put in their opinion about whether the verdict was just or not. And then, indifference. A few days later, the caravan of the press and the cameras had moved on. Did it really make a difference whether MJ was guilty or not? Only to him. Only to HIS life. But the spectacle was over. What really happened didn't matter anymore. Jackson could have been thrown in jail or not. It would have been all the same to everyone else (more or less, except for MJ's true fans). The outcome is really irrelevant. It's only the spectacle that counts.

P.P.S. The "Indians" at the Boston Tea Party dressed up like Mohawks, who lived nowhere near Boston but rather in the Great Lakes region of New York, where they were members of the five-nation Iroquois Confederacy.

CHAPTER 12

Early in the morning, with the bright rays of orange sun pushing with speed over rows of corn and warming dewdrops on the grass behind the Zaliya Rashna meditation retreat, a group of meditators was hopping up and down, shaking their limbs from side to side, trying to disencumber the stresses of "modern living."

The instructor for the morning class, which wasn't exactly tai chi but a variant developed especially for the patient-retreaters at the institute, was none other than Buffalo Man himself. He stood in front of the twenty-four students—willing to wake up before the sunrise, to greet the sun when it finally "kissed the earth with its radiant beams" (as Buffalo Man put it)—and as he opened his arms wide, forming a buttercup greeting the sun, his followers leaped first on the right foot, then on the left as they moved their arms with one palm saluting the sky and then the other like go-go dancers trying to hail a cab to heaven.

"Oh sun, you are powerful," Buffalo Man started to chant. "Oh sun, you give us warmth and life to all manner of fruits and vegetables. And as even the great scientists of the earth understand—who believe we can all simply eat vitamin capsules someday to sustain our bodies—there is no true source for our life but you. There are no solar panels without you. We are all made of atoms from stars that have exploded as supernovas, and so without you we are nothing."

It was mid-August, when the heat of the Iowa earth incubates corn, and as rays of the sun "kissed" the tops of the tasseled corn rising to great heights—which could bury an innocent wanderer into the corn—the sky lightened from dark, and all who felt the energy of the sun as they hopped knew the earth was good; it was only humans who made it seem each day might be a struggle. The warm sun heated the dew that stuck to the feet of the meditators and promised fertility, the regenerating power of the ground.

The group of meditators formed three rows of eight, all following Buffalo Man as he tilted his eyes to the sky, and only Paul wondered in the last row as he watched the other meditators hopping in a smooth euphoria, why the promise of the sun could feel so hot on his face and why the dew of the earth could feel so warm on his feet, yet why the warmth and promise of Buffalo Man's words failed to enter his fearful heart.

Buffalo Man continued: "The great god of the sun has smiled on us this morning, and certainly he smiles on *all* of you, but he's also sent me a message that one of you refuses to feel the warmth of his powers. Fear inevitably shuts all our senses and causes us to fail to see the gifts we have already been given. But to the person this morning who fails to feel the sun, I promise you that with a proper conquering of fear, the fullness of the senses can be reopened. For just as the pores of an animal get clogged—leading to a painful eruption within the skin as an acne of trapped poisons—the pricking of that trapped fear releases the pore and allows the full healing energy of the body to resume its natural course."

If ever there was a strained metaphor, this was it, Paul thought. What could be more strained than equating his fear to a clogged pore? He tried to catch up to the hopping pace of the devoted followers. He listened to the pounding rhythm of their feet bouncing off the grass of the lawn behind the main building. The unity of feet pressing from the ball to the heel as they landed and then lifting with arms raised worshipfully toward the sky, and then landing back on the other foot, was truly a wonderful sound to hear. It reminded him of the synchronized drums of the Nigerian drummer Babatunde Olatunji. The drums pounded. The feet pounded. The hearts beat and the sky absorbed the arms reaching toward it. The sun rose. The rays spread. And Buffalo Man's arms spread slowly, slowly, so slowly they barely seemed to move; yet slowly they opened wider and wider into the sky above like a lotus exposing its delicate yet resilient petals.

A cloud of sleepiness fogged Paul's brain, however, and he was reminded yet again he had never been a morning person. His fast-beating heart clashed with the smooth rhythm of the morning sun dancers. Would there be no gong to let him know just how long he had to endure this torture? How long would he have to stress his body, pretending he liked this kind of physical activity? What he really wanted was a plate of greasy eggs over easy, griddled with a side of three flapjacks smothered in syrup, followed by half a dozen pieces of bacon, washed down with lukewarm coffee drenched with cream and sugar—no Sweet'N Low, please—just like he'd had in the truck stops as he'd hitchhiked his way across country from Boston. He didn't want to romanticize truck stop food, but he felt it was fantastic; not that it always tasted so good, but when it was right, it was hard to beat the fried chicken. And although the iceberg lettuce sometimes looked like it had nothing to do with the word *lettuce,* whenever he saw the six choices of salad dressing at the salad bar, it didn't matter the sauces looked like they'd been reformulated or opened from an enormous plastic jug; the sweet orange candy of French dressing was a pleasure he looked forward to with spoonfuls of Baco-Bits thrown on for good measure and a greasy, buttery roll next to an order of fried chicken to top it off.

Why had he hitchhiked when he probably could have found a cheap car, or even borrowed Ned's if he had to? He wasn't sure, but if he had to guess, he would have said it had something to do with putting his impending mortality back in the closet. *I mean,* he thought while riding in one of the trucks, *the thing that people who* pick up *hitchhikers fear is that they'll get killed by a freak, but for the hitchhiker it's the purest form of life, something for nothing, not feeling you have to be anywhere in particular at any time, knowing a new encounter is just at the next leg of the road when you have to find someone new to take you down the highway.* What all those guys like Jack Kerouac had understood, Paul thought, was that hitchhiking extended life and allowed the hitchhiker to stay one foot ahead of his troubled mind.

So he had hitchhiked from Boston to Iowa, and he'd even managed to get a ride all the way to the Rashna Retreat; and the other purpose of hitchhiking, Paul realized, was to decontaminate himself from Buffalo Man's original curse, because hadn't all his problems begun when he *picked up* a hitchhiker, which had led him to the retreat? So now instead of *taking* someone, he would be *taken to* the retreat and reverse the curse of the prophecy that had predicted not only the death of his first brother and the end of his marriage and the breakup with his second brother, but that also predicted his death in the middle of the fourth ring of his life—which was now. Only recently he'd had his birthday, on the 20th of July. He'd turned thirty-six, an age he felt was far too old for someone who had already failed at so many things, while others such as astronauts on the newly relaunched space shuttle *Discovery* were already up in the heavens Buffalo Man prayed to, walking in space, risking life and limb to further the cause of humanity's great adventure.

At the end of the morning sun salutation, the dancers fell silent together in one final jump, and Paul—who had already stopped jumping a few minutes before—suddenly felt a tapping from behind on his shoulder.

It was Brad Rashnaji, the assistant to Buffalo Man who had summoned Paul during his last visit to the Rashna Retreat to receive his palm reading. "According to our records," Brad Rashnaji said now, "that check you claimed should have come in the mail eight years ago never quite appeared. Our computer files show your behavior was unenthusiastic—meaning too skeptical upon your last visit to warrant readmission to the Rashna Retreat. As Buffalo Man always tells us, a proper and healthy attitude is required before the healing process can begin . . . However, two circumstances have permitted you to be checked in this morning. The first is there has also always been a permanent record on your file in our computer with a message from Buffalo Man stating that if you ever wished to stay with us again, this would imply a tacit admission the prophecy he gave you was true and that therefore you should be readmitted so the two of you can discuss your future further. Buffalo Man is informing me he continues to find your prophecy interesting and that he wishes to help you over-come the gravest challenge you will now face in the fourth ring of your life."

"Buffalo man is telling you this all right now? I thought he was just over there," Paul said, pointing to Buffalo Man as he spoke to the other retreaters toweling off after the morning salutations.

"Yes, exactly. He has already intuited these things, and so he has told me to welcome you. And he also wishes you to know it's not out of any generosity he's doing this service for you. He stands strictly by his payment policy and by the standards and obligations of the Rashna Retreat, but he wishes you to know that a number of years ago your ex-wife, Zoe—who was still your girlfriend then—paid up the money you owed in the hope this might lift what you call 'the curse of Buffalo Man' and that she also left instructions recently, after your wild esca-pade in the food court in Boston, that she would pay for you to have another one-week stay at the retreat to finally resolve your issues."

"She did that?" Paul said. "But she won't even let me stay in our apartment. Why would she do anything like that?"

"According to your file, once she saw you go literally ballistic on TV, she knew it would only be a matter of time before you came back to the Rashna Retreat to resolve your issues with Buffalo Man. If I were you, I would simply accept her offer, be thankful, and move on."

And so it was all a bit clearer now why the woman who was at the reception desk had taken so long reading her computer screen as Paul had tried to check in at five o'clock this morning. Paul had decided to play it straight and not to sneak into the retreat. There was no chance he would ever be able to talk to Buffalo Man that way, so he had simply told the woman at the reception desk he realized he had some unresolved issues from his last visit but that if she could speak to her boss, he was sure everything could be worked out. After the woman read her screen for what seemed a long enough time for a literacy-training course, she'd told Paul she would have to speak to the management first before she could check him in but that it *might* be possible to work something out. She told him to take a seat in the lobby, and he complied. Then she disappeared. And since it was taking her so long to return, he had finally wandered out of the main building until he found the group of morning meditators getting ready to greet Buffalo Man and the sun. He put his few belongings down. He was unshaved. His jeans were too tight for making such morning moves. As usual, he felt he lacked the Lycra warm-up pants and other gear of professional yoga exercisers, but since he was unwilling to be denied access to the Rashna Retreat, he did his best to go through the morning sun greeting; and now here was Brad Rashnaji telling him he could stay at the retreat, that a room was ready for him, and that Zoe, of all people, had paid for him to be able to meet Buffalo Man again to resolve his problems.

"Buffalo Man will be ready to see you for the first of your tests at eleven o'clock this morning," Brad Rashnaji said. "Please remember to show up promptly for your first session."

"Tests?" said Paul.

"Yes. Three tests. It's all part of the necessary purification process. There's no gain without pain. Since you are firmly rooted in the Western tradition, Buffalo Man has suggested I use the analogy of Odysseus going home to get his wife, Penelope, after he has abandoned her for years. I take it you probably had to study the epic poem in college? In any case, you'll recall that in order to win back his wife's love, he had to first prove himself through a series of tests—the last and most dangerous of which involved killing all the men who were her suitors. Of course, there's also the *Star Wars* movie version of these tests. The hero fights his inner demons. He fights his father. He acquires the force and wins goodness over the dark side. Or in Hong Kong action movies and in tales of Zen Buddhism, the same thing arises. Every culture has these tests, and it's the only way to get to happiness."

"And if I succeed at the three tests, will Buffalo Man guarantee this will get rid of the curse he gave me?"

"Buffalo Man never gives any curses. He simply reads the palms of a select few and then shares his wisdom. You should meet him in front of the Kiva Hut at eleven o'clock in a bathing suit."

"In a bathing suit? But I just came across country hitchhiking and I don't like to swim."

"Suit yourself. No pun intended. But if you want any hope of over-coming your prophecy, then I suggest you meet him in something that resembles a bathing suit by eleven o'clock on the dot."

Was Paul in a hurry? Yes. The sooner he could meet with Buffalo Man and find out whatever stupid tests he had to go through to give him his life back, the sooner he could regain his freedom. He'd been trapped for years now by this stupid, fucking prophecy, some words uttered and divined by only the shape and feel of his palms, no less, and how could a life be wholly dictated by the shape of one's body? After getting instructions from Brad Rashnaji, he dropped off his few belongings in his assigned room, which—all too intentionally, he felt—was the exact room he'd slept in the last time he'd come to the Rashna Retreat. They're trying to trap me, he thought. They want to throw me back into the corncrib and make me think I'll sleep in again and wake to find out that Zoe isn't really paying for anything and that I owe them a pile of money, and then I'm going to get another fricking prophecy that more bad things are going to happen to me.

When he entered the room—with its teak-framed futon and fruit still piled high on an altar to placate the gods, and butterfat candles still burning with incense that was supposed to be oh-so-soothing but that just reminded him he had once been called away from a cool shower by Brad Rashnaji and told to go get a free palm reading that had screwed up the rest of his life—he almost didn't leave his belongings. He almost latched the door and planned to flee again to some other place that would provide an answer to his existential crisis.

But where would he go? Who else could cure him but the devil? *The only way to eradicate this curse of my life, this stinking pot of the dregs of my inabilities, is to go to the man himself.* He couldn't nap, which was certainly unusual for him. He couldn't shower. He could think only of removing the curse and getting to Buffalo Man as quickly as possible to kung fu kick the prophecy into the gutter. Whatever tests there were, whatever crazy activities they might be—whether keeping his eyes open with bamboo sticks as water slowly dripped onto his forehead, or sitting in a lotus position for hours and hours—he would contort himself, he would do whatever it took to have his life back again under his control.

He went to the main building of the Rashna Retreat, and surrounded by others calmly eating fresh fruit out of handmade bowls that were clearly supposed to be contemplative pieces of art, he sat at the end of a low table on a tatami and ate his granola as quickly as possible, barely chewing, slurping up the milk, doing anything to get the meal over with so he could get closer to the time he would meet Buffalo Man one-on-one and begin the process of reacquiring his life.

At least the man was willing to meet with him voluntarily and lead him out of his mess. *I should be more thankful, shouldn't I?* he thought. *Some guru-dudes might just have abandoned me to my fate. And even though he gave me this shitty fate to begin with, at least he's willing to help me get out of the trap now.*

He walked fast around the facilities, alternately cursing Buffalo Man and thinking he had some good sides. At the pool behind the central building he remembered this was the first place he had seen Zoe, reading her book about Andy Warhol. If only he could go back and start over—still meet her, marry her, but lose his anxiousness along the way, be liberated from his constant need to analyze, be liberated of his jealousies of his brothers, have more ability and focus and be able to complete his book, or some project, any project. The students at B_____ Community College would be heading back to class soon, and although he didn't really want to teach students who came and went to class randomly, depending on their whim—much as he seemed to live his own life—wouldn't it be nice if he could be headed back to his classroom this fall again with the approval of Chairman Kominski, with some feeling he was accepted by fellow colleagues and that his thoughts and ideas mattered to someone in the world?

At the pool, he realized suddenly he had yet to find a bathing suit and he walked up to one of the retreaters and asked the guy if he had an extra suit he could borrow, and when he was told, not surprisingly, the guy didn't have one, he asked if he could just use the bathing suit the guy had on. "I just need it for a day or so," Paul said. "Maybe even just until tonight. I'm not sure what the tests are Buffalo Man is going to give me. Would you mind? I'm kind of in a weird position. I'm kind of desperate."

"Hey listen, I'd like to help you out," the guy said, "but it's really the only suit I have."

By now it was ten minutes to eleven, and if Paul didn't get a suit soon he wouldn't have one at all. At the far end of the pool, near where Zoe was sitting when he'd been with her his first time at the retreat, he saw some woman had forgotten a red shawl with a few gold threads. After looking around for the owner and finding it definitely abandoned, he took it and went into the pool changing room and wrapped the cotton shawl around his legs and loin until he was swaddled in some kind of red cloth diaper, or primitive clothing, that made him look like he was ready for an ancient wrestling match. He was ready to fight off his prophecy. He was ready, if necessary, even to wrestle with Buffalo Man. He had some idea of something like an Indian leg-wrestling match, where the two would lie on their backs and struggle with interlocked legs, until Paul could prove his strength. When Paul came out of the changing room, he looked over at the man who wouldn't lend him his bathing suit and he beat his chest like Tarzan.

"Hey, I wasn't trying to get personal about this," the man said to Paul.

"Aaargh," Paul roared. He slapped his chest and headed toward the Kiva Hut, where he'd been instructed to meet Buffalo Man promptly at eleven.

The Kiva was an earthen, round room built underground and had a top covered with mud, wood, and sticks. A wooden ladder descended into the sweat room, where people taking long sweats usually sat in groups as they meditated with a retreat leader. Sometimes they stayed in there for hours before coming out, covered in sweat. *I'll just have to outlast him,* Paul thought. *He'll try to use his yoga powers to outsweat me.* He looked around for Buffalo Man, and there was no sign of him. He wondered if he'd come to the right place. He was naked except for the loincloth that he'd wrapped over his underwear, and he had a pair of flip-flops on that he kicked in the dirt, psyching himself up to withstand the tests Buffalo Man was going to give him. He looked back toward the main center, expecting to see Buffalo Man coming in his usual assured, bouncing-step way, but instead a deep voice, amplified by the interior of the Kiva Hut like the inside of a drum, boomed out Buffalo Man saying, "Come inside. Your purification will now begin."

The voice startled Paul and he obeyed instantly. He went to the ladder into the Kiva and stepped down, lowering himself backward slowly, feeling the ladder rungs as foreign territory that might not support him, until he finally clomped to the earth floor below ground. "Come closer and sit by me," he heard the voice of Buffalo Man say. Was it really Buffalo Man? The room was dark and his eyes had yet to adjust. The only light was from a candle at the other end of the round cavern and from the hole at the top of the ladder. But the ladder was removed and the hole above sealed, so he was faced with the shock of going from the brightness of an Iowa summer into the dark of what felt like potentially hell.

Why does he always torture me this way? Paul thought. Why can't he just give me some prescription like a doctor or meet with me in some lit room with a comfortable couch like a modern Western psychologist? Why the need for earth floors and dust? The basic assumption behind these kinds of retreats, Paul felt, was that there is something cold and insufficiently soulful about the modern world. The retreats proclaimed human beings were made of organic material and, therefore, only organic material could heal humanity's discomfort. The cure was in natural oils; the cure was in natural massages; the cure in releasing the natural chi in the body; in letting the blood flow naturally. But why were they so sure the cure came from nature, when the problem seemed to reside in nature also?—in the voracious desire to fight in the wild, in the desire to be the alpha dog, in the voracious desire for nature to overcome its own limitations by creating an artificial world that was meant to overcome the limits of what was natural. The grain of the destruction of man seemed, then, inside himself and not without. It was within the beast. And being in an earthen hut couldn't change any of that, or make Paul feel any better, he felt, for being unfocused, or lazy, or jealous.

"Sit down," Buffalo Man said. He motioned Paul to a bench of baked mud that ringed the inside of the Kiva Hut. Paul sat close to the man who he'd felt for years was the cause of his misfortune—a small candle sputtering on the bench between them—and he had the desire to reach forward and strangle him, slowly. But what would that accomplish? Nothing. So he sat beside Buffalo Man, trying to keep his mind open so he could take in every word clearly rather than being clouded by the anger he felt within.

"It is such a pleasure," Buffalo Man said. "Such a pleasure to see you again. Honestly." He placed his hands together in front of his face and gave *namaste* greetings. "Welcome. Welcome back to the Rashna Retreat. The entire staff welcomes you back to a restful and recuperative stay here."

"You do realize who I am, don't you?" said Paul.

"Yes, of course. Of course, I do. You were the hothead who ran off before trying to come up with any plan to face your fate properly. And for that reason you left behind a big bill to pay. And you wished for others to take the responsibility for what you had done. Fortunately for you, your ex-partner, Zoe, *did* help you out. But she shouldn't have. You, alone, must take responsibility for your actions . . . Naturally, I understand why you wanted to run off that afternoon. The shock of such a prophecy was bound to have made you fearful like a deer caught in headlights. But sadly, as you can see, the prophecy has all come true. It is all true, you see. And just so you understand, it is not so often I receive such a prophecy—and receive is the *correct* word, for it is not really me who has been causing all of your frustration, as you think. I am not the *cause* of your frustration, I am merely the conduit to the enlightener who brings you knowledge of yourself and of what your trajectory is to be."

"Yes," Paul said, "but what made me so angry was that you just told a pile of horrible things that were going to happen to me and then you told me I should simply get rid of all my possessions and run off to the Himalayas to study with some other guru who was supposed to teach me while I stood naked in the wilderness. How does *that* fit into your model of healing? It seems more like an ambush than any kind of retreat. Imagine if you had been me. Would you have believed anything that you yourself said until it all came true?"

"True, true," Buffalo Man said, "no one truly believes their fate until it actually comes to pass. But nevertheless it is true . . . How can I help you, then? What are you here for?"

"I want to avoid my early death, of course," Paul said. "And I want happiness."

"Yes, surely," Buffalo Man said. "But no one can really avoid their death at the appointed hour. And to say that you want happiness is far too vague. But perhaps we can help you avoid your discomfort by focusing on your specific fears. For it is *fear* that man really wants to eliminate. For example, if I do not fear, then I do not mind death. Animals spend no time thinking about death because they cannot, and therefore they are not imprisoned by the fear of death. They simply live. Likewise, it is always our fears that poison our lives and that create all our problems. Therefore, once you can speak of your fears openly to me, then we can create the tests that will overcome those fears. So what do you fear?"

But the better question might have been what didn't he fear? Paul thought. Now that the question was posed so bluntly, he closed his eyes and spoke out a torrent of fear. "I fear that I am as insignificant as a gnat on the face of the earth," Paul said. "I fear that my brother Cyrus doesn't love me. I fear that my brother Cyrus is better than me. I fear that I only begin things and never finish them. I fear that my parents don't love me. I fear that everyone can see I am a fraud, that I have called myself a drummer in a band and a college professor, but that I have no ability in either. I fear that Zoe doesn't think I am attractive. I fear that

Zoe doesn't think I am good in bed. I fear that the beauty of the earth has never seemed quite as beautiful as it was supposed to be, or as I have always been told that it is. I fear that I am too weak to appreciate the beauty of the earth in its fullness. I fear that I am not an artist. I fear that I am not a scholar. I fear that I am acted upon and that I do not control my own destiny. I fear that I have become so cynical because the world is ugly and it seems wiser to deny any love for anything than to surrender to love. I fear my skepticism. I fear death. I fear that I am a man of fears more than of courage," Paul said.

"Good," Buffalo Man said. "You are now beginning the process of purification that is necessary to fight all these fears. First you must cleanse yourself of these fears and then you can begin to conquer them."

"But the problem is I fear any simplistic notion of conquering my fears as well," Paul said.

"Well, if you are saying that you reject the idea of wisdom or of someone who can teach you the way out of these fears, then you have become simply a nihilist," Buffalo Man said. "And the Rashna Retreat is built around the entire idea that modern life has created feelings of hopelessness that can only begin to be healed through proper nutrition and meditation and purification."

"But what if I reject you as a teacher? If I'm skeptical of you as the person who could be my real guru?" It was a risky thing to say, Paul thought, but if they were going to get to the heart of the matter, then he had to be honest in all ways.

"Then reject me. The choice is yours. The choice is always yours, of course. But you have seen what happened the last time you rejected my words, and so I must encourage you not to do so again."

Was this simply another Faustian bargain, then? Yet another teacher to get him out of a tight jam, like The Modern Cyrano? Yet another wishful hope in a string of wishful hopes? It seemed pointless to follow a guru one knew in his heart was just a wishful hope. And yet, at that moment, sitting in the Kiva Hut which was becoming hotter and hotter, to the point Paul was now beginning to sweat profusely, there didn't seem any other better hope or any other better gurus around. At least Buffalo Man had already proved, in Paul's estimation, that he had a window into his future.

"So what kind of tests do you have planned for me?" Paul said. "Brad Rashnaji said something about some kind of tests I would have to take."

"True, true. Yes, yes. The conquering of one's fears must begin with a purification process, a complete cleansing of the system. Naturally, this can often involve sweating out the toxins in one's body. A five-day sweat without food, for example, in a Kiva Hut such as this one with only water. Or in some religions, such as with Zen Buddhists, a complete emptying of the mind is required first by contemplating conundrums such as the sound of one hand clapping. But in your case, after considering your life story, I think it would be best if you engaged in a series of three tests that I would call Sex, Drugs, and Rock and Roll. The exact origin of your fears can always be traced back to an antecedent. Shamans such as Freud—I like to think of him as a shaman because he was really a healer—like to go all the way back to infancy for the source of one's fears and problems, but this gives us little in the way of tests that can be given to overcome one's fears. And for this reason, I prefer to focus on you when you were already a wounded adult, just after the breakup of your band, I.C.N."

"I.C.N.? Really? Why then?"

"Because that was the moment when you first fully internalized that you were not going to be a success in this life. That you were just like everyone else in this world. That you were a mere mortal. The quest for fame gives hopes of immortality and of being special, and when you lost that chance for fame, you were confronted with the shortness of life that all of us face on earth. So really, when I gave you the prophecy your life would be short and that you would die in the fourth ring of your life, I was simply confirming what you subconsciously had already realized when the band broke up."

"You're suggesting, then, that if I could simply purify myself of the origins of my quest for immortality that I would be ready then to face my own impending mortality?"

"Exactly," Buffalo Man said. "You must renounce your desires—for fame and sexual prowess and the need to be loved and for the lazy happiness that is symbolized by a drug-induced stupor. Your desires must be renounced through purification by an overstimulation of sex, drugs, and rock and roll. Most humbly, I suggest we should not waste any time and that the first of your tests should begin tomorrow morning."

Whereas the day before Paul had been instructed to show up at his meeting in something resembling a bathing suit, now, as he was on the verge of taking his first test—the sex part—he was instructed by Buffalo Man to take off all his clothes in a locker room with soothing yellow light and quiet meditative music, and then to enter the "Decontamination Chamber" at the end of the changing room.

Paul looked at his naked body in the mirror in the dressing room, and the chubby image reflecting back at him was something he both saw and did not see at the same time. He scrutinized his body, and he saw a man five feet eight inches tall, whose short blond hair was twisted with sweat from a night without sleep, brown curves under his eyes. He saw a man with a medium to small penis. More of an average penis, he thought. It might be on the small side or on the average side. He had read once that the average penis was five and a half inches when erect, and he'd even measured his penis to see where he fit on the scale of manhood, and he'd found that he was, amazingly, exactly five and a half inches, but whether he was really bigger than other men or not he didn't know because he could only guess when he glanced at other men's penises in locker rooms. Glanced is the word he'd use, not only because he didn't want any man to think he was checking him out, but also because he didn't want any other man to check *him* out. He preferred to remain unseen. Unevaluated. Left to decide his own value of his penis size. For something so personal and vital to one's self-esteem, he reflected how little he really knew about the true scale of men's penises. But hadn't he done what all men did when they were young? he thought—looked in porno magazines at the models to size himself up by comparison. Judging by the enormous cocks of the men in the porno mags, he was certainly nothing. For a long time he had believed his penis was small, but then he eventually read the study on the length of the average penis. And yet, with the images of the cocks in the porno mags still in the back of his mind, he felt his penis must be somewhat smaller than average. Sexually, he knew he had an appetite. He definitely liked to see sexy women and he masturbated regularly, as he felt most men did, and he had learned with Zoe to slowly become more relaxed and to enjoy letting himself go by engaging in whatever fantasy he might have. But he knew his sex life with Zoe had become routine, and for this reason he had understood when she had gone to sex-therapy classes that she was simply trying to attain something more. She was simply trying to fulfill *her* fantasy, and that seemed fully acceptable to Paul as long as she still *loved* him. But now it seemed she didn't love him anymore—although she had sent word to Buffalo Man she was expecting he was coming, which certainly showed more than a little compassion for his current fears and predicament. Insofar as Paul was *not* looking at himself in the mirror, it was that he simultaneously tried to see who he was and to disassociate himself from the reflection that came back at him.

Feeling naked and desiring to put on some clothes, Paul opened a cedar door like to a sauna, and he entered the "Decontamination Chamber." Buffalo Man was waiting for him in the middle of the room. The Decontamination Chamber had a wood floor that was smooth from pounding, exercising feet. It had hundreds of TV monitors lining all sides of the rectangular room and a high ceiling with heavy wood beams. It looked like the training room of a martial arts dojo, with the odd difference there were so many TVs along the walls.

Buffalo Man was dressed in a bright saffron dhoti, and he held a mesh wire mask in one hand and a bamboo sword that looked like it was for competing in the sport of kendo. Paul felt the cool air of the room swirl around his naked body and he wished he were clothed.

"What's the kendo sword for?" Paul said.

"Questions. Questions. Wonderful, wonderful," Buffalo Man said. "I'm so glad to see you here this morning. And I wish to assure you that—though you may *feel* awkward being naked at first—this is simply the natural sense of inadequacy that causes you to desire so strongly to be sexually successful and famous in the first place. The source of your desire to be 'something' rather than a 'nothing' or a 'loser' resides, as with almost all my retreat patients, in a feeling you are inadequate. In your particular case, this may be a feeling of sexual inadequacy, or perhaps feelings of inadequacy toward your parents (which is, of course, very typical), or feelings of inadequacy in comparison to your brothers, but whatever the source of these feelings, the great Guru Satyajit—who has taught me much—has taught me that the source of this human suffering is not only a feeling of inadequacy but of *jealousy*. And for this reason we must overcome those things we desire too much, in order to achieve some balance. In this first test, therefore, what you must do is beat off, or fight, with all those images of lust that have made you feel so inadequate. You must fight off the very feeling your penis is small by allowing yourself to feel it is in fact *your* penis, that it is perfectly adequate, and that you have every reason to be happy with it in its current condition."

"You said you want me to 'beat off' those images?"

"Yes, but not as in 'jerk off.' If there is one thing I do not believe in it is jerking off, which is simply a waste of the precious fluids god has given us. *No,* what I am suggesting is that you put on this kendo helmet and that you take this kendo sword, and in a minute, when Jennifer Rashnaji comes in, I want you to use your stick to attempt to beat her away with all your might. Naturally, like any desire, she will fight back, and only if you can win in this first test will you have begun to cure yourself of your desires. In the meantime—to remind you of all the images polluting your brain since you were a young boy, when you no doubt saw your first porno movie—there will be a continuous and rapid display of pornographic images on the TVs that surround you. Such images can be quite overwhelming when shown on one hundred and eighty-nine television sets all at once, and as you fight with Jennifer Rashnaji, I hope you will keep in mind you are symbolically fighting all this pollution that has entered your system."

"And why are there a hundred and eighty-nine TVs?" Paul said.

"Because the number—as revealed by Guru Satyajit—is a holy number of ritual purification."

"Got it," said Paul, and he thought Buffalo Man must be aware of the skepticism in his voice.

"You see, there you go again—skeptical, skeptical, skeptical," Buffalo Man said. "But has not the prophecy that was revealed to you via the voices of the world who know one's fate before it is known already proven its truth to you?"

Buffalo Man instructed Paul to put the kendo helmet on, and he complied. Paul held the bamboo sword in both hands, and it was surprisingly heavy. The bottom of the sword was wrapped with a worn piece of black leather and had a small logo of the imprint of female lips puckering to give a kiss with red lipstick. The body of the sword consisted of thin, dried-out bamboo slats tied together with what looked like rolled-up condoms.

From one of the far corners of the room, Jennifer Rashnaji came out another cedar-wood door with her kendo helmet already on and with a bamboo sword that looked the same as Paul's, except hers was tied together with used straps of lingerie, and like Paul, she was naked. The one hundred and eighty-nine TVs suddenly turned on and an image of moist red lips puckered all around Paul. They were sensuous lips. "You're a star, baby," the lips said, "and I want to suck you so dry you'll feel like the Sahara." The next image was of a woman giving a blowjob to a man with an enormous cock. She was going down on him mechanically, and his cock was bigger than the leg of an elephant, and she was stroking his penis and telling him he was an animal, just an animal, just a great fucking enormous animal.

So this is it? Paul thought. *This is what I've come hitchhiking all the way across country to get? These are the great words of wisdom I've been seeking?* Basic words about abnegation and celibacy and turning away from the feelings of inadequacy that he felt because of a lifetime of a media-saturated culture. *But I already knew all of that,* Paul thought. *I've known it for years. And none of that has made me feel any less inadequate.*

And yet there wasn't much time to think because Jennifer Rashnaji spread her legs wide like a male Kabuki dancer in front of him. Her body was fit from daily yoga, and there was little to dislike about her. The lips of her vagina were wide open, revealing the goal of every move men attempted in a bar. *There* was the holy grail of sexuality. The holy pussy that every man wanted to shoot at and score. Her breasts were fit and looked ready to seduce any lustful man. She let out a battle cry, stomped first one foot and then the other, held her sword in front with tremendous focus, as if sizing Paul up, and then she rushed toward him running as fast as she could, aiming her sword at his meek, naked, fairly flaccid body, and as she came closer Paul realized she was aiming at his penis.

Was it mere protection of his little sack of jewels, then, that made him take up his sword to protect himself from Jennifer Rashnaji's attack? Whatever it was, Paul lifted his sword high around his ear like a baseball player winding up, and when Jennifer Rashnaji came close he swung forward with all his might. His sword connected with hers. The bound strands of bamboo rattled sharply and clapped. Condom hit wrapped-up lingerie straps and the two jostled together. The woman on the TVs moaned, "Oh baby, oh baby, oh baby, you're so big. You're a star. You're a bright shining star." And the man on the TV screens cummed into her mouth in a hundred and eighty-nine ejaculations.

"Excellent, excellent," Buffalo Man said. "You are finally letting out your anger and aggression at all the sources of lust that have been placed into your heart. You are decontaminating now. In half an hour I'll come back."

A half hour went by with Jennifer Rashnaji alternately splaying her legs and attacking Paul. Paul hit back with as much force as he could muster, but he never could come close to hitting the kendo sword of love out of her hand. At the end of thirty minutes the porno video went off, and the screens all went blank at once. Jennifer Rashnaji pushed Paul to the floor with her sword and said, "That's it. Time's up. Session is over. The next one will be later this afternoon."

"Will it be the same thing?" Paul said.

"Yes, you'll have a repeat sexual-decontamination kendo session with me, and then tomorrow you'll continue with the drugs, and the day after that you'll have the rock and roll."

"But I don't feel anything," Paul said. "I don't think this is doing anything for me."

"Perhaps, but it's all part of a process. Part of a twelve-step decontamination process. And you're only in the first phase." Jennifer Rashnaji bowed to Paul.

Paul was too tired to bow back. He walked—or more accurately limped—toward his own locker room. He felt no more adequate or less inadequate than before. In the dressing room, he stood naked in front of the mirror with the soft yellow lighting, with recorded wind chimes and flutes blowing faintly in the background, and as he looked at his flabby chest and flaccid average-to-slightly-smaller-than-average penis, he felt it looked the same as it always had.

Is this it, then? Paul thought. Is this the end of the road? It certainly felt like the end of the road as he walked into the cornfield behind the Rashna Retreat. For where were the answers to his problems? He had hitchhiked all the way to Iowa to overcome the curse Buffalo Man gave him, and all he'd been given in return was equally trite advice, as vague, really, as the idea he would die somewhere in the fourth ring of his life. The idea that he could simply hit a sword against Jennifer Rashnaji some more and that this would make him feel strength was preposterous. He had thought, at first, Buffalo Man was tailoring his medicine to him as an individual—with his references to I.C.N. and Sex, Drugs, and Rock and Roll—but now he realized, after talking to a few of the retreaters at lunch, that Buffalo Man used this same "therapy" with at least a few others. And what had he expected? Of course Buffalo Man used the therapy with others, because how else would he have the porno movies all set up. Did he really think Buffalo Man had stayed up all night trying to get together the videos just for him? No, he was just getting a variation of the same therapy all the other retreaters got.

I've been lying to myself, Paul thought. *All these years, ever since I came to this place the first time, and I've been lying to myself believing this man actually has given me a real prophecy of my life.* So why had he been lying to himself? Why had he let himself believe in the prophecy? *Because then I'm not responsible for my failures and misfortune,* Paul thought. *Then someone else is.*

But it was his *own* fault he had been part of a band that failed. It was his *own* fault he hadn't been able to complete his book. It was his *own* fault he had been fired from B_____ Community College. And it was his *own* fault he had ticked Zoe off by failing to find any discipline, until she finally reached the point she couldn't be with him anymore. And yet, at the same time, as he accepted this responsibility now, could he also deny the selfishness of his parents and of his brother (kidnapping him, no less, for purely political ends) or deny that Zoe, too, seemed not to know what was truly valuable in life as she chased after some kind of acting stardom that would probably never come?

So how could he find a meaningful way out of his *own* failure?

It was August, and by now the corn should have been so tall he wouldn't be able to see over it once he entered the field behind the Rashna Retreat. The corn along the border of the retreat was well watered, presumably by one of the gardeners who kept up the bonsai next to the yoga room. Therefore, the corn appeared robust and healthy along the fence of the neighboring farm field, just as it had looked robust by the field of watered grass where Buffalo Man had led the morning sun greeting the day before. (Paul had mistaken water from the sprinkling system for morning dew.) But beyond this decorative wall of corn, when Paul entered the farm field behind the retreat, he saw sicker corn with roots struggling to find and suck out moisture in the parched earth, and the corn grew in uneven, spotty patches. There was a NO TRESPASSING sign blowing in the hot wind of what was proving to be one of the driest summers in years. News reports, which Paul had only glimpsed in truck stop cafes as he hitchhiked across the country, told of a shockingly depleted Missouri River and of barges that could barely make it up the Mississippi to deliver coal and oil. There were headlines the corn harvest was going to be weak, and the price of corn was shooting up. When Paul had read those headlines they had just been headlines, and even when he'd seen corn looking prematurely beige on their stalks as he rode in the trucks, the full magnitude of the dying plants hadn't connected to his feelings until he entered the cornfield. The dirt beneath his feet was dry and crumbly, and it didn't seem any worm could survive. Now that he was beyond the wall of watered corn at the retreat, he heard the leaves of the corn rattling in the wind like the sound of maracas made of dried gourds. It reminded him of the Día de los Muertos, when dead spirits were supposed to be in the presence of the living. For Mexicans and Indians of South America, the Day of the Dead was supposed to be a happy day to connect with the spirits of their lost loved ones, but since Paul didn't believe in the religion of those people, he felt only the presence of death to come rather than the spirits of the dead returned. Yet the corn was not all dead. It formed rising and falling patches that seemed to live or die on the fate of whether a little more moisture had fallen onto one patch of ground or another. Some areas, only a few inches lower, must have been places that captured a little more water, and there the corn survived. Other places, a little higher, received too little water, and before dying the corn grew less than normal and then prematurely expired. The effect was to make a dry, brown and green patchy field, an unruly garden of death sweeping before Paul that nevertheless impressed him with the strength of some of the plants as they resisted the drought and somehow managed to survive.

He could see much further than normally possible in a cornfield because of the low corn, yet it was his sense of sound that momentarily proved stronger than his ability to see. A sudden gunshot clapped a short violent thwack that was quickly muffled by dirt, and then another clap and thwack followed in the distance to his right. After the initial startle, Paul thought, *It's probably nothing. It's probably just some teenage farmer shooting cans.* But for someone who was shooting at cans, there was a long pause between the first two shots and the next. Paul turned from the sound and decided to walk through the uneven, dry corn, across the furrows of parched dirt, away from the violent noise. It seemed unlikely this was a hunter of any kind. Legally—even though Paul wasn't a hunter—he knew the hunting season for pheasants and deer wouldn't begin until fall. He had been asked once, by Zoe, why, and he had given his best shot to make a reasonable reply: "I think it's to protect the animals' young. Since the babies are born in the spring, by holding off until the fall, the young get a chance to grow big enough to be independent before they're shot." Now that he thought about it, it seemed an odd form of morality—making sure the young were big enough to become orphans and claiming enough sympathy for animals to leave them alone until it was a good time to kill them. The more likely explanation was simply to make sure there were enough animals coming down the pipeline to continue to be slaughtered.

The sound of gunshots was coming closer, though Paul was trying to walk away from them. And then another sound came after the shots; the high-pitched buzzing of a motor, like a dirt bike revving at high speed, whined and nagged in the distance. Paul stopped with the dust of the earth around his feet, his tennis shoes crushing the roots of a dying stalk of corn, and he looked for what might be making the sound. In the distance, to his right, kicking up dust, he saw a man on a three-wheel off-road motorcycle bouncing up and down over rows of corn, flying before the thick fat tires of his machine reconnected with the ground and tore through the earth, pushing the bike forward closer toward its prey. Occasionally, the three-wheeler suddenly stopped. The rider pulled a rifle around from his shoulder. He aimed into the corn, somewhere, toward a target Paul couldn't see, and then fired off a couple more.

He must be hunting illegally. He must be hunting for something, Paul thought. Or maybe he wasn't. Maybe he was just firing randomly into the ground. But that seemed unlikely. Given Paul was trespassing, he wasn't sure if he should go back or continue. Either way, he was afraid the guy might see his pale white flesh in the sun and think he was an animal.

The three-wheeler came closer. The dust was piling up into the air, and though the man had seemed far off only a couple of minutes ago, he was coming suddenly much closer. The three-wheel dune buggy was covered with red and white stripes of the American flag, and the front of the buggy was blue with white stars. The rider was bare-chested; he had a red bandana tied around his long hair to keep it pulled back, and he looked like he might have drunk half a gallon of peppermint schnapps for breakfast. He headed straight toward Paul, and when he was within twenty feet, he slammed on the brakes and scooted forward until the fat front tire burrowed into the ground.

"This is private property," the teenage kid said. He couldn't have been any older than seventeen. "It's my uncle's fucking farm and he don't want no one poaching any of his animals. That deer is mine."

"No problem," said Paul. "Which way do you want me to go?" He pointed back toward the Rashna Retreat.

"The road's closer," the kid said, and instead of pointing behind Paul to the retreat, he spit to the left, where he said there was a road.

"OK," Paul said. "No problem." If there was one thing he had learned a long time ago, it was to stay away from fights with rednecks and just do what they told you. That was definitely the best way to safety. He turned to the left and started walking slowly enough to try not to bug the kid anymore, but also fast enough to let him know he was fully complying.

Just get me outta here. I just wanna get home as soon as I can, he thought. He had already dismissed Buffalo Man's prophecy as a bunch of crap now that he could see the medicine to cure him was so absurd. And yet, with this quick near brush with death, how could he be so certain Buffalo Man was wrong? The approach of the kid with the gun had made it all seem that perhaps he *would* die young and prematurely, like the corn, in the fourth ring of his life. For more than fifteen minutes he walked in the direction he was ordered, toward the "road," and he wondered if it was the same interstate he'd encountered so many years before in the night when he'd gone behind the Rashna Retreat just after Buffalo Man had given him his prophecy.

The kid on the three-wheeler had turned into the distance, but by the sound of his engine Paul could tell he was coming back toward him and he decided to run. He ran perpendicular to the furrows of corn, and it was easy to trip on the dirt and roots. The pale green of the corn turning slowly to brown left the stalks with razor-sharp leaves that cut him against his cheeks.

He was running hard now. His heart was beating. The corn was to all sides, sometimes low enough so he could see far ahead and other times so close he ran directly into plants, running into a wall that parted and parted but that remained a barrier.

The three-wheeler buzzed closer and closer and Paul ran to the point he could run no faster. As he pushed through the corn, he came all of a sudden to the edge of the same high embankment he had sat on years before when he'd felt the fear of death and the bad speed on the interstate. Was it bad speed that he felt now as he tried to outrun the three-wheeler? Perhaps. But in the thrill and mindless focus on running to the road where he had been instructed to go, he felt exhilaration, too, the pumping of blood firmly through his arteries and heart.

At the edge of the interstate he stood at the top of a twenty-five-yard embankment of dry grass and dirt that sloped at a steep angle down to the concrete pavement. And as he came out onto the highway he realized, for the first time, that he had not been running alone. A male deer, with a white buck tail and two youthfully smooth long ears, came out of the corn running at full speed down the embankment. The deer didn't contemplate failure for a moment. It didn't seem to contemplate death. The deer ran down the hill, kicking up dirt as it went, barely stumbling as it moved in a controlled yet pursued fashion to the interstate. For once without hesitation, Paul ran down the embankment, following the deer. A culvert passed beneath the highway to the right, a place where he might be able to find safety from the three-wheeler above if he was truly trying to follow him rather than the animal.

With its legs at the edge of the interstate, the deer looked to the left, toward the oncoming semitrailers and cars rushing in a blind speed at the animal. Yet without hesitation the deer ran onto the unnatural pavement and placed itself in the middle of the road. The animal seemed to wait for him. It certainly had no reason to wait. It seemed to call Paul forward, and with the cars coming closer from the distance Paul ran up to the deer and stood momentarily with the animal on the concrete pavement before it rushed safely across to the other side, free from the hunt of its predator on the three-wheeler.

Planted firmly, with his feet on the long dotted lines that ran in the center of the blind speed of the highway as it rushed toward the Pacific, Paul heard the trucks and cars coming closer, and he did not move out of the way. It was an auditory speed. It was the sound and compression of air. It was a car rushing to one side and then a truck to the other. The cars and traffic honked and swerved around him as he stood firmly without moving in the center of the highway. So this is it, Paul thought. This is how the blind speed is overcome. He opened his eyes and looked firmly at the traffic approaching and swerving around him. It was necessary to take risks to overcome failure.

He walked calmly over to the side of the pavement just next to the yellow line that bordered the fast lane and lay himself down on the ground. He looked up at the parching heat of the sun, which did not blind him in his happiness, and as the cars ran and burned past him, their hot tires running at an annihilating pace into the pavement, he thought that the border between the blind speed and the good speed was faint but it was still discernible. *Since the problem is from within,* he thought, *I must change myself.*

ACKNOWLEDGMENTS

Thanks to the National Endowment for the Arts, Saul Bellow, Tom Perrotta, Frank Conroy, James Alan McPherson, Lan Samantha Chang, George Packer, Connie Brothers, and Martin Sherwin. Special thanks to Chris Walsh, Danielle Lapidoth, Leo Espinosa, Steve Smith, and Jeff Posternak.

This book is dedicated to Joel, Sandy, Bronwyn, and Laura.

ABOUT THE AUTHOR

Josh Barkan was awarded a literature fellowship from the National Endowment for the Arts in 2006. He has taught writing at Harvard, NYU, and Boston University and is the author of the story collection *Before Hiroshima*. A graduate of the Iowa Writers' Workshop and Yale, he lives in New York City.